Memo

Louisa Scarr studied Psychology at the University of Southampton and has lived in and around the city ever since. She works as a freelance copywriter and editor, and when she's not writing, she can be found pounding the streets in running shoes or swimming in muddy lakes.

Also by Louisa Scarr

Butler & West

Last Place You Look
Under a Dark Cloud
Blink of an Eye
Seen to Be Believed
Out of the Ashes

PC Lucy Halliday

Gallows Wood
Memorial Park

LOUISA SCARR

MEMORIAL PARK

First published in the United Kingdom in 2025 by

Canelo
Unit 9, 5th Floor
Cargo Works, 1-2 Hatfields
London SE1 9PG
United Kingdom

A CIP catalogue record for this book is available from the British Library.

Print ISBN 978 1 83598 075 0
Ebook ISBN 978 1 83598 076 7

Cover design by Dan Mogford

Cover images © Alamy

Look for more great books at www.canelo.co

Printed and bound in Great Britain by Clays Ltd, Elcograf S.p.A.

1

For my writing life support:

Fliss, Heather, Jo, Rachael, Kate, Niki and Clare.

'Whereof what's past is prologue, what to come
In yours and my discharge.'

William Shakespeare, *The Tempest*, 1611

PROLOGUE

They find the body at seven fifty-eight in the evening. Rain pours in sheets, soaking everyone to the skin in seconds. But cocker spaniels don't care about the rain; their fluffy undercoat is built for jumping into muddy streams, for battling wind and freezing temperatures.

Moss doesn't hesitate. Nose to the ground, he ignores the open front door, the broken bottles and fag ends on the cracked paving, taking Lucy straight around the back of the house. Brambles and stinging nettles attack Lucy's legs in the overgrown garden, while Moss pulls left and right, detecting the odour he was trained to find. A scent that has lain undisturbed for far, far too long.

The dog stills, and in that moment, Lucy knows.

It is over.

PART ONE

DAY ONE – WEDNESDAY

CHAPTER ONE

Before the police arrive, before it all begins, Maria is wishing for excitement. That's what she will remember later, lying in bed, unable to sleep – she wanted this. It was all her fault.

The Wednesday starts like every other. Maria wakes at half-five with the patter of little footsteps, the door to their bedroom opening, a gummy face next to hers. Tony rolls over with a grunt; Maria squints at her daughter, eyes half-open.

Rosie's blonde curls are standing up, an electric shock on one side of her head, squashed to her skull on the other. She is sucking her thumb. Rupert – the well-loved bunny toy – is clutched tightly in her other hand, his fur worn to a dingy grey.

'It's early, sweetie. Go back to bed.'

But Maria knows it's pointless. She can smell the warm tang of a full nappy, and she gets up, shivering in the freezing air and pulling on tracksuit bottoms, slippers, hoodie, picking Rosie up and carrying her back to her bedroom.

Clean, dressed, their day begins. In the kitchen, Maria's priority is the coffee machine. Once that's percolating, she settles Rosie in front of *Bluey*, unloads the dishwasher, tidies away the mess from Eddie's late-night snack, and puts a load of washing in the machine.

The rest of the house bursts into life at seven. Running water overhead as Tony has a shower; loud music from Eddie's room as the first of many alarms goes off. He will ignore them all. Her now-adult son is irresponsible and wayward – lazy, with nothing to do now that university is out of the picture. Any suggestion of getting a job is received with grunts and eye rolls.

Rosie is coaxed to the table for Cheerios, followed by toast and jam. High in sugar, but she's eating. Isn't that the main thing? Maria makes a mental note to google nutritious breakfasts for three-year-olds, already aware that any attempt will be met with tantrums and abandoned after a day.

Tony comes downstairs in a Hugo Boss suit and a cloud of aftershave, taking the last mug of coffee from the machine and swigging it as he ties his shoelaces. He dodges his daughter's sticky fingers as he gives her a kiss on the top of her head. A peck on Maria's cheek and he's gone, the BMW 8 Series roaring as he guns it out of the driveway.

'Happy fucking Valentine's Day to you too,' Maria mutters sarcastically. Some acknowledgement would have been nice. Maybe he'll come home tonight with a card and flowers, guilted into it by someone at the office. Probably not. She picks up her phone, sends a text. She can buy her own goodies.

She sits at the table next to her daughter, exhausted even though the sun has barely risen. The hours stretch out in front of her – she can't stand another day trapped between these four walls, her daughter shrieking for television, for food, for yet another toy she's seen advertised who knows where. Her phone beeps – the message returned. It's brief, but she wasn't looking for conversation. He has what she needs, and it distils the plan in her mind. After breakfast, she resolves: *we will get out in the fresh air.*

We will go to the park.

–

The declaration is met with enthusiasm from Rosie, so they don their winter coats and hats, Maria plonks her daughter in the buggy, and away they go.

Maria is buoyed by the sunshine as she walks quickly through the town, heading for the recreation ground and the gaudy swings and slides. They pass through the large, wrought-iron gates – the stone pillars engraved with the names of the war dead and strewn with leftover poppy wreaths. Rosie squeaks to be released from the buggy once they're clear of the road. Maria lifts her gently, laughing as her daughter toddles off towards the swings, Rupert clutched in her hand.

Maria takes a seat on the park bench. She glances around, waiting for him to arrive. Maybe today won't be so bad, she thinks. She'll get what she needs, pass over a few twenties, and then, transaction done, she'll wait for the café to open. Buy a coffee for her, and a babyccino for Rosie. Maybe even treat her to a chocolate flake. She watches her daughter fondly. She has placed Rupert in the swing and is gently pushing him, talking to the bunny in jumbled, indecipherable words. Her cheeks are pink in the cold, her hair wild.

Maria turns, looking for Rosie's missing hat – they can't lose another one – and spots it next to the gate. She gets up to fetch it; her phone rings.

No Caller ID, the screen says. She's tempted to ignore the call, but it could be important – could be Tony, phoning from work. She presses the green button.

'Hello? Maria Logan here?'

At first, there's nothing but static. She glances at the screen to see if the call is connected, repeats her greeting: 'Hello?'

And then the woman speaks. Her voice is measured and calm, telling a story as old as time. Maria doesn't believe it at first, screws her face up in annoyance.

'Who is this?' she snarls. 'What's your name?'

'You know my name,' the woman replies. 'Stop pretending. You know full well what's going on.'

'How dare you… How did you get my number?'

'This is for your own good, Maria. You need to accept this. This can't go on any longer.'

Maria starts circling the park, asking questions, then shouting obscenities when the woman won't give any more information. She just repeats the same phrase, the accusation that Maria can't possibly believe. Won't allow herself to believe. Not again.

And then, the woman's gone. Three final beeps and the line is dead.

Maria stares at her phone for a second, her mouth gaping. Her first reaction is to phone Tony. Confront him with this ridiculous accusation. Have him laugh it off, put it out of her mind. But what if the woman is telling the truth? What then?

She stands motionless for a moment, processing what she's just been told, when her subconscious twitches. A prickle of dread. A shiver, working its way from her head, down her spine, to the pit of her stomach. The park is quiet. Too quiet. She looks up from her phone.

'Rosie?' she calls. Hushed, at first. 'Rosie?'

The slide, the roundabout. The swing shifts slightly in the breeze. Empty. Her gaze shifts, blinking, as she searches for her daughter. For a thatch of blonde curls. For the bright red of her coat. The blue of her wellies.

'Rosie?' Louder now. 'Rosie, honey?'

She starts to walk, checking under the slide, anywhere Rosie could be. Her pace getting faster, her movements more desperate.

'Rosie, don't hide from Mummy. Come out now? Please?' The last word is a frantic plea, a shout across the empty grass. She walks further, still no sign. Every muscle is rigid with panic, the coffee from breakfast acidic in her stomach. She rakes her hands through her hair, turning in panicked circles. Nothing.

Nothing.

'Rosie!' she shrieks.

A woman appears by her side. Older. Grey hair. Thin, almost gaunt. Wearing a navy-blue coat and matching woollen scarf. Maria recognises her, but can't work out from where.

'Are you okay?' she says.

'My daughter. Rosie. She's gone. She was just here… and… she's gone. She's gone. She's three. She's only little.'

The buzz of disquiet has grown into a full-blown panic. Hot blood races in her veins. Maria's dizzy, can't think, can't talk. Just wants her daughter. *Please*. Let her find her daughter.

'Where was she?' the woman says calmly.

'Just here!' Maria shouts. The woman hesitates, but starts to walk across the grass, checking everywhere Maria's already been. The futile gesture angers Maria. She needs help. Real help. Not this useless woman.

Maria's running now. The length of the park, hoping, praying that Rosie will pop up, laughing. Chortling at the fun she's had, hiding from Mummy. *Please. Please. Please*, Maria whispers. *Please.*

But the park is empty. Nobody here. Nothing – except for the busy road on the far side. The fast-flowing river next to them. Dangers she hadn't considered. How naïve she has been. How stupid.

Her legs weaken and she collapses into the mud. Tears now – crying from pure fear and desperation. *Please.*

The woman touches her shoulder gently. And through her horror Maria can hear the woman talking.

'Police,' she's saying. 'A child's gone missing.'

CHAPTER TWO

By the time PC Lucy Halliday arrives at Memorial Park, the place is packed with police. Patrol cars line the road, a mass of yellow and blue, interspersed with unmarked vehicles like her own. She's directed through to the car park for the rugby club – the rendezvous point for the search, known as the RVP, and her first point of call.

She pulls her Ford Mondeo estate into the closest space. No sirens so the dogs are calm in the back, and she leaves them, zipping her coat up and walking across to the squat white building where the police search adviser is waiting.

She's worked with PC Brian Miller before. An experienced PolSA, he's ex-army, ex-dog unit. He knows his stuff. Black cap on, this morning he's swathed in a thick Arktis coat. He called her, just after half-nine.

'Missing child,' he'd said. 'Name of Rosie Logan. Three years old. Bring both dogs.'

His instruction had an ominous air. A missing person search would often involve Iggy – her two-year-old, general purpose German shepherd – but the fact that she has to bring Moss too throws a black cloud over proceedings. Moss is officially a victim recovery dog, or VRD, but the title is a misnomer. The only victims Moss recovers are dead – the little black spaniel is trained to find blood and cadavers. She mutters a silent prayer that they won't need Moss today.

Brian Miller nods a greeting as she approaches. He's standing out the front of the building, a mug of coffee steaming in his hand, deep in conversation with a uniformed officer – the two pips on his shoulder tell Lucy he's an inspector, and the man in charge this morning.

Miller introduces her.

'Inspector Greaves, this is PC Lucy Halliday. Dog handler.'

The inspector doesn't pause to say hello, just gives her scruffy uniform and mud-caked boots a quick up and down then turns straight back to Miller. 'You said we had a full dog team,' he snaps.

'PC Nash is en route,' Miller replies.

Lucy can't help the smile that creeps onto her face. PC Pete Nash is also a member of the dog unit, and – if she's being honest with herself – her nearly boyfriend. Maybe, kind of, not quite – a few dates and dog training with follow-up drinks does not infer a steady commitment, but it's the best she can do at the moment.

The inspector leaves, striding over to the group of uniforms standing a distance away.

Miller turns to Lucy. 'The scene's a fucking mess. You can see that already?'

Lucy nods. The park is full of people. Flooded with response and patrol, even a few curious members of the public. Heavy boots would have trampled over each square inch of this space, leaving confusing, conflicting scents on every blade of grass. The dogs need a sterile scene in order to track effectively, ideally fresh dewy ground, untouched by any other human. There is too much of a scent picture here for a dog's sensitive nose.

'Give me the lay of the land,' Lucy says, gesturing inside. 'And a coffee.'

Miller leads the way through the double doors, into the main reception room of the sports club. It's a well-loved place, with a scuffed wooden floor, a bar at the back, and bare brick walls decorated with trophy cases and photographs of football and rugby teams over the years. Black, gold and white balloons hang from curtain rails, streamers limp.

'There was a sixtieth birthday party last night,' Miller explains. 'The caretaker was here to clean up when we took over.' He gestures to a long trestle table where a huge map has been laid out.

Miller takes wire-framed glasses out of his pocket, puts them on, then places a bitten nail in the centre of the map. He points out key locations as he talks. 'Park, here. Rosie was last seen next to the swings, to the right, wearing a red coat and blue wellies, possibly holding a grey rabbit toy. This area consists of the children's playpark, a memorial garden bordered by hedges, some outbuildings, then the sports field and building here. There's a path that runs the length of the river, popular with fishermen and dog walkers, but we have no witnesses, as far as we know at the moment. The play area's enclosed with a low green fence, except for where it joins the river, here.'

Lucy glances up, meeting Miller's grim expression with her own. She'd noticed the river on her walk over: fast -flowing, wide, deep – and freezing cold at this time of year.

'Marine unit on their way?' she asks.

'As we speak. Ringwood Road to the east, car park surrounded by woodland, then the A338 just above it. No idea on last direction of travel. It's a bloody nightmare.' Miller looks out the long windows at the now pacing inspector. 'Do you know Greaves?'

Lucy shakes her head.

'Rumour has it, just been promoted. Stressed as hell and it's only early. Hate to think what he's going to be like as we move out of the golden hour.'

Lucy nods, knowingly. The golden hour – the short period of time after a crime is committed or a person goes missing, when forensics are fresh and witnesses are at their most cooperative. Outside of that, the risk gets exponentially worse. Especially for a young child.

'Just do what you can,' Miller finishes. He points to the large silver urn, white mugs next to it. 'Hot drinks and biscuits are there. Take Iggy for a walk. Over the far side of the park, along the length of the river and the undergrowth beyond. I'll get Nash to cover the other side of the road when he and Dax arrive. Radio if you find anything.'

'Will do.'

'And Lucy? Good luck. We're going to need it.'

Lucy returns his frown, and leaves the warmth of the rugby club, pulling her coat around her as she heads back to the car. She opens the boot, and her two dogs look at her, eager.

'Sorry, Moss,' she says. 'Iggy, you're up.'

She opens the crate, grabbing the German shepherd's collar as he jumps from the car. She puts his harness on, clips his lead to the top, then crouches down to his level, pushing her fingers into his thick fur. Underneath the brown and black, he's toasty warm; built for this job.

'You know what you need to do, mate,' she says to him. His ears are pricked, his tongue lolling, keen to get going.

She straightens up, but just as she's pulling on her gloves and hat, she spots an old black Mercedes pull in. She knows that car. What's he doing here?

She waits as he parks up.

DCI Jack Ellis is pristine as he climbs out of the car, an anomaly among the bustle and mess. He pulls a smart black coat over his grey suit, buttoning it up to the neck, then running a hand through his dark-blond hair. He spots Lucy and walks across; with anyone else Lucy would be wary of Iggy's reaction, but when Jack reaches them, the dog is relaxed and happy, stepping forward to greet him like an old friend, leaving a trail of wet nose on the wool coat.

'I thought you'd be here,' Jack says. He holds out a paper bag; she recognises the branding and takes it eagerly, opening it and taking a long inhale of the contents. Pastry, chocolate, sugar and grease. Just what she needs. 'Knew you wouldn't eat breakfast.'

'You know me too well.'

'For my sins.' Lucy puts it in the car, promise of a treat for later, while Jack reaches down and strokes the shepherd's ears. 'Yes, hello, Iggy. Thank you very much,' he adds sarcastically, brushing off the dog hair.

'Why are you here?' Lucy says. 'Is there anything I should know?'

Jack's presence indicates something more sinister. This is still a misper, not a murder; there's no need for Major Crime to be involved. Unless a body has been found.

'I'm not here in an official capacity,' Jack replies. 'I was having coffee with Inspector Greaves when the call came in. Thought I'd come down and take a look. See if I could help.'

'Professional or personal?' Lucy pushes.

Jack gives her a look. 'A bit of both. Don't let me stop you,' he adds. 'The main thing is that we find this girl.'

Jack's comment needs more interrogation but he's right, there are more important things. Lucy says a final thank you and goodbye and calls Iggy away from Jack. Dog at heel, they cross the main road, heading to the park. She keeps Iggy on the lead, walking him around the edge of the main activity.

She's been on enough missing person searches over the years to know what's going on. The instant the 999 call came through, officers would have been deployed to the park. A grade one, high-risk misper, like this one, dictates an immediate response – the dispatcher sending as many units as possible, while the call taker logs the important information: name, age, description, last seen, what Rosie Logan had been wearing.

The little girl's photograph would have been sent to all units, and Greaves will have others back at the station looking for CCTV, traffic cameras, any sighting of the girl. A three-hundred-metre search would have been undertaken. Officers would have been sent to the home address and the hospital, every friend or family member contacted.

The majority of misper calls are closed within the hour. A member of the public phoning in: 'I have a little girl here. She's lost her mummy.' Or a simple misunderstanding between family members. 'I'm sorry, I thought I was picking her up from school today.' The fact they have nothing doesn't bode well.

Brian Miller was right when he said they needed luck. Lucy knows the rugby club would have already been cleared, but the job for the next few hours is to search the whole park. It's a big area. A three-year-old may not appear nimble, but given the right motivation they can toddle surprisingly far. A dog in the distance, a stray balloon from last night's festivities – any number of things could distract a young girl.

It's freezing out here today. Even in her thick Arktis coat and gloves, the winter's air is biting, nipping at her nose and ears. She hopes Rosie Logan has a warm coat, because if not…

Lucy needs to focus. She looks across to the middle of the park, searching for the mother. That must be her – long, curly blonde hair, like her daughter's, poking out the bottom of a bobble hat, ski jacket, boots. Next to her an older woman in a navy coat lingers, trying to offer comfort but looking just as upset as the mother – the woman that raised the alert, Lucy assumes. She hands the mum a tissue, and she clutches it to her face as a uniformed officer speaks to them. Lucy can't imagine what this woman is going through. One moment, one mistake, and her whole life has been turned on its head.

Lucy moves away. As callous as it sounds, the mother is not her worry – she has a job to do, and Iggy is the best dog to help her do it. Forty-two kilograms of brown and black German shepherd, with hundreds of years of breeding to ensure he is perfect at this. She steers him away from the bustle and noise, walking him slowly to the football pitches. No commands, just her and her dog on a lead, letting the dog sniff, find his own way. On a lead locate, she's looking for a change in his behaviour. A subtle shift that will tell her the dog has found something out of the ordinary.

She looks for trails – maybe an unusual footpath or track; somewhere a three-year-old might toddle. The conditions are in their favour, a light wind, wet grass, no rain.

The dog isn't trained to look specifically for Rosie. It's not like on TV. They're not presented with an article of the child's clothing to sniff, before the dog goes hurtling down the nearest path. The Scent Article Method – or SAM, as it's known – is too narrow, too unreliable. Instead, this is footstep tracking, hoping the dog finds a human scent, something new, something that doesn't belong on the grass on this freezing cold morning. And that could be anything – people, property – that might help an investigation.

Rosie could be out here in the freezing cold. She could have hurt herself. She might be scared and hiding, concealed in the undergrowth where a human eye won't see her.

But a dog's nose will.

All she needs is a nose in the air. A tensing of his muscles – an indication that Iggy has caught a scent. She leads the dog as he sniffs, weaves this way and that. But he's relaxed. Nothing out of the ordinary here.

'Come on,' she whispers to the universe, willing something to happen. 'Where are you, Rosie?'

CHAPTER THREE

Inspector Greaves isn't happy to see Jack, and Jack can't blame him. Greaves is early thirties and wants to prove himself on his first case as an inspector; the last thing he needs is a DCI looking over his shoulder.

'I appreciate the advice and coffee earlier, but there's no need for you to be here. I'll keep you informed, *sir*.' Greaves leans hard on the sarcastic 'sir'.

'Pretend I'm not here. I'll just observe,' Jack replies.

Greaves is quiet for a moment, no doubt biting back a response that could get him suspended.

'Don't you have a busy Major Crime team to head up?' he says instead.

'They're fine,' Jack says, waving his question away, only too aware of the unanswered messages on his phone – the assault from last night he hurriedly handed over to DS Amrit Gill as he left. 'Have you called the marine unit?'

'On their way.'

'Search and rescue?'

'They're gathering a team.'

'What about—?'

His question is silenced with a glare. 'We have every available officer on the scene. Because of our location here, on the county border, Wiltshire are on alert, ready to send units if we need them. Drones will be in the air in thirty, NPAS will follow with a plane from Herne if we need them. Analysts are scouring CCTV, checking all and every vehicle that has passed before and since. Dog units have been deployed. What else would you have me do?'

Jack ignores his tone. 'Teams are searching the house?'

'As we speak. Perhaps you'd like to go there? Cast your professional eye over the residence.'

'I will,' Jack says. 'Give me the address. I'll head straight down.'

Jack's being a pain in the arse, and he knows it. Greaves writes down the address, passes it to him and then stares, wordlessly, until Jack walks away.

A quick check on Google shows Jack it's a ten-minute walk, and he takes the streets at a brisk pace, keen to warm up in the cold. This isn't the first time he's stuck his nose into a child misper case; in one of his old postings, the teams went out of their way to hide ongoing investigations, actively blocking his involvement until his boss had to intervene.

As he walks, he chastises himself for being so obvious. No repressed psychological damage here – just a deep scar, worn front and centre for all the world to see. Missing person investigations are his kryptonite, and after the events of last June, everyone knows why.

At the age of eleven, Jack's childhood best friend, Theo, went missing, never to be found. Jack was the last person to see Theo alive. He ended up the prime suspect, and even though he was eventually cleared, the resulting investigation swept Jack and his family in its wake, inadvertently destroying his life in the process. He had to change his name, go into hiding, but last June the press got hold of the details again. His worst fears came true – and now everyone knows. The head of MCIT was once a murder suspect.

But that was then. Rosie Logan is now. The press coverage faded; the gossips at the nick found someone else to talk about. He has no wish to bring that all up again, but still. Ten minutes. He'll supervise the search here, and then he'll head back to the nick. He's sure the little girl will have turned up by then.

-

The Logan house is huge – three floors, double-fronted, red brick, the expansive driveway full of patrol cars, blocking a white

Land Rover and a flashy BMW. A rusty Renault Clio sits alongside.

As he walks closer, he hears raised voices – the grand front door is open and a man in a black suit is arguing with one of the uniformed officers.

'She's not here. She's not in the loft. She's not in the garden. Why are you tramping through my house?'

'But sir, as we discussed—'

'Rosie went missing at the park, you need—'

'Can I help?' Jack says, straightening up to his full six foot two and standing in the doorway. The two men stop immediately. 'DCI Jack Ellis,' he says, holding out his ID. 'What seems to be the problem?'

'Mr Logan here is refusing—'

'I don't see the point of you wasting your time searching my house. My daughter's out there.' Mr Logan points past Jack's shoulder. 'She's out there… And you should be… You should…' The man sags, the air whooshing out of his lungs. 'Why aren't you trying to find her?' he says finally, his voice no more than a whisper.

Jack steps forward and gently encourages the man into the closest room – a lounge, decorated in shades of grey and cream and white. He slumps onto the sofa, his head in his hands.

Jack directs the uniform towards the kitchen, then sits next to Mr Logan.

'You're Rosie's dad?' he asks, softly.

'Yes. Tony. Tony Logan. I'm… I'd just started work when Maria called. Said Rosie was missing.' He looks up, his face stricken. 'Please. They won't tell me anything. The police told me to come here and wait. Where's my daughter?'

'We're looking for her. Your wife – Maria? – she's at the park, assisting the police with the search. We are doing everything we can to find Rosie. We have all officers at our disposal, dog teams, officers scouring CCTV back at the station. We're phoning round hospitals, doing a house-to-house. Finding Rosie is our highest priority right now.'

'She's only three. What was Maria doing? How could she have lost her? And then I get back here and that guy—' He jabs with one finger towards the kitchen. 'Tells me they need to search the house. Why? She's not here!'

'It's standard procedure, Mr Logan. You wouldn't believe the number of missing children that show up safe and sound at home. Dropped back by a well-meaning neighbour, collected by another member of the family. Is there anyone—?'

But before Jack can finish his sentence, Tony Logan is on his feet, shouting.

'Eddie! Eddie, are you home? Get down here this second!'

Jack follows the father as he sprints up the staircase, still bellowing at the top of his lungs. He barges into a room at the top, the door flying open and revealing a darkened bedroom, the curtains closed. A bleary face pokes out from under the duvet, squinting as Logan puts the main light on.

'Tony, man, what the fuck—'

'Where's Rosie? Have you seen Rosie?'

'Rosie? No. You've just woken me up…'

Eddie pulls himself to a sit, running his hands through his mop of unruly black curls. Late teens, Jack guesses. Certainly old enough to be doing something more productive than lying around in this smell and mess at this hour of the day. He stares at Jack.

'Who are you?' he says. 'What's going on?'

Tony slumps against the wall, his hands over his face.

Jack introduces himself to the confused kid. 'We're here because your sister, Rosie—'

'Half-sister,' Tony interjects.

'Rosie's missing.'

'Missing? What? How?'

'Your mother bloody well lost her this morning,' Tony snaps. He turns and goes back down the stairs.

'Eddie? Is that your name?' Eddie nods. 'You've been here all morning?'

'Yeah.' Eddie swings his bare legs out of bed, dressed in boxer shorts and a T-shirt. 'I'm a heavy sleeper. I was out last night.' His gaze shifts guiltily to his desk, where a huge green glass bong sits on the top.

Jack gives him an indulgent smile. 'I'm going to pretend I haven't seen that. But you may want to get dressed. Your dad might need some support.'

'Tony's not my dad,' Eddie retorts. 'He met my mum when I was twelve.'

'But he's Rosie's dad?'

'Yeah. For what use he is. Bank account, that's all.' Eddie stands up. 'I'll get dressed,' he says wearily, and Jack takes it as his cue to leave.

'Which room is Rosie's?' he asks before he goes.

'Just there. Next to Mum and Tony's.'

Eddie flaps his hand in the general direction, then pushes the door shut with a hairy foot.

Jack takes a few steps and pushes down the handle. There's always something sad and eerie about looking around the room of someone who's missing. Beds unmade, books half read, clothes discarded on the floor, worse case never to be worn again. Rosie's is no different.

Jack has little experience in this area, but the bedroom looks typical for a three-year-old girl. Pink walls, an animal frieze marching around the top. Pink curtains. Pink duvet on a small white single bed. A riot of stuffed toys are stacked on top of a chest of drawers, some spilling to the floor; books are shoved higgledy-piggledy in a bookcase, some Jack recognises – *The Gruffalo*, *The Very Hungry Caterpillar* – some he doesn't. The mess is in direct contrast to the pristine house below, and more in keeping with the residence of a small child. Miscellaneous toys scatter the plush light grey carpet – Jack picks up a small red plastic cup, from a tea set, he assumes. Wonders who was playing with Rosie. Her mother? He can't imagine either of the men he has met so far sitting cross-legged, offering imaginary tea and biscuits to a teddy bear.

Jack places the cup on the windowsill, looking out to the garden. Tony Logan has given his permission to start the search; outside the window, black figures scour the lawn, peering over the back fence, looking through the shed.

Jack opens a few drawers, but nothing seems out of place so he leaves the room, taking a detour into the bathroom. He looks at the two toothbrushes on display, picking up the pink dinosaur-shaped one and putting it in an evidence bag he takes from his pocket.

Back downstairs, uniformed officers methodically move their way through the house. One passes Jack, heading up, no doubt to check the loft. Jack joins Tony back in the sitting room, where a cup of tea is cooling on the table.

Jack holds out the toothbrush. 'Is this Rosie's?'

Tony peers at it. 'Yes. Why—?' Then he stops himself. 'DNA,' he says, answering his own question, his head tilting down to his hands.

'Mr Logan, can you think of anyone else who might have Rosie? Friends, relatives?'

'No, it's just us,' he says to the floor. 'We moved here a few years ago, just after Rosie was born. For me, for work. Maria hasn't got many friends.' He looks up, his mouth downturned. 'If any.'

'Rosie's grandparents?'

'Both my parents are dead. Maria's mum died when she was seventeen, dad a few years earlier.'

'And Eddie's father? Where is he?'

'Sean? Waste of space. Like his son. Not seen Eddie for as long as I've been around. Probably doesn't even know Rosie exists.'

'Full name?'

'Sean Madden.'

'Does Maria ever speak to him?'

'No. Absolutely not. Can't stand the sight of him.'

'And what do you do, Tony?'

'I'm the sales director for a company in Winchester. Hammerton-Clyde? Have you heard of it?'

'No, sorry. That must take you away from home a lot?'

But before Tony can reply, a uniformed officer sticks his head around the door. He glances at Tony, then tilts his head at Jack, indicating he should come and speak to him.

Tony notices the unspoken message pass between the two cops. 'What's going on?' he says. 'Tell me.'

'I'll be right back,' Jack says, attempting a reassuring smile. 'What is it?' he whispers to the PC, once they're both standing in the hallway.

'You need to go back to the park,' the PC replies. 'And bring the father. The dogs… they've found something.'

CHAPTER FOUR

Lucy feels all eyes on her as she walks Iggy around the sports field. The dog trots at her side, his concentration darting to and fro: too many distractions, too much noise. The bustle of police uniforms; the crackle of radios; overhead a drone buzzes, surveying the area. She leads him further away – *think like a three-year-old*, she tells herself, look for something that might have caught Rosie's eye. An animal in the bushes, a glint of something shiny. But there's nothing.

PC Pete Nash arrives at the far side of the park – a tall figure in black, the huge form of Dax, his German shepherd, next to him. Even from this distance Pete's attractive, broad-shouldered, excellent hair. She can imagine the dark shadow of stubble across his chin, the simple scent of him – shampoo, toothpaste, and the faintest hint of warm biscuity dog. He looks her way; she raises an arm in greeting. He does the same, then points towards the woodland on the opposite side of the road, north of the car park. Heading over there, he's saying.

Another truck has drawn up – black, unmarked – the marine unit, towing a red RIB on a trailer. They draw focus. Already a few journalists have arrived, curious, with their notebooks and cameras. A press release won't go out yet, not until the inspector knows what he's faced with, but the more attention they get, the sooner he'll be obliged to make a statement. And then the full force of the nation will fall on his shoulders. A missing three-year-old. White, blue eyes, blonde angelic curls. Guaranteed to be noticed by everyone.

Still. That's not her problem. Once it might have been, but her days as a detective inspector are behind her. Life is simple now.

Necessary, after the abduction and murder of her husband, Nico, resolved last summer when his body was finally found after two years missing. Still the memories of him flicker, impinging on her consciousness, threatening to derail her.

It's no wonder she can't get past first base with the delicious Pete Nash; there's just too much baggage.

Iggy pulls her back to reality. The shepherd has paused at the end of the concrete path, amber eyes on her, checking for permission before he moves on to the wooden area, just beyond.

'Come on then,' she says, and they push into the trees.

The path evolves to gravel and mud, unattractive for a three-year-old, even one in wellies. Out of the sunshine the air is chilled; she pauses to zip her coat to her chin and that's when she spots Iggy. His whole body has tensed; nose to the ground, he's huffing at the dry leaves on the path.

'What you got?' she says to him.

That's the permission he needs: he starts to move, still hoovering at the dirt, his head zipping this way and that, losing the scent, then catching it again.

She follows him – giving slack on the lead but keeping him within reach. Every muscle in his body is poised, 100 per cent focused on the scent trail up his nose, and she feels the same way, wishing, hoping, her heart thumping hard in her chest. But there are no guarantees here. Iggy might lose the scent, or it might just be some other human who's walked that way this morning. Some nameless, insignificant person, long gone.

Lucy is still following the dog when he stops abruptly and drops into a down position. She praises him, gives him a pat and a stroke then pulls him away. She doesn't want to contaminate the find.

Because what's in front of her dog is significant. A small, well-loved, grey bunny rabbit toy. Belonging to Rosie Logan.

–

She waits while Miller is summoned; he arrives with Inspector Greaves and the two men stand over the rabbit, looking at it gravely. The inspector snaps a photo on his phone.

She shouts across to the PolSA. This changes the focus of the search – assuming this is Rosie's, they have a live scent. A start point for the dog to follow.

'Brian? Can I…?'

She points away, into the woodland. He nods. If Rosie passed through here, she needs to get Iggy back on the trail before precious scent is dispersed. She pulls her dog away, this time directing him with a hand to the ground and a command, 'Seek.'

She lets the dog lead her, sniffing, searching, but they circle, aimless. After ten minutes, Iggy looks up at her, tongue lolling.

Whatever he was following has gone.

She spends another half an hour walking Iggy through the woodland to no avail. Disheartened, she returns to the rendezvous point at the rugby club where Miller is waiting. He looks up from the map as she arrives.

'Good find with the toy,' he says.

'It's hers, right?'

'Greaves is confirming with the parents, but yes, we think so. DCI Ellis is with them.'

'Ellis is still here?' She glances to the line of journalists outside the cordon, stamping their feet in the cold. 'That'll get tongues wagging.'

'Hmm.' Miller frowns, his brow lowered. She doesn't have to ask what he's thinking.

They're into the second hour of a misper search. It's three degrees out, barely above freezing. They've deployed dogs, drones. Lucy can hear the *thub thub* of the helicopter overhead, searching the area with a telescopic zoom and infrared. The marine teams are now out on the river, studying the flow, estimating where Rosie – where her body – might be, before deploying the divers.

And they have nothing.

'What would you go for?' Miller asks. 'If you were in charge?'

She meets Miller's gaze. He's asking which misper category she would put Rosie into; which of the four she would choose.

Lucy sighs. The first, missing voluntarily, they can rule out – Rosie's three, she's no errant kid, running away from home.

'If we assume the rabbit is Rosie's,' Lucy says, 'why did she drop it?'

Miller nods. 'You're going for box number two? Missing through illness or injury?'

'Or generally lost – category three. Wandered away from her mother, couldn't find her way back?'

'But the location of the rabbit was a good two hundred metres away from the park. She walks all that way, and nobody sees her? Her mum doesn't spot her? And where is she now?' Miller turns back to his map before Lucy can answer. Any appetite for speculation has gone – neither of them wants to mention the fourth category: missing through third-party involvement. Someone has her.

But if she's been found, why haven't the police been called? If Rosie is out here alone, it's freezing cold, and the displaced rabbit is an ominous sign. The river is deep and fast; the main road on the other side would quickly take any would-be abductor to the motorway and north.

The prognosis doesn't look good for the missing Rosie Logan.

CHAPTER FIVE

Maria Logan collapses to her knees the moment Greaves shows her the photograph of the soft toy bunny. Her hands go over her face and her shoulders convulse.

The husband goes white. 'Yes, that's Rosie's,' he confirms with a croak. 'She didn't go anywhere without Rupert.'

They're standing in the park, Jack by Tony Logan's side. The husband reaches out and places a hand on Maria's back. Jack observes with interest as she shrugs it off, gathering herself together and standing up, wrapping her arms around her middle, refusing any comfort from her husband.

'What happens now?' Tony asks, in an officious tone.

'Rosie's rabbit is being processed by our forensics team as we speak. Looking for evidence, foreign DNA, anything that might give an indication as to Rosie's whereabouts. Could you both provide a sample, Mr and Mrs Logan? Just a simple swab in the mouth. For elimination purposes?'

'Of course, anything we can do.'

'The search is still ongoing,' Greaves continues. 'We are doing everything we can to find your daughter, but if you would be so kind as to go to your home, we can update you from there.'

There's a clamour from the far side of the cordon. Voices shouting.

'Inspector Greaves, who's gone missing?'

'Who are you looking for?'

'Is it a child?'

Greaves regards the journalists with an icy glare, then turns back to the family. 'We will be making a statement to the press soon, just to make you aware. Nothing detailed at this stage, something simple to say that your daughter has gone missing and a number to contact if anyone knows anything. Is that okay?'

Both parents nod silently.

'You may receive calls of your own. If you do, please don't share any details with the press. Just hang up or say, "No comment." Understood?'

More nodding.

'Thank you,' Greaves finishes. 'Now PC Hammond here will drive you home, and take a DNA sample once you get there. We'll arrange for a family liaison officer to come by shortly.'

'I don't want a stranger in my house,' Tony says.

'Mr Logan—'

'The FLO is there to help you,' Jack interrupts. 'To update you on the investigation, answer any questions you might have. While Inspector Greaves here continues to run the search.'

Tony's face is still stony, but Maria interjects before he can speak again.

'Let them do their job,' she says, and he stays quiet, allowing himself to be led away by the PC.

Greaves watches them go, then turns to Jack.

'I assume the house search is complete? And you'll be leaving?'

Jack chooses to ignore the unsubtle hint. 'Not yet. The officers are still going through the bedrooms. Drawers, wardrobes, that sort of thing.'

Greaves stares. 'That's a bit detailed, isn't it?'

'Maybe. Worth being thorough, don't you think?'

'These are nice people, DCI Ellis. This isn't your run-of-the-mill council house mental case. They don't deserve this sort of scrutiny.'

Jack blinks at Greaves's blatant prejudice. He collects himself before he speaks.

'Every parent, every victim, deserves our respect and sympathy, Inspector,' he says, his voice low and quiet, his tone icy. 'And none deserve our judgement. Do you hear me?'

Greaves goes red. 'Yes,' he mumbles.

'Yes, what?'

'Yes, sir.'

'We will treat Mr and Mrs Logan in the same way as we would anyone involved in an investigation of this nature. In that we will cover every base, tick every box. But we will do it with respect and care. Do we understand each other?'

'Yes, sir.'

'Now do your job. Update the press. I'll head back to the house. I'll update you if we find anything.'

Greaves walks away without another word, Jack's stare boring into his back.

'DCI Ellis.'

He jumps. 'What?' He turns. It's Lucy, with Iggy by her side. 'Sorry. How's it going?'

She looks after the departed Greaves, ignores his question. 'You need to take over.'

'There's no reason—'

'I heard – the toy belongs to Rosie. You know what that means: something awful's happened to her.'

'We don't know why Rosie dropped the rabbit. She's young. Three-year-olds drop things all the time.'

'So where is she?' Lucy glances at her watch. 'It's been two and a half hours.'

Jack doesn't need Lucy to say it – the fact that Rosie is still missing after all this time infers a third-party involvement, and that means a crime's been committed, taking the investigation in a whole different direction. But Jack's also aware he needs to be careful. Keep his personal feelings to himself. Rosie is not Theo. One missing child does not mean history is repeating; procedures exist for a reason.

'It sends the wrong message if MCIT take over,' he says, taking great pains to keep his tone measured. 'We have no proof—'

'Why are you holding back, Jack?' Lucy stares at him, disbelieving. 'You had no qualms sticking your nose in this morning, why are you so reticent now?'

'Lucy—'

'Is this about Theo? What are you afraid of? You didn't fail him then, and you won't fail Rosie now—'

'PC Halliday!' Jack snaps, then lowers his voice straight away. 'Please remember where you are and who I am. You have no right to tell a DCI what to do. I will take over this investigation as and when protocol dictates I should do so. Do your job. Stop telling me how to do mine.'

She stares at him, fury in her eyes. 'No, you're right. *Sir*. You do what you believe is correct. You stick to your precious protocol.'

And with that she stalks off, Iggy locked to her side.

'Shit,' Jack mutters. That's two people he's pissed off in the space of ten minutes, all because he's interfered with this investigation. He could be in his nice warm office, his team around him, dealing with crimes that fall squarely within his remit. He's lucky he didn't get bitten – that Iggy didn't take his raised voice as a threat to his handler and munch a good solid chunk out of his arm. He would have deserved it.

He turns and watches Lucy leave, Iggy looking up at her, gusts of warm breath turning icy in the air as he pants. Heading back to the rugby club, no doubt. To do their job.

But is finding Rosie Logan his? He hunches his shoulders, rubs his hands together, trying to get some feeling back in his numb fingers, then thrusts his hands into his armpits. As it stands, the investigation lies with Greaves – as much as Jack dislikes him. There is no evidence a crime has been committed, although Lucy is right – the more time ticks on, the less likely it is that they will find Rosie safe and well.

But something – *someone* – holds Jack back. Lucy knew it, and deep down, Jack knows it too. Theo. The worry that if he gets too close, he will be swept up in something bigger than him. That it will hurt. And this time, it will be more than he can bear.

No, he is right to keep his distance. He will go back to the house, do as he said and finish the search. Then he will return to the nick until he gets the call. Until the boxes are ticked and the process is followed, he will let Inspector Greaves do his job.

Even though every nerve fibre in his body tells him that Lucy is right.

Something's happened to that girl.

CHAPTER SIX

Maria sits next to Tony in the back of the police car, feeling exactly like the criminal she is. Guilt thrums in her veins, churns her stomach. Ever since Rosie disappeared she's felt nauseous, but she will never be sick – her body is drained and empty with her daughter gone.

Her mind cycles through disaster after disaster. Each one as terrible as the last. Rosie broken, dead in a ditch. A paedophile desecrating Rosie's innocent body. Rosie fallen in the river, drowning as the fish and creatures eat her. And in each one, Rosie is calling out her name, her wails of *Mummy* going unanswered. Lost, confused, cold, afraid.

Maria can't cry any more. Her body is dry, a desiccated husk from all the tears she has shed since nine this morning. She longs, prays, wishes that the call will come and Rosie will have been found. But the universe is stubborn; the car remains eerily quiet.

They pull into the driveway. The door is opened and Maria climbs out, Tony following. Maria's distracted by the number of police officers in her house. She knew they were searching but she didn't think they'd be this thorough. This dedicated. They must think they're involved. That more is going on. And they'd be right.

She takes her phone out of her pocket, checks the screen. One new message. With shaking hands, she unlocks the phone.

what u talking about u stupid bitch saw the cops got outta there

He's replied, but he hasn't answered her question.

Have you got my daughter? she types again.

The reply comes back straight away: *what you talking about no delete my number*

'Maria?' She jumps. Tony's at her elbow. 'That policeman is on TV.'

She pushes her phone into her back pocket. The television is on as they walk into the sitting room. Sixty-five inches of Inspector Greaves's stern face, projected across their big-screen TV. A banner runs along the bottom. *MISSING GIRL*, it says, then a reference number. Greaves looks sweaty and uncomfortable, stuttering through every word. Is this the man that's going to find her daughter?

Eddie is sitting on the sofa, watching. He's dressed, but his grey T-shirt has a line of food down the front, his hair is dishevelled and uncombed. Maria sits wordlessly next to him. His cheap deodorant barely masks the smell of bubble gum vape, but she hasn't got the energy to scold him for it now. She reaches out for his hand and for the first time since he was a little boy, he lets her take it.

'...now missing for nearly three hours,' Greaves is saying on the screen. 'Rosie Logan is three years old, with curly blonde hair, wearing a red coat and blue wellington boots. She was last seen at Memorial Park, just after nine a.m.'

A photograph of Rosie takes over. The one Maria gave the first officer that showed up – a shot from her third birthday party. She's smiling, clutching Rupert, a smudge of chocolate cake around her mouth.

'I thought that other guy was in charge,' Eddie says, pointing to the screen. 'The tall bloke.'

'Which one?'

'He came here. Helped with the search. Said—'

'Shush,' Tony hisses.

'He was better than this guy,' Eddie whispers to Maria.

'...police teams have been called and we are using all resources at our disposal to search the area. We ask that members of the public remain vigilant and report any sightings or information on 999 as soon as they can, quoting the incident number on the screen. We will be taking no further questions at this time.'

The press conference ends, and the newsreader shifts to the next story.

'That's it?' Tony says. 'That's all they're going to do?'

'They're doing all they can,' Maria replies.

'Fuck all. They haven't found her. And I hate to say it, but Boy Wonder here is right for a change. Why isn't that detective in charge?'

Maria doesn't have an answer for that. She doesn't have an answer for any of it. She's weary, her muscles aching.

'I'm going to go and have a lie-down,' she mumbles, standing up.

Tony's stare follows her as she leaves the room. She's felt his gaze the whole journey here. The judgement, the questions. The blame – and rightfully so. Five minutes of distraction, and Rosie had gone.

She can't bear to be around him. The hypocritical bastard.

Because she knows: it's his fault.

Whatever happens, it will always be his fault.

CHAPTER SEVEN

Lucy strides towards the rugby club, seething with every step. Iggy hurries at her side, looking up with concerned eyes, sensing the furious mood of his handler. How dare Jack talk to her like that? Pulling rank, even though he damn well knows she's right? Jack – and the MCIT – should be in charge of this search. He's just hiding, afraid of being front and centre of yet another missing child investigation.

Once she gets in the warm, she pours herself a coffee and helps herself to two digestive biscuits, dropping one to Iggy, who eats it in a single bite. *Do your job?* she thinks, remembering Jack's bitten words and cursing him all over again. She'll help find this child even if he's going to stand by and do nothing.

Her phone rings in her pocket and she pulls it out. *Fran*, it says on the screen; she answers it.

'Are you working this?' Fran asks. 'The missing girl?'

'Me and the whole constabulary.'

'Am I going to be needed?'

Lucy pauses. Dr Fran Rosetti – Lucy's best friend, and a forensic pathologist – would be the first person called to the scene if they find a body. A body. The elephant in the room that nobody wants to address.

'I don't know,' Lucy says, slowly. 'We're still searching, nothing yet.'

'Rumour has it her toy has been found.'

'In some woodland. Far side of the sports field.'

'Near the river?'

'Yes.'

Lucy turns her attention to Inspector Greaves, outside, pacing on the worn patch of grass in front of the rugby club, a phone clamped to his ear. His stress must be through the roof, ratcheting up as each new press van parks up outside the cordon. People are watching. Minutes tick by and the child still isn't found.

'Greaves doesn't have a clue,' Lucy says.

'Never did. Even when he was a PC. Miracle he's got to where he is now.'

'Well, I think he's starting to wish he'd turned down that promotion. I told Jack he should take over this investigation.'

'DCI Ellis?' Fran says. She's not police, but even a forensic pathologist knows about rank. 'He's there?'

'Just passing by, he said. Bollocks,' she adds, with feeling.

'Go easy on him. Every missing child is a reminder of Theo. It must be difficult. Even though he was a child when it happened, losing his best friend in that way would have scarred him to an unimaginable extent.' Fran lets out a long sigh. 'You gave him both barrels, didn't you?'

Lucy feels awful. 'I've got to go,' she says hurriedly, taking a convenient out as Miller heads towards her.

'Call me later. You're off after today, right? Come round for dinner?'

'Four whole days of solid rest. And yes, I would love to.'

'Make sure you do,' Fran finishes, and hangs up.

'Drink up,' Miller says, gesturing to her mug of coffee. 'We're expanding the search. Greaves wants us to cover the other side of the road. Up to the boundary of the A338.'

'He's thinking a three-year-old crossed the Ringwood Road? All by herself? In rush hour?'

'He wants to be sure. Take Iggy over there. Start with the outbuildings.'

At the mention of his name, Iggy sits up, ears raised. Miller leaves and Lucy zips up her coat, walking back into the cold.

She trudges alongside Iggy, across the soft grass, pausing for a second to consider the fast flow of the river; the wide tangled depths. The marine team are hard at work. Two men in black sit in a red RIB, solemnly regarding the inky swell as they ebb and flow with the current. Another few are huddled around a laptop on the shore, a serious group, people with PhDs who know about tides. Who know where the body of a three-year-old might wash up, if that's where she's fallen.

In Lucy's mind, sadly, this is still one of the most likely scenarios. She doesn't envy the police divers. She finds the bodies, as they do, but hers are on solid ground. Not underwater, breathing air from a bottle, trapped in whatever confined space they are allocated to search. The thought alone makes her breath hitch with claustrophobia. No, she'll stick to above ground, thank you very much.

She starts walking again.

He's right, of course. Jack. Right to tell her to wind her neck in. Fran knew it; she should listen to her friend. Out here he is a detective chief inspector, in charge of an army of cops. Structure and rank exist for a reason. Coppers need to do what they're told; what Jack says, goes.

In this case, *do your job*.

They haven't searched the opposite side of the road with dogs. Mainly because of the improbability of the area. At nine a.m., the road would have been heaving. It's the main thoroughfare out of the town, heading towards Ringwood. How could a three-year-old have crossed without someone noticing?

She can see Pete Nash on the far side, searching to the north. She heads south, to the large outbuildings on the edge of the car park.

They're mainly concrete – two ugly boxes with plain grey plastered walls and a corrugated iron roof. She patrols the outside, Iggy on a long line, his nose high, looking for a scent on the wind. The first, bigger opening, is a set of metal shutters, secured at the bottom with a heavy padlock. She bends down and pulls; it won't move more than a few inches upwards. No space to get in, not even for a small child.

She continues – the next building has two solid wooden doors, a thick chain and padlock woven though each handle. But this time Iggy stops, places his nose against the gap between the ground and the door, and sniffs. A long full snort, something in the air. Something he likes.

Lucy tugs at the doors to reveal a dark interior, enough of a gap to slip through. Easily big enough for a German shepherd and his five-foot-three slender handler. Lucy wrenches the doors as far apart as she can, then ducks under the chain. Inside, she takes her torch out of her pocket and clicks it on.

The narrow beam of light shows what Lucy expected. Numerous old football goals, their poles and nets entwined. Netball posts. A ride-on mower.

Lucy starts to call, softly, 'Rosie? Rosie, are you here?'

She runs her torch around the space, as Iggy continues his search. There's something new in his body language – he's tense, his nose quivering, tail high.

He swings his head, trying to catch it, then down to the ground, snorting and huffing at the dry leaves and dust on the concrete. He shifts again, moving as if guided by an invisible line, following the scent, pulling Lucy along in his wake.

Until she sees what he's found.

A flash of yellow. Low down, hidden by a lopsided picnic table. The curve of a shoulder, the pink of skin. Adrenaline pulses in Lucy's veins. Could this be Rosie? Surely...?

She stops Iggy – 'Finish' – and takes a step forward. Iggy is on alert, his posture strong, his mouth open and panting, but too well trained to move without her command. Reassured with the dog by her side, she crouches down in front of the discarded furniture.

'My name's Lucy. I'm a police officer. I can help you. Could you come out, please?'

The person shakes, but otherwise doesn't move.

'You're not in trouble. But you need to come out.'

'I don't want your dog to bite me.' A small voice, high. A boy. Disappointment flares. It's not Rosie, but an older child.

'This is Iggy. And he won't bite you, I promise. What's your name?'

'Lewis.'

'Hi, Lewis. I'm Lucy,' she repeats. 'Could you move closer so I can see you?'

There's a clatter, and a small boy emerges. He's pale and shivering, his arms wrapped around his body. He eyes the dog warily.

'He won't hurt you,' Lucy says. 'How long were you in there, Lewis?'

'I don't know,' the boy mumbles. 'An hour or so?'

'Why were you hiding?'

'Because of them.' He points to outside, then to the white letters on her jacket.

'The police?'

'Dad says I shouldn't speak to the police.'

Lucy swallows a retort. She's sure Lewis's father has his reasons – illegal ones, probably – but teaching children to avoid the police makes her job immeasurably harder.

'We can help you,' Lucy repeats, her voice soothing. 'We can take you home. Do you want to go home?'

The boy looks unsure.

'Or somewhere else? Do you know the rugby club? Just over there. We have drinks. Hot chocolate, biscuits.'

The boy's eyes light up. 'Do you have Coke?'

Lucy laughs. 'We can find you a can of Coke.'

She holds out her hand, but the boy ignores it, pulling himself to his feet. Now he's upright she can see he's older than she initially thought. Maybe eleven or twelve. Should be at school. Should not be hiding in a locked building, on a freezing Wednesday morning.

She walks him slowly out of the building, the boy on one side, Iggy on the other. She keeps a wary eye on Lewis, not wanting him to run as they get closer to the rugby club.

Once they're in sight, conversation stills as the other police officers see them approach. Brian Miller lowers his wire-framed glasses to watch; Greaves stands straight in anticipation. Lucy hasn't asked Lewis any questions – it's not her place to do so – but she wonders how much these coppers will get out of him.

Leaving Iggy with Miller outside the rugby club, she steers Lewis inside, picking up someone's spare coat and draping it over his shoulders. She gestures to a fold-up chair.

'Here, sit there. I'll get you that Coke. Sure you wouldn't like something warmer?'

'Nah-ah,' he says. 'You promised Coke. And not that diet stuff, neither.'

'Right you are,' Lucy says with a smile.

She digs into her pocket, pulls out a few quid and hands it to the nearest uniformed officer.

'Go to the Co-op,' she whispers. 'Buy this kid a can of Coke. And some chocolate – a Mars bar or something. Make it quick.'

The policeman doesn't quibble and jogs off in the direction of the town centre.

She turns back to Lewis. 'It's on its way. Now, if I could introduce you to someone?' Greaves has appeared by her elbow, bristling with self-importance. 'Lewis, this is Inspector Greaves. He has a few questions for you.'

'Questions?' The kid glances from Lucy to Greaves, nervous. 'I didn't agree to no questions.'

'What's your surname, Lewis?' Greaves asks, almost pushing Lucy out of the way.

The kid clamps his mouth shut and shakes his head.

'A three-year-old went missing from this park today. Did you know that?'

Lewis glances past Lucy to the sports field, to the police cars and the bustle. His eyes widen with fear.

'I didn't see no girl,' he says.

Greaves tenses. 'I didn't say it was a girl.'

'I didn't— It wasn't—'

'When did you see her?' Greaves snaps. 'What did you do?'

Interviewing the kid here, like this, breaks every rule in the book. Even as a potential witness, they should be at the police station, with an appropriate adult present. Greaves's desperation is obvious. He's shaking, sweating like an addict at rehab, almost as anxious as the child in his charge. And whatever his approach is, it's not working – there's no way Lewis is going to talk.

He's curled up on the chair, knees up to his chest, recoiled from the inspector, shaking his head, faster and faster. Greaves notices it and steps backwards, and it's then that Lewis takes his chance, springing to his feet and attempting a getaway.

He sprints for the door, but Greaves slams it shut, the boom echoing around the room, standing in front of it, his hands on his hips. The boy screeches to a halt. He's breathing heavily, his hands in tiny fists; a cornered animal, ready to attack.

'You're not going anywhere until you talk to us,' Greaves says.

Lewis isn't the only one scared – Lucy's terrified. She's never seen anything like this – the inspector in charge has lost control. And he's threatening a child.

'Sir!' Lucy shouts. And for the first time, Lucy notices the stain on Lewis's coat. Streaks of dark red, spotted and smudged.

'I'm going to tell my dad,' Lewis says, backing away. 'You can't keep me here. I know my rights.'

'Tell us what you know,' Greaves snaps again, and the kid starts to cry.

'My dad's going to sue you,' he snuffles through his tears.

Lucy looks at Greaves, then back to Lewis. Surely Greaves must know that scaring a kid won't get results? Inexperience is making the recently promoted inspector panic; the trace of what can only be blood and the fact the kid has clearly seen Rosie adds to the fact that Greaves is, at best, an arsehole, producing a melting pot of disaster.

Outside, the noise has attracted interest – coppers stopping dead, looking through the windows; Miller doing his best to restrain an agitated Iggy. This stand-off has to end now, but they can't risk losing their witness. This kid might know something about Rosie; there's no way they can let him go.

There's only one person Lucy can call.

CHAPTER EIGHT

Jack is on the way back to the park when he answers the phone, his face darkening as he listens. An unaccompanied child, a potential witness, and a senior officer losing his shit.

He doubles his pace, making it back within five minutes. While he walks, he sends a message to DS Gill, asking for a favour, and all the while Lucy's messages arrive. A continuous stream – *The kid knows something, but no way he's talking to Greaves*, *Come now*, and a final, desperate, *Where are you???*

He sprints the last hundred metres across the muddy grass to the rugby club, but when he gets there, he pauses. His heart is racing, his breathing fast. He can't go in like this – the last thing this kid needs is another stressed copper.

He pushes the door open to the rugby club and takes a left turn, away from the main room. He finds himself behind the bar, surrounded by large metal barrels and opened boxes of soft drinks. The smell of old beer and sweat in the air.

He waits. He can hear the conversation in the next room – Greaves's insistent demands, the high-pitched squeak from a child, and Lucy, trying to intervene. He takes another step; he can just see Greaves through the shutters.

Lucy's right: Greaves is stressed. His shirtsleeves are rolled up, he's sweating, leaning forward to the kid sitting on a chair in front of him. The child is pale-faced and still. Lucy is in between them, shielding the child.

'You saw Rosie, you told us that,' Greaves is saying. 'Whatever you did, you're only making matters worse by not talking.'

'I didn't see her. I don't know—'

'You told us you did.'

'I didn't.'

'Sir, can I have a word—' Lucy glances at her phone. 'You need to stop—'

'I'll stop whenever this kid tells us what he did to Rosie. And you should go back to your *dog*, Constable Halliday.'

The words, the situation, drag Jack back in time. He remembers being that kid, eleven years old, brought in for questioning over the disappearance of his best friend. Tired, confused, full of worry. The night before he'd been pulled out of his bed in the dead of night, questioned in his living room. *What time did you leave Theo? Did anyone see you when you walked home? When did you get home? Where did Theo say he was going?*

Before that day his biggest concern had been whether he could cobble together enough pocket money for him and Theo to see *Jurassic Park* again, and there he was, being threatened with arrest for murder. His memories blurred, and confused, he changed his story, again and again, until the detective was shouting with frustration. He'd cried, pleaded to go home, but nobody – not even the appropriate adult to his left – did anything to help.

Why am I here? Jack asks himself. This missing child feels personal; how can he keep it separate to maintain the professional distance he needs? There's no doubt Theo's disappearance when he was eleven has driven his whole career – that determination to succeed where detectives at the time hadn't – and up to now it's worked in his favour, albeit to the detriment of his personal life. But he's done mispers before, why should this one be any different?

For nearly thirty years, Jack ignored his past. But the events of last summer brought it all to the surface, and since then he's been struggling to keep Theo out of his head. The dreams have returned, a constant reminder of the boy they couldn't find. Events out of his control; the tight grip he keeps on his life has been weakening, and he doesn't like it.

His phone beeps again – *You need to stop this!* – rousing Jack from his past trauma. He retraces his steps, and pushes the double doors open into the room.

Greaves turns. His face is puce, his expression a mixture of guilt and fear.

'Can I have a word, Inspector?' Jack says evenly.

'I'm in the middle of something—'

'Now.'

Greaves throws a furious look to Lucy, then follows Jack into the corridor.

'This kid knows something. He saw Rosie,' Greaves snaps. 'He's a witness, at the very least. Maybe even a suspect.'

'So you're interviewing him without an appropriate adult present, in the middle of a rugby club?'

'I cautioned him.'

'Have you contacted his parents?'

'He won't give us his full name.'

'I'm not surprised. He's probably terrified.' Jack raises himself to his full height. 'You should return to the station, Inspector Greaves. I'll take over from here.'

'Now we have a lead, you want the case?' Greaves hisses. 'Is that it?'

'From where I'm standing you don't have a lead. You have a scared kid and a potential complaint on your hands.'

Greaves stays quiet.

'What's he told you?' Jack asks.

'He saw her. He's got blood on his coat. He did something.'

'He said that?'

'No, but—'

'But nothing. You wouldn't treat an adult in custody like this. You certainly shouldn't be doing this to a young boy.'

'He's a murder suspect.'

'He's a *child*,' Jack stresses.

'What if he's hurt her?'

'What if he confesses? And because you haven't followed PACE the whole damn thing gets thrown out? What then, Inspector Greaves?'

Greaves throws his hands up in disgust. 'Fine. Take him. Take the whole damn investigation. See if I care.'

And he storms through the main doors with a bang.

Jack takes a long, deep inhale and looks down at his hands, stretching his fingers wide, willing the shaking to abate.

A uniformed copper appears at his side, clutching a Coke and a Mars bar. He hands them to Jack. 'Halliday said to get these for the kid.'

'Great, thanks.'

Jack closes his eyes, takes a calming breath, and goes into the room.

The kid looks up in surprise as Jack approaches. Jack crouches down to his level. 'I'm sorry about that,' he says. 'My name is Jack. I hear you were promised this.' He passes Lewis the Coke and the chocolate.

'Yeah...' Lewis glances up at Lucy, who smiles, warmly, then snaps the ring pull open and presses his mouth against the stream of fizz. He takes a few long gulps then burps.

Jack laughs. 'Better?'

'I want to go home.'

'And you will. We'll call your parents, get them to pick you up. Do you have a number for them?'

Lewis looks hesitant, then capitulates. 'My mum works at the library. Call her. Not my dad,' he adds quickly.

'What's her name?'

'Sarah. Sarah Nicholls.'

'So you're Lewis Nicholls?'

The kid nods, taking another swig of Coke.

'We'll call her now.' Jack nods to the PC waiting at the door, who notes the name.

'There's a woman to see you,' the PC adds. 'She says you requested an appropriate adult.'

Jack breathes a sigh of relief at Amrit's fast work. 'I did, thank you.'

Jack shows the woman into the room. She looks confused at the unusual set-up, but introduces herself and sits next to the boy. He doesn't give her more than a cursory glance, opening the chocolate bar and taking a large bite.

The full responsibility of the investigation now falls squarely on Jack's shoulders, and he's acutely aware of every one of the four hours Rosie's been missing. He looks at Lucy. He should have taken over sooner. Proof or no proof, they all know this isn't going to end well.

And as much as Jack identifies with him – remembers himself, aged eleven, in this same appalling situation – he must stay objective. There's no guarantee this kid's innocent. Blood on his jacket, bunking off school? Young children can do terrible things, Jamie Bulger taught us that.

Jack grabs a chair and sits down.

'Lewis?' he says to the chewing boy. 'While we wait for your mum, do you mind if we have a chat?'

'Are you in charge?' he asks through his mouthful.

'I am now.'

'Okay, whatever.'

'Do you know how cold it is out there today?' Lewis shakes his head. 'Three degrees Celsius. Nearly freezing. How long do you think you can stay out in that before you get ill?'

'Not long,' the boy mumbles. He slowly places the half-eaten chocolate bar in his lap.

'Not long at all. So we need your help. I'm worried. About that little girl… about Rosie. We need to find her, before it's too late.'

The kid stares at his hands, picking at a hangnail.

'Lewis?' Jack repeats. 'You're not in trouble. We just need to know.'

'I'm not in trouble?'

'No.'

'Even though I was bunking off school?'

'Let's not worry about that for now,' Jack says with a sigh. 'That's the least of our problems.'

Jack sits back in his seat. He clasps his hands tightly in his lap, trying to contain his impatience. *Wait. Just wait*, he tells himself.

Lewis picks up the Coke then puts it down again. He's on the edge of tears as he looks up at Lucy, then to Jack.

'I didn't do anything to her, I swear. She was like that when I found her.'

'Like what?'

'Her hand. She'd cut her hand, it was bleeding.'

'Was the cut bad?'

'I don't think so, but she was crying. I didn't know what to do.'

'Where was this? Near the park?'

'No, in the woodland. On the other side of the car park. Closer to the houses. There's a cut through – to the estate. Through the trees. Nobody ever goes that way because there's no path, but if you know it, you can find it.'

'Can you show us on a map?'

'Yeah, sure.' Jack glances to Lucy and she gets up, hurrying out of the room.

'What happened? Take me through it, slowly.'

'I didn't hurt her.'

'I believe you, Lewis.' The kid meets Jack's gaze; he seems to trust Jack – his shoulders slump and he picks up the Coke again.

'I was heading to the copse. It's a good place to hang out. When I should be at school,' he mumbles. Jack nods, encouraging him on. 'And she was there. Wailing and screaming.'

'What time was this?'

'Half-ten? I dunno. Her hand was bleeding, and she was crying about Rupert. I don't know who that is.'

'It's her toy rabbit.'

'Oh, okay. I didn't know that. I took a tissue out of my pocket, tried to help but she was just wailing. I thought she'd probably come from the park, so I tried to take her hand, lead her back that way, but she wouldn't move. Just sat on the ground, bawling and bleeding. I panicked. I didn't know what to do. I don't have a phone. My dad won't let me. If I had one, I could've called you guys.'

'Would you have?' Jack says with a smile.

Lewis returns the grin. 'Probably not. But I could've, I dunno…' The smile drops away. 'I didn't know what to do so I told her to stay where she was and ran towards the park. But when I got close the park was full of coppers, and then I realised I had her blood on me, on my coat, so I thought it would be better if I had the girl, so nobody would think I'd hurt her, so I went back to where I'd left her, and… And she'd gone.'

Lewis finishes his garbled sentence with a rush of breath.

'Gone?'

'I looked around, but I couldn't find her.'

'Why didn't you speak to the police then?'

'And say what? "I found this girl. She had blood on her. But now she's gone"? That guy you just kicked out – he would have gone postal. Banged me up for sure. By then the place was crawling with cops. And me, covered in blood. Thought I'd hide until the kid showed up and you left. But you never did. And then that dog got me.'

Lewis meets Jack's gaze. 'You haven't found her, have you?' he says, quietly. 'Does that mean she's dead?'

Jack glances up to the clock and frowns. One p.m. Rosie's been missing for four hours, and nobody has any idea where she is.

'I hope not, Lewis,' Jack replies. 'I really do.'

CHAPTER NINE

Lucy returns with a map. Lewis looks much improved in Jack's company, finishing off his Coke and chocolate. Jack thanks Lucy, then hands the map to Lewis.

He studies it for a moment, turns it this way and that, then points to a patch of ground, just south of the car park.

'There's nothing there,' Jack says. 'They checked. It's fenced off.'

'Yeah, sure. To adults. But if you're a kid who doesn't mind getting grubby, you can get through.'

'And that's where you last saw Rosie?'

'Yeah.'

Jack passes the map to Lucy. 'We'll get on it.'

Lucy doesn't wait for an instruction, but heads straight out, dialling as she goes. Pete answers on the first ring.

'Are you still here? I've got an area we need to search.'

–

Brian Miller hands Iggy to Lucy and the two of them meet Pete in the car park. Lucy shows them the map.

Brian looks towards the patch of woodland. 'If the opening's where you say it is, then the scene's sterile. Nobody's been in there, but it's been a good few hours. I wouldn't hold out much hope of finding a track.' He looks at Pete. 'Nash, you take Dax. And Lucy.' Brian pauses. 'Maybe bring Moss?'

The three of them exchange an unspoken understanding. A last resort. Nash and Dax will cover off the search for a walking, talking human. And she and Moss will look for blood. Or a body.

She walks to the car, loading a happy but tired Iggy into the boot and opening the cage to Moss's half. The black fluffy spaniel looks at her eagerly as she picks up his harness, his paw already raised in readiness as she puts it on him.

They walk across to the copse, Moss cheerful beside her. Pete's found the opening already and gone through; Lucy can see why everyone missed this – the gap in the fence is low, bordered by a length of barbed wire and hidden by a holly bush. She peers at it for a moment, a scrap of red catching her eye. Lucy calls Miller over.

'Rosie's coat?'

He squints. 'Maybe. You know what this means? If that kid is telling the truth, you need to be looking for a blood trail. Go through and leave this with me.'

Moss might have a job after all.

Lucy pushes her way through, Moss following.

Inside the light is dim, the winter sun blocked by the thick spiderweb of branches. It's a small patch of trees – mature oaks and sycamores, leaves fallen, crunching underfoot. There is no formal path – more a track worn between the undergrowth, weaving this way and that to avoid the worst of the puddles and thorns. She can hear crashing to her left as Nash and Dax force their way through. Pete will be walking Dax around, looking for a scent to track. Keen to keep out of their way she heads right and directs Moss with the command, 'Look, look.' Off they go, Moss pulling on the lead, sniffing, concentration locked on the task at hand.

They find their way to a small clearing – in the centre a patch of black remains, charred sticks surrounded by crisp packets, fag butts, vape wrappers, litter from a McDonald's and empty bottles from a range of cheap spirits. A hangout, somewhere to smoke and drink, underage no doubt. Moss sniffs but the teenage dirtbags are long gone, leaving nothing of interest behind.

She turns away, redirecting the dog and suppressing a shiver as she bends down, running her fingers through Moss's thick black coat. He's reassuringly warm, warmer than her on this chilly

February afternoon, and she thinks again about that small girl, out in this cold.

But she doesn't have long to reflect before Moss stops, frozen, his nose down. And there, barely visible against the leaves, is a single red droplet. Blood. She releases the dog with an enthusiastic, 'Yes!' and calls it in through the radio.

'Hold tight, I'm on my way,' comes Miller's reply, and before long he joins her in the woodland.

She points to the spot; he marks it with a red flag.

'We need more blood dogs,' Lucy says. 'Moss can't do this alone.'

'Moss is the only VRD on day shift. You'll have to do what you can.'

'Fantastic,' Lucy mutters, and leads Moss away.

The spaniel is soon back on the trail. Lucy directs his search, pointing here and there, as Moss's frenetic activity yields results. Three more scenes, Miller marking them in turn, each one further into the woodland than the last.

Poor Rosie. Lucy imagines her hurting her hand on the barbed wire, crying, bleeding, as she stumbles through the copse. But how did she end up this far from the park? Lucy can see droppings here and there; maybe she was following an animal – a rabbit or a squirrel. Maybe she was playing hide-and-seek, running away from her mother. But whatever the reason, only her blood remains.

Moss shows no sign of tiring, hauling Lucy along in his wake. Lots to find today, plenty of reward for a small spaniel, doing what he loves. And then he stops. Hesitates at the edge of the trees, the last droplet marked a few metres behind them, his dark brown eyes looking up at Lucy, asking for direction.

'Look, look,' Lucy repeats, and he searches briefly, then pauses again. They've covered this ground already. The next step is through the gate and into the housing estate where pedestrians may have walked, camouflaging the blood with hundreds of other scent patterns of their own. Lucy decides to try but the spaniel circles, unfocused. Too many routes, too many smells.

Lucy calls through to Pete and heads back into the woodland; she doesn't have to wait long, in minutes he's next to her, Dax close to heel. Unlike Iggy, Dax is a predominantly black, long-haired German shepherd. He's a formidable dog – older, more experienced. Trained in firearms support as well as his usual work in general purpose.

'Blood?' Pete says.

'Three scenes, but nothing out there,' she says, pointing towards the houses. 'Dax coming up empty?'

'Yeah, nothing. I thought he had something for a while, but he lost it. Conditions aren't great, maybe it's just been too long.' Dax barks. 'Not your fault, buddy.'

But then he pulls on his lead, and Pete's attention is diverted. The shepherd is looking down, deep into the foliage.

'What've you got?' Pete says to Dax. The dog pulls forward, his nose in the brambles, then crouches down on his haunches, frozen in position.

Pete frowns and gets down on his knees.

'Well, hello,' he says. 'Help me, will you?'

Lucy does as she's told, tugging at the brambles and foliage, not caring about getting scratched. Pete's response tells her it's not a dead body, and as they clear the space, she realises what the dog has found.

It's a small box, painted in beige and green, camouflaged perfectly into the surroundings. To Lucy, it looks like a walkie-talkie with holes on the front – some sort of technology. A padlock secures it shut; webbing straps hold it to the base of the tree.

'It's a camera,' Pete says. He leans into the radio on his shoulder, calling Miller, then points at the front. 'See that? That's the lens. Night vision, motion-activated, waterproof.' Lucy is still looking blank, as Pete explains further. 'A wildlife cam. For videoing badgers and foxes and the like.'

'Do you think it's captured any footage of Rosie?'

'Only one way of finding out.'

Pete praises his dog – Dax receiving a squeaky plastic King Kong action figure, to his glee – as Miller arrives, crouching down and peering at the camera.

'Bloody good work, both of you,' Miller says. 'I'll get this to DCI Ellis – he can take it back to the nick, ASAP.'

'MCIT are taking over?' Pete says. 'Since when?'

'Since now,' Miller replies. 'And thank fuck for that. Someone decent in charge. You both go on a break. I'll shout if I need you.'

Pete and Lucy walk to the car park taking the long way around, avoiding the teams now in the woodland. Lucy knows that once forensics have finished Miller will have licensed search officers going over every inch with their fingertips, looking for anything else that might indicate where Rosie had gone.

Pete breaks the silence after a few moments. 'You know Ellis well, don't you?' he says.

'I guess.'

'You think he can make headway on this?'

'If anyone can, Jack will. And the team.'

Pete nods slowly then pauses, taking something out of his coat pocket. He hands it to her with a sheepish grin. 'Happy Valentine's Day.'

'Oh, shit. Is that today?' She looks at the small white envelope in her hand with horror. 'Did you get me a card?'

'Not exactly. And it's okay. I didn't expect anything… I know… we're not…' He shrugs awkwardly and points towards the rugby club. 'I'm going to get a coffee. Do you want one?'

Lucy declines and watches him stride away, Dax at his heels. Shit. *Shit.* Nervously, she opens the envelope, dreading some sort of pink, slushy card, and laughs out loud with relief. Inside is a car sticker showing a German shepherd, the words *You Might Get In, You Won't Get Out*, written beneath. It's perfect – sweet, not sentimental – and it makes her feel awful.

She hadn't even considered getting him something. There's no reason why she should have – even though it's been nearly nine months it's still a tentative dance. She's never been to his house;

she's never invited him to hers. They meet in neutral territory – pubs, parks, training grounds. All blushes and banter. And desire. Definite desire. But despite that, she and Pete haven't got further than a snog at the end of a date. A long, drawn-out, gropey snog – yes. But no more than that, before they go their separate ways.

But if they're going to move forward, she needs to think about this stuff. The little gestures, the tokens of affection that say *I like you, let's do this*. Because she wants to – bloody hell, does she want to – but something is holding her back.

She's not sure exactly what. Could be a number of things, and she runs through them in her head as she gets to her car and pours water for Moss. The fact her husband has only been in the ground – properly – for nine months. Or that she's got so used to being by herself, she can't imagine what it would be like to have someone in her life again.

She likes things simple. A quiet house. Two dogs. Days taken up with work and training and long walks in the New Forest. Nights – going to bed early with nothing more demanding than a good book and a cup of camomile tea. Could she risk this new-found peace?

But Pete Nash? Gorgeous, single Pete Nash, who understands the demands of her job and has no problem with her spending all her time hanging out with two demanding mutts? What would be so wrong with falling in love with Pete?

Her musings come to an end as Moss finishes his water and she loads him into the car with an enthusiastic leap. He circles and settles, looking out the door of the cage. Iggy has got to his feet, once again keen to get out there and work – she laughs at his lust for life. Eager anticipation, doing what he loves.

He's not scared. Iggy is in danger every day, hurling himself at every bad guy at her command, but he's not held back by the thought of what *might* happen or who could hurt him. He just trusts her, throws himself in there, keen to discover what's in store for him next.

And – not for the first time – Lucy thinks she could learn a lot from her dogs.

CHAPTER TEN

Jack stands in front of his team, their stern faces meeting his. This belongs to MCIT now; finding Rosie is their responsibility, and theirs alone. Jack feels the importance of that: a dull ache in his chest, a barely contained beating of his heart.

But there is no more time for hesitation. The whiteboard has been cleaned; the most recent recruit – DC Emma Bates – stands next to it, a black pen in hand, ready to capture the pertinent points of the case. She's a newly qualified detective – eager, repeatedly pushing the unruly black curls that have escaped from her tidy bun back behind her ears.

Jack appraises the group. DC Phil Lawrence, young, tentative, but growing in confidence. DC Emma Bates. And finally, his second-in-command, DS Amrit Gill, recently promoted but with the best instincts he's seen in a copper. She began at Hampshire Constabulary just before he did, nine months ago now, and has proven herself as smart and dedicated. They've had problems recruiting, and as a consequence they're a small group, but loyal and hardworking. He trusts them. If Rosie's out there, Jack would put money on these detectives finding her.

'Let's start from the beginning,' Jack says, pointing to the timeline that's already been drawn up. 'At nine thirteen this morning, Rosie Logan was reported missing by a passer-by helping Maria Logan, her mother. Officers were on the scene by nine twenty-six and the official search began.' An enlarged map of the area is on an adjacent board, and Jack points at this now. 'The search began with a three-hundred-metre radius, including the playpark, the memorial garden, the sports field and rugby club to the south and the car park and woodland to the east. The grey rabbit toy was found here—' he points to a red pin in the woodland to the south, next to the river, 'and has been confirmed as belonging to Rosie by her mother. The only witness to Rosie's disappearance is Lewis Nicholls, an eleven-year-old boy, who has since been picked up by his mother.'

'We're certain he had nothing to do with it?' DC Phil Lawrence asks.

'Nothing's ever a hundred per cent. But he seemed genuine and I believe him, yes. He found Rosie injured, just after ten thirty. He tried to alert her mother to her whereabouts, got scared by the police presence, and when he went back for Rosie, she'd gone.'

'He was the last person to see her?'

'That we know of, so far. On his say-so, we extended the search into a further section of woodland, previously ignored because we didn't believe there was access. And it's there that the dogs found a blood trail, and a badger cam. We are waiting for footage from that camera now. Family consists of Maria Logan, thirty-eight, her husband, Tony Logan, forty-five, and Maria's son from her first marriage, Eddie Madden, twenty.'

'The son's twenty and still lives at home?'

'That's not unusual,' Amrit counters. 'Cost of rent and housing now?'

'I agree with Amrit,' Jack says. 'Living at home isn't unusual in itself, but he's an odd character. I might be wrong, but he doesn't seem to have a job, doesn't go to college or uni. Stays in his room all day smoking pot.'

'Shall we check him out?'

'Please. Now, Rosie Logan has been missing for five hours. The golden hour has gone. Give me your theories.'

The team look nervous. Nobody wants to start.

'Come on,' Jack says. 'Doesn't matter how wild or ridiculous. I'll begin. The mother, Maria Logan, did something to Rosie, either at the park or before, and reported her missing to cover her tracks.'

'Has she got a history of mental illness?' Bates asks. 'Can we get her medical records?'

'Not without permission or a warrant. And no, not as far as we know.'

'But it can't be her,' Amrit says. 'CCTV shows Maria and Rosie walking to the park. We know they arrived. And you've searched the park. What about the river?' she continues without taking a breath. 'It's the most likely scenario. The water's high and fast-flowing, the dive teams are still out there.'

'A definite possibility. Write it up,' Jack says to Bates, who prints *RIVER* below *MOTHER* in neat capitals on the board.

'Some random's taken her,' Lawrence says.

'The husband's done something to her.'

'The son killed her. Jealousy.'

The theories come thick and fast; Jack can't argue with any of them. They've all seen it – the majority of murders are carried out by the person closest to the victim. Their family or partner, in other words. And that probability increases when it comes to young children.

'Do we believe she's still alive?' Jack asks.

The room falls silent. He notices Amrit glance up to the clock.

'Outside in this cold,' she says quietly. 'She doesn't stand a chance.'

'So our best hope of finding her alive is that someone has her?' Lawrence says.

'If not, we're looking for a body,' Amrit adds grimly.

'Let's not work to that certainty yet,' Jack says, knowing that in another twenty-four hours that situation may well change. 'Coppers and intel have been scouring CCTV and traffic cameras all morning – nothing so far, although, Lawrence, I'd like you to take point on this. Ensure that all available cameras have been located, Ring doorbells, dashcams, the lot. Double-check that all footage has been watched. We know there's ANPR and traffic cams on both directions of Ringwood Road – this will have captured every car going in or out of there at the time. Someone needs to go through every one of those plates.'

Lawrence nods in acknowledgement.

'Bates,' he says to the new DC, 'you and I are going to head back to the house and the family. By that point hopefully the dog unit will have concluded their search. We'll interview them all again, together. I want to see how they interact. And then I'd like you to stay. Your background was as a FLO, right?' A family liaison officer; Bates nods. 'You'll be their support, as well as our eyes and ears on the inside.

'Amrit, you'll run point from here. Check alibis for the whole family, see if children's services have a file on them. Find out where the search for known RSOs has got to. I want to know if we've got any paedophiles in the area.'

'Will do,' Amrit confirms. 'But boss…'

'Yes?'

'The family has money. Tony Logan's a sales director, must earn a decent wage. You've seen the size of the house.'

'You're thinking Rosie's been kidnapped?'

'Maybe.'

'It's a good shout. I'll get on to IT, see if we can get a tap done on their phones. What do we know so far about Sean Madden, the ex?'

'Nothing on the RMS, but he has a record as long as your arm on the PNC. Arrested for theft in 2004, escalating to aggravated burglary in 2006. Got thirteen years, had a few altercations inside so spent twelve in Winchester at Her Majesty's Pleasure. Out in 2018.'

'That's a long time inside for agg burglary?'

'They broke into a house at night. Pre-planned, the whole family was there, he had a knife, children were threatened. Previous conviction.' Amrit shrugs. 'The judge threw the book at him.'

'So he would have spent most of his son's life inside?'

'Looks that way.'

'And he's now where?'

'Current address has him down in Cornwall. Bodmin. So not nearby.'

'Get on to Devon and Cornwall constabulary, see if they can pay him a visit. I want to know exactly where that man is, especially with his history of violence. In the meantime, I'll speak to the chief about getting someone from intel assigned. Get them looking into the family. Tony Logan said that neither of them has surviving parents, and that Maria doesn't have any friends. I want to know why.'

'No friends at all?' Amrit says, echoing his surprise. 'Not even other mums? Neighbours? Isn't that a bit odd?'

'That's what I thought.'

Jack turns as there's a gentle knock on the door.

A face pokes around, then comes into the room. Raj Johal from the digital department smiles at the team; Amrit Gill blushes a deep shade of red.

'DCI Ellis,' he says. 'Sorry to interrupt, but as you're now SIO, I thought you should know as soon as possible...'

'The wildlife camera. You have something?'

'Currently loading at my desk. If you'd like to follow me?'

He makes an exaggerated flourish; Jack already has his jacket on.

'Team,' he says, as he follows Raj out of the door. 'You know what you're doing. Get to work.'

CHAPTER ELEVEN

'Show me,' Jack says the moment they set foot in the digital department.

'Give me a chance,' Raj replies. 'The footage is still downloading.'

'But you have something?'

'We have video. No idea what's on it.'

Raj takes a seat in front of his monitor; Jack pulls up a chair alongside. He picks up the small plastic case in its evidence bag, now open, the padlock a mess of splintered metal. He turns it over in his hand, studying it.

'Standard equipment for a job like this,' Raj says. 'Good kit, but not too costly. Don't want to buy anything too expensive if you're going to be leaving it unattended in the woods. How's Amrit?' he adds. 'Getting on okay in her new role?'

Jack gives him a look. 'Ask her yourself. I thought you two were dating, or whatever you call it nowadays.'

'We were, but—'

'Any sign of who the camera belonged to?' Jack interrupts, regretting bringing up the subject.

'None, although if you leave someone waiting in the woods, I'm guessing whoever it was will come to you. All footage records on an SD card, they'd need to visit to swap out the card and put new batteries in at some point.'

'But you've got the SD card?'

'Watching it as we speak.'

Raj gestures to the screen where a black and white film plays out. The camera captures a narrow patch of foliage, low down, nothing but leaves, grass and mud in shot.

'It's motion-activated, but that doesn't help as the slightest shifting branch seems to set this one off.' Raj fast-forwards; trees quiver, the time clicks on. A badger lumbers into shot, pointed black and white face, fat furry body. It sniffs in the undergrowth, digging with big black paws in the mud.

'Confirms what the camera was there for,' Raj says.

'Fast-forward,' Jack replies, and everything moves into double speed again.

The footage jerks onward, the scene brighter, the sun coming up.

'There. There! Stop,' Jack says, as a blur encroaches on the screen. 'Go back.'

Raj does as he's told, then pauses.

Jack stares at the image on the screen. Blood drains from his face.

For there is Rosie Logan.

The camera doesn't capture much – even at her height, the shot is too low, so they only have a view of her middle, downwards. But it's unmistakably her. The image is surreal; like seeing a ghost in real life. A mythical creature. Their unicorn. Small welly boots, a coat, pudgy fingers. *No gloves*, Jack thinks. The image is in black and white, but even at this definition, they can see patches of a darker grey across her soft white hands. Blood?

Raj presses play again, this time in slow motion. She walks one way across the shot, then back, her hands flapping, clearly distressed. Then another pair of legs comes into view. Trainers, jeans. Unmistakably Lewis. Jack glances at the timestamp.

Ten thirty-two a.m. The kid was telling the truth.

The boy kneels down, eye level to Rosie. They seem to be talking. He tries to take her hand, but she pulls away. He gets to his feet, then leaves.

'Gone to get help?' Raj asks.

'As he said.'

Rosie is alone again. She collapses to the ground, sitting in the mud, and they can see her face now. Mouth open, cheeks wet, the poor kid is crying. Her hair is a mess of white curls – *no hat*, Jack thinks again – and she glances this way and that, wailing.

Until she stops. She looks up, and another pair of legs comes into shot. Black trousers, or maybe jeans. Heeled ankle boots. They stop just in front of Rosie.

Jack leans forward, his face close to the screen, not wanting to miss a single shot. He barely breathes.

A hand reaches down and pulls Rosie to her feet. The child seems calmer, her movements have slowed. The two of them walk out of shot.

'Rewind,' Jack says.

Raj does as he's told, and they watch it again, Jack's eyes glued to the screen. But there are no identifying marks, no way of knowing who this person is.

'Again.'

Raj rewinds, Jack barely blinking as it plays out for a third time. The boots, the cut of the trousers look feminine, but apart from that, Jack doesn't have a clue.

'Who is that?' Raj says, his voice coming out as a croak.

He pauses the video, the people frozen in hazy black and white.

'And where have you taken Rosie?' Jack whispers to the screen.

CHAPTER TWELVE

The chocolate twist is as delicious as Lucy imagined it would be. She sits in her car, silently praising Jack as she eats the pastry, picking the chocolate chips out of pieces before she passes them back to her dogs. With two excited, panting hounds, the windscreen has steamed up, so she wipes her sleeve across it, watching the search continue in the park.

The manpower from officers on the ground has tapered off, replaced by volunteers from search and rescue. The marine unit are still on site, along with the forensic teams and the LSOs in the woodland, painstakingly picking through the undergrowth.

A light knock on the window from Pete diverts her attention; Iggy goes nuts in the cage behind her, barking right in her ear.

'Iggy, enough.' She climbs out of the car, and closes the door, muffling Iggy's excitable yelps.

'Miller's told me I can go,' Pete says. 'I'm going to head back to Netley, apparently there's a new pup they want me to look at.'

'It's alright for some.' She holds out the last mouthful of her pastry, offering it to Pete.

He takes it, pops it in his mouth with a smile. 'Do you fancy a drink later?'

'Fuck, yes. And I'm off after today, so I get to stay up well past my bedtime.'

'You are?' Pete tries to suppress a grin and fails. 'Drinks on you, then.'

'Whatever your little heart desires,' Lucy replies. She gives him a flirty smile, but the moment is ruined by her phone ringing. She pulls it out, surprised when she sees the name on the screen.

'I'll call you later,' Pete says as Lucy gets back into the warmth of the car and answers the phone.

'Cal?' she says. 'How are you?'

'Hi Lucy. It's been a while.'

'Haven't heard from you since Nico's funeral.' She glances back through the windscreen, watching Pete drive off. 'How can I help?' she asks, although she has a good idea why Calvin Watson, Home Affairs editor at the *Guardian*, and her husband's former boss, would be getting in touch. Today, of all days.

'Rosie Logan. What do you know?'

Lucy rolls her eyes. 'Nothing I can tell you.'

'But you're involved? It's Hampshire. A big misper search. You must be.'

'I'm just a lowly dog handler, Cal. What do I know?'

'Don't give me that crap, Luce. You know everything. And I heard DCI Ellis has taken over. Does that mean you've found a body?'

'No, Cal,' Lucy says firmly. 'I'm sure Jack will update the press in due course.' She leans forward, squinting through the smeared windscreen at a lone figure walking towards the park. 'I've got to go,' she says, and she hangs up as Cal protests.

She gets out of her car and jogs towards the woman.

'Mrs Logan?' she shouts as she approaches. The woman pauses, looking around, confused. 'Mrs Logan, I'm PC Halliday – Lucy. I've been helping with the search for your daughter. Why are you here? Aren't you supposed to be at home?'

'I... no... I didn't want to be at home. I want to help.'

'We have the best officers on the case. You need to be with your family.'

'My family.' She scoffs, looking over at the park, then back to Lucy. 'You hear about these missing children on the news. And you think – how stupid are the parents, to lose their baby like that.'

'It wasn't your fault.'

'I looked away for a moment. Couldn't have been more than five minutes.'

'I know.' Lucy takes her elbow, gently steering the woman towards her car. 'Did you walk here? Shall I drive you home?'

'Walk? Yes. Or if they're not stupid, they're neglectful. I was as guilty as everyone else for judging those parents when that little girl went missing. Madeleine McCann, do you remember? I thought, how could they leave her? Go out drinking and leave her alone. I would never do that.'

Lucy carefully helps the woman into the front seat. She's wearing leggings and an oversized woollen jumper, a coat over the top, and Lucy gropes for the seatbelt, trying to do it up, as if she were a child.

'They still haven't found her. Can you imagine? How long has it been? Ten, fifteen years?'

'Mrs Logan—'

'Maria, please.' Lucy starts the engine, drives towards town. 'You're the one with the police dogs, aren't you? Rosie will be sad she missed you. She loves dogs.'

'They're working dogs. Rosie wouldn't have had much time to play.'

'I didn't kill her. You know that, don't you?'

'I know,' Lucy says, trying to placate the woman. Her voice is wistful, distracted, her head bent. To Lucy it feels like she's on something – a benzo or similar.

'Left here,' Maria says, indicating the turn. 'Are you married, Lucy?'

'Me? No.'

'Lucky. Stay that way. Waste of space, the lot of them. They say they love you and then let you down at every opportunity they get. Kids?'

'No.'

'Do you want them? Sorry, that's too personal.' Maria blinks for a moment, as if confused as to how she got there. In a police car, with two dogs breathing down her neck.

'I've got two crazy mutts, that's enough responsibility for me.'

'Very sensible. Right at the T-junction,' she adds, pointing. 'Number thirty-six. I wanted to get a dog, for Rosie. But Tony said no. Maybe we'll get one. After Rosie comes home.'

And then she starts to cry. Light, feminine sobs, her hands over her face. 'Oh, God. I just want to find her. I just want her home.'

Lucy reaches out and pats her arm. Hardly a comfort, a useless gesture. Lucy can't imagine what Maria is going through, but she knows something about loss and uncertainty. Her heart goes out to this woman. Why is there nobody with her? Offering reassurance and love and tea and biscuits. Lucy's a loner, always has been, but even she had Fran to pick up the pieces when Nico disappeared.

Lucy slows the car, looking for number thirty-six. It's not difficult to find – the drive is full of patrol cars, the front door open, people spilling out onto the tarmac. Uniformed officers and Tony Logan. All arguing.

Lucy and Maria get out of the car, Maria lingers nearby, while Lucy goes up to the officer at the epicentre of the disagreement. They've worked together before – PC Chester. Young, but experienced; she trusts he's done a good job.

'What's going on?'

Chester holds out an evidence bag; inside is a blue rectangular tin.

'Found it in the wardrobe in the main bedroom,' he says.

'What were you even doing in the main bedroom?' Tony Logan shouts.

'As I said, sir, wardrobes are a common hiding place for small children. And this was in plain sight.'

'What's in it?' Lucy asks.

The officer holds up a second evidence bag.

'Shit,' she says.

Because inside is a small baggy of white powder.

'It's not mine,' Tony says. He points an accusatory finger to the bedroom above them where a young man is watching out of the window. 'It must be his.'

'Who sleeps in the main bedroom?' Lucy asks, glancing over to Maria – she's hardly registering the fracas, staring into the middle distance, a vacant look on her face.

'Me and my wife,' Tony replies. 'But he must have put it there.'

Lucy thought she had seen it all, but shopping your stepson to the police on the day your daughter has gone missing is a new one on her.

'We can work that out for ourselves,' Lucy says. Then to PC Chester, 'Is the search complete?'

'Yes.'

'Then let's get out of the way, shall we?' Lucy has no authority over this search, or even this PC, but a little bit of decisiveness goes a long way. Chester walks back to his police car. 'Now if you would be so kind?' she says to Tony Logan, pointing towards the front door, where Maria is now waiting.

'You can't think… I don't…' Tony says, as the officer goes out of sight. 'I don't do drugs.'

'We'll be out of your way shortly,' Lucy repeats.

Tony and Maria Logan go inside. There's a pause, and a tall young man comes barrelling out of the front door in his joggers and T-shirt.

'It's not mine, whatever he says,' he shouts, gesticulating back towards the house. 'I smoke a bit of weed now and again, but not… not whatever you found.'

'What did we find?' Lucy asks.

'Tony said it was a white powder. Coke, or heroin, or something? I'm not into that shit. I'm not. Fingerprint it. Run it for DNA. You can do that, can't you? And you'll see. It's him. It's all Tony.'

'We will,' Lucy confirms.

He watches them for a moment longer, then goes back into the house. Lucy walks over to PC Chester.

'I'll notify Miller,' Lucy says. 'Tell him the search is complete. A negative on Rosie Logan but a positive on whatever we have here.'

'Thank you.' PC Chester's smile fades. 'That poor kid,' he says, as he puts the evidence in his boot.

Lucy looks up to the windows of the huge house, imagining the expensive interior that no doubt lies within. She thinks about the children that live there. The son, locked in a toxic relationship with his stepdad. And Rosie. The little girl, whose disappearance is revealing more secrets by the hour.

CHAPTER THIRTEEN

DC Bates takes the wheel, while Jack uses the drive to Fordingbridge to make calls. First to his boss – Detective Chief Superintendent Andrew Weaver, an affable man in his late fifties, happy to have done his time on the street and spend the rest of it battling politics. Drinking finest scotch in members' clubs, in other words. He doesn't interfere with Jack's ways of working, likes a chat but instinctively knows this is not the time.

'You need more detectives to work a high-risk misper like this one, Jack,' he says, when Jack explains the problem.

'Just keep the officers from response and patrol on the case and assign me someone from intel.'

A pause, followed by a slurp as Weaver drinks his coffee. 'Fine,' he concludes. 'But when this is done you and I need to have a chat about your high standards. A DCI of your calibre needs more officers.'

So I can sit behind a desk all day, like you? Jack thinks, but instead agrees, and hangs up. Next, an update from Brian Miller, Jack raising his eyebrows at the news of the drugs found in the master bedroom. And then, on to Amrit.

'Still nothing, boss,' she confirms, after he's explained about Rosie and the woman on the video. 'House-to-house is quiet, everyone's at work, and even the general public are being restrained. Children's services have nothing on the family.'

'Thanks, Amrit. Keep me up to date,' he concludes as Bates pulls the car into the drive.

They can hear the shouting the moment they get out of the car. He glances to Bates with raised eyebrows, then presses the doorbell. The commotion stops immediately. Footsteps, and the door is opened.

Tony stands on the mat. His face is red, his muscles taut. He blinks at Jack. 'You again. Where's the other guy?'

'Circumstances have changed. I've taken over the case.'

'What sort of circumstances?'

'Can I come in? Can you get the others?'

Tony holds the door open and ushers them into the kitchen. Jack and DC Bates take a seat at the polished table. Tony leaves for a moment, there's the thumping of feet up the stairs, then restrained voices, hissing. He comes back down and sits opposite them. After a moment, Maria appears at the doorway, her face blotchy and red, her eyes swollen with tears.

'What's going on?' she asks.

Jack introduces himself and Bates again as Eddie joins them, slumping down in the chair furthest away from his stepfather.

'The drugs aren't mine,' he mutters. 'You should be arresting him.'

'We're not here to arrest anyone. We need to talk about the drugs, but they aren't the most important thing right now.'

'She's dead, isn't she?' Maria blurts out, then begins to cry. Her husband makes no effort to comfort her, just stares, pale-faced, at Jack.

'We haven't found Rosie, no, Mrs Logan,' Jack says gently. 'The search is ongoing and we're working under the assumption that Rosie is very much alive. We're here to show you some video footage we've found.'

Bates takes the laptop out of her bag and puts it on the table. She finds the static photo then turns it around to show the family. They crane forward; even Eddie shows interest.

'This is a screenshot taken from some footage we recovered this afternoon,' Jack says. 'A camera had been placed in the woodland – we believe to video wildlife – and we discovered this.'

'But that's Rosie!' Maria says. 'What time...?'

Her husband points to the screen. 'Ten forty?' Tony says. 'That was hours ago. You've been searching the whole morning, and this is all you find?'

'We've traced Rosie's movements after she went missing in the park. She hurt herself on some barbed wire, we don't believe too badly, and was found by a young lad. He tried to find you, Mrs Logan, but got spooked by the police. And when he went back to get Rosie, she had gone.'

Jack nods to Bates and she presses a button. A new image comes on the screen – the one including the mystery figure.

'We believe Rosie is currently under the care of this person.'

'Who the hell's that?' Tony bellows.

'Do you recognise them?'

'This is a leg and a foot. How are we supposed to tell?'

'Given the type of boot, we are working on the assumption that this is a woman. Do you recognise it? Do you know anyone that owns something similar?'

'No. Nobody,' Tony says quickly.

'What about Chloe?' Maria says. She looks at Eddie. 'Does Chloe have boots like that?'

'Who's Chloe?'

'Eddie's friend. She babysits for Rosie sometimes.'

'Can you give me her information?'

'It's not Chloe,' Eddie snaps. He sits up straight, jabs at the screen with his finger. 'These are old lady boots. Chloe wouldn't be caught dead wearing those. Only old people wear boots like that.'

'Old people?' Jack asks.

'People your age,' Eddie says.

Charming, Jack thinks. He feels nothing but sympathy for this family, and the horror they're going through, but stuck in between Tony's aggression and the son's immaturity, his patience is starting to wane. 'I'm still going to need Chloe's information,' Jack repeats.

'Fine.' Eddie types on his phone then slides it across to Bates, who writes the information down.

'Can you think of anyone else who might know Rosie? Friends, family?'

'I don't have any friends,' Maria says. 'And I've told you before, no family.'

'It's probably another one of his whores,' Eddie mutters.

'Eddie!' his mother snaps.

'That's what you guys were fighting about. Before the detective showed up. He's done it again, hasn't he?'

'Eddie—'

'It's true. That's why we're here. Because he couldn't keep it in his pants.'

'How dare you… You little shit…'

Tony has turned puce, his body shaking, staring down his stepson until he realises he's being observed. He pushes his chair back with a loud squeak and walks out of the room.

'It's true though,' Eddie says. 'We do everything for him, and he treats you like crap.'

Maria reaches over and places her hand over her son's. She squeezes it gently.

'Why did you move to the area, Mrs Logan?' Jack asks. 'Your husband said he got a new job.'

'He had to,' Eddie says. 'He had a sexual harassment claim—'

'Eddie,' Maria interjects. 'That's not why—'

'It is. I saw it. The letter—'

'Eddie!' He stops. Maria takes a deep breath. 'Tony had… some problems with his previous job. A woman—'

'Not just one woman—'

'A few women,' Maria corrects with a glare. 'Put in a sexual harassment claim to the boss of the company. Tony denied it at first. Said it was all rubbish, but they gave him an ultimatum: quit or they'd fire him. So we moved down here.' She glances at her son. 'Away from Eddie's school… his friends. It's been hard on us all.'

'And later?' Jack asks. Maria looks at him, confused. 'You said Tony denied it at first. What did he say later?'

She sighs. 'He'd had a number of affairs. Slept with a few of them, and obviously they didn't like being used in that way. Put in the complaint. But that has nothing to do with Rosie,' she adds quickly. 'None of those women know where we are, let alone would harm a child.'

'And now?' Jack looks to Eddie. 'Your son said he's done it again?'

'It's nothing,' she mumbles.

'Mum, you have to tell them.'

She stares at Jack for a moment, then down to her hands. She picks at her soft pink nail varnish. 'He's having an affair,' she says, more to her hands than to Jack. 'That's why I wasn't watching Rosie. The latest one phoned.'

'That dickhead,' Eddie spits. Maria holds his hand tightly, calming him.

'She called you?' Jack prompts.

'Just after nine. No caller ID. Said that she slept with my husband. And that she wanted me to know that he was leaving me.'

Jack's about to ask another question when they hear heavy footsteps on the stairs and Tony appears in the doorway. Tony looks at Jack, then his wife.

'You told him?' he snaps. 'You told the cops?'

'It might be relevant,' she bites back. 'It might help them find Rosie.'

'Why? You can't possibly think that some one-night stand from two months ago has taken our daughter?'

'She was psycho enough to find my number and call me. Why not?'

'Because... because...' Tony splutters for a moment. 'This is not my fault.'

Jack stands up, meeting Tony's eyeline. 'What's her name, Mr Logan?'

'This is ridiculous.'

'Just tell him her fucking name!' Maria screams, then bursts into tears, sobbing into her hands as Eddie storms out of the room. A slam follows from upstairs.

Tony glares, then lets out a long exhalation of air. 'Bridget Daley. It was a one-time thing, but these women… they get it in their heads.'

'Her number?'

He takes his phone out of his pocket and pulls up her contact information. He holds it up to Jack and he makes a note.

'Where did you meet her?'

'A bar. In town. We got talking. Flirting. You know how it is.'

If he's trying to create some sort of macho kinship with Jack, it's not working: Jack wouldn't know how to flirt with a woman in a bar if he tried.

But Tony takes Jack's silence as confirmation. 'She gave me her number and then next time I was out, I went back to hers. Once. It was only once,' he directs to his distraught wife. 'And that was months ago.'

'Why did she call your wife now? Why today?'

'I don't know. You'll have to ask her,' he says. 'But she's got nothing to do with Rosie. If you had just watched her more closely. If you—'

'This is nobody's fault,' Jack interrupts. 'Will you give permission for us to access your mobile phone and bank records?'

'Will I—? No! We're not the criminals here. And how dare you contact my work. Checking my alibi, were you?'

'Just following procedure,' Jack confirms.

'I'm not the bad guy. You act like you're so innocent,' he directs to Maria, 'when I know you've been speaking to Sean again.'

'Sean?' Maria protests, through her tears. 'You're bringing up Sean now?'

'He's been calling you.'

'He's Eddie's father!' She glances upstairs to where heavy metal music is now thumping. 'And keep your bloody voice down.' She looks at Jack. 'Sean got out of prison about six years ago. I haven't told Eddie. I didn't want to…' She shrugs, turns back to her husband. 'He wants to see Eddie. Be a part of his life. And he will. When the time's right.'

'It's just an excuse. To get close to you.'

'It's nothing like that. He knows I'm married. And that I'm faithful – unlike you.'

'Maybe if you weren't still flirting with your ex-husband, I wouldn't need to look elsewhere,' Tony replies. And with that, he strides out in a flurry of expensive aftershave and self-righteousness.

Jack looks to Bates, who raises her eyebrows. Maria sees the exchange.

'I'm sorry. You didn't need to witness that. Things haven't been right in our marriage for a while. But I honestly thought Tony was beyond it.'

'I'm sorry, but I have to ask. Have you seen your ex-husband lately?'

'No. Not since he went inside. But Tony's right. We have been talking. Every now and again, since he got out. But I haven't heard from him in six months.' Her gaze shifts to the frozen picture on the screen. 'It's better that it's a woman, isn't it?' she says. 'A woman will look after Rosie.'

Jack stares at the ankle boot. He thinks about Rose West, about Myra Hindley. And the fact that despite the news appeal, this woman hasn't called the police.

'You have no idea who this woman is?' he asks.

'None,' Maria says again. 'But you'll find her, won't you?'

'We'll do our best,' Jack confirms, knowing that right now, their best just isn't good enough.

CHAPTER FOURTEEN

Jack leaves Bates in charge of the domestic battlefield – 'I've seen worse,' she says as he leaves – and heads to Bridget Daley's house. Wednesday, mid-afternoon, he assumes she'll be at work but when he rings the doorbell, she answers dressed in a trouser suit and a white top. She reels when he shows his ID.

'DCI Jack Ellis,' he says. 'Bridget Daley?'

She nods, going pale. 'I wasn't serious. I just wanted to scare her, that's all.'

Jack's skin prickles. 'Can I come in?' he asks, keeping his voice level.

She nods, directing him down a corridor to the far end of the house, to a compact kitchen overlooking a small but perfectly formed garden. He stands next to the table, while she leans on the kitchen counter, as if readying herself to flee.

'Can you tell me what happened?' Jack asks, as vague as possible, the police caution on the tip of his tongue.

'She didn't need to call the police,' Bridget says. 'I wasn't going to do anything.'

'Maria Logan?'

'Yes. You say these things, don't you? When you're angry. It's Valentine's Day, I missed Tony. I wanted to be with him. I wasn't actually going to kill her.'

'Who did you threaten to kill?' Jack asks slowly.

'That bitch. Maria. She's why we can't be together.'

Jack feels some of the tension in his chest lifting. She doesn't have the girl. 'You don't know anything about Rosie?'

'Rosie? Tony's daughter? Why would I threaten a little girl?' She seems genuinely confused. 'I just wanted Maria to let Tony go. That's why I called her. To tell her to piss off so we could be together. What's Rosie got to do with anything?'

'She's missing,' Jack says.

'Missing?' Her face is stricken. 'Since when?'

'Since this morning.'

Her hand flies to her mouth. 'And you thought... that I...? No! I don't know anything about that. Oh, my God. Tony. He must be distraught. He must be...' She picks up her phone but Jack interrupts.

'I think it's best if you leave him be for the moment.'

She looks at the phone, then at Jack.

'Yes,' she says, quietly. 'I think you're probably right.'

She takes two slow steps and slumps at the kitchen table, putting her head in her hands. Jack sits next to her.

'How did you meet Tony?' he asks.

'Night out. I was with friends. Tony stood next to me at the bar. We started talking. But our connection was instant. Some people you meet and... and you know.'

Jack nods, encouraging her to continue.

'We went out a few times after that. Drinking, dinner, all the nice places in town. I could see the ring. I knew he was married. But he said they were splitting up, that things hadn't been great since their little girl was born.' She smiles, her hand playing with the silver pendant around her neck. It sparkles in the overhead light. 'He doted on Rosie. We planned that they would come and live here – him and Rosie – and that was fine by me. But *she*...' Her face turns bitter. 'Maria said that if he left them, she would make sure he never saw Rosie again. Would tell the courts that he hit her, make up all sorts of lies.'

'And did he?'

'Hit her? No! That was bullshit. But it was enough to scare Tony into staying.'

'And you were angry about this?'

'With Maria, yes. But not Rosie. Poor kid, having that bitch as a mother.' She picks up her phone, selects an app and scrolls.

'Oh, no,' she says, as she reads from the screen. 'I didn't know. I hadn't seen. Oh, Tony,' she says, under her breath.

'You're telling me Maria knew about you and Tony,' Jack says.

'Yes. He told her last week.' She turns to look at him. 'Is she saying otherwise? She's lying. She's manipulative and evil and I wouldn't be surprised if she's hidden Rosie somewhere, just to get back at Tony. Have you searched the house? Spoken to her son? Useless, he is. Tony told me about him.'

'Eddie?'

'If that's what his name is. From her first marriage. Have you spoken to the ex-husband? Someone else who makes Tony's life a misery.'

'How?'

'Stalking Maria, watching the house. And Eddie's going the same way as his dad. Stealing money, taking drugs.'

'Tony said that Sean's been at the house?'

'Yeah. That's why he can't stay over. Why he can't leave Maria alone.' Her phone beeps, and she looks at it. 'I'm sorry. It's work. I have to leave. I don't know anything about Tony's little girl.'

'Of course. Could I use your bathroom before I go?' Jack tries his most trustworthy smile.

Bridget looks at him dubiously, but points upstairs. 'First door on the left.'

Jack thanks her and heads up. It's a small house. An open door leading to a small living room at the front, two bedrooms and the bathroom upstairs. The doors are open, and Jack sticks his head into them all. No toys, no locked doors. Nothing that points towards a child having been here.

His phone rings. He glances downstairs, worried about being found out for his snooping, but there's no noise from the kitchen. He answers it.

'Devon and Cornwall have come back on Sean Madden,' Amrit says immediately. 'No one's home. But his boss says that's not out of the ordinary. On his days off he's often out camping in the middle of nowhere.'

'In February? Can they find him?'

'They're trying, but unless we have evidence of him being here this morning, they're reluctant to go tramping around Dartmoor.'

'Get on it,' he replies. 'I'll be back in the office in about an hour. I'll help when I'm back.'

He goes through the motions of using the bathroom, flushes the chain, runs the water, then heads back downstairs. Bridget is waiting by the front door, shoes on, her hand on the lock.

'Would you mind if I show you a photo before I go?' Jack asks. He takes his phone out and pulls up the shot of the leg and the boot, Rosie just out of the frame. 'Do you recognise this person?'

'This foot? No. And it's not me, before you ask. I couldn't afford boots like that.'

'You recognise the brand?'

'Sure. They're Burberry. Distinctive buckle. Over five hundred quid. I wouldn't go walking around in the woods if I was wearing those.'

'Has Tony ever bought you gifts?'

Her hand goes to the necklace again. 'Some.'

'And on your nights out with Tony, has he ever done drugs?'

She blinks. A blush of red sneaks up her neck. 'Never,' she says. 'Now, if you wouldn't mind...' And she practically closes the door in Jack's face.

Jack sits in his car, processing what he's just heard. An unfaithful husband, buying expensive gifts for his new lover. And who's to say he's not doing the same with someone else. Expensive boots? Maybe. He texts the brand of boot to Amrit at the station. It's a step forward, but solves nothing. If anything, what they've discovered in the last hour has muddied the waters rather than putting them closer to finding Rosie.

Nothing about this family is simple. Tony Logan is having an affair, one of many if the past is anything to go by. Maria Logan may or may not be sleeping with her ex. There is no way that Maria Logan, Tony Logan and Bridget Daley are all telling the truth. Did Maria know about the affair before this morning? Had

Tony Logan told his wife he was leaving her, or was that a line to keep Bridget Daley interested?

He could well imagine Tony snorting a line of coke on his nights out, but did the drugs found in the Logan house have anything to do with Rosie's disappearance, or were they just a symptom of a man trying to revisit his youth?

It's clear: somebody is lying. And in a missing child investigation, that fact could be deadly.

CHAPTER FIFTEEN

Maria lies in her bedroom, alone. The pill she took earlier has worn off; the anxiety returns. She listens to the noises in the house, thinks about her family, and what's brought them to this point.

Next door, Eddie is still blasting his music at full volume. He's twenty, angry, and who can blame him? He doesn't get on with his stepdad; he's been dragged around the country, away from his friends and his college just when it mattered the most. His A level results were woeful; he couldn't get into university. He hates being here but where else can he go? No prospects, no ambition bar spending every day smoking weed and pissing off Tony as much as he can. He needs mates, someone to hang out with. Maybe even a girlfriend. Her thoughts drift to Chloe – the only person his age who hangs around with him. It's an odd match – the smart young girl, and her messy son. She wonders what Chloe sees in him.

But at least Eddie has one friend. She has no one. She noticed the look on the detectives' faces when she told them. They didn't believe her.

She did, once. Workmates at the supermarket, women at the mother and baby group she went to with Eddie. But things were so easy in your twenties, weren't they? All that self-reliance. That confidence. And since meeting Tony, people have just dropped away. A woman who accused Tony of coming on to her – gone. Declining invitations out because Tony wants a night in – after a while they stop asking. They don't care. Being a mother second time around is different – she had nothing in common with the spoiled young women at Music with Mummy, but watched with envy as they all went for a coffee after without inviting her. She has no job, nowhere to go. How would she even start making friends now?

And what of her husband? Tony's in his study; she can hear the click of his keyboard, the scraping of his chair on the wooden floor. Tony has gone into work mode – trying to solve problems, make people work harder, smarter, whatever. He's not good at sitting still, her husband, never has been. Probably why he has so many affairs – always looking for the next best thing. She doesn't care that they're fighting; she doesn't want his comfort, his excuses, his apologies. She should have known – once a cheater, always a cheater. Their marriage is over, but the thought of starting afresh drags in her bones. She's too tired, too old. She can't do this again.

Not without Rosie.

The absence of her daughter is a constant rock in her stomach. A weight around her neck, pulling her down. It's been six hours since she was abducted – because that's what's happened, isn't it?

That woman in the video. She has taken Rosie. But who, and why, and where?

Maria likes this other detective – this DCI. He has a way about him, a calmness that gives her confidence. But he's a murder detective, what does that mean? Do they expect to find her daughter dead?

The tea she drank earlier roils in her stomach. An acidic burn, making her nauseous. Her brain spits possible futures. The detective turning up, his eyes downturned. Rosie's body has disappeared, never to be found. Or worse: dead and defiled.

Maria can't hold it in any longer. She leaps to her feet, throwing the door to the en suite open and vomiting a wave of bitterness into the toilet. She retches until her body is empty, and collapses on the tiles, her energy spent.

Footsteps, then a gentle knock on the door.

'Maria?' a voice says. 'Are you okay?'

It's that woman, the detective they've left at the house, supposedly to look after them. But she's watching, Maria can feel it.

'I'm fine,' she croaks back. 'I'll be out in a moment.'

'Do you want a cup of tea?'

No, she doesn't. Not another fucking cup of tea. She wants to turn back time – not go to the park that morning, keep her gaze firmly locked on Rosie. She just wants her daughter back.

She pulls her shaking legs into a stand. She opens the door; the bedroom is empty, that detective's gone, thank goodness. She can hear her downstairs in the kitchen – the rattle of mugs, the bubble of the kettle. She's singing softly; the noise grates. Maria needs to get out of here.

She descends the stairs slowly, quietly, grabs boots, then sneaks past the door to the kitchen and out of the bifold in Rosie's playroom. She slips through the garden and out the back gate.

She walks quickly, glad to be out in the fresh air, however freezing it is. She realises she's forgotten her coat, and wraps her arms around herself, walking faster. She doesn't care where she's going. Not back to the park this time. But away. Away.

Her phone rings in her pocket; she ignores it, expecting it to be that detective or Tony. But the buzzing doesn't stop, and when she finally pulls it out she stops dead in the street.

No name, she deleted his contact ages ago, but she still knows the number. Eleven digits, embedded into her brain.

She stares for a moment, then presses the green button.

She holds the phone to her ear, just listening. She doesn't say anything, not even a hello. He wouldn't have expected that.

Thirty seconds pass, maybe a minute. She can hear him breathing on the other end of the line.

Then, 'Are you okay?'

His voice is calm, deep. But just hearing it makes her burst into tears. He's always had this effect on her – an instant bond, an almost innate urge to want to be with him. That was the problem when she was seventeen, the same twenty-one years later.

'I'm here, Maria. I'm a street away from your house.'

'You can't—' She's onto the main road now and frantically looks around. Past her own driveway, past the turn-off into her street.

'I can see you. I'm in the green Toyota.'

There's an old truck parked a few metres down. A figure sitting in the rusty cab; a ripped tarpaulin fluttering over the flatbed at the back. That's him, that's his style.

'I don't want to make things worse for you, but I'm here. For you.'

'You can't—' she repeats, but she can't bring herself to tell him to leave. 'Drive around the corner, to the Co-op. I'll meet you in the car park,' she says, and hangs up before she can change her mind.

She watches as the truck slowly pulls away from the kerb, moving out of sight.

As she gets closer to the shop, her heart beats faster. He gets out when she's next to the truck, holds his arms out and she can't help but fall into them. He smells the same: smoke, sawdust, shampoo.

He releases her and she remembers where she is. She glances around, but nobody's watching.

'How are you holding up?' he asks. 'I saw it on the news. I drove straight here.'

'I don't know,' Maria says, her voice cracking. 'Rosie… she's… She's just gone. They can't find her. And now the detectives are involved, and they searched our house, and…'

She dissolves into great gasping sobs; he steers her into the passenger side of the cab of his truck. He gets in the other side and waits while she takes short halting breaths.

'That's standard procedure,' he says. 'Searching your house. They want to be sure she's not hiding.'

'But Rosie… she's three. She doesn't know the way back from the park, she couldn't have walked home.'

'It's just standard,' he repeats. Then he pauses. 'How's Ed?'

'Eddie, now,' she corrects him. 'And he's fine. Six feet tall, skinny as a rake.'

'Six feet? He didn't get that from me,' he chuckles. 'Nineteen? Is he at uni?'

'Twenty,' she corrects him. 'And no. He didn't apply. Wanted some time off.'

'Time off, right,' he says, then descends into silence.

They sit for a moment. Maria watches the customers of the Co-op going in and out of the store; she envies their banal little lives, the simplicity.

'I miss you,' he says.

She tries not to hear it. He repeats it, louder this time.

'Sean, we can't do this. You shouldn't be here.'

'I'm sorry—'

'You said that.'

'I mean it.'

'A few apologies doesn't make up for twelve years of… just nothing, Sean.'

'I was in prison.'

'And who put you there?'

He stops, looks down at his feet. 'If I could change what I did, I would. I shouldn't have taken that knife with me, I shouldn't have—'

'You shouldn't have gone there in the first place.'

'I was trying to provide for my family.'

'You could have got a job.'

It's an old argument. Rehashed over the years – sometimes face to face, in the septic atmosphere of the prison visiting room. Sometimes just in her head. Nothing changed then, nothing will now.

'I'm not that man anymore,' Sean says. 'My life's better. I'm better. I have a job – at a farm. They give me a house. And a dog.'

'Sean—'

'Just think about it. It would be different this time.'

'I can't think of anything right now. Not while Rosie's missing.'

'But when she comes back. When they find her. We could be a family again.'

Maria likes the way he says that. Like there's no doubt in the fact her daughter will return safe and well. But Sean lives in a fantasy world, always has.

'Eddie doesn't want to see you,' she says. She's lying; it's becoming a habit.

'He will. He'll come round.'

'I'm *married*, Sean. To a man who loves me and has a steady job, and who puts a roof over my head.'

'And you love him?'

The slight pause betrays her. Maria's not sure why she's even defending Tony, why she bothers.

'He looks after me,' she says.

Sean scoffs. 'Apparently so,' he replies, gesturing to her expensive cashmere jumper, her leather knee-high boots. 'I didn't realise you were that sort of woman.'

'Fuck you,' she throws back as she opens the passenger side door.

'I'm sorry, I'm sorry, Maria.' He leans over and grabs at her arm. She pauses. Looks back to her ex-husband, to the man she married much too young, to the father of her son.

Sean's aged, but the added years have done him the world of good. His hair is cut short, cropped against his head, but it's still dark, only his stubble showing the slightest hint of grey. He's wiry, tough; a hard life written in the lines on his face. But his eyes are still a soft blue, his calloused hands are gentle as he holds onto her arm, stopping her from leaving.

She remembers how she felt when she was with Sean – like life was theirs for the taking and anything was possible. They could have travelled, seen the world. But instead they ended up in a mobile caravan where the roof leaked and Eddie screamed all hours. Until Sean went out that night and didn't come home. And the police came.

'I have to go,' she says, softer now. 'Thank you for coming to see me. I mean it.'

'Anytime,' he replies. 'Can I call you? Text?'

'I'll call you,' she confirms. 'Things are tough at the moment. I don't need you making it worse.'

He nods and releases her arm. She climbs the rest of the way out of the truck and closes the door, walking quickly away from the Co-op. She doesn't look back. Because if she did, she might turn around, get straight into that truck, and never return.

CHAPTER SIXTEEN

The mood in the incident room is down when Jack returns. There is a low hum of activity – people typing, the click of a mouse, quiet conversations on the phone – but backs are hunched, and coffee cups are plentiful.

Amrit follows him into his office.

'Still nothing on traffic cams or ANPR,' she says. She points to where Lawrence is working. 'But we're still looking. Plus, we're running all registered sex offenders in the area against the ANPR. We should know soon. What did the mistress have to say?'

Jack slumps in his chair and updates Amrit on Bridget Daley's side of the story, the contradictions between her and Tony Logan.

'Do you believe her?'

'There's no reason to think she's lying. She seemed genuine. Shocked that Rosie was missing, full of vitriol towards the wife.'

'There's something going on in that house,' Amrit says. 'Bates called – apparently Maria went down to the Co-op this afternoon. Sneaked out. When she got back, she said she went to buy milk.'

'Let me guess – they had a fridge full already.'

'Four pints.'

'But does it have anything to do with Rosie? She could have just wanted some fresh air.' Jack glances at the clock, then out of the window. The sky has dimmed, edging closer to the end of the day. 'Phone Bates. Tell her to get the family ready for a press conference first thing tomorrow. I'll speak to the duty sergeant on response and patrol, and call Miller now. PolSA should have an update.'

Amrit leaves and Jack picks up the phone to Brian Miller. He answers on the first ring.

'She's not here, guv,' he says immediately. 'We've searched every corner, every blade of grass. Run the dogs over it all. Boxer one-zero did a fly by. Drones are coming up blank. No trace.'

'And the river?'

'The divers have been out all afternoon. Anything detected on the sonar was a false alarm. They can come back tomorrow if you want, search further downstream, but after the recent rain, that river's fast and deep. If she went in, she could be anywhere by now.' He pauses. 'Where do you want us to go next?'

Jack sighs. 'Stand down for now. All signs are pointing to an abduction. I don't want to waste any more budget on the search.'

Miller grunts down the phone. An acknowledgement that if that's the case it could be either good, or horribly bad. 'I'll close the RVP for the night. Keep a few guards on scene, but otherwise I'll be back on shift tomorrow at first light. Call me zero seven hundred hours. Available if you need me.'

Jack says his thanks and hangs up. Brian Miller is a good egg – if he says the area has been searched then no stone has been left unturned. Rosie Logan isn't there. Jack turns in his chair and looks out of the window at the darkening sky. He can't help but think about Theo, all those years ago. The disappearance of his best friend was similar to this one – no trace, no leads. He says a silent prayer to a god he hasn't believed in for years.

Please may she be safe.

–

The hours tick by. Jack tells Lawrence and Amrit to go home, get some sleep; other officers take over their posts, raking through the CCTV and the cameras. He knows that he should do the same, but he can't help thinking about that little girl. Somewhere. Lost.

He scours reports and updates for something he might have missed. He's just toying with the idea of taking a look at the CCTV footage for himself when a familiar face pokes around the door.

'I thought I'd find you here,' Lucy says. She's still in uniform, a smudge of mud down one leg, her hair in a high ponytail.

'No dogs?'

'They're fed and having a well-earned kip in the car,' she says. 'You should be doing the same.'

'I wouldn't fit in your car.'

She gives him a wan smile in appreciation of his poor attempt at a joke.

'Even if I go home, I won't be able to sleep,' he says.

'Have some dinner with me.'

'Canteen's shut. I can't bear another vending machine sandwich.'

'Good job I'm here then.'

She brings a paper bag out from behind her back and plonks it on his desk, right on top of the paperwork. The smells coming from within are so tempting he doesn't even object.

'Where did you get hot food from?' he says, pulling out steaming plastic containers.

'I can't take the credit. Fran dropped it off.'

'Even better,' he replies, grinning as Lucy hands him a fork.

Inside are portions of macaroni cheese, garlic bread, and a meat-filled ravioli covered in tomato sauce that Lucy takes from him straight away. He ravenously opens the box, digging into the pasta, cheese coming away in strings as he shoves a forkful into his mouth.

Lucy waits for him to take a few bites, before she says, 'Someone's got her, haven't they?'

He nods as he chews and swallows. 'Looking that way. A woman, with expensive tastes.'

He fills her in on the brand of boot, showing her the printout of the exact one that Amrit has identified from the website.

'They must have sold hundreds of these.'

'If not more,' Jack says, watching with mild disgust as Lucy dips garlic bread into the tomato sauce, then drips it down her front. He hands her a napkin. 'The Logans are doing an appeal first thing tomorrow. If they can avoid killing each other before then.'

'Do you think they're involved? I saw the drugs they found.'

'MDMA,' Jack confirms. Lucy raises her eyebrows. 'You thought it would be coke?' She nods, her mouth full. 'Me too. Two strong latents on the tin. Just need to get the family to let us print them.'

'They're refusing?'

'So far. Bates is working on it. Apparently, Tony Logan said they're not the ones at fault, so why should they be treated like criminals?'

'Because they have illegal drugs hidden in their house?'

'Less than half a gram. Personal use. We could charge them for possession of a class A, but what would be the point? Doesn't help us find their daughter.'

'Unless you use it as leverage to get them to talk.'

'And what then, if they have nothing to hide?' Jack says. 'All we know is Tony Logan likes to put it about a bit. It's hardly proof of abduction. We need to work with them, not piss them off. And imagine the PR on that.' He shudders. 'And for what it's worth, I don't think it belongs to Eddie. He's a pothead. Likes to slow things down, not speed them up.'

'Maybe Tony Logan likes a night out.'

'Mistress said no.'

'And you believe her?'

'Not for a second.'

They sink into silence, finishing off the rest of their dinner. Jack enjoys Lucy's company. For the past nine months, to his surprise, their friendship has gone from strength to strength. A coffee in the canteen; drinks in the pub; even dinner, once or twice. She's straight-talking, honest to a fault – and because of that Jack trusts her. A strange concept, but one he's enjoying.

And she seems better, the last few months. He remembers when they first met. Her house was a mess, her life on hold, desperately waiting for news of her missing husband. And since his fate was confirmed, she's pushed her shoulders back and got on with her life. Even started dating Pete Nash – a similarity between the dog handlers that Jack can see works.

It's in calm moments like these – the easy exchange, the trust between them – that something else comes into Jack's mind. Something important, that Lucy should know. Their friendship was cast in stone after the events last June, but he hasn't been completely honest. The man who confessed to killing Lucy's husband had a bargaining chip. Nico's last words, recanted with his dying breath: *She needs to know what happened to her sister.*

To Jack's knowledge, Lucy doesn't have a sister. Two half-brothers, living in Newcastle, but no sister. He's even done a few quiet checks on the police databases, searching for *Holmes*, Lucy's maiden name. But it's a common surname, too many to sift through without any additional information.

So he's let it be. Written it off as the ramblings of a dying man; and what good would it do, telling her? Everyone involved is dead, he doesn't want to put her life into a tailspin all over again. What you don't know can't hurt you. *But would I want to be told?* he wonders.

'A quick thought,' Lucy says, distracting him from his musings. 'Just because Tony has owned up to one affair, it doesn't mean he isn't having another. He had more than one woman on the go where they lived before, didn't he?'

'And what? This new woman has Rosie? With or without his knowledge?'

'Could be either. Revenge, or maybe they'd planned it. Take Rosie, and Tony will join them later. Rosie miraculously turns up, fit and well. Show Maria as a neglectful mother for losing her, apply for custody, job done. Instant family.'

Jack sits back, stomach pleasantly full, considering it. 'We'd need to access his phone records to find out for sure. And he'd never give us permission.'

'Maybe he doesn't need to. They might have a family plan. And if that's the case—'

'We only need Maria to say yes.'

Lucy points a finger at him with a smile. But before he can do anything, they hear the sound of thudding footsteps, and Amrit appears in the doorway.

Flushed and out of breath, she clutches a piece of paper in her hand.

'One of the number plates came back,' she gasps. 'Seen in the area, near the park, just after nine.'

Jack's already on his feet. 'Back to who?'

'Long story short – a guy called Gary Ballard. Registered sex offender. Convictions for possession and distribution of prohibited images of children. Only got out six months ago. Teams are assembling as we speak.' She turns her focus to Lucy. 'And we need your dog.'

CHAPTER SEVENTEEN

The house is foul: the stuff of nightmares. It stands in the middle of a row of terraces, the front door pale and peeling, the garden no more than a patch of concrete, full of weeds and empty bottles.

Lucy's dread for Rosie intensifies. If she was brought here, things may be worse than they thought.

Lucy waits next to her car as the house entry team go first. A squad of burly PCs, all in black, heaving the red 'enforcer' against the door. The battering ram makes light work of the lock, splintering it open instantly, and in seconds the team are inside, aggressive shouts of 'Police, get down on the ground' echoing around the empty street.

Lights have gone on in neighbouring windows, but the street stays empty. Nobody wants to get swept up in the trouble, put themselves in the firing line for future repercussions.

Her body is tense, all muscles on high alert as she waits for the house to be given the all-clear – for Rosie to emerge in the arms of a police officer. But the place is silent.

She glances across to Jack. Like the rest of the team, he's wearing a black coat with POLICE emblazoned on the side, but unlike the others he's standing straight, focus locked on the house, the radio held against his ear.

And then the news comes that nobody wanted.

'All clear, all in order. State nine, one in custody.'

Jack's shoulders visibly sag.

'Roger that. Dog team, stand by. VRD only.'

Lucy opens the boot to the car; both dogs rise to attention, mouths open, teeth and jaws on display. But it's the nose she wants now – Moss's specifically.

She opens the grate to Moss's side and slips the harness over his body. Moss's tail wagging, his ears up, his eyes bright. He doesn't understand the aching disappointment that the girl isn't here. Or at least, she's not here alive. It's Moss's job to see if the alternative is true.

Lucy encourages him down from the car and shuts the boot. She walks across to the house, Moss trotting eagerly by her side; the sergeant of the house entry team greets her at the door.

'What am I facing, Sarge?'

'It's shit in there, so be on alert. No broken glass, no needles that we can see, but you never know.'

Lucy nods in acknowledgement. 'I'll do a quick sweep,' she says as Jack joins them. 'Look for any obvious presentations of blood, and...' She doesn't want to say it. Jack nods, head down.

'What was the arrest for?' Lucy asks, tilting her head towards the tubby figure now languishing in a patrol car.

'Possession of extreme pornography.'

'Children?' Jack asks.

'Not that we've found. But take a look for yourself. We've barely scratched the surface.'

Lucy exhales slowly, preparing herself for the worst. Behind her, Jack is pulling on shoe covers and gloves, but she and Moss are going in as is. Their job is to ascertain if there is a crime scene within these four walls. Then let the SOCOs take over if there is.

She steps through the front door. Inside, the house smells of damp and sweat, an undertone of cigarettes and marijuana seeping through. Black mould coats every ceiling, the floorboards bounce as they step across.

Moss doesn't need to be told, she can see his nose is already twitching, but she gives the command 'Look, look,' and the dog starts darting this way and that, his attention alternating between the ground and the air. She hates to think what his sensitive smell receptors are picking up; the pervading odour is almost overpowering to the human nose.

She allows the dog to lead her into the living room containing a sagging sofa and a scratched coffee table. She sees why it didn't take the officers long to make an arrest; the table is covered with pornographic images – women and men in various states of undress, engaging in sexual acts, some involving knives, guns and a hangman noose. Lucy leaves them where they are; luckily Moss is already steering her away, his nose pulling him into the adjacent room.

The kitchen next, coated in a thick grey slime of rotted food and abandoned takeaway containers, a bin overflowing onto the stained lino floor. Lucy is starting to feel this is a wasted search – there is no way they're going to find anything in this hovel.

Moss sets his sights on the stairs, pulling her in his wake. This cornucopia of foul stench is a dog's playground; she doesn't dare let him off the lead in case he sticks his nose in something harmful.

There are two rooms at the top of the stairs. The first is a bathroom, so black and foul-smelling that Lucy closes the door and refuses to go near. The second is a bedroom. A bare mattress lies on top of a carpet, worn and filthy, and it's impossible to make out the original colour. A stained sleeping bag lies on top, a grey pillow next to it. Moss gives it all a good sniff but shows no signs of indication. Three built-in wardrobes line the far wall and Lucy resolves that this will be it. She'll let Moss have a sniff inside then get the hell out of there. They can't do a proper search in these conditions and she's starting to worry about the risk to her dog's health.

She opens the first wardrobe – completely empty, bar a few metal coat hangers. No interest from Moss. The second is chock full of clothes, heaped almost to the top. Moss gives them a good sniff but doesn't pause. There could be anything in there, she's not about to start going through it to get a needle prick, or worse. She shifts Moss to the third and final – and already she notices a difference.

This door is sturdier than the others. Solid wood rather than cheap MDF. And there's a padlock over the latch.

She gives it a quick tug; it seems sturdy. She glances back to her dog. Moss has stilled, his nose pressed against the bottom of the door, sniffing fast. And as she watches, he freezes.

She frowns. The dog looks up at her.

'Show me,' she says, and his nose goes straight back to the bottom of the locked doors. Her skin prickles.

'Jack?' she shouts without taking her eyes off her dog. 'DCI Ellis?'

Jack appears in the doorway and is quickly by her side.

'What have you got?'

'Moss indicated here.' Lucy points to the spot. 'Twice. Clearly. And it's locked.'

Jack's eyes narrow. He reaches forward and tugs on the door; the handle comes off in his hand. He shouts back to the entry team, demanding a crowbar. It's brought swiftly, applied to the lock and with a splinter and a grind of metal it pulls away.

They should wait for the SOCOs, but this is a missing child and time is of the essence. Lucy pulls the dog back as Jack opens the door.

There's nothing there. Lucy passes her torch to Jack, and he shines it into the space; goosebumps bristle on Lucy's skin and she sees immediately why Moss had given an indication.

The space is bigger than a normal wardrobe. Wooden walls finish halfway, evolving into brickwork and ending a few feet back with a breezeblock wall. It must have been expanded into the room next door, hidden somehow, behind wardrobes or cupboards. The floor is made up of wooden boards, and every surface is covered with dark brown stains.

There are a few items in the far back. In the gloom, Lucy can't see what they are. She turns to Jack to get him to redirect the torch when she realises what he's staring at. He's motionless, frozen, the torch pointing at the walls of the box. Faint white lines – scratches – score the surface.

'Someone had been trying to get out,' Jack says, his voice no more than a whisper. 'They kept…' He clears his throat. 'Someone was imprisoned here. Someone who…'

Was bleeding. Was injured.

But it's not possible. The wardrobe is small, cramped. You couldn't keep someone locked up in here.

Unless it was a child.

Jack's gaze has turned to the rubbish at the back. He focuses the torch, lighting up the pile. Crumpled plastic bottles. Litter. And a few items of clothing – a shoe, and something else.

Jack almost folds himself in two to climb inside. He takes shuffling footsteps, then reaches down and picks up the piece of cloth. He backs up, holding it out between two fingers.

It's small. What was once a white T-shirt is now stained and grubby and falling apart. But it's possible to make out the picture on the front.

It's a dinosaur – a toothy *Tyrannosaurus rex* with a car between its teeth. Dark brown streaks stain the front. It's too big to be Rosie's. This belongs to a boy, and it looks to Lucy like it's been there for a while. Years, maybe decades.

And then she realises. 'Jack…' she begins. She reaches out to touch his arm, but he's fixed on the dinosaur cartoon, his face pale.

And with it, all of Jack's worst fears have been confirmed.

'It was Theo's,' Jack whispers. 'Theo was here.'

PART TWO

CHAPTER EIGHTEEN

In the hours that follow the discovery of the T-shirt, Lucy doesn't leave Jack's side, watching him alternate between barking frantic instructions to overworked SOCOs to periods of frozen contemplation, head down, arms by his sides. As if his body has shut down and can't process any more.

After the house has been taken over by the crime scene manager, Lucy gently ushers him outside and into the passenger seat of her car. He doesn't complain, doesn't even comment on the dog hair and the dried mud, just sits down and lets Moss clamber into the footwell next to him. The spaniel rests his jowls on Jack's leg, looking up at him with brown baleful eyes. Jack rests a heavy hand on his head.

'Are you sure it's Theo's T-shirt?' Lucy asks gently. 'If it is, it must have been there for… for decades.'

'Nearly thirty years. And yes, I'm sure. The dinosaur on the front – his dad brought it back from South Africa. Some trip to see the family. So it's unique – or as good as, over here.'

Lucy's not convinced but doesn't want to push Jack further.

'We'll know more in the morning,' she says. 'Let the SOCOs do their job.'

Jack nods, slowly. His fingers work circles in the dog's fur. 'Is this where he was all this time?' Jack says. 'Barely thirty miles from where we grew up?'

'Where was that?' Lucy asks.

'In Gathurst, just outside Portsmouth.'

'Is that why you took this job? To move closer to your family?'

Jack chokes out a bark of laughter. 'No, never that. My parents are still up north. Berwick, on the border of Scotland. Mum keeps in touch with Sophie, but apart from that they have no ties to where we used to live.'

'And Sophie lives in Portsmouth?'

'Yeah.' He stops again, massages Moss's ears. 'Maybe I came back for her. Maybe because I thought I could find Theo. So where is he, Lucy?' He turns to face her for the first time, his face haggard with fatigue and stress. 'If he was there, in that *cupboard*,' he spits that word. 'Where is he now?'

'They'll have to reopen the investigation. They'll find him.'

'Who? Who will? You and I both know there's no appetite for cold cases. We don't have the resource to investigate crimes committed yesterday, let alone ones from thirty years ago.'

'New evidence—'

'One T-shirt.' He looks at her. 'That could have belonged to any boy of that age. I'm not stupid, Lucy. I know what people will say. I'm seeing what I want to see.'

'Forensics will confirm. And the people who lived in that house—'

'They'll be long gone.' Jack presses his fingers into his eyes, then slowly runs his hands down his face. 'No, what's done is done. Theo's dead.'

'You need to know for sure.'

'Why? Forgiveness? Closure?' he says scornfully. 'We've survived for thirty years. What you don't know can't hurt you.'

'Jack—'

'Leave it alone. Besides, we have more pressing matters to attend to. Rosie Logan, for one. We need to confirm if she was ever even in that house. And work out where on earth she is right now.'

The car plunges into silence. He's right: they're no further forward in finding Rosie. A number plate led them here – someone with ties to this address was near the park when Rosie disappeared, and that's what they need to focus on.

Lucy's phone vibrates in her pocket; she ignores it. The buzzing cuts through the silence in the car; Jack looks at her.

'Answer it,' he says.

'It's Pete. He'll be wondering where I am.'

'You're supposed to be out with him?' Lucy nods. 'Answer it.'

And with that he opens the car door and, giving Moss one last pat, climbs out, closing it behind him.

Moss clambers onto the passenger seat and sits, peering out of the windscreen, his ears up. The house is a crime scene, it swarms with people – uniforms, white suited SOCOs – and Jack is quickly lost in the melee.

Her phone has stopped buzzing, but she takes it out of her pocket, looking at the messages from Pete. Her thumb hovers over the call button, but she pauses, thinking of Theo.

Four days off. She can achieve a lot in four days.

MCIT might not have any time to investigate, but she damn well does. She was a detective once. She could be one again.

DAY TWO – THURSDAY

CHAPTER NINETEEN

New day, new challenges. And for Jack – the press conference.

He can't have got home before two a.m. last night, stripping down to his boxers and collapsing into bed. But he couldn't sleep. Thoughts of Theo strummed against his brain – he *knows* that the T-shirt is his. And that means he'd been alive, imprisoned in that godforsaken cupboard. Cold, scared, in pain – and for how long?

The police should have done more. *He* should have done more, but he'd been eleven, what difference would he have made? He had his own demons to contend with: labelled a murder suspect, driven across the country by his parents, desperate to resurrect their normal lives. He changed his name: Jason Kent became Jack Ellis. A detective chief inspector.

And here he is.

He can't do anything for Theo now. But he can find Rosie.

The Logans arrive at the police station at nine, driven from home by Bates. Jack escorts them through. They stand, stiff, grey-faced, waiting in the middle of the family room; Maria in a long navy dress and heels, Tony Logan in a suit, looking every inch the serious businessman. They don't touch, don't even look at each other.

There's no sign of Eddie.

'We don't need him here,' Tony says, when asked if he'll be joining them. Jack glances to Bates and gets a look that says, *Let it go*. She's obviously been over that already.

He offers drinks; Tony wants coffee, while Maria asks for water. Jack nods and Bates follows him outside.

'They hate each other,' he says to Bates as they stand in the corridor, waiting for the vending machine to dispense a cup of noxious caffeine. 'They can't go on live television like that.'

'This is *good*,' Bates says. 'You should have seen them when I turned up at breakfast – they were refusing to go in the same car. They've been arguing about everything. Tony's affairs, the drugs we found in the bedroom, the fact that Maria lost Rosie in the first place.'

'Bloody hell,' Jack mutters. This is all they need. He takes the coffee in one hand, the cup of water in the other, and heads back.

They're sitting on opposite sides of the room. Jack hands them their drinks; Tony takes one look and places the cup of coffee on the table, untouched. Jack can't blame him for that, at least.

Jack sits in between them. Rests his arms on his knees, leaning forward, looking one way then the other.

'Emma has briefed you already, but I want to be doubly sure you know what you're getting into. The aim of today is to present the personal – the human side of this disappearance. You're Rosie's parents, and the public out there need to see how important it is that we find her. The room is going to be full of journalists. Cameras will go off. Questions will be fired constantly. Now, I'll answer those, but you'll need to make a statement. Do you know what you're saying?'

'I'm doing the talking,' Tony says, patting his top pocket where a sheet of white paper juts out the top.

'Good.' Jack turns to Maria. 'And that may well be, but you need to present a united front. You both need to be as calm as you can, given the circumstances. The most important thing is we get the message out. You want Rosie returned, as soon as possible. To you. Her loving parents.' He stresses that last point with a stare. 'You might not love each other much at this moment in time, but you love her. Right?'

Maria nods. She looks to Tony, who does the same. There's a knock on the door and Emma Bates sticks her head around.

'They're ready,' she says.

–

Jack goes first, walking in front of Maria and Tony, up to the stage. A Hampshire Constabulary backdrop behind them; a blue cloth draped over the long table. Microphones in front. One for each of them. The lights are dazzling, the watching faces blurred.

Jack takes a moment to settle himself. He's wearing a clean, crisp white shirt, fresh suit, navy tie. He places the folder in front of him, opens it to the first page, and looks at the words. Double-spaced, clean type.

He takes a deep breath and begins.

'Good morning, thank you for coming. My name is DCI Jack Ellis and I'm from Hampshire Police. We are here today to appeal for information to help trace a three-year-old girl, Rosie Logan, who has been reported missing. The last known sighting was yesterday, Wednesday the fourteenth of February, at Memorial Park in Fordingbridge at approximately nine a.m. Her current whereabouts are unknown.

'She is three years old with blonde curly hair and blue eyes. She was wearing blue wellington boots and a red coat. At the time of her disappearance, she was holding a grey soft rabbit toy – but this has since been recovered.'

He pauses, looks out into the sea of faces and camera lenses. Vultures, poised, looking for fresh meat to attract readers to their story.

Jack swallows his nervousness and continues, talking directly to the public: 'If you were in that location at that time or just after, please check your dashcam footage or any personal CCTV. If you can support us in finding Rosie, contact us by calling 999 and quoting the incident number on the screen. And may I reassure you, there is no indication that there is any criminality involved in Rosie's disappearance at this time. Search and rescue teams remain at the location, but we are keeping an open mind and haven't ruled out the possibility that Rosie is currently with a family member or friend. If you are with Rosie, please come forward to let us know as soon as you can so she can be reunited with her mum and dad.

'Police are continuing their enquiries and are working with the parents, Tony and Maria Logan, here today, who would like to say a few words.'

Jack looks across to Tony Logan with what he hopes is a reassuring smile. Tony looks at his wife; Maria's gaze stays locked on the tabletop. The piece of paper in his hand shakes; he places it back on the table and looks out into the audience.

'Rosie is a bright, chatty, three-year-old girl. She loves unicorns and all animals, especially dogs…' His voice cracks, he clears his throat. 'We miss Rosie and would give anything for her to be back with us again. Please… please call the police if you know anything, so she can be returned home to me and my wife.' He grabs at Maria's hand and clutches it; she doesn't look at her husband, continues to stare numbly downwards. 'Thank you.'

Jack almost lets out a sigh of relief. Nearly done. 'Thank you,' he concludes. 'We have a few minutes for brief questions.'

Hands go up, but a voice shouts from the front row: 'Rosie's been missing for twenty-four hours – does the fact that a DCI from MCIT has taken over mean you suspect foul play?'

Jack feels Maria's gaze. 'MCIT is simply the best resourced department to run this investigation. As I said before, we have no reason to suspect—'

'Where do you think Rosie is?'

'I can't comment at this time, but we ask anyone—'

'You have some experience with missing person investigations, isn't that right, DCI Ellis?'

Jack blinks. He looks out into the audience but the light blinds him. 'As a detective within the MCIT, I have extensive experience on missing person cases—'

'But one in particular? From your childhood?'

'I heard progress had been made last night on the Theo Nkosi case?'

'DCI Ellis, where's Theo?'

The questions come thick and fast. Jack grits his teeth, forces his exhausted mind to focus.

'We are here to talk about Rosie Logan, and that is all. Thank you for coming today. And to reiterate, I would urge anyone with any information to come forward by calling 999, and help us find Rosie.'

And with that he gets up and walks from the room.

CHAPTER TWENTY

Lucy watches the press conference from her sofa, a sleepy Moss curled into a ball next to her. She sees the tension in Jack's jaw, notices the narrowing of his eyes when the journalist asks the questions about Theo, but she knows Jack well. Anyone else would see a dedicated detective, trying to do his job.

Maria and Tony Logan are another matter entirely. They come across as stiff and uncaring. Posh, manicured, brought there under protest. Even the untrained eye can spot there is something rotten in their marriage.

The coverage ends and the newsreader takes over, showing a photo of Rosie and a map of the location where she went missing. Jack's keeping his cards close to his chest – no mention of the woman leading Rosie away. Not wanting to start a media circus; still hoping that whoever she is will come forward of her own accord.

Lucy finishes her coffee, planning her day. She calls Pete; he answers on the fourth ring.

'So we're not doing drinks, then?'

'I'm sorry,' she replies. 'Had to work.'

'I thought you got off at six?'

'I did. But I was at the nick when the call came in, and I had Moss with me.'

'What were you doing at Southampton?'

Pete's confusion is warranted. As dog handlers, their HQ is down in Netley, not at the central police station. Pete takes a slow breath in, realising.

'You were with Jack?'

'Fran made him dinner. I was dropping it off.'

'And then you went with him on the call?'

'I did. I'm sorry, Pete. I should have messaged.' There's a long pause. She can hear his heavy footsteps, a whistle as he calls his dog. 'Are you training?'

'Down at Broadlands. In the river.'

'Can I join you?'

'On your day off?' His words are brief, but she can sense him softening.

'Got to walk them anyway.'

Another beat, then an expulsion of air. 'Jesus Christ, Lucy. You are insufferable.' He laughs and she knows she's forgiven. 'Bring your wetsuit. You're going in.'

–

German shepherds aren't like spaniels. Any suggestion of water, from a trickling stream to a deep, fast-flowing river, and Moss will have hurled himself in, gleefully paddling after whatever might be in there. But Iggy? He needs to be persuaded.

It's not a great trait in a general purpose dog.

A GPD needs to be prepared to enter any environment after their track. Pitch-black warehouse, open field, nothing is off limits. So if the offender they're following goes in the water, then so must Iggy.

And this is how Lucy finds herself up to her waist in the middle of the River Test at ten a.m. on this freezing cold Thursday.

The water is arctic; her legs and feet are already numb, even in the neoprene, and she can feel mud and who knows what under her feet. She's wearing a large padded sleeve over her right arm, holding it above the water.

'I don't like you right now, Nash,' she shouts.

'Feeling's mutual,' he laughs from the riverbank.

Dax is up first and standing next to him, alert and ready to go.

'You're supposed to be running,' Pete hollers.

'Fine,' she grumbles, and turns, moving as quickly as she can in the rushing water. Behind her, she hears Pete shout 'Stop!' and knows that in a moment, ninety pounds and forty-two teeth of German shepherd will be slamming into her.

She holds the padded arm up high and braces herself; the impact sends her flying and she loses her footing, falling face first into the water as Dax pulls the sleeve away, chomping joyfully and swimming back to the bank. She stands up again, choking and cursing, pushing her hair out of her eyes as she turns to face Pete. He's called Dax and is now doubled over with laughter.

'Yeah, yeah,' she mutters, as she wades over. 'Your turn next.'

He's still chortling as he holds out a helping hand and pulls her onto solid ground. Next to them, Dax is shaking himself dry, the sleeve still in his mouth. Pete extracts it with a single command, and the two of them walk back to the cars to change dogs.

As Lucy awkwardly pulls off her wetsuit and gets dressed, she has to admit, it was worth coming here today. Firstly, for Iggy's training goals, but also so she can appreciate the fine form of Pete Nash, getting ready next to her. She's trying not to stare, but it's tricky not to – the skin-tight wetsuit as he pulls it up toned thighs, over his shorts, nice arse, hard abs.

Fuck's sake, she needs to get laid by this guy.

A wet nose nudges her hand where it's paused on the door to the cage. She shakes her head, waking herself up, and lets her dog out, putting his harness on.

'You ready?' she says to Pete.

'Always.' He grins. Dammit, he knows how good he looks right now and, as if making his point, walks in front of her to the river.

To Lucy's dismay, Pete manages to keep his footing every time Iggy goes for the bite, and the dog does her proud. He shows no reluctance throwing himself into the water, swimming decisively towards Pete and launching himself joyfully at the sleeve, bringing it back to Lucy when she calls.

'A few more sessions and I'd say that goal is ticked off,' Pete says, clambering out of the river. 'He's an excellent dog.'

'He is,' Lucy says, giving the wet shepherd a fond stroke of the ears. They walk back, Lucy towels down Iggy then loads him into the car. She pauses, watching Pete as he dries himself off, briefly wondering if he needs help.

'Tonight?' she asks instead. 'Are you free?'

He stops, the wetsuit around his waist. 'Are you going to show?'

'If you come dressed like that, I will.'

He snorts out a laugh. 'The Anchor, half-seven?'

'I'll be there.'

Reluctantly, she pulls herself away with just a quick kiss and gets in the car. Why hasn't she done more with him, she asks herself for the hundredth time. But their relationship will progress further than a snog, the butterflies in her stomach tell her. Soon.

–

The day has evolved into a beautiful one, sun pushing out from behind the clouds. Nothing but a blue sky and a rest day in front of her. These are the times she enjoys the most: just her and her dogs, heart beating, lungs full of fresh air from the environmental training at the river. But today her mind just won't empty. She can't stop thinking about Theo.

It was July 1994 when Theo went missing – close to thirty years ago. What does not knowing do to a person? Her own husband had been missing for nearly two years before he had been found the previous June, and that state of limbo had been torture.

She has to question the T-shirt. Whether, desperate for an answer, Jack saw what he wanted. But who else could it belong to? What other possible explanation could there be? Still – it's with the lab now, they'll know soon enough.

Lucy thinks about Theo's family – his parents, siblings – what have they been going through for three decades? They will have been notified about last night – about the house and the T-shirt, presented with a photograph and asked to identify it, no doubt. The questions they will have asked as a result, and still, no answers.

Jack's reaction last night had been strange, but she understood it. He had been Theo's best friend, and the last person to see him alive. Seeing that cupboard – the blood and the stains on the walls and floor – wouldn't have helped the guilt coursing in his veins. The last vestiges of hope, gone. Assuming that is Theo's T-shirt, Jack would know that, most likely, they won't be finding a living, breathing person, but a body.

Finding a body, as Lucy knows, is gruelling, but it's closure, of sorts. You can move on. Grieve. Hold a funeral and celebrate their life. In the absence of that confirmation, you're stuck; caught forever in your own personal circle of hell.

She considers the crossroads ahead. What should she do?

Despite the morning's work, Lucy's energised, cosy in her coat and jeans. The dogs certainly aren't tired; she could go home and collect Moss, then head into Ashurst for a walk in the New Forest. Or she could turn left, for Theo.

Lucy pauses. She thinks of Jack, and his apathy. Of the family, waiting for news.

'I'd want to know,' she mutters.

And decision made, she turns left. Heading towards the nick.

–

Detective Chief Superintendent Weaver is in his office when she arrives, talking on the phone. She knows him from her previous job, remembers what makes him tick. He likes being in the warm and dry, likes to chat. Likes it when things are made easy.

She pokes her head around the doorway; he waves her in, holds up his fingers. *Two minutes*. She sits down in the chair opposite his desk while he talks, seemingly about nothing work-related, then ends the call with a cheery goodbye.

'Lucy Halliday,' he says. 'Long time no see. How's life with the canines?'

'Simple,' she replies with a smile. 'No people.'

'How lovely. How can I help you?'

'Theo Nkosi. The T-shirt recovered last night. Do we have the results yet?'

'I heard about that. That's a turn-up for the books. And no. No news from the lab as far as I know.'

'But you've reopened the case? It must have been Hampshire who conducted the original investigation?'

'It was. And no.'

'No?'

'Not yet. We're waiting for confirmation from the lab. And we have our hands full with the Rosie Logan disappearance, in case you haven't noticed? We can't spare any resource with that going on – there's nobody free to look into it.'

'But I could.' She says it without thinking. Weaver looks sternly over the top of his glasses. 'I'm on four rest days. And I'm owed holiday, if I need more. I could dig out the original case files, get up to speed. Prepare some summary documents for MCIT once Rosie has… Once it's all over.'

His brow furrows. 'And why would you do that?'

'He's been missing for nearly thirty years. What that does to the family. I know what that's like.'

'You could be wasting your time. That T-shirt could have nothing to do with Theo Nkosi.'

'Then that's on me. No impact on your budget,' Lucy adds with a sweet smile.

Weaver grunts. 'We don't want the press getting wind of this. Digging up all that shit again. Have you spoken to Jack Ellis?'

'He's got enough on his plate.'

He regards her a moment longer, then slowly nods. 'Fine. Do it. On your own time. And yes, report to me – leave Jack alone for now.'

'Yes, guv. Of course. I'll let you know what I find.'

She backs out of his office before he changes his mind and walks quickly to find a spare desk, somewhere she can sit and work.

She opens her laptop and for a moment, she pauses. She thinks about Jack. Her friend, working hard in the MCIT office, a few floors above her. She went behind his back, spoke to his boss – lied to his boss – about a case personal to him.

Weaver's right. The last thing Jack needs right now is the press latching onto what happened back then. Having the finger pointed at him for murder ruined his life when he was eleven and threatened to do the same when it all came out last June. The journalist in the press conference earlier was the start of a slippery slope – it can't happen again.

She tells herself it's okay, that she's doing him a favour. Find out what happened, once and for all, and he can start to put the whole thing behind him. But as she types the case number into the RMS she knows she's kidding herself.

Jack's not going to like this. He's not going to like it at all.

CHAPTER TWENTY-ONE

The journey home from the police station passes in complete silence. Eddie meets them at the door. Tony pushes past him, heading straight to his study.

'You both looked like psychopaths,' Eddie mutters.

Maria scowls at her son. 'Make me a cup of tea, won't you?'

'Isn't that what she's here for?' he comments, pointing to DC Bates, who has followed them in.

Maria cajoles Eddie into the kitchen; she hears the kettle go on, then Eddie talking on the phone, whispering in one-syllable words. She catches one question: 'Do they think it was us?'

Do they? she wonders. Surely not. What mother would arrange for the abduction of her child? But then what sort of mother is she? Funny, but when she was a single mum, living in a draughty caravan park with a screaming Eddie and a husband out every night, she thought herself a good mother. She kept Eddie warm and dry and fed, spent her days playing with him on the worn blanket. Tummy time, reading to him – all the brain-enriching activities she was told about by her health visitor. But when Rosie arrived, it was as if she had forgotten all of that.

Rosie was an easier baby. She slept, she giggled, she smiled. She had all the toys that one small girl could ever wish for. But, still, Maria had felt she was failing. She noticed the judgemental stares from every woman at the mother and baby classes. She was too thin, too posh, too old, to fit in with these women. She stopped going. Her only company on those lonely days was Eddie and Chloe – and Chloe was better with Rosie than she ever was. More natural. More relaxed. And then they moved away, so it didn't matter that she hadn't made any friends.

She realises she's still standing in the hallway, her shoes on, her coat in her hand. She's been like this ever since Rosie disappeared; losing chunks of time, distracted and numb in the face of such impending disaster. As if, any moment now, DC Bates will tell her the terrible news.

She looks up to Tony's study. She can hear tapping behind the closed door; Tony working. How can he concentrate at a time like this?

She takes her phone out of her pocket, presses on the Safari logo and types in *Rosie Logan*. Immediately, the screen is full of articles, some from official news sites, some not. Her daughter's face, the same picture, over and over. And the comments. She reels in the face of the vitriol, the anger.

Stop wasting time – arrest the mother!

That bitch! She doesn't even care.

I hope that girl has gone to a better family, cos this one don't love her.

'What are you…?' DC Bates is next to her, looking over her shoulder. She gently prises the phone out of Maria's hand. 'Stop looking at that.'

'They… they hate me,' Maria gasps. 'How can they think I would harm my baby girl?'

'They're nobodies. Keyboard warriors with nothing better to do. Stay away from the internet.'

DC Bates gently ushers her into the living room and down onto the sofa. Eddie appears with a cup of tea, places it on the coffee table then sits down next to her. She'd like a hug, but her son hasn't done such a thing in years; she settles for the feeling of his solid body next to hers.

'They're all wankers and perverts, Mum,' he says.

'But someone might know something,' Maria replies. 'You're monitoring this, right? In case someone knows where Rosie is?'

'The team are on it. But listen, we need your help,' Bates says. 'We need permission to access your mobile phone records and your bank.'

Maria's head snaps up. 'Why?'

Bates glances out of the door, then back to Maria. 'We're worried that Tony might have…' She clears her throat awkwardly. 'Other women. Ones he's not telling us about.'

'And you think one of those has Rosie?'

'We're exploring all angles. It's a joint bank account. Your mobile phones are on a family plan. If you give permission, we can access Tony's records and his credit cards.'

'And Eddie's. And mine.'

Bates frowns. 'Yes, and yours.'

'You're going to go through every number?'

'Not every single one. Just those we think might be important.'

'Mum,' Eddie says next to her. 'I don't care. Let them have it. Tony's lying to us – to you. Wouldn't you like to know for sure?'

Maria glances guiltily out of the door, then down to the phone in her hand.

'But what about his work phone? Wouldn't he contact women on there?'

'He wouldn't,' Eddie replies. 'Don't you remember? He said that because it's a work phone his HR department can see every call. He wouldn't dare. He wouldn't even let me borrow it to call Chloe that day my mobile broke. He gave me his shitty Android.'

She thinks of the call she made yesterday morning. The text she sent after. But there's no way she can refuse. Two sets of eyes burrow into her. She can't be the shitty mother they're all saying she is.

'Fine,' she says. 'Do it.'

Because the lies, the guilt don't matter. Not now. She just wants to find her daughter.

CHAPTER TWENTY-TWO

In the flurry of the aftermath of the press conference, Jack can lose himself in the case. It's easy to forget Theo when there are calls to assign, new leads to follow up on.

Appealing to the public for information has brought out the usual crazies. Rosie was taken by a UFO; Rosie is Madeleine McCann reincarnated; Rosie has been taken by a cult and is living in California. Knowing someone else has already been through in detail, Jack skim-reads, his interest caught by the sheer volume of opinions about Maria and Tony Logan. The comments below the social media feeds are the same, screaming a litany of blame and judgement.

It's always the parents.

They don't care about Rosie.

They hate each other, you can tell by looking at them.

Jack has to agree with that last one. Looking back over the coverage, Maria comes across as uncaring, Tony as arrogant and domineering. It wasn't the heartfelt plea they had been hoping for.

Jack finds the parallels to Madeleine McCann interesting. Same age when they disappeared. Both are pretty, blonde-haired girls. Both white. Both from affluent families. Newspaper coverage is only just taking hold in Rosie's case, but Jack knows if her disappearance goes on for much longer it will draw the same level of media frenzy as the McCann investigation did in 2007, and indeed, continues to attract to this day. The police need the eyes and ears of the general public, but the intense scrutiny of the family, and indeed the work done by the SIO, isn't helpful.

Jack's starting to feel a squeeze of his stomach, a fresh wave of nausea, when the front desk calls up. Instant relief: Chloe Winters is here. Eddie's friend, and Rosie's babysitter.

Jack leaves Amrit in charge, and heads down to meet her. The woman waiting in reception is petite, with vivid, dyed red hair and large doe-shaped eyes. She doesn't look older than sixteen, but confidently shakes his hand when Jack introduces himself.

He shows her through to the family room, offers her a drink – she declines.

'I've felt sick since I found out,' she says. 'Can't sleep, just thinking of Rosie out there. Eddie called me straight away. I was in a lecture, had to leave halfway through.'

'College?' he says, trying to gauge her age. She's fidgety, nervous – repeatedly tapping her first finger against her thumb.

'Uni,' she says. She manages a proud smile. 'Second year at Southampton.'

Same age as Eddie. 'And how do you know the family?'

'Eddie and I met at school. Back when we both lived in Swindon. Doing our GCSEs. That place was like *Lord of the Flies*, everyone for themselves. You had to find a tribe, and fast, or they'd pick you off.' She offers a weak grin. 'A lame gazelle at the mercy of a pack of lions.'

'And you and Eddie became friends?'

'I guess so. Eddie – you've met him, right?' Jack nods. 'He's different. And more so then. Dressed all in black, wore eyeliner, had his hair long. We were the outcasts.'

'Forgive me for saying, but you don't seem like a typical outcast?'

Her face turns dark. 'Oh, I was. It was… a bad time. Things are better now. Eddie and I – we were close.' She catches Jack's expression. 'Not like that! Good friends. That's all.'

Jack wonders whether Eddie would like more from the attractive young woman.

'How well do you know Maria and Tony?' he asks instead.

'Pretty well. They moved away to Fordingbridge a few years ago but I'm close to them again now I'm at Southampton Uni.

I babysit for Rosie when I can. I can't get over what's happened. Have you any idea who's taken her?'

'Why do you think she's been taken?'

'Just because…' Her face flushes, eye contact shifting to the floor. 'Eddie said there was a video. Of someone with Rosie? Was that confidential?'

'No, it's fine.' Jack takes the still of the ankle boot out of his file and pushes it across to Chloe. 'Any idea who this is?'

Chloe picks it up, studies it closely. She looks at Jack for a moment, then back to the photo. 'When was this taken?'

'Yesterday. Just after half-ten.'

'In the morning?' She goes quiet again. 'It's not me, if that's what you're thinking. I don't own boots like that.'

'Any idea who does?'

'No clue. Sorry.'

'What's Rosie like?'

Chloe's face lights up. 'She's a sweetheart. Absolutely adorable. Smart, funny. Knows what she wants and isn't afraid to argue her case, even at three. A good trait to have in a little girl.' Her chin wobbles, and her eyes brim over with tears. 'I promised myself that I wouldn't get upset when I came to talk to you. That I would do everything I could to help you find her.'

'You're doing a great job,' Jack says. 'And Maria and Tony?'

'What about them?'

'What are your impressions of them?'

She wipes a tear away, wrinkles her nose. 'They're always lovely to me, but they're not a close family. Eddie and Tony don't see eye to eye, they're always fighting. But Maria and Eddie have a lovely relationship. Eddie dotes on Rosie, they're sweet together. But.' She stops.

'But?' Jack prompts.

'But Maria and Tony don't get along. I didn't realise when I first met them, but once Rosie arrived the cracks started to show. Tony was distant, always at work. Out every night. And…'

'And?'

'He used to drive me home after babysitting. I didn't like it. He never did anything, but I always got the feeling he might, you know? So I got friends to pick me up – made an excuse and said that they were passing. Until I got my own licence, that is.'

'Is Tony ever violent with Maria or Eddie?'

She shakes her head.

'With Rosie?'

'Absolutely not.'

'Have you ever seen anyone in the family use drugs?'

'No. And whatever you found – that's not Eddie's. He's not into that shit.'

'What is Eddie into?' Jack asks. Chloe flushes. 'We know about the weed.'

Chloe breathes out. 'Just that, then.'

'Any idea whose it is?'

'Eddie said you found it in Tony and Maria's room?' Jack nods. 'Probably *his*,' she says, with a curl of her lip.

'Do you babysit a lot?'

'When I can. More in the early days. When Rosie was a baby. I think Maria struggled. Rosie was sweet, but Maria couldn't cope with the sleepless nights and the routine that comes with a young baby. Tony was never there. She was lonely, so I stepped in when I could. And I didn't mind,' she adds quickly. 'The extra cash was welcome, and I liked spending time with Maria and Eddie and Rosie. Thinking about it now, Maria might have been depressed. I'm studying medicine.' She smiles. 'And Maria showed all the signs of someone with postnatal depression. If I'd known…' Her gaze drifts to the middle distance.

'Did Eddie tell you much about his dad?'

'Sean?' Chloe narrows her eyes. 'Not much. I know he's been in prison Eddie's entire life. He's never met him.'

'He's not now.'

'No?'

'He was released in 2018.' Chloe looks blank. 'Eddie didn't mention it?'

'No. As far as Eddie knows he's still locked up. I asked him once if he thought about visiting and Eddie said no. He said, "What would be the point? He's a stranger." He only has his surname because he hates Tony more. If he's out, Eddie has no idea.'

Jack frowns. Yet more lies. He pushes the photograph back towards Chloe. 'Are you sure you don't recognise this boot?'

Chloe looks again but shakes her head. 'How could this happen? How could this have gone so wrong?' She starts crying again, ever more frantic. 'Please. You have to find her. Rosie – she's special. To me. To her family.'

'We're doing everything we can.'

Jack leaves the distraught woman with a sympathetic PC, and trudges up the stairs to the incident room, stopping off at the canteen on the way. While the server makes coffees for the team, he ponders Chloe's answers.

A fractured family at each other's throats; a mother struggling to cope; a lonely, isolated son, kept in the dark that his father is out of prison. And at the centre of it all: Rosie.

The consensus seems to be that everyone loved her – a sweet child, well looked after. No mention of violence within the home; no record with children's services. Even Chloe, no more than a babysitter, seems unusually attached. But she's young, probably fortunate enough to have never experienced tragedy in her life. Everything's emotional when you're that age.

He's still thinking about the interview with Chloe when Amrit arrives in the canteen. She spots him and hurries over, nearly knocking the coffees out of his hand.

'Boss, your phone,' she gasps, her face pink. 'Your phone's off.'

'I was in an interview.'

'Rachel Lennon called.'

She doesn't have to say any more – the crime scene manager, with something to report. He leaves the coffees with Amrit and walks quickly away, turning his phone on and calling Lennon without checking his voicemail. He pushes through a door and stands in a stairwell, desperate for a shred of peace and quiet. She answers on the first ring.

'Jack,' she says. 'I'm so sorry.'

'It's him?'

'Yes. Blood on the T-shirt is a match to Theo Nkosi.'

The news barely registers – he knew the moment he saw the dinosaur on the front. Theo's favourite, worn until it was filthy with dirt and his mother insisted on putting it in the wash.

Theo's mother.

'Have the family been notified?' he asks. 'That it's a definite match?'

'Someone's on their way to speak to them now. Who should I forward the report to? You, or Halliday?'

'PC Lucy Halliday?' he exclaims. His voice echoes in the empty stairwell.

The CSM registers his tone. 'Weaver said she was looking into it,' she says, warily.

'Me,' Jack replies. 'Send the results to me.'

He ends the call, his stomach rolling with unease. He wants to be with Theo's family – he *needs* to be with them – but he's here, miles away, dealing with yet another child he can't find.

His worry manifests in anger. He dials Lucy; it goes to voicemail. He tries again, same result but this time he leaves a message.

'What did I say?' he growls through gritted teeth. 'Leave it alone, Lucy. I don't want you digging into this. That's an order.'

He's not her boss, but he does outrank her. Not that that's ever stopped her in the past. He slumps onto the hard staircase, resting his head in his hands. He doesn't want Lucy investigating. She's a good detective, she'll find out what happened to Theo.

And that's exactly the problem.

CHAPTER TWENTY-THREE

The files were easy to find; buried at the back of the storage room, carefully catalogued and labelled. Lucy pulls the old cardboard boxes from the shelves – two, remarkably few given the situation. She places them on the floor, takes the lid off the first and runs her fingers through the documents and notebooks.

In 1994, there had been no social media, no drones, no ANPR. CCTV would have been slower, probably operating on a time lapse rather than a continuous feed. There would have been searches, public appeals, press conferences, but the resources available to the detectives were a fraction of what they work with now.

She pulls out the first folder and sits cross-legged on the floor, opening it on her lap. A colour photo of Theo Nkosi rests on the top. A formal school shot: chubby cheeks, a broad grin. His collar is half tucked into his jumper; there is a smudge of ink on his chin. He was a cute kid. Eleven years old when he went missing on Thursday 28 July 1994.

Lucy thinks of that stinking dark cupboard. The T-shirt discarded on the floor and the report she still hasn't received. She picks up her phone and calls Rachel Lennon. It rings out. She tries Fran.

'Yes, the results are back,' Fran says, once Lucy has explained. 'Rachel mentioned it. The T-shirt belonged to Theo. But why are you so interested? Aren't you supposed to be on a rest day?'

Her tone is suspicious; Fran knows Lucy well. Sticking her nose into cases that don't belong to her is an ongoing trend. And something that doesn't generally end well.

'I've spoken to Weaver,' Lucy says. 'He knows I'm looking into Theo Nkosi's disappearance.'

'Does Jack?'

Lucy wrinkles her nose. The furious voicemail on Lucy's phone tells her all she needs to know.

'He told you to leave it be, didn't he?' Fran says.

'Yes. But Fran,' Lucy adds quickly, 'this is the first proof in thirty years that Theo was abducted. That Jack had nothing to do with it. He won't be complaining when I find out what happened. When I clear his name once and for all.' Lucy stops. Their relationship works both ways: Lucy can tell when Fran's keeping something back herself. 'What else did they find?'

Fran makes a loud huff. 'Theo's DNA also came back as a match to the blood spatter and the pooling in the cupboard.'

'He was held there,' Lucy says.

'It looks that way.'

'Killed there?'

'Nothing else of relevance has been found in the house or the garden, let alone a body. They're still searching.'

'Has anyone told the family?'

'They should have by now.'

'Any other DNA profiles in the cupboard?'

'Not that they've found.'

'So Theo was the only child kept captive there. His abduction was a one-off?'

'Possibly.'

'What else have they found in the house?'

'I don't know—'

'Tell me.'

'I don't. Honestly, Lucy. You want to know more, phone Rachel Lennon.' Fran sighs. 'But listen. This is not your job. Jack's well-being is not your responsibility.'

'He's my friend.'

'Which makes it all the more important that you respect his wishes and leave it the hell alone.' More silence. 'You're not going to, are you?'

'I'll just review the case. See if there's anything obvious that pops out. And then I'll hand it over to another detective in MCIT.'

'Make sure you do. And come over for dinner soon. You can even bring Moss.'

'Not Iggy?'

'Iggy will eat my cat.'

Lucy hangs up with a chuckle, but the moment Fran's off the phone her mood sours. She looks at the photo of Theo.

It feels wrong, raking over Theo's last moments in this cold, dusty storage room. And if she's going to keep away from Jack, she needs to take these well away from the nick. She needs to get the dogs home – there's only so long she can leave them in the car park. She can't stay here.

She heaves the boxes into her arms, signs them out, then awkwardly carries them out to her car, hoping with every step that she won't cross paths with Jack. Her prayers are answered, and she shuts the door with a sigh of relief. She doesn't like deceiving Jack in this way, but if she gets some answers then surely it will have been worth it. He'll forgive her. Won't he?

–

She spends the rest of the day with Moss, Iggy content in his kennel outside. At first the spaniel was ecstatic to have her home, but his excitement soon evolved to boredom when he realised she wasn't going to move from the sofa. He settles next to her, snoring quietly, every little movement eliciting an open eye, checking that Lucy wasn't daring to go somewhere without him.

But apart from going to the kitchen to refill endless mugs of coffee, she doesn't leave the room. Slowly, methodically, Lucy makes her way through the files and the boxes, jotting notes of the salient details on the pad next to her. It's surreal, reading about this case. Seeing it through the investigating officer's eyes, when her only viewpoint up to now has been Jack's. His name appears often, the name he left behind when the UK press hounded him and his family across the country. Jason Kent, aged eleven. They feel like different people – the Jack she knows now, and Jason, the boy then.

By the time the sun goes down, she's been through it all. Moss has long given up, now upside down, his feet in the air, back leg jerking. A puddle of soft warm dog, letting out small, snuffed breaths. She leans over and rubs the silky fur under his chin. An eye opens, a reproachful glance. She reads the last page, squinting in the semi-darkness, then stretches. Moss turns the right way up and looks at her as she reviews her notes.

Thursday 28 July – Theo and Jason left their respective homes to play in their local woods. It was 1994, and hardly a rarity that kids would be left to their own devices during the day – especially in a suburb as sleepy as Gathurst. Theo's parents said Jason and Theo would spend every moment together – more so given it was now the summer holidays. The weather was a sticky thirty-two degrees – the middle of a heatwave that had left reservoirs dry and people grumpy. Theo and Jason would return at the end of the day, filthy from the tops of their heads to the soles of their feet, frequently shirtless and shoeless, covered in sticky blue sugar from ice pops.

Theo's mum, Wendy, remarked she would often run a bath ready for Theo's return so she could put him straight in it, leaving a grimy rim of grey once he'd finished. That night, the bath was run, dinner was ready, but Theo didn't come home. Wendy didn't worry. This was the summer holidays – it was light outside until well past nine and Theo had probably lost track of time.

Two hours later, just before eight, Wendy sent her eldest daughter, Sophie, out to look for him. She returned half an hour later, saying the woods were deserted, and neither Jason nor Theo were anywhere to be found.

Wendy called Jason's house. Jason's mother – described as tight-lipped and rude by Wendy – said that Jason had returned home hours ago, at about a quarter to seven. That's when Wendy started to worry. She asked to speak to Jason – he came on the phone and confirmed that Theo had indeed been headed home. And no, he didn't know where else Theo might have gone.

Wendy Nkosi called 999 at ten minutes past nine. A uniformed officer showed up at their house at half past.

Lucy reads the initial statements again. They're thorough, and cover everything Lucy would expect. What Theo was wearing, who he was with, when he said he'd be back. Units were dispatched to the woods, and then to Jason Kent's address. The resulting statements were brief – there was no sign of the boy.

Detective Inspector Maguire took over the investigation just after midnight.

Lucy pulls her laptop over and looks up the name on the police database. Stanley Maguire, now retired. Still living in the area. Definitely someone to speak to. She makes a note of his number then calls it, leaving a brief message requesting him to phone her back. His notes are here, but it's the things he didn't write down that Lucy wants to know. The little suspicions, the hunch. That instinct that all coppers nurture.

She puts his notebooks aside and turns her attention to the tapes. In 1994, they used cassettes; hell, in some nicks they still do. She picks up the old plastic cases and is surprised to find a VHS tape at the bottom.

Jason Kent – interview 1 29/07/94.

A cassette deck might be out of the question, but a VHS player is not. Her husband was a stickler for old technology, loving vinyl and floppy discs, resisting the new for as long as he could. She looks over her shoulder towards the garage, where his old boxes of junk still reside.

'Maybe you had your uses after all,' she mutters to the ether.

CHAPTER TWENTY-FOUR

Lucy emerges from the garage an hour later – filthy, dusty, but clutching a huge lump of brown plastic and metal, a bundle of wires stacked on the top. Technology has never been her forte, but she's old enough to remember how VHS players worked, and manages to connect the cables. The old player whirrs into action.

It's an antiquated thing, almost as heavy as a modern-day television. She looks at the VHS tape in her hand, gives the spools a quick tighten, then pushes it into the slot.

It makes a few grinding noises before the machine spits it out.

'Fucking hell,' Lucy growls. She puts her head down and blows into the hole – the only solution she can think of – then tries again. This time the tape stays in. She crosses her fingers and presses play.

Black and white static fills the screen. The indecipherable snowstorm continues for ten seconds or so, and just when Lucy is about to lose hope, it cuts to film. The grainy image shows a room: beige walls, orange plastic chairs and an MDF table. A man in a suit sits on one side, a young boy on the other. Lucy cranes forward to the screen. It's hard to make out much, but there are aspects about this child she recognises. Jason Kent is white-blond with a deep tan – clearly a kid who spends all day out in the sunshine. He's stick thin, but the child has the same rigid posture, and with a glance to the camera, Lucy spots the same strange blue-grey eyes. But there is one thing that distinguishes him from his adult counterpart – she has never seen Jack scared. This kid is terrified.

His legs jump under the table, a constant *tap tap*, keeping double time with the clock. His skinny arms shake under the

T-shirt, all the way down to his fingertips as he picks up the can of Lilt in front of him. He puts it down without taking a sip.

There's a woman next to him – young, dark hair – an appropriate adult, Lucy presumes. But she's doing nothing to help or reassure him: just staring dully at the notepad in front of her, twiddling a pen.

'Tell us what you were doing with Theo,' the detective says, resuming a conversation dissolved in the damage on the tape. 'And you can go home.'

'I… I don't know what you mean. We weren't burying anything.'

'A witness saw you when she was walking her dog. First the both of you, at five o'clock. Then later, when she walked back, just you. Digging a hole.'

'W-when?'

'About half-six, she said. What were you burying, Jason?'

'Nothing.'

'Our officers are out in the woods now. With dogs, metal detectors. Whatever it was, we'll find it. And it'll be much better for you if you come clean with us now.'

A long pause. The detective leans in closer. 'I can tell you're lying,' he says, so quietly the tape only just picks it up.

'I'm not. I don't know what you're talking about.'

There's a quiver in his voice; he chews on his lip.

The detective sits back again. 'Fine. Let's talk about what time you left Theo.'

'I didn't leave Theo. We left the woods together. I thought he was going home. I-I thought it was about six.'

'Your mum says you got home at quarter to seven.'

'Okay.'

'How long does it take you to walk back from the woods?'

'About ten minutes.'

'What time did you leave?'

'I don't wear a watch.'

The detective points to the Casio digital on Jack's wrist. 'So what's that?'

'I-I wasn't wearing it yesterday.'

'Why not?'

'I didn't want it to get damaged.'

'How would it get damaged, Jason? What were you planning to do?'

'I-I—' The kid sniffs loudly, runs the back of his hand across his nose. He glances at the woman next to him, but she stays quiet. 'Nothing. Just playing. You know. Mud and sticks and—'

'Why didn't you walk home together?'

'We live in opposite directions.'

'Yes, of course.' The detective pulls a map from a file, puts it in front of Jack. Lucy has seen that same map in the box, the edges soft and wrinkled with age. 'You live here,' the detective says. 'In Hampton Gardens? And Theo lives at Tower Park?'

'Yes.'

Another long pause. The detective's constantly shifting from haranguing the boy, barely letting him answer, to long, uncomfortable silences. After a moment, he asks: 'Do you know Theo's family, Jason? Have you met his parents?'

'Yes.'

'Can you imagine what they must be feeling now? How upset they are? Just tell us what happened, Jason. Where is Theo's body?'

'His… his body?'

'Did you fight? Did someone get hurt?'

'We didn't fight!'

'Was it an accident then? Cowboys and Indians, cops and robbers? You pretended to hit Theo but this time things went too far. You hurt him—'

'I would never hurt Theo. I didn't… I didn't…'

He's crying properly now, tears running down his face, dripping from his chin, and at last the woman looks up. 'I think it's best if we leave it there,' she says.

The detective scowls, studying Jason's face closely.

'Don't think this is the end,' he says. 'We'll find out the truth.'

The woman leads the sobbing child out of the interview room; the detective gets up and walks to the video camera. He rolls his eyes, as if confiding in a friend, then reaches forward and turns it off. The screen goes black.

Lucy can see from the records that this wasn't the only interrogation Jason had to endure. They spent the day bringing him in and out of the interview – Lucy has copies of the transcripts. He wasn't arrested, but Lucy can imagine him being left for long stretches in a grotty family room, nothing but his own dread and fear to keep him company.

It's no wonder Jack doesn't like to talk about Theo; no wonder he shuts out that time in his life. This terrifying day at the police station was only the beginning – after that the press got hold of confidential details and the onslaught began. Innocent until proven guilty only works in a court of law; a year after Jamie Bulger had been killed by two kids, journalists only saw the guilt in Jason Kent's eyes. The little white rich kid killed the poor, mixed-race boy, and they were damned if they were going to let facts stand in their way.

Lucy finds it astonishing that Jack's experience at the hands of the police that day led him to become an officer himself. They've talked about it – how he wanted to make sure it didn't happen to another child – but Lucy can read between the lines. He wanted to right some wrongs. Solve the crimes, get closure for families that were as unlucky as Theo's.

The detective on the tape – Maguire, Lucy assumes – was cold and calculating and a bully. She knows how the desperation to find a missing child can corrupt an otherwise solid police officer – she's seen it first-hand with Greaves. But what on earth did he think had happened for him to go after Jason Kent so hard?

She needs to speak to Maguire. She leaves another voicemail, then turns back to the files. She reads the notes, the transcripts – they never even got close to finding that squat in Southampton.

But this is the chance they need. They know now. Thirty years ago, Theo Nkosi was abducted and kept captive in a cupboard. There will be DNA, council tax records, voting register. They will find out who lived there.

It's a solid lead. And one she will follow. To the bitter end.

CHAPTER TWENTY-FIVE

It seems that when Maria Logan told her husband that her mother was dead, it wasn't strictly speaking true. Unless the woman in front of Jack in the reception of Southampton Central police station is a ghost, Adelaide Pope is alive and well.

'Dead to her, maybe,' Adelaide says, using a long, red-polished nail to shift a curtain of bleached blonde hair away from her face. 'Saw her on the press conference. We haven't spoken in eighteen years. I was hoping you might be able to do something about that.'

'And how would that work?' Jack asks.

'I could help find her little girl. She'd like me then, wouldn't she?'

'Help, how?'

'I dunno. I know what she was like as a kid. How she grew up. Maybe you'd like to hear about that?'

'Did you know Sean Madden?'

'That good-for-nothing? Sure.'

Jack's still waiting on the mobile phone and bank records for the family, and as much as he doesn't fancy being in a confined space with this woman, knowing some background might help. He escorts her through to the family room, and as he expected the room is quickly suffused with the scent of her perfume and the pervading smell of cigarettes. She shrugs her black and white leopard print coat from her shoulders, and crosses one skinny leg over the other.

'I guess a coffee would be out of the question?' she asks. 'Unless it's that vending machine shit?'

'It is, I'm afraid.'

'Never mind. Doesn't matter – as long as I get your company for a bit.' She smiles, showing the lipstick on her teeth. 'No ring, I see. You're not married?'

'Tell me about Sean,' Jack says, trying his best to steer the conversation back on track. 'How old was Maria when she met him?'

'Seventeen,' she says. 'It was his fault, you know. That she moved out. Not that we were best mates before that point. Teenage girls. My fault, I was the same. Rebellion runs in the family.'

'And how old was Sean?'

'In his twenties. Twenty-two? Twenty-three? They met at some club, I think. He saw her, he wanted her. Not that I blame her – he was quite the catch. An attractive guy. Tattoos and swagger. I wouldn't have kicked him out of bed. Knew he was trouble though, from the moment I saw him. He was known by the police, even then.'

'What was he doing?'

'Vandalism, graffiti. Saw his tags all over town. Nicking stuff.'

'Drugs?'

'No, that was the one thing in his favour. Not his style. He even got Maria off them.'

That catches Jack's attention. 'What drugs was Maria using?'

'Oh, I don't know what they were called, love. All different from my day. Pills and white powder but what she didn't swallow, she'd put up her nose. That's what we argued about. That, and she didn't like Derek. My husband. Her stepdad.'

'Any idea why she didn't like Derek?'

'She didn't like to see me happy. That's all. First chance she got – off she went with Sean. Didn't see her then for a few years.' She picks up her handbag, rifles in the contents and pulls out a packet of cigarettes. 'Assume I can't smoke in here?'

'Sorry, no.'

More scrabbling, and she emerges with a pack of gum. She puts one in her mouth, offers it to Jack. He declines.

'I knew he'd get her pregnant. Then, sure enough, there she was. In Asda – pushing a buggy. Edward must have been – what? One, two? Cute kid. I offered to buy her some stuff, but she wasn't having any of it. Said Sean was looking after her. Yeah, sure. Couple of years later, he was in the paper. Nicked for sticking a knife in someone's face. Thought she'd come home then, but no, said she was fine. That was eighteen years ago. I tried to track her down a few times – found her in Swindon, and Derek went up to see her. He used to work over there a lot, said he didn't mind. Tried to make her see sense and visit me. She wasn't having none of it. She's doing alright, yeah? Saw her on the television. She looked posh. And that new husband of hers. Bet he earns a pretty penny. She always could fall on her feet though, my Maria.'

She stops then, chewing loudly. She reminds Jack of a dairy cow, in her black and white coat, hair puffed up like ears.

'Do you have any idea where Rosie is?' Jack asks.

Adelaide regards him with heavily black-lined eyes. 'No. But don't you go pinning this on my Maria. I know what the papers are saying, the Facebook. And it wasn't her.'

'What wasn't her?'

'The kid's dead, right? After twenty-four hours – I've seen the crime shows. Well, it wasn't Maria who did it. Whatever she got up to in the past, she's a great mum. Having Edward changed her.' She points a red nail towards Jack. 'You find Sean. Leopards don't change their spots. It'll be him, I'll bet ya.'

–

Jack escorts Adelaide out, promising to put in a good word about her to Maria, whatever that means. He trudges up the stairs to the incident room, thinking about leopards and spots, Maria and her former drug use. They need to find out who that MDMA belongs to, but how that will help them find Rosie, he's not sure. Amrit meets him in the doorway.

'Gary Ballard is ready for his interview,' she says. 'The guy we traced back to that house last night? Sturridge from the HTCU has asked if I'll join him, but do you want to?'

'No. I'm involved. Theo,' he adds with a shrug, and she colours, realising she's forgotten how her DCI had once been a murder suspect. 'I'll watch though,' he adds, and she smiles, relieved.

'Lead the way.'

CHAPTER TWENTY-SIX

Gary Ballard, registered sex offender and all-round shitbag, is not proving helpful. His answers have been confused and disjointed, punctuated by hacking coughs that make Jack want to put a face mask on, even through the video monitor.

DC Sturridge from the high-tech crime unit is keen to know where the porn came from, and has agreed to lead the interview; Amrit's there to find out the connection to Rosie. Both are getting frustrated.

'You're in big trouble, Gary,' Sturridge says. 'You've only been out for six months, and here you are again, under arrest for possession of extreme porn. We found the bloodied T-shirt from a missing child in the cupboard in your bedroom. You're going to be back inside, never to see the light of day again, unless you give me an incentive to say nice things to the judge.'

'I said, I don't know. That porn was there when I moved in. And I don't know nothing about a cupboard.'

'You never asked why there was a padlocked door in your bedroom?'

'Nah. I don't stick me nose in. Learnt that in prison. Don't know why I'm even here.'

Sturridge sighs in frustration. 'Let's go back to the start. Again. The registration plate for a red Ford Focus was recorded on ANPR in Fordingbridge at nine-oh-eight yesterday morning. That car was registered to your mother. We called her. She said you nicked the car two months ago.'

Gary looks abashed. 'Was she pissed off?'

'That you'd stolen her car? Yes, I'd say so. Not so much that she told the police at the time though, so still a chance to make amends.' Sturridge throws an eye roll to Amrit. 'She didn't know where you were, so we looked up your records and traced you back to the house.'

'Needed a place to stay. And I have to give you coppers an address, don't I? Now I'm on the sex list.'

'Yes, yes you do,' Sturridge says, patronising. 'Thanks for that.'

'Not my house, though. And I've sold the car. Last week.'

'You sold a stolen car?' Amrit sits forward. 'To whom?'

'My mate. He gave me a hundred quid for it. I needed the cash. Fordingbridge, you say? Yeah, that'd make sense.'

'In what way?' Exasperation is starting to creep into Amrit's voice.

'He lives in the town. Works out in the New Forest. Said he needed a car to get around.' Gary shrugs. 'Nothing to do with me.'

'And you didn't think to give it back to your mum?'

'Like I said. Needed the cash.'

'Didn't he ask for the paperwork?'

'What paperwork?'

'The DVLA… Never mind. What is his name?'

'Dave. Dave something.'

'Thought you said he was a mate?'

'Pub mate. Shared a few drinks. Just know him as Dave.'

'What pub?'

'Coach an' Horses. Down in Ringwood.' Jack watches as Amrit makes a note. More scumbags to find.

'Excellent, thank you. Moving on,' Sturridge says, sighing. 'You needed a place to live. Who let you stay at this house?'

'This geezer. Met him at the same pub. Said I could squat there while I was getting on me feet.'

'A different geezer to Dave?'

'Yeah.'

'And did this geezer have a name?'

Gary looks vacant. 'Can't remember.'

'A pub mate?'

'That'll be it,' Gary says with a grin. 'You're getting me now.'

'What did he look like?'

'Skinny guy, sick-looking. Old. Wore jeans.'

Like every man in that neighbourhood, Jack thinks. Jack knows Sturridge is struggling to find the source of the porn; the DI has already confessed to Jack that intel on that house is sparse. Land registry comes back to a man called Robert Chaplin, but it's a common name and the address for him on record is long out of date. Council tax hasn't been paid since 2009, electricity and gas are cut off. They're waiting for forensics to come back on the porn, and Jack's sure there'll be prints – and who knows what else – from a wide range of sources. He doesn't envy the lab having to handle that one.

'Do you know the name Robert Chaplin?' Sturridge asks.

'Nah.'

'Not the guy you met at the pub?'

Ballard squints, rusty cogs turning. 'Nah. He said his name was Jimmy. Remember that now.'

'Jimmy what?'

'No idea.'

Another sigh from Sturridge. 'Have you ever seen anyone else at the house?'

'Loads of people. Don't speak to them. Keep to meself.'

'So you said,' Sturridge says, wearily.

This is a waste of time. Gary Ballard is no more than one in a long line of idiots, offending and reoffending, living the majority of their pathetic lives in prison. The lab has found no evidence that Rosie was ever there, and Ballard wasn't living at that address when Theo was abducted. They'll track down the elusive 'Dave Something' to corroborate the story, and try and find 'Jimmy', the man who let Ballard stay, but Jack doesn't hold out much hope. Gary Ballard knows nothing that can help them.

Jack leaves them to it, turning off the video feed and heading up to the incident room. In his office, he checks his emails and reads the reports sent through to him from Lawrence, still trawling CCTV. He opens the video files, and presses play on the first.

The timestamp is just before nine, a video taken from a Ring doorbell on a house on Main Road. It shows Maria walking by, pushing Rosie's buggy. Although there's no audio, the child is clearly talking, her mouth opening and closing, her hands waving animatedly. The soft bunny rests on her lap. Maria pauses at the zebra crossing, bending down to push a bobble hat over her daughter's mass of curls, and then they're gone. Out of sight, heading towards the park.

Jack consults Lawrence's notes – CCTV tracks Maria and Rosie the whole way. They take the most direct route from their home to the park. They don't stop. They don't talk to anyone.

Amrit appears in the doorway, leaning against the frame.

'Sturridge is going to charge him with possession of extreme porn, and the likelihood is that Gary will go straight back inside.'

'Don't pass go, don't collect two hundred pounds,' Jack replies.

'Exactly. But we got nowhere. Did you see?' Jack nods. 'Guy's a moron. He's either lying or he's got no idea who he sold his car to, no idea who owns that house – and I think the latter. Dead end. I've asked for someone from R and P to go down to that pub this evening and passed it back to intel to try and find Robert Chaplin, so fingers crossed. Intel are going to send someone down this afternoon to work with us, did Weaver say?'

'I hoped. Who have we got?'

'New guy called Gus Harman. Any idea?' Jack shakes his head. 'Hope he's good. What have you got there?'

'CCTV of Maria Logan yesterday morning.'

'Dead end, Lawrence said.'

'I just can't see how she's involved. Or any of the family,' Jack says, frustrated. 'The Ring doorbell on the Logan house shows everything playing out as the family stated. Tony goes to work at eight fifteen, his work confirms he arrived just before nine. Eddie doesn't get out of bed until I arrive and wake him up. Rosie was alive and well when Maria arrived at the park at nine o'clock. If they're involved in Rosie's abduction, it's via a third party.'

'We're still going through the traffic cameras. Every car registration is being checked. We'll find something,' Amrit says, and heads back to her desk.

'But what if they didn't come in by car?' Jack says quietly to himself, but before he can shout out to Amrit, his phone rings. He answers it. It's the front desk and Jack dreads the news – another witness coming forward, a time-waster like Maria's mother. But the clerk confirms an altogether nicer visitor.

'I'll be straight down,' Jack says.

–

Jack can see her through the window of the double doors. He pauses for a moment, watches how she pushes her hair behind her ears, folds her arms across her chest. The same mannerisms, the same beautiful woman he's known for all these years.

He pushes through; she turns. Up close he can see how the last few days have taken their toll – she looks tired, her eyes strained. She's wearing jeans, a thick grey woollen cardigan over a white top, and when he gives her a kiss on the cheek, she smells of summer.

'I won't stay long,' she says. 'I know you're busy.'

'It's fine. Shall we…'

'Can we get a drink somewhere?' she says. 'Just not tea. I've had enough sodding tea over the last few days to last me a lifetime. Why do you coppers always insist on making tea?'

They leave the nick, walking side by side towards the shopping centre. They stop at the first place that's open – a gaudy TGI Friday's, mercifully quiet after the lunchtime rush. Sophie takes a seat on the far side; Jack orders two Diet Cokes at the bar and carries them over.

'I wanted to see you,' Sophie says. 'I saw you on the press conference this morning – it's awful, that girl. Have you made any progress?'

'Not much,' Jack admits.

Sophie takes it as a rebuff. 'I'm sorry, I shouldn't be taking up your time.'

She goes to stand up, but Jack stops her, his hand on her arm. 'It's fine. I have a team. It's good to get a break sometimes.'

She nods, sits back down again.

'How are you?' he asks. 'I was going to phone but… I didn't know if you wanted to hear from me.'

'I always want to hear from you, Jay.' She smiles, warmly. 'Mum asks after you.'

'Tell her hello. And how are you all?' he asks again.

'We're…' Sophie's jaw clenches, she looks up to the ceiling for a moment, blinking back tears. 'We expected it, one day. That someone would find a body.'

'We haven't found him.'

'You will.'

Jack thinks of the stalled investigation, the lack of resource. And Lucy, feeling a flash of appreciation for her persistence for the first time.

'It's been thirty years, Sophie,' he says softly. 'There are no guarantees.'

'I know. I know. And it shouldn't matter now, should it? We know he's dead. He's not coming home. But it would be nice…'

She starts crying then, small, delicate sobs. He wants to reach out and take her hand, but feels awkward – unsure of how things stand between them.

'You want to bring his body home,' Jack says softly. 'I get that.'

She looks up at him, her eyes wet. She reaches for a napkin, dabs at the mess.

'He should have some peace,' she replies. 'That house… where the T-shirt was found. The copper wouldn't tell us much, but… They hurt him, didn't they?'

'We don't know anything for certain,' Jack begins. The image of the cupboard comes into his head, as it has regularly since last night. 'But you need to be sure you want to know what happened. The places I've been, the stuff I've seen. It stays. I don't want that for you, Soph.'

'I want to know what happened to my brother,' Sophie says. Their eyes meet and he sees her resolve.

'Then I promise you. I'll tell you everything. But not here.'

'Hell, no.' She makes a choke of laughter. 'Not in fucking TGI Friday's.'

They share a smile. Words form in Jack's head. *I miss you. We should… We could…* But he doesn't dare articulate the mix of hope and despair he feels in Sophie's company. So much has passed between them. A couple for five years, another ten without her. Then last year – briefly getting together, before he pushed her away again.

They split up for a reason. His career came first, and there would always be the fact that he was the boy who came home, while Theo didn't. Love can only get you so far. It doesn't overshadow lingering resentment, or guilt, or the unknowable truth of what happened to Theo that night. Except it might not be a question for much longer.

He and Sophie finish their drinks; they walk back to the police station in silence. Side by side, dread and worry nagging in Jack's guts.

The time has come. To tell the truth.

Soon.

CHAPTER TWENTY-SEVEN

Retired detective inspector Stan Maguire calls Lucy back from the nineteenth hole of the golf course, and agrees to meet her there. By the time she arrives, he is already on his second pint, a half-eaten plate of chips in front of him.

He looks her up and down, noting her casual jeans and sweatshirt.

'PC, you say?' he comments. 'This some extracurricular project to get credit for a promotion? Because if so, you might want to choose another case. This one's as cold as a polar bear.'

Lucy decides to avoid the truth, knowing that her ex-detective turned dog handler background will raise more questions than it answers.

'New evidence has come to light,' she replies.

He pauses, chip halfway to his mouth. 'What sort of new evidence?'

'We now believe Theo Nkosi was abducted and held in a house in Randall Road, Southampton.'

'For how long?'

'We don't know.'

'But you have a body?'

'We have blood. And a T-shirt.'

He replaces the chip on the plate. 'Bloody hell,' he mutters, staring out of the window to the golf course. On the first tee, a golfer shanks it into the bushes. Neither of them comments.

'Can you tell me more about the investigation?' Lucy asks. 'I have your notes from that time, but it would be good to know what you didn't write down. Who did you suspect?'

Maguire takes a long breath in. 'That kid, of course. The best friend. The bloke who now works as a copper in MCIT.'

'But why?'

'We had nothing. A child that vanished into thin air. All we had was one witness who said she saw the white kid digging in the mud. Finding her in the first place was pure luck – she was the one car in the path of the camera that day. My theory was he was burying something.'

'You thought an eleven-year-old boy could bury a body?'

'I thought it was possible. Look, Jamie Bulger had just been murdered by two eleven-year-olds, that blew all assumptions out of the water. As far as I was concerned, I couldn't rule anything out.'

'But you searched the area?'

'Top to bottom. Dogs, full fingertip search. All we found were sweet wrappers and lost football stickers. In the end, all that woman did was muddy the waters and waste our time.'

'Do you still think he did it?'

'Honestly? No. If you killed your best mate, moved out of the area and changed your name, why would you put yourself back into the limelight by becoming a murder cop? Unless he's a complete psychopath. In which case he would have done something else and got arrested for that.' He shakes his head. 'No, my instincts were wrong, then. And not much use now.'

'What about the family?'

Maguire frowns. 'We checked them out. Thoroughly. The oldest daughter was thirteen at the time, the twin brothers were seven. The mother was home with the kids, the father at work. We had alibis for all of them, and we searched the house and garden – nothing. If the best friend was to be believed, Theo left the woods just after six and was abducted somewhere between there and his home. And that was another thing: the timings didn't stack up. Jason Kent didn't get home until quarter to seven. You've seen the map, I assume. That was a ten-minute walk for both of them. At most.' He turns introspective again, running a fork through the grease left on his plate. 'I always thought we'd find something one day.' He looks up, meets Lucy's gaze. 'We did our best. I did my best. We had nothing. I had pressure from those on high to find the kid. The papers were reporting institutional racism, that we weren't trying because the kid was mixed-race, but I promise you, we threw everything at that search.' He glances to the television screen above their heads, where the news is reporting on Rosie's disappearance. It's on mute, but a photo of Rosie's beaming face is showing full screen.

'Same pressure as those sods are getting now. A kid goes missing and all hell breaks loose. As it should do. But it doesn't help the investigation. That girl's hot property. How long's it been? Thirty-six hours?' He looks grimly into his pint. 'She's dead. Or shipped off to another country. No getting her back. No, this case will haunt that SIO for the next thirty years. Same as Theo Nkosi did me.'

He looks at Lucy. 'Review that cold case. Do everything you can. But promise me you'll let me know what you find?'

Lucy nods. 'Of course. Was there nobody else you suspected?'

'Nope. We looked into his teacher at school, his classmates, his neighbours. We walked the route – we interviewed every resident of every street Theo would have had to walk down to get home. If he left the woods at the time Jason Kent said, he should have been home by ten past six. But nobody saw him. And nobody gave us any reason to suspect them. But you do it all again. Speak to the family, have a look around the woods where he was last seen. Good luck.'

Lucy thanks him and leaves, none the wiser. The old investigation seems solid – everything Maguire has told her ties up with what she's read from the case files. But something niggles in Lucy's mind. Something about the witness.

All that woman did was muddy the waters and waste our time.

She takes her phone out of her pocket and makes a call.

DS Amrit Gill answers on the first ring. 'Are you the reason my boss is in such a bad mood?'

Lucy grimaces, remembering Jack's voicemails. 'Could be. How is he? Is he eating?'

'Barely. Looks like shit. And you're not about to make things better, are you?'

'Sorry.'

Lucy waits, hears the resigned sigh at the other end of the line. 'Go on then. What do you want?'

'I need you to find someone for me. A witness. Angela Burns.'

CHAPTER TWENTY-EIGHT

Amrit and the team have enough on their plate, but Lucy's confidence in the clever DS was warranted: Amrit phones back within the hour.

'I shouldn't be telling you this…' Amrit begins, tentatively.

Lucy presses the phone closer to her ear. 'But?'

'Angela Burns, now known as Angela Joseph. Still living here in Southampton.'

'Amrit, you're a genius.'

'I can't take the credit. We've got a new guy from intel working with us – and he's brilliant. A looker, too. But Lucy, you're not going to do anything that'll get you in trouble?'

'Absolutely not.'

'Or me? I didn't mention it to Jack. He's got enough on his mind as it is.'

'No. I promise. I just want to know what happened to Theo. Same as you. Same as Jack.'

'The boss was clear – our priorities lie elsewhere—'

'Yours do. But mine don't. Come on, Amrit. I'm just going to reinterview her. What's the worst that could happen?'

Another pause, then, 'Fine.' And Amrit reels off an address. Lucy reviews the map: no more than a quarter of an hour's drive. Her dogs will be fine. And with that thought in her head, she heads towards town.

-

The house is huge, part of a new-build estate outside Southampton. Tastefully designed, with just the right amount of garden for the residents but not enough to eat into profit margins. The front door is navy blue and glossy, the door knocker shiny silver. Lucy presses the bell, imagines someone watching her as it lights up blue. After a moment she hears the soft pad of footsteps, and the door opens on the chain.

'Hello?'

'PC Lucy Halliday, Hampshire Police. I'm looking for Angela Joseph?'

'That's me. Can I see some ID?'

Lucy pokes her warrant card through the gap. The door closes for a moment, the clatter of the chain, then it reopens, revealing a petite blonde woman. Hair in soft waves, an ageless face, made up with a natural look that takes hours to do.

'What's this concerning?' she asks, her voice soft.

'I need to speak to you about a witness report you gave in 1994. In reference to a boy that went missing near Portsmouth?'

The woman pales. The door closes slightly.

'Do you remember that, Mrs Joseph?'

'Yes. Yes, I do.' She glances at her watch, then out into the street. 'You'd better come in. I don't have long.'

'Thank you.'

Lucy is shown through to a cream living room. Cream carpets, cream walls, cream sofa. A soft cream shaggy rug. It's pristine, and Lucy wonders how much mud and dog hair she has on her jeans. She hesitates before she sits down on the butter-soft suede sofa.

'Can I get you anything? Tea, coffee?' the woman says.

'No, I'm fine.' Lucy takes out her notepad and gives a reassuring smile. 'This won't take long – we're just reviewing the case. Standard procedure. Could you tell me what you saw that day?'

Mrs Joseph watches her for a moment, then perches on the edge of the opposite sofa, crossing one leg over the other and folding her arms. 'It was nothing. And it was so long ago, I'm not sure I can remember much. I was walking my dog. And I saw those two boys. Theo, wasn't he called? And the other one. The blond kid.'

'What time was this?'

'It was still light. Middle of rush hour. So just after five, maybe?'

'Just you?'

'And my dog.'

Lucy considers Mrs Joseph. Like her decor, she's dressed in a white cashmere jumper, light grey leggings with cream Ugg boots. Not an outfit – or a house – belonging to someone who owns dogs.

'What breed was it?'

'My dog? It was… oh, I forget.'

'Small? Large?'

'Small. Oh, yes. A cocker spaniel. One of those fluffy things with the ears.'

'Did you walk far that day?'

'Not really. Just ten minutes or so. It wasn't a big fan of walks. Much preferred being at home, on the sofa.'

'And it was near to where you lived?'

'Oh, no. I lived… further away. Had to drive about half an hour to get there.'

'You drove half an hour to Gathurst for a ten-minute walk?'

'I wanted to go somewhere different. Look, what's this about? I walked out one way, saw the two boys. On the way back, it was just one, burying something. That was thirty years ago. I thought it was all done with.'

'We have new evidence. We're reopening the investigation. What was the name of your dog?'

'What was…? I don't remember. Why does that matter?'

Up to this point her manner has been calm, her voice measured, posh enough to cut glass. But with her annoyance comes a harsher undertone. A few dropped t's, edges of an accent creeping in.

'We just need to confirm facts, Mrs Joseph,' Lucy says sweetly. 'Everything's important in a murder investigation.'

'Murder?' Her eyes open wide, her shoulders leap up to her ears. 'You've found a body?'

Lucy dodges the question. 'We found a bloodied T-shirt belonging to Theo at a squat in the middle of Southampton. We believe he died there.' Lucy watches the woman's body language with interest. 'Do you have a dog now?'

'A dog? No. Why these ridiculous questions about dogs? I'd like you to leave. My husband will be home soon. He has a difficult job, he doesn't need you adding to his stress.'

'Just routine, as I said, Mrs Joseph,' Lucy replies, but she gets to her feet. 'Were you married in 1994?'

'No. I was barely out of my teens. It was a long time ago.'

'It was.' The woman has the front door open and is practically forcing Lucy out to the street. 'If you remember anything else…' Lucy manages before the door is closed in her face, '…don't hesitate to get in touch,' she finishes to the painted wood.

Lucy pauses for a moment, listening for any noise in the house. The place remains silent. She hesitates, then walks back to her car, biding her time. Something about the woman's reaction tells her it's worth sticking around, and while she waits, she phones Cal. He answers on the first ring.

'I was hoping you'd call,' he says, the conversation and bustle of the newsroom in the background. 'I heard a rumour – that the investigation into one missing child has led you to dust off the file of another?'

Lucy laughs. 'One day I'm going to get you drunk and you're going to tell me who your sources are.'

'Take more than a few whiskies to give up that sort of information. Is it true?'

'Might be. Depends how you can help.'

'I'm listening.'

'I've got all the old case files, but I want to know what's not in there. What were the papers reporting at the time? What were the theories making the rounds?'

'You can dig up the archives yourself.'

'I have. And all that shows is a load of unsubstantiated theories about Jason Kent. What was going on behind the scenes?'

There's a pause. The background noise abates as Cal moves somewhere he won't be overheard.

'Have you spoken to Jason Kent-slash-Jack Ellis about this?'

'I don't need to. It wasn't him.'

'Is that what he said?'

Lucy winces. 'He's reluctant to share anything at all. Doesn't want me looking into it.'

'What does that tell you? Look, Lucy. I know you and he are mates, and you owe him for everything that happened with Nico, but there was a reason the papers went after Jason Kent. He was the last person to see him alive.'

'You're starting to sound like them.'

'I'm just saying… Keep an open mind.' Cal stops. Lucy imagines him, brow furrowed, running his hands through his receding grey hair. 'And Lucy…'

His tone is hesitant; she doesn't like it.

'What?'

'I'm glad you called, I was going to phone you. Someone on my team has a renewed interest – in Jack. Or should I say, Jason Kent.'

'That's old news, surely?'

'Not now new evidence has been found. And the simplest way to sell papers—'

'Is to go for the previous prime suspect.'

'Exactly.' There's a long pause. Lucy curses silently in her head. 'I'm sorry, Lucy, I know it's not what you want to hear.'

'Aren't you in charge? Can't you stop it?'

'It's a good story. I agree with him.'

'Even though it's not true?'

'So you say.' She can almost see Cal's shrug. 'Look, Lucy. I need news to print. I can hold it until the weekend. Next week, tops. Unless you find me something new.'

'Fucking hell, Cal. Fine. Send me what you have. And you'll be the first to know.'

'And when is that?'

Lucy's focus is diverted as the shiny blue front door opens and Angela Joseph emerges. She pulls her long wool coat tightly around her, glancing about.

'Lucy?' Cal prompts.

'I told you – it's yours. But not if you publish shit on Jack.'

Lucy hangs up, cursing all journalists everywhere. But she pushes her worries about Jack out of her mind, starting her engine as Angela Joseph gets into her expensive Audi and screeches down the road.

Whatever Angela Joseph is doing, she's not dutifully waiting for her husband to come home; something about the conversation with Lucy has her rattled.

Lucy drops her phone onto the passenger seat and follows.

CHAPTER TWENTY-NINE

Angela Joseph isn't hanging around; she's driving fast, taking corners at speed, paying little regard to traffic laws.

Something Lucy said has rattled her. Lucy follows at a reasonable distance dialling Amrit over the loudspeaker.

'I need everything you've got on this woman,' Lucy says when she answers. 'What was she doing in 1994? What's she been doing since? Known associates, any aliases, previous addresses.'

'I do have a missing child case of my own to follow up on, Lucy,' Amrit replies. 'And I outrank you, strictly speaking.'

'It's important,' Lucy says. And she shares everything she's just heard from Cal. Amrit was there last June. She experienced the disruption it caused, hauling Jack into the limelight. It's a distraction they don't need right now.

There's a long pause. 'Fine,' Amrit says bitterly. 'But you better find something good.'

'I will. There's something off about this woman.'

'What?' Amrit says, curiosity creeping into her voice.

'The timings were wrong. The statement in 1994 has an hour and a half between seeing the two boys together and then just Jason on her return. And today she says she was only walking for ten minutes.'

'It was a long time ago.'

'And the dog-walking thing doesn't add up. She didn't live anywhere near those woods, yet she was walking her dog there. She says it was a cocker spaniel that didn't like walks. What spaniel do you know doesn't like *walks*?'

'Maybe it was an old dog. Maybe it wasn't a typical cocker spaniel. You can't base an entire investigation on your knowledge of one dog breed.'

'She couldn't remember its name.'

'It's been thirty years—'

'What was the name of your first pet?'

'Thumper. Okay, so you have a point—'

'And now she's bolted from her house – her very nice house, I have to say – and driven to the arse-end of Southampton.'

'You're following her?' Amrit squeaks.

'Yes, and…' Lucy's distracted as the silver Audi makes a left-hand turn. 'She's stopping. I'm at Fletchers.'

'That tower block in Southwood? Lucy, be careful around there. Not a good place for a female cop to be single-crewed.'

'I'm not in uniform, I'm fine. Just get me that info,' Lucy finishes and hangs up, parking the car a little distance away from the Audi and watching.

Angela Joseph gets out of her car, eyes flitting around her, an anomaly in the insalubrious surroundings. This is no posh new build. This is a run-down pebble-dashed tower block covered in freshly daubed graffiti, the broken paving slabs littered with fag ends and bright silver nitrous oxide canisters. Lucy doesn't have to move from her safe warm car to watch where Mrs Joseph is going – all the staircases and corridors open out to the elements; all the better to reduce the smell of piss and cigarette smoke.

Mrs Joseph takes the concrete staircase at the far side, her cream wool coat a perfect contrast against the grey as she ascends. Two floors, then across the balcony. She pauses in the middle, glancing this way and that. Unsure of which door? Or just nervous of being mugged? Whatever the reason, she chooses, and knocks.

Nothing happens, she hammers again. This time someone answers. Lucy winds down her window and listens.

She doesn't need to wait long. The shouting starts straight away. Angela Joseph is furious – gesticulating and screaming at whoever has opened that door. The words are lost in the echoes and angles of the tower block, but the cause and effect are clear. Something Lucy said made Angela Joseph come here. And she's not happy.

The shouting concludes, and Mrs Joseph storms away. Lucy ducks down in her car, considering her next move. She could go after her, call her bluff, but she needs to know more before she can push. Angela Joseph returns to her Audi and screeches out of the car park; Lucy looks up at the second-floor balcony. Without further thought, she retraces Angela Joseph's steps, looking down the row of front doors, trying to guess which one the woman was standing in front of.

Thirty-one, or thirty-two? But as she's prevaricating, the door opens, and a wrinkled man steps out.

'You can fuck off an' all,' he says to Lucy.

'Was a woman just speaking to you?'

'Shrieking more like. An' I'll tell you what I told 'er: no idea who lived here before. But it weren't me.' He shakes his head. 'Two beautiful women turning up on me doorstep, and neither wanna see me. Shame.' And he closes the door with a slam.

Thirty-one, Lucy says to herself, then dials Amrit.

'Find out who lived at number thirty-one, tower B, in 1994,' she says. 'Thank you,' she adds sweetly, then hangs up before Amrit can protest.

CHAPTER THIRTY

While Jack wished for the mobile phone and bank records from Maria and Tony Logan, now they're here he's starting to regret it. Pages and pages of numbers have arrived, columns and rows turning his screen into a jumbled haze. DC Phil Lawrence has been assigned to go through them, but Jack has idly loaded them onto his screen, scrolling through the mobile phone bills for both Tony and Maria that fateful morning.

A single number is common to both – one Lawrence has already identified. Bridget Daley. She called Tony at eight twenty-four that morning and they'd spoken for twelve minutes, presumably as he drove to work. A half-hour gap – Jack imagining Bridget fuming – then the incoming call to Maria Logan.

Jack casts his eye back over Tony's phone bill. Bridget's number pops up again and again, confirming that Tony was lying – he and Bridget were speaking regularly. It wasn't water under the bridge, and Jack's inclined to believe Bridget's side for the rest of the story, given Tony's track record with women.

Mixed among the conversations between Tony and his mistress are multiple other numbers. Maria's, Jack recognises, but the rest are a mystery to him. And he makes pages and pages of calls. Jack can't remember the last time he received a call that wasn't about work, but Tony's constantly on the phone, chatting away about who knows what, and this isn't even his work mobile.

Jack flicks to Maria Logan's – they are the opposite of her husband's. One or two calls a day, if that. A few texts. But something catches his eye. A number, reoccurring. Every week or so she sends a message, gets one in return. The last: yesterday morning.

An hour and a half before Bridget Daley phoned, Maria had a text exchange with this person. A few calls to Tony, then there's nothing until a flurry of messages just before midday.

Jack leans forward and shouts out of his office door. 'Phil?' Lawrence looks over from his desk where he's squinting at the monitor, next to the new guy that Jack still hasn't said hello to. 'Can you both come here for a moment? And bring the mobile bills?'

Lawrence does as he's told, followed by the analyst from intel. Up close, he's not what Jack was expecting. Tall, well-built, with the upper body of a lumberjack and the beard and man bun to match. He's even wearing a flannel checked shirt. He holds out his hand.

'Gus Harman,' he says.

Jack participates in the bone-crunching handshake. 'DCI Jack Ellis. Sorry I haven't been out before.'

'No problem, boss. You've got a lot going on.' He sits next to Phil in front of Jack's desk. 'I'm guessing you want to know what we've found from the call logs.'

'That, and a few other things. What can you tell me about Tony Logan?'

Gus looks to Phil Lawrence, who gives him the nod. 'Ongoing calls with Bridget Daley. This was no one-night stand. And, for the record, she wasn't the only person he was calling. There are at least two other numbers he phones with alarming regularity, all at certain times of the day. About half-eight in the morning...'

'His drive to work?'

'Right. Then between twelve and one, and at about half-six in the evening. Lunchtime and his drive home. The most telling, though, are the ones he calls at night. Half-ten, sometimes at midnight. Those go on for a good half an hour, longer sometimes.'

'More women, more affairs?'

'That would be my guess. We're waiting for confirmation from EE. Plus, Phil found something odd in their joint bank account.'

Phil takes over: 'I was focusing on this while Gus did the phone bills.' He pushes the page across to Jack. 'All the usual outgoings, as you'd expect. Amazon, Waitrose, a few fancy clothes shops. And then this.' He points – a line has been highlighted.

'The same every month?' Jack comments. 'A grand? Who to?'

'Not sure yet. Waiting to hear back from HSBC. It's not your usual bills, I've got those covered.'

'Bit blatant to send money to a mistress from the joint account.'

'Child payments?' Gus asks. 'Is there another sprog out there somewhere? I can take a look.'

Jack rolls his eyes. Honestly, this man. Tony Logan has a lot to answer for. 'Yes, do.'

'Should we get them in for interview?' Phil asks.

'No. Not yet. I want to know what we're dealing with before we confront them. Find out who it is. Same with those numbers for Tony. Give me an update by the end of the day. But what about this one?' He shows them the page he was just looking at. 'This number on Maria Logan's phone. Any idea who it is?'

Rustling of paper, as Gus considers that particular line. 'I haven't got to Maria yet. I was still on the husband. You want me to find out?'

Jack nods. 'As a priority, thank you. Plus this incoming call – just before three, yesterday?'

Phil smiles at Gus, knowingly. 'That's Sean Madden's number. Devon and Cornwall gave it to me.'

'So she has been speaking to her ex-husband? And as recently as yesterday.' Jack huffs, annoyed. 'Is anything these people have been telling us actually true?'

But before Phil can answer, Amrit sticks her head around the door.

'Boss, good news. ANPR on Sean Madden just came back.'

'And?' Jack says.

'And it captures the number plate of his work truck a number of times yesterday. A Toyota Hilux. Driving to and from roads leading to the Logan residence. So either he's stalking his ex-wife—'

'We know Maria Logan is lying.' Jack glances to Phil. 'We have his number on her mobile phone records.'

Amrit nods. 'So they have been in touch. And that's not all. The team kept looking. And widened the search to the M27 and the A31 – there's an additional sighting.' She pauses, with a smile. 'On the A338, just before nine a.m. Heading towards Fordingbridge.'

'Just as Rosie Logan goes missing. Well done, Amrit. Excellent work, all of you. Put out an all units alert. I'll get Bates to speak to Maria Logan. We need to find Sean Madden.'

CHAPTER THIRTY-ONE

Time crawls. One simple hour now feels like a lifetime to Maria, a purgatory that will never end. She hides in the bedroom, listening to the noises from the rest of the house. Tony in his study, quiet except for the occasional mutter on the phone, the tap of his keyboard. Eddie, denied his usual weed by the policewoman downstairs, vapes like a maniac in his bedroom, sticky fumes oozing from the gap under the door, heavy metal blaring. The presence of the copper in the kitchen is unnerving. Silent, observing. Drinking endless cups of tea.

It's too quiet.

When Rosie was around, the house was never peaceful. An array of sounds: fake chirpy voices from the television, electronic buzzing from whatever piece of animated plastic was the favourite of the hour. Rosie's incessant questions, her laughter, and even the screaming when she didn't get her way. The whole house howls from the vacuum of her absence.

A mobile phone rings downstairs. The cop: her murmured voice impossible to comprehend. Not good news, Maria assumes, but not the worst, as slow footsteps trudge up the stairs.

A gentle knock on the door. 'Maria?' Whispered.

Maria sighs. Ignoring it will get her nowhere. 'Come in,' she says, then repeats it louder. The door opens slowly, and DC Bates sticks her head around.

She annoys her, this woman. She's young, seems to be sympathetic but what does she know? She has no ring on her finger, hasn't mentioned a child. Maria already had a baby and a failed marriage by her mid-twenties. She lived in a freezing caravan and ate beans out of a can. Life had dragged her down, beaten her by the time she was the same age as this chipper little bit.

'Maria, can I have a word?' the copper says.

Maria gestures for her to come inside. She closes the door behind her. Interesting. So it's about Tony or Eddie, rather than news about Rosie.

But Maria's wrong.

'We need to talk about Sean.'

'Sean? My ex?'

'Yes. Traffic cameras spotted him in the area yesterday. Have you spoken to him?'

'No. I told you that.' Maria feels her face flush. She's a terrible liar.

The policewoman frowns. 'We have your mobile phone bill, Maria. We know you have.'

A burn of anger at that.

'Why did you ask? So you could catch me out?'

'Yes.' The policewoman's honesty surprises her. 'You need to be truthful with us, Maria. When did you last speak to Sean?'

Maria gives up, throwing her hands in the air and slumping back on the bed. 'He phoned me yesterday. We met at the Co-op around the corner. There? Happy now? But Sean doesn't have anything to do with this. He's Eddie's father, not Rosie's. He was just checking that I was okay.'

'What time was this?'

'About three?'

'You didn't meet up with him before that?'

'No. Why?'

Bates takes a long breath in. 'We need to speak to him. Urgently. Could you call and ask him to come by?'

'Here? He's an ex-con. He won't want to speak to the police. Besides, he was in Cornwall when Rosie went missing. He only drove up when he heard what'd happened.'

'I'm afraid he's going to have to. We have him on traffic cameras much earlier than that. Around the time Rosie went missing, in fact.'

'When?'

'Just before nine a.m.'

She thinks of the truck. Of the flatbed in the back and the tarpaulin draped over the top. Could Rosie have been in there?

'You think he has her?'

'It's a possibility. But if he has, we don't want him to do anything stupid. Could you call him? Ask him to come here?'

Sean lied to her. He said he drove up as soon as he heard Rosie was missing, but there's no way that's possible. She hadn't realised it before, but Cornwall is hours away, he couldn't have got here that fast.

'But there was a woman in that video. That wasn't him.'

'He might be working with someone. Please, Maria? The sooner we can speak to him, the sooner we find Rosie.'

'You only said it was a possibility.'

'It's our best lead.'

She meets Bates's gaze, sees the resolution in her eyes.

She doesn't want Eddie to see Sean, but Eddie's locked in his room, heavy metal thumping. He won't even realise.

And Rosie. That's what's important here, she thinks as she picks her phone up, dials. It rings once, twice. He answers.

'Maria? Is everything okay?'

The concern in his voice makes bile rise in her stomach. If he's got Rosie, swear to God, she'll kill him.

'Sean, I need you to come to the house. I need to speak to you.'

'But what about Tony? The police?'

'I'll meet you around the back. Just come now. Please.'

And before he can protest, she hangs up. She looks at Bates. 'He'll come. But if he knows police are here, he'll run. Let me speak to him first. Then you can step in.'

Bates looks unsure, but nods. They head through the house, out the bifold doors, into the garden. There's a gate there that leads to an alleyway around the back. If she knows Sean, he'll find it. The wily little bastard.

Sure enough, after ten minutes she hears the grumble of his old Toyota and the slam of a car door. She opens the gate and ushers him into the garden, closing it behind him.

He's suspicious, glancing around. 'Where's Tony?' he says.

'He's gone out,' she lies. She can't bear it any longer. 'Sean, where's Rosie?'

'Rosie? What do you mean? I have no idea.'

'If you've taken her—'

'I haven't! You know that. I drove up as soon as I saw the news.'

'There's no way you could drive up from Cornwall that fast—'

'I was closer. I was working in Dorset—'

'Bullshit!' Maria can't help but shout. 'The police have you on their cameras. You were in the area, even before Rosie went missing. You were here, Sean! Don't lie to me.'

Sean goes pale. 'I'm not. I swear. I know nothing—'

'I don't believe you. You're lying. Same as you always have. The police are here.'

DC Bates makes her entrance. She's not in uniform, but her stance, just the look about her, marks her out as a cop. Sean stares at the two of them, then behind him at the closed gate, as nervous as a trapped animal.

'Sean, please,' Bates says. 'We need to speak to you. Just a quick interview at the station.'

'Fuck no. I'm not going to the police station. I know nothing about Rosie.'

'What's going on?'

They all turn. Tony stands behind them, his hands on his hips, legs wide like a gunslinger. He glares at Maria. 'What's he doing here?'

'The police want to speak to him,' Maria says.

'About Rosie?' Tony takes two steps forward. 'What's Sean got to do with Rosie?'

'It's not true,' Sean protests. 'I was here, yes. But I had no idea...'

Sean doesn't have a chance to finish his sentence – Tony's on him in seconds, careering across the lawn, fist outstretched. His first hit misses; Sean, the scrappier of the two men, lands a retaliatory punch on the side of his head, then one right in the stomach. Tony howls with anger, grabbing him around the middle, and the two men fall to the ground, messily smacking at each other until Bates weighs in, grabbing Sean's arm and pulling it roughly behind his back.

Maria watches, appalled, as the copper expertly separates the two men. Tony lies on the grass, gasping.

'Do him for assault!' Tony shouts. 'You saw that? He hit me.'

'You went for me first!'

'Mum?' Eddie appears in the doorway, confused. 'What's going on?'

Maria goes to him, but as she does, her son's gaze rests on Sean, his clothes muddy and askew, his knuckles bloody. Eddie frowns.

'Dad?' he says.

'Hi, Ed,' Sean says, sheepishly. 'I'm sorry, this isn't how I wanted us to meet again.'

'You're out of prison?' He stares at Bates, who's still restraining him, his arm behind his back. 'You're being arrested again?'

'I'm—' He looks up into Bates's face.

'He's helping us with our enquiries,' Bates replies, releasing the pressure slightly.

Eddie looks to Maria. 'And you knew? You've been in contact with him?'

'I—' She reaches out to her son, but he pulls away. He looks younger than his years, the vulnerability etched on his face. 'I'm sorry, Eddie. I was going to talk to you, but Rosie…'

'I was the last thought on everyone's mind. As usual.' His head drops; he heads back into the house.

Maria glares at the two men. She points at Tony. 'You. Get indoors. And you…' To Sean. 'Go with the police. Tell them what you know. Get my daughter back.'

She can't do this anymore. The worry, the frustration. The burning red-hot anger at the world who took her daughter from her. Tears prickle as she goes back into the house. She trudges up the stairs to the bedroom, watching out the window as Sean is escorted into Bates's car.

So many lies. So many secrets. Already her marriage has gone to shit, and now her son hates her.

Everything has gone wrong. And she only has herself to blame.

CHAPTER THIRTY-TWO

As much as Lucy hates it, Theo's case will have to wait. She has a date.

She walks the dogs, has a shower. Rakes through her wardrobe looking for a dress, ends up in jeans and a nice top. Blow-dries her hair for once, puts on jewellery, a touch of make-up. Even she has to admit, the final look isn't bad. And she could do with a glass of crisp refreshing white.

Moss, who still breaks the rules and is allowed in the house, watches from where he's lying by the door. Head on his paws, eyes locked on her, he waits, always the loyal companion.

'You like him, don't you, Moss?' she says, and he raises his head, his ears lifting. 'You think he's a good bloke?'

But they all are, at the beginning. Nico was charming, handsome. He brought her flowers on their first date, then all the ones after that when he slapped her, when he dragged her down the stairs by her hair, when he pushed her up against the brick wall, his large hand leaving red bruises on her face. A good bloke, his friends said at his funeral. A good man.

She drops to the carpet, an invitation for Moss to clamber in her lap. She allows herself to be comforted by the warm mess of black fur and buries her face in the soft fluff behind his ears. He smells reassuringly of malty dog, of home and safety and acceptance.

'You'll bite him if he does anything?' He looks up at her, his black fuzzy face impossibly cute. 'Or Iggy will,' she says, giving his ears a final scratch.

She gets wearily to her feet. Checks her hair in the mirror then screws her face up at her reflection. Not all men, she tells herself, sitting on the bed to zip her boots up. But some, her reflection says back.

–

In the pub, two hours later, all thoughts of Nico have evaporated from her mind. She's on her second glass of wine, Pete his second pint. The Anchor is off the usual trail, neither wanting their time to be hijacked by colleagues popping in after shift. Wooden beams, Old English vibe, with real ales on tap and small tea lights on the table. The flickering light throws Pete's stubbled face into appealing shadows. His hair is washed, falling in his face, and he's wearing a shirt and clean, unripped jeans.

'So you can imagine it,' Pete's saying. 'The door's blown, red dots are dancing in the smoke, all the officers shouting "Armed police. Come out now. Last chance."'

Pete's telling Lucy about Dax's first outing as a firearms support dog. A local drug dealer, the top of the chain, known to carry guns. A warrant out for his arrest, and a firearms team sent to bring him in. She's heard the story apocryphally around the nick, but the in-person recital beats it hands down.

'But nobody's coming out, right? Nobody's shouting, there's no noise at all coming from that penthouse. So, the sarge – you know Brixton? Grizzled, takes no shit?' Lucy nods. A formidable bloke. 'He tells me to send Dax in. I get down to his level, give him a pat, "off you go". You know, fingers crossed behind my back, because he's been trained but who knows what the fuck he's going to do in the field.

'We hear the noise straight away. Growling, then this thumping. Falling furniture, bashing. We still can't see shit in the smoke, but it sounds like Dax is hurling someone around in there. I call him out, and what happens?'

Pete holds the tension, grinning.

Lucy can't help but ask, smiling already, knowing what's coming next. 'What?'

'He comes out, red dots focused on his head, holding a four-foot Mickey Mouse. One of those massive plush toys, almost as big as he is. And fuck, that dog is pleased with himself, strutting out, holding this bloody toy in his mouth.'

Lucy is enjoying the story, loving the light relief. 'Then what?'

'Everyone's trying not to laugh, but I think, okay. Intel said the bad guy was in there, maybe he's hiding. So I take it off him, throw it down the stairs, and send Dax in again. Same thing, bashing and growling, and what does he come out with this time? Minnie Mouse.'

Pete's laughing along with Lucy now, almost creased in two. 'So yeah, that was Dax's first call-out as an FSD. You want to do this amazing job, show your dog off, and all you get is an embarrassing story, told to new recruits for years to come.'

'He's improved since then,' Lucy snorts.

'Barely. And don't you laugh. Iggy's got the potential.'

'To be an FSD, or to embarrass the shit out of me?'

Pete smiles. 'Both.'

She meets his grin over the top of her glass. It's nice being here, with him. Better than nice. She's forgotten what it can be like, this lightness, to enjoy someone's company in this way.

Pete leans back and takes a swig of his beer. His expression changes – serious all of a sudden. 'Are you okay?' he asks, peering at her in the half-light. 'I heard that the T-shirt belonged to Theo Nkosi.'

Lucy raises an eyebrow. 'You heard?'

'Phil Lawrence told me.'

'Ah. And yeah. Plus a shitload of blood spatter. Looks like he was held there before he died.'

'Fucking hell. A thirty-year-old cold case. Like anyone's got time to take that on.'

Lucy sips at her wine. It's not like Pete to try and catch her out, but she doesn't want to lie.

'I've started looking into it. Weaver gave me permission.'

Pete tilts his head, curious. 'Officially? Or in your spare time?'

'The latter. What else have I got to do until Monday?'

'Sleep. Eat. Catch up on series two of *The Traitors*?'

'But as you said – nobody else has time. Rosie Logan is still missing, and she has to take priority. MCIT aren't going to give it any consideration.'

'But why you? Did Jack ask you to?'

'No. In fact, he told me to stay away.'

'Yet here you are, doing the exact opposite. I thought you were settled now you had Iggy?'

'I am. I don't want to go back to MCIT, that time of my life is over.' She pauses, not sure how she's going to make Pete understand. Pete's been a dog handler since he was in his mid-twenties, transferring from response and patrol as soon as he was able. He's never wanted to be a detective, never had a yearning for the big cases. 'This boy has been missing for thirty years. *Thirty*,' she stresses. 'Nico was missing for nearly two and it was agony, I can't even start to imagine how his family is feeling. They deserve to know what happened – this is the first opportunity to make some headway, and it seems criminal that it could slip through our fingers.'

'But why now? Surely it could wait a week or so until someone from MCIT has the hours?'

'But you lose the surprise. I went to see the witness that saw the two boys today. She hadn't heard about the T-shirt being found and the look on her face… It spoke volumes. Nobody can hide that emotion. Also, I phoned Cal earlier. He knows what's going on already. If we wait a week or so, the information will be out there and those involved will have time to work out new alibis, new lies. I can't take that risk.'

Pete nods slowly, no emotion on his face.

'So it's got nothing to do with Ellis?'

Lucy winces. 'Cal said one of his team's looking at putting a piece out. Digging up all the stuff from last June. He said he'd delay if I could find something new.'

'So you are on a crusade to clear his name.'

'No! I mean… Yes, if that happens as a result, then great. But that's not my end goal.'

'And what happens if you discover the opposite?'

Lucy frowns. 'What do you mean?'

'I mean, if you discover that Ellis was involved, what then?'

'Jack wasn't involved. The T-shirt was found at the house of a known paedophile, that has nothing to do with Jack.'

'I'm just saying. There's a reason we don't work on personal cases. We can become blinkered, deny the information right in front of us—'

'I'm not blinkered!'

'I'm not saying you are. But you're not impartial, are you?'

Pete's looking at her levelly. Frustratingly calm. As if proving his point, she leans back, grabs her glass of wine and takes the final gulp.

'I need another. You?'

'Yeah, sure.'

She gets up and makes her way to the bar. He's annoying her, with his questioning and his sane, bloody rational viewpoint. Dammit. He's spot on. If it wasn't for her connection, her friendship with Jack, Theo's case would be just another in a long line of tragically sad, but all-too-common unsolved mispers.

She senses someone behind her as Pete joins her at the bar. She turns.

'I didn't mean to piss you off,' he says. 'I'm just saying, be careful, that's all.'

His capitulation soothes her. 'Look, you're right,' she says. 'I want to find out what happened. For Theo and his family, yes. But also for Jack. And if I find something that compromises my investigation, then I'll hand it over.'

Pete smiles softly, then frowns. His gaze shifts away from her.

'What?' Lucy prompts.

'You and Jack.'

His tone is slow, cautious. The barman comes over, interrupts as he asks for their order. 'Large glass of Sauvignon Blanc?' Pete looks to Lucy, she nods. 'And a pint of Ghost Ship.'

'What about Jack?'

'Are you… Did anything…' Pete shakes his head. 'Nah. Forget it.'

'No, Pete. What? Is there anything going on between me and Jack? Is that what you want to know?'

'Yeah.' He looks embarrassed. 'It's just… you and I… I know we've only been on a few dates. And stuff. And if you're seeing other people, that's okay. I just want to know.'

Lucy almost laughs but sees his abashed face and restrains herself. 'Pete,' she says softly. She takes a step towards him. 'I barely have time to see you, when would I have a chance to go out with anyone else?'

'So… you're not?' A small smile creeps onto his face.

'No. And definitely not Jack Ellis. We're just friends. Never anything else. Not my type.'

'Not your type?'

'No.' She laughs. 'He's too… buttoned up. Too stressed.'

'So who is your type?' He leans forward, towering over her, his body almost resting against hers.

'I don't know. Maybe I have a soft spot for tall men smelling of dog.'

'Eau d'Alsatian.'

'Best there is.'

He leans down and kisses her softly on the lips. 'Good to know,' he almost whispers.

She wants to do more of that, but they're interrupted by the barman, bringing their drinks and clearing his throat loudly.

'Fourteen-sixty, please, mate,' he says with a cheeky smile.

Pete pays and they carry their drinks back to the table, mood improved.

'Tell me about this witness then,' Pete says. 'I may not have detective training, but I can spot a bad guy.'

'Bad woman, in this case,' Lucy says, and she tells Pete about the posh house, then the trail to the tower block.

'A history she wants to keep hidden?'

'That's what I thought,' Lucy says. 'She's all cream and cashmere now, but what if her background is less wholesome?'

'Doesn't mean she's lying about what she saw.'

'True. But whatever it was, it was enough to have her running out of her house.'

Lucy's phone rings and she pulls it out of her pocket. She gives Pete an apologetic smile, then gets up to answer it.

'Cal, did you find anything?'

'Good evening to you, too, Lucy,' Cal says, sarcastically. 'And yes, I dug out the files. There's not much there, most of it focuses around Jason Kent – Jack, whatever – and his horrible parents. You'll want to have a read – I'll email it to you – but the inference was that if Mr and Mrs Kent were awful then the apple didn't fall far from the tree.'

'He was eleven!'

'Didn't matter. Not to the guys investigating at the time. They were rich, white and privileged. The general feeling was that it didn't grant a free pass and Jason Kent should have been charged for Theo's murder. Theo was poor, black and the child of an immigrant. They saw the race angle and went after it.'

Lucy remembers Pete's words. Was she being blinkered to Jack? 'Do you think they were right?'

Cal pauses, sucking air over his teeth. 'I don't know. There's not much of any substance. No proof one way or another. Would I have run it?' He sighs. 'Probably. Missing kids sell papers. And a good rich–poor, black–white divide? It would sell even more. Still will,' he adds pointedly. 'I'll send it all across to you, Lucy. See for yourself. The stuff about Jack's parents – it makes for good reading.'

Lucy's curiosity is piqued. 'Thank you, Cal.'

'Don't thank me now. Thank me with something I can publish. Soon.'

And the editor hangs up.

Lucy stares at her phone for a moment, waiting for the familiar ping of a new email. Sure enough, it arrives ten seconds later.

She goes back to the table.

'Let me guess,' Pete says, leaning back in resigned defeat. 'You have to go.'

'That was Cal, from the *Guardian*. He has something. I'm sorry.'

Pete shrugs. 'It's a nice night. I'll stay here, finish my pint.' He stands up, leaning over the table and kissing her. Another soft kiss, one she would like to prolong, and she's tempted to ignore Cal's email. Sit down for another drink. Maybe go back to Pete's after…

But her phone beeps again and Pete breaks away. He smiles.

'Tomorrow night?' he says, as if reading her mind. 'Pick up where we left off?'

She feels a blush work up to her face. 'You're not working?'

'I finish at six.'

She nods, grabs her coat, and heads out of the pub, feeling Pete's eyes on her back. A strange buzz starts up in her stomach, a warm glow of fun anticipation, like she's a teenager when she's around him.

How much she would like to stay, but Cal's words have got her thinking. What secrets do those files hold? And more to the point – how much do they incriminate Jack?

CHAPTER THIRTY-THREE

Sean Madden does not want to be in a police interview room, under caution, under arrest for assault. In Jack's view, Tony Logan deserves a good punch in the face for a number of reasons, but it gives them a convenient excuse to hold Madden.

Jack starts the recording, confirms that Sean has turned down his right to a lawyer, and introduces himself and DS Gill.

He doesn't waste any time. 'Sean, we know you were driving down the A338 at eight fifty-six on Wednesday morning. We have your Toyota on ANPR, with cameras showing you in the front seat. Where is Rosie Logan?'

Madden pales. 'I don't know anything about Rosie.'

'What were you doing there? It seems a remarkable coincidence you were driving down that particular road the very morning your ex-wife's daughter goes missing. Who has her?'

'I don't know. Look, I turned down legal advice because I want you to see I have nothing to hide. I want you to find her. I care about Rosie. I care about Maria.'

'You're still in love with your ex-wife?'

Sean juts his chin. 'Yes, if you must know. Being locked up was the biggest mistake of my life. I lost everything that day. My wife, my son.'

'You're using Rosie to get Maria back?'

'No! I don't have her. It was Valentine's Day yesterday. It used to be special for Maria and me – we'd do something nice, even if all we could afford was a takeaway. I was going to try to persuade her to leave her husband.' His face clouds. 'That absolute douchebag. Speak to my boss. I've had the holiday booked for weeks. If I'd known, I wouldn't have got caught up in this, I would have stayed well away. I can't go back inside.'

'Twelve years, wasn't it?'

'Yes,' he says. 'And I've turned my life around since. I have a good job. A home. A dog. I'm settled. I wanted to make sure I had all of that before I saw Maria. I wanted to show her that I'd changed.'

'So you punched her husband.'

'He came at me! Ask that cop that was there. She'll tell you. I was defending myself.'

Jack waves his objections away. That's not what they're there for. 'How long have you been in contact with Maria?'

'A while. I phoned after I got out. 2018.'

'That long?'

'On and off. I first messaged because I wanted to see Ed. Sorry, Eddie. Build a few bridges between us. He would have been fifteen, sixteen then. But Maria said no. He was going through some stuff, and she didn't want me to make matters worse.'

'What sort of stuff?'

'I don't know, she didn't say. Teenage things, I assume. I did what she asked. I kept away, but I stayed in touch. Called, messaged every now and again.'

'Meeting up? Having an affair?'

'No! Nothing like that. Just chatting on the phone.'

'You expect us to believe that yesterday morning was the first time you and Maria had seen each other since you went inside?'

His face colours. 'Okay, maybe once or twice. But we never slept together—'

'Is Rosie your child?'

'No! Maria—'

'Did you see Maria yesterday morning? When Rosie disappeared.'

'I didn't see Maria until the afternoon.'

'But you were in Fordingbridge just before nine a.m. Why did you wait?'

'I wanted to get some breakfast – I'd been driving for hours. I parked up and got a fry-up. You can ask them – nice place on the High Street. Bridges, it was called. By the time I'd finished the place was overrun with cops. I kept my distance until someone told me what was going on.'

'Did you see Rosie?'

'No.'

'Would you like another child? Another chance at being a family?'

'I already have a family. Maria and Eddie.'

'So Rosie was getting in the way?'

'You're twisting my words.' He runs his hands over his short hair in frustration. 'I didn't mean that.'

'What did you have in mind if Maria agreed to go back with you? How did Rosie fit into this cosy picture?'

'I hadn't thought about it. I only found out about Rosie recently – she kept it quiet. To be honest, I was surprised. I didn't think it was possible.'

Jack's senses twitch. 'What do you mean? Think what was possible?'

Sean looks up, sensing Jack's manner change. For the first time Jack's not just baiting the man, asking him quickfire questions to get him to crack. He genuinely wants to know.

'Eddie's birth – it was a mess. Maria was in labour for hours. Driving to the hospital, being told to take her home, that she was still hours away from giving birth. Maria was writhing around in pain. In the end I begged the doctors to admit her. And the moment they did, it all started to go wrong.'

He meets Jack's gaze, the memory of the panic hovering below the surface. 'I've never seen so much blood. It was pouring out of her. They pushed me away, rushed her up to surgery. It was touch and go they'd get Eddie out alive. They did, and Maria was okay, but they had to carry out an emergency… you know.'

'Hysterectomy?' Jack says.

'That's the one. She couldn't have any more children.'

Jack glances to Amrit; her face echoes his. Sean Madden reads their confusion.

'She didn't tell you?' he says. 'Rosie's not hers. There's no way Rosie's her biological child.'

CHAPTER THIRTY-FOUR

'Did we ask?' Jack directs to the team as soon as the interview is over. 'Did we specifically ask?'

Blank faces.

'We just assumed...' Bates replies, trailing off under the full force of Jack's stare. 'Do you want me to speak to the family?'

'No, not yet,' Jack replies. 'Maria and Tony Logan didn't directly lie, but they omitted something pretty bloody important to our investigation. Along with everything else we know they've misled us about.'

Silence from the team. From their faces, they feel the same way as him. Annoyance, that the Logans hadn't mentioned it earlier, and self-recrimination, that nobody thought to damn well *ask*. An unconscious bias coming into play – the Logans are well-to-do, a *nice family*. Why would they lie?

'We have their DNA?' he says. 'From where we took them for elimination purposes against the rabbit toy?' Amrit nods. 'Test them against Rosie's samples. I don't care that it's not what they gave permission for – the number of potential charges against them are adding up. Possession of a class A, and now obstructing a police investigation. And run Rosie against the database – in case a familial match pops. Tell the lab to bump it up the priority list – I want to know those results by first thing tomorrow.'

Amrit gets straight on the phone.

'Bates, get back over there but keep this to yourself for the time being. And don't let either Tony or Maria Logan out of your sight. No more trips to the Co-op.'

'What are we thinking, boss?' Bates asks. 'That she was abducted by her birth mother?'

'Possibly. Rosie could have been adopted?'

'That would have come out via our original search,' Amrit interjects, phone against her ear. 'There was nothing on record with children's services.'

'A private adoption?'

'Or done illegally. Which is why they didn't want to tell us?'

'Maybe Rosie was abducted as a baby?' Lawrence suggests. 'By Maria, or by someone else. All the more reason to keep quiet.'

It feels unlikely, but Jack's willing to consider anything at this stage. 'Check against missing persons from 2020. A blonde, blue-eyed baby would be tricky to miss. Any other theories?'

'It could all be perfectly innocent,' Amrit says. 'Conceived using a surrogate. An egg donor, but Tony Logan's sperm?'

All eyes shift to the photo of Rosie on the board. The blonde curls match Maria's, but looking at her now, Jack has to admit there's nothing in her facial features that ties with either parent. Eddie Madden has the fine nose, dark complexion and wide mouth of his father, the curls and slim build of his mother. But Rosie? It's difficult to say.

Either way, the deceit has pissed Jack off. Impossible to carry out a misper investigation with one arm tied behind your back.

'Did we make any progress with the elusive Dave from the Coach and Horses?' Jack asks Amrit. 'The man Gary Ballard sold his car to?'

'Yes,' Amrit replies, checking her notes. 'And Ballard was telling the truth. David Horst. Lives in Elisa Court, in Fordingbridge. Works as an electrician and had a job in Blashford that morning. His alibi checks out. Says his van had broken down and he needed the car as a stop gap. Had no idea Ballard had nicked it. Says he'll return it to Ballard's mum.'

'Someone's going to be happy, at least. And the "Jimmy" who let Ballard stay at the house?'

'No idea. Still working on it.'

'What do you want to do with Sean Madden?' Lawrence says, holding out the phone. 'Custody sergeant wants to know if we're charging or releasing.'

'We'll probably release,' Jack says. 'But keep him here overnight while we go over his truck for any sign of Rosie. Get Devon and Cornwall to search his house. It'll be nice to know we have one of our suspects under lock and key. And monitor his phone in the meantime. Tell me if anyone calls.'

Lawrence relays the message down to custody. Amrit has got through to the lab at last; Bates gathers up her stuff and leaves to spend the evening with Maria and Tony.

Jack rubs his eyes. When he opens them again his gaze shifts to the video image – the owner of the boot, walking away with Rosie. Her absent biological mother, wanting her back? Or a different sort of abduction – nefarious and scary.

It's late. Day two, and Rosie is still missing. It doesn't bode well. At this point the investigation shifts. The possibilities narrow. She's out there alone, or someone has her. Someone who hasn't come forward. Either way, when tomorrow comes around, they could be searching for a body.

CHAPTER THIRTY-FIVE

The only thing on Lucy's mind as she arrives home from the pub is looking at whatever Cal has sent her. After the initial email, she had received two more, and as she walks through the house to the garden to check on the dogs, she casts her eye briefly over the subject lines.

Press conference – Nkosi family

Notes and research – Jason Kent

Response from police

She's particularly interested in the last one – nowadays any attempt by the press to get off-the-record statements from detectives would be met by a stony 'no comment', but maybe back in 1994 they were less discreet.

She lets the dogs out into the garden and stands in the darkness. Residual light drifts from her kitchen as Iggy and Moss sniff and make a half-hearted attempt to play. Iggy, ever the boisterous bully of the pair, shoulder barges Moss, then nudges him with his nose when the easy-going spaniel fails to respond. Lucy picks up Iggy's toy to distract him, and throws it down the garden. While Iggy joyfully hurls it in the air, she thinks about Pete; about his jealousy over Jack. And why she's never felt any attraction to someone who, she has to admit, is now one of her closest friends.

She met Jack during a time in her life when romantic relationships couldn't have been further from her mind. Jack saw her at her worst – confused, grieving, breaking every rule in the police handbook – and she at his. Buttoned up and closely guarded, he had been forced to trust her and come clean about his history with Theo. She had faith that he'd been telling the truth.

But Pete's words come back to her now. What if he was involved in Theo's death? Murder seems a stretch, but they'd been young boys, playing in the woods with sticks and stones. What if something had happened?

She shakes her head. No, it's ridiculous. She's read the files. They searched those woods, and they came up with nothing. No eleven-year-old boy could kill someone and hide the body so effectively that an army of police and dogs and ground-penetrating radar couldn't find him. Plus, there was the T-shirt at the squat. He was there when it was discovered, so he hadn't been involved with that, had he?

She calls the dogs to heel, gives them a final pet and puts them to bed in their respective kennels, heading back into the house. No, Jack's reservations about her investigation were simply him not being able to face reality, or the trauma of what she might find.

She changes into her joggers and hoodie and gets comfortable on the sofa with a cup of hot chocolate and her laptop. She loads the first email – a video file. It fills the screen, jumping into life with a hiss and a blast of static.

The quality is bad, the fashions dated. A young DI Maguire sits with a couple on the stage, in front of a sea of journalists. Unlike the Logans, this pair are nervous, sweating and clutching each other's hands. Lucy checks her notes – Wendy and Junior Nkosi. Theo's mum and dad. Junior is black, wearing a dark grey suit and a white shirt. Wendy is white, and Lucy knows the press picked up on this fast. A white British woman marrying a black South African wasn't rare in those days, but it was still unusual, especially in a town like Portsmouth where the majority of its residents would have been white. And the fact that the police hadn't found mixed-race Theo and were reluctant to charge or even arrest their prime suspect – little white Jason Kent – was something they seized on like hyenas fighting over a carcass.

The press conference goes smoothly at first. The standard statement, Maguire looking into the camera with practised ease, although Lucy can see the first signs of strain starting to show in the bags under his eyes, the slightly ruffled hair. Junior Nkosi gives a heartfelt plea, his voice, with the heavy South African accent, cracking with emotion as he talks. The couple's hands stay locked the entire time, their solidarity obvious.

And then the questions come. They start easy. *What is Theo like? Does he enjoy school?* Wendy answers, her face infused with love as she talks about his obsession with dinosaurs and football, his slightly less than ideal attention span in class. *Who was Theo with that day? Were there any witnesses?* Maguire tackles these, deflecting with standard statements. *We aren't at liberty to divulge that information at this time. Witnesses are helping us with our enquiries.*

But the journalists won't let it go. *Who was Theo's best friend? What does Jason Kent have to say about Theo's disappearance?*

Maguire ends the press conference, but the stage had been set. Lucy pauses the video and clicks on the next email. A number of documents are attached; Lucy opens each one in turn. Some are rough notes, hastily written and scanned in at a later date. Others are half-formed articles or ideas, complete with spelling mistakes and incomplete sentences, but Lucy can get the gist. The journalists assumed that Maguire's reticence about Jason Kent was because of his guilt. In the absence of any additional information, they went down hard on the eleven-year-old, quoting the same psychologists who had given evidence at the Jamie Bulger trial. He was labelled a budding psychopath, a calculating cheat; school friends and even teachers interviewed described him as sly and conniving. The line between fiction and truth blurred as journalists reported whatever they chose, hiding behind quoted 'close friends', 'allegedly' scatter-gunned through the prose.

The final email contains only a few files. Jotted notes, a few official press releases, giving bland progress updates. One is a .wav file. When Lucy clicks, she hears two voices behind the hissing. Two men – they talk casually for a few moments, then one goes in for the kill.

'Go on, tell me,' he says. 'I won't quote you.' A long pause. 'We know you think it's Kent.'

Another gap. 'Yeah,' the second man says. His accent is northern, not Maguire but Lucy assumes another detective from his team. 'Creepy little kid. Quiet, but smart. You can see him thinking.'

'Weird eyes.'

'Yeah.' Mutual laughter. 'Cold little fucker. Did you hear what his dad said?'

'No?'

The voice lowers, confiding a secret. 'The dad said he never liked Jason hanging around with the kid. That he – and I quote – "wasn't their kind".'

'What did he mean by that?'

'Black, I guess.'

'Fucking hell.'

'Yeah. Jason Kent killed him, alright. We just can't prove it.'

The damage was done. As far as the press were concerned, the Kent family were racist, and Jason was guilty. Jack's life, from that point on, would never be the same again. No wonder he changed his name.

Lucy sits back on the sofa, processing everything she's read. As far as she can tell, Maguire did everything right. He followed every lead, scoured the streets of Portsmouth, but the investigation was run by the journalists and the public. Jason was the prime suspect, and they destroyed him for it.

What would she have done differently? Lucy wonders. Her thoughts turn to Rosie Logan. The case is different due to the age of the children – while an eleven-year-old has independence and could feasibly have run away from home, a three-year-old is considerably more vulnerable. An eleven-year-old can survive on the streets. A three-year-old cannot.

She picks up her laptop and runs a simple Google search. *Rosie Logan*. Immediately the screen is full of links. News articles, tweets from Hampshire Constabulary appealing for information, but also blogs, YouTube and TikTok videos, posts on Reddit and Facebook. Mainstream and social media is alive with theories and speculation, a handful joining the dots between Rosie Logan's senior investigating officer and the missing Theo Nkosi from thirty years ago, a few even speculating that Jack might be involved.

But the majority blame the parents. Tony and Maria's stone-cold façade at the press conference has been screenshotted and used as evidence, their background has been analysed and regurgitated in a litany of blame and scandal. It's trial by kangaroo court, which can't be helping the investigation.

Lucy picks up her phone, about to call Jack, when she notices the time. Hours have flown by, it's well past one a.m. She can't phone now; even if Jack is awake, she doesn't want to disturb him.

She closes her laptop and gathers up the paper and notes strewn around her. Reading Cal's notes have helped; she knows what she needs to do next.

Return to the scene of the crime. Head out to the woods, where Theo Nkosi was last seen alive.

DAY THREE – FRIDAY

CHAPTER THIRTY-SIX

A new day, and dogs need to be walked no matter what else you have in mind.

Lucy wakes, groggy, and after a pot of coffee, loads an enthusiastic Moss and Iggy into the back of her estate and heads out to the suburbs of Gathurst, in Portsmouth. To the woods where Theo went missing.

It's not an easy location to find. She parks the car in a lay-by at the edge of a field, and puts both dogs on their leads, walking towards the place she identified earlier on Google Maps. It's a small woodland skirting the edge of a row of fields. This time of year, they're ploughed and muddy, but she remembers Jack's description of the heatwave: rows of desiccated crops, desperate for a hint of rain. She walks down the path, letting the dogs pull ahead on loose leads, desperate to get stuck into the new smells on offer. She comes to a shallow ditch, a hedge on the other side. After a moment of searching, she finds an opening and ducks through, discovering a sheltered forest, a thick canopy of trees overhead, mud and brambles underfoot.

A narrow path leads to an open space; she takes her phone out of her pocket and compares the crime scene photos at the time to the view in front of her. The woods were less overgrown, but the clearing was the same. Now filled with empty bottles and cigarette butts, then, sweet wrappers and litter. A place now populated by teenagers, but it would have been paradise to two small boys in 1994.

She lets both dogs off their leads and they run free, enjoying the delights of the forest. Sun dapples through the gaps in the trees; Lucy's breath blows in icy gusts as she strides through. Moss has long gone – the spaniel following tantalising scents into the trees, returning periodically, soaking wet and brown with mud. Iggy remains closer to her side. Loyal, never fully letting his guard down. But relaxed, his mouth open, tongue lolling, his walk jaunty, tail high. She's not worried about them disturbing unsuspecting members of the public – there's nobody around. She's struck by how remote it is. There's simply nothing here.

They went over the area with dogs at the time, but she keeps an ear out for Moss. The chance of the spaniel finding anything after thirty years is achingly remote, but you never know. He's nose to the ground, tail high, but it's more likely he's picking up on rabbits, deer, squirrels. A wealth of delicious smells to a spaniel.

Her thought goes back to Angela Joseph and her witness statement. Her car was the one plate they managed to capture on camera at the time – close to the road that Lucy herself parked on. And something doesn't sit right. It's not an obvious place to walk a dog. There are no footpaths or bridleways. This is no publicly owned forest – given the fields Lucy assumes it's a patch of land owned by the farm and left to grow wild. The dogs don't care about brambles or nettles, but Lucy's already scratched and stung. She had to struggle to find the woods – only a local would know to come here, and Angela Joseph wasn't that. She lived in Southampton, even then.

She claimed it was a short walk, but Lucy has first-hand experience with spaniels and 'a short walk' isn't something in their vernacular. Even if it was an old dog, it seems strange Angela Joseph would drive all this way. Why wasn't it questioned more at the time?

Lucy takes her phone out of her pocket and checks her notes. Angela Joseph claimed she walked in this direction, passing the clearing where the boys were playing, then the sole figure of Jason Kent digging on the way back. And yet the dog didn't go up to them, she didn't even say hello? Jason's statement was unambiguous – they saw nobody all day. They were alone.

After an hour in the freezing cold and biting wind, Lucy's had enough. Both dogs have had a good sniff and a shit, it's time to make a move. She checks her phone and takes the quickest route out, adding new scratches to the leaves in her hair and the mud on her boots. Dogs on their leads, she marches back to the car.

She pours the dogs a water bowl each, then loads them into the boot. Both settle quickly, satisfied and happy, and Lucy considers her next move. She's seen the map – the routes Jack and Theo would have taken as they walked home. It's worth a second look.

Jason Kent first. Heater blasting hot air, she drives slowly around residential streets, looking for his old house.

She finds it easily. It's a huge place – manicured lawns, tall metal gates. Thirty years on, Lucy estimates it's worth millions, but even back then Jason's family would have been considered well off. The gates are closed, and she peers through from the open car window. The house is austere and foreboding. Lucy can't imagine growing up somewhere like this. She knows Jason's parents moved away when Theo disappeared; she's not going to learn anything new squinting through gates. She puts the car into gear and heads in the opposite direction.

Barely a mile to the west, and the neighbourhood couldn't be more different. Where before the houses were isolated – their own plot of land, single, secluded – these flow into one another. Gardens with no definable boundaries, rickety walls, music blasting from open windows and an aroma of spice in the air. A woman leans over a low fence in her front garden talking to her neighbour, their chat punctuated with loud cackles and laughter. A man is working on his motorbike, overlooked by a teenager, trying to seem cool but desperate to have a go. This is a community.

Lucy leaves the dogs sleeping in the car and walks down to number twelve. Mid-terrace, a ramshackle collection of pots scattered on the small paved front garden, green shoots sprouting through, some already showing the familiar heads of a daffodil. Stickers in the window – a faded *Remain*, a Ukrainian blue and yellow flag.

Lucy pauses, looking up at the top windows where the curtains are drawn. She's just debating knocking when the front door opens and a woman stands in front of her, arms folded over a plentiful bosom.

'Can I help you?' she says, assessing Lucy from top to bottom. She's wearing a yellow and gold apron and the smell coming from the kitchen makes Lucy's mouth water. 'If you're a journalist, you're not welcome.'

'I'm not a journalist. My name's PC Lucy Halliday. I'm investigating Theo's disappearance. I was hoping we could talk.'

'Why aren't you in uniform? We were told it would be months. Years, if they found anything new at all.'

'That might be the case. But...' She pulls her shoulders back. 'I'm a friend of Jack's – Jason's.'

Her face softens at the mention of Jack. 'He asked you to come?'

'No – Jack's busy.'

'With that missing girl. I saw on the news.' She nods slowly. 'Come in, then,' she says. 'I'm Wendy. Sorry to be so rude. But those journalists... They've been sniffing around again. Pack of wolves, the lot of them.'

'Lucy,' she says again. 'Thank you.'

The house is warm and cosy as Wendy leads her into the kitchen and gestures for her to take a seat at a battered wooden table. The chairs are decorated with brightly coloured cushions; the walls are covered with an array of artwork – some obviously daubed by children, others painted with an expert hand. The muddle is pleasing – nothing taking a prominent place, each one as important as the last.

'That one was Theo's,' Wendy says, catching Lucy looking at a primary-coloured scribble as she makes the coffee. Two taller figures, four smaller. 'That was us, he said. He loved to draw. Rare that he didn't draw a dinosaur.'

'Jack said they both loved dinosaurs.'

Wendy brings two mugs over, sitting opposite her at the table. She shakes her head at the mention of Jack. 'Still feels strange, calling him that. To us he was always Jay. A little bird, pecking at food, fluttering around Theo.' She laughs at the memory. 'Is he still like that?'

Lucy thinks of Jack. His stillness, his quiet. 'Not so much. More like a watchful eagle now.'

'Guess he has to be. Given his job.' She takes a long breath in, focusing on Lucy. 'What would you like to know, love?'

'Tell me about Theo. What was he like?'

She smiles softly. 'A ball of energy. Always getting into trouble for talking in class and dragging Jay into it with him. Those two, joined at the hip – obsessed with dinosaurs and football stickers. We'd just had the World Cup – it was all they went on about. But he was never really naughty. Just had a brain that wouldn't switch off. Wanted to know everything, go everywhere. Nothing was out of bounds to Theo. He couldn't sit still. His brain was always buzzing. They'd probably call it ADHD now, but back then he was just a lively little boy.'

'He was the second oldest?'

'Yes, Sophie first. Then Theo, then Leo and Harry. Twins. If Theo wasn't enough of a handful, those two kept me busy.' She gets up to stir the saucepan on the hob and Lucy gets another delicious waft as she lifts the lid. 'They're doctors now, those two. Cardiology and a GP. Who would have thought it? And Sophie's a teacher.' Her gaze drifts into the middle distance. 'He would have been forty-one this year,' she says quietly, then turns back to Lucy. 'The T-shirt they found. That means he's dead, doesn't it? You're looking for a body.'

'Yes, that's the most likely outcome.'

She sets her jaw, nods. 'Thank you for being honest. That cop that came around before – he was vague. Wouldn't answer any of our questions.' She turns and looks Lucy right in the eye. 'Did he suffer?'

'Mrs Nkosi—'

'Wendy, please. Did he?'

'It's possible, yes. I'm sorry. Mrs Nkosi – Wendy, sorry – what do you think happened to Theo?'

She sits down again, clasps her hands together on the table. 'I've been over this so many times in my mind. So many theories, thoughts, questions. It killed Theo's father, the not knowing.'

'I'm sorry to hear that.'

'It was cancer, obviously. Five years ago now. But the stress, the constant fretting. Junior just couldn't let it go. I try not to let it take me in the same way.'

She looks towards the front of the house as a door bangs and a voice calls out, 'Mum?' followed by the clatter of shopping bags.

'In here, Soph.'

A tall, dark, astonishingly beautiful woman appears in the doorway. She heaves the bags to the work surface, then turns to look at Lucy.

'Sophie Nkosi,' she says, holding out her hand.

'This is PC Halliday, Sophie,' Wendy says. 'She's helping out on Theo's case.'

'Lucy,' Lucy replies, shaking her hand. Sophie regards her through narrowed eyes.

'Aren't you the dog handler?' she says. Wendy turns quickly. 'You were in the papers last summer. I'm sorry about your husband.'

'Thank you. And I am,' Lucy confirms. 'But I used to be a detective. I'm helping out.'

'Are those your dogs in the car outside?' Sophie asks. 'The big one keeps barking at the neighbours.'

'Oh, Christ. I'm sorry. He does that. I won't be long—'

'Bring them in,' Wendy says.

Lucy looks at her in surprise. 'They're police dogs. Working animals, high-energy. We've just been for a walk, they're filthy.'

'I'd love to meet them. I miss having dogs. I had terriers, as a kid. Luna and Mason. Theo always wanted one, do you remember, Soph? But Leo, with his asthma. We just couldn't. Bring them in,' she repeats.

Knowing her dogs, Lucy's not sure it's a good idea, but she doesn't want Iggy pissing off the whole street. Sure enough, the shepherd is having a wonderful time defending the car from all possible offenders, greeting Lucy proudly with a lolling tongue as she lifts the boot. She puts both dogs into harness and brings them inside at heel.

Wendy's face lights up when she sees them. 'Can I?' she asks. Lucy nods, telling Iggy to sit. Iggy does what he's told but Moss can't contain his excitement, wriggling in circles as Wendy says hello, bending down to the dog and getting a lick in her face for her troubles. She laughs, turning her attention to Iggy, the shepherd wasting no time by trying to clamber all forty-two kilograms of him into her lap.

'Iggy, no. I'm sorry, he doesn't know his size.' But Wendy waves her apologies away.

'They're lovely dogs. You must enjoy your job.'

'I do.' Lucy cradles Iggy's big heavy head in her lap, giving the dog an enthusiastic scratch behind his ears. 'Alpha male this one, takes his job seriously, but he's a softie at heart. You know you're brilliant, don't you?' she says to the dog, while an envious Moss tries to nose his way in. 'You too, jealous pots.'

Sophie puts the shopping away, keeping her distance, but once she's done, she turns, a smile at her mum's obvious joy.

'Jack mentioned Moss,' Sophie says. She puts the last can away and joins them at the table. 'Even he had to admit he liked him.'

Lucy settles the dogs at her feet. 'He definitely needed some persuading.'

'You still speak to Jay?' Wendy asks.

'We keep in touch,' Sophie replies. She turns back to Lucy. 'What do you need to know?'

'We were talking about Theo. Do you mind me asking – would he have gone somewhere else that day? It's just the investigating officer failed to find anyone who saw him walking home.'

Wendy shakes her head, definite. 'Nah-ah. Not our Theo. He did as he was told. Always a good boy. Strong sense of right and wrong – do you remember, Soph? Would dob you and your brothers in, no hesitation.'

Sophie smiles, fondly. 'Remember when he caught me smoking? First time I'd tried it, just after my thirteenth birthday, behind the bike sheds at school. And by the time I got home, you guys knew. Grounded for a week.'

'And think how much better your health is as a result,' her mum retorts.

'What do you think happened to Theo, Sophie?'

Sophie glances to her mum, nervously. 'Someone took him. By force.'

Wendy nods. 'We were always so strict about that. Never get into a car with strangers. Even if it's someone you know. And be home in time for dinner.' She smiles, reaching under the table. Lucy realises Moss has slid under and is resting his muddy head on her leg. 'Theo was always home in time for dinner. He loved his food, that boy.'

'Were you ever contacted?' Lucy asks, considering kidnap. 'Someone asking for money, for example?'

'From us, love?' Wendy chuckles. 'Jay's family maybe, but nobody who saw Theo would think he came from money.'

'Letters, strange phone calls?'

Wendy frowns. 'No letters – but you're right. We got hang ups for a while.'

Sophie turns sharply. 'You never told me?'

'You were thirteen, Sophie. We had a number of calls – from the press, a few members of the public.' Her face darkens. 'Racist stuff, I'm sure you can imagine,' she directs to Lucy. 'We were a mixed-race family. Some people didn't like that – even in the nineties. So we changed our number. I assume the hang ups were part of that. Although there was one.' Her forehead furrows and she gets to her feet. Lucy and Sophie watch as she goes out of the room. Slow footsteps as she heads upstairs. Sophie's gaze falls on Lucy.

'You better not be stirring this all up for no reason,' she says in a whisper. 'Mum's been through a lot. We all have.'

'I just want to help,' Lucy says, silencing as Wendy comes back into the room. She has an A4 file in her hand. She passes it to Lucy.

'Here,' she says. 'The police told us to keep a record of all the phone calls we received. They said they would try to prosecute the worst offenders but after we changed our number it went quiet. And we said we'd rather they focused on finding Theo.' She shrugs. 'Useless, all of it – but I kept the file.' Lucy opens it. 'First page.'

Lucy takes out the sheet of A4. It's a simple list – time, date, and what was said. A litany of terrible racist slurs.

'This is awful, I'm so sorry,' Lucy murmurs. Wendy points to the second page.

'There,' she says. 'That was the odd one. A woman. All she said was, "I'm sorry", and then hung up.'

'Did you tell the police?'

'Yes. I think they traced the number – see here? – but it came to nothing.'

Lucy runs her finger down the list. '01703?' she mutters out loud. Not an area code she recognises.

'Southampton,' Wendy says. 'The numbers changed… I don't know… late nineties? It used to be 01703.'

Lucy frowns. Three occurrences, all over the same day. Two hang ups, one apology, then nothing. Could it be more than a random crazy? Southampton again. Could it all be linked?

'Can I keep this?' Lucy asks, as Iggy sticks his head up, nudging her with a wet nose.

'Of course,' Wendy confirms as it becomes clear just why Iggy lives in his kennel. A large German shepherd has no place in a small terraced house, and he practically knocks Wendy off her chair as he tries to get out from under the table. Moss nimbly jumps up onto an empty chair, Lucy's swift intervention stopping him from overturning the coffee mugs.

'Oh, I'm so sorry. These two should not be allowed in polite company.' Lucy gets to her feet, pulling her dogs after her. 'Thank you for speaking to me.'

'I'll see you out,' Sophie says. Lucy gives a final smile to Wendy, then follows Sophie to the front door. She pauses in the hallway.

'I'll be in touch,' Lucy confirms.

Sophie nods slowly. 'It's been thirty years. Why do you think you'll find him now?'

'Police work has come a long way since 1994. Forensics, expanded police databases. There are no guarantees, but it's worth a try.'

Sophie still doesn't look convinced. 'Jack trusts you. And he doesn't trust anyone, so I'm willing to give you the benefit of the doubt.' She glances back into the house. 'For thirty years, we've told ourselves – it doesn't matter that they've never found a body. The likelihood is he's dead, so what difference does it make? But it does, you know?' Lucy gives a quick nod. 'Of course you know. Your husband. Sometimes, in those lonely hours, I imagine that he did run away. That Theo's out there, living his life. Or he banged his head and got amnesia, with no idea that his family even exist, let alone that we're here, waiting for him.' She shrugs. 'It's ridiculous, but that last shred of hope – it defeats all rational thought. If you find a body, I'd like to see him. And I know – after this long it won't be more than just bones, but I need it. I need to see him one last time. Will you promise me that?'

Lucy nods. 'I'll do everything I can.'

The two of them exchange numbers. Lucy says a final goodbye and gets into her car; Sophie waits until she's heading away before she goes back into the house.

Lucy drives home, thinking about Sophie's words. When Nico was finally found, Lucy didn't want to see her husband's body, preferring to remember him as the living, breathing force of energy he was, but she knows how important it is to have that choice. The pathology team can only do so much; sometimes it's impossible to avoid the sunken eyes, the decomposition, the skin slippage, but families of the victim don't see what we see. They see their child, their father, their loved one. And they want to say goodbye.

Lucy stops at traffic lights, takes roundabouts, lost in the facts of the case. Mothers can be biased, but Theo sounds like a good kid. A stable family, loving parents, and nothing Jack has told her contradicts what she heard today. So assuming Theo did what he was told that day and walked directly home from the woods, what happened?

Her thoughts turn to the crank caller – the apologetic woman. There was no mention in the file. She dials a number on hands-free. Cal answers.

'Can you do me one last favour?' she says. 'Could you look up a number? A landline, from 1994?'

CHAPTER THIRTY-SEVEN

Maria sits silent in the back of the police car. She clasps her hands together to stop them from shaking but only succeeds in making the tremors worse. She feels like a common criminal. It doesn't matter that Bates said it was just a 'routine interview', that they 'have a few discrepancies they need to address'. She's been cautioned, and she's here. They know something. They know.

A male detective with a shaved head meets her outside the front of the police station. That's something, isn't it? That they're not taking her around the back. The detective introduces himself as DC Lawrence, and gives her a reassuring smile. He offers her tea, coffee, even a sandwich, but she declines. She can't eat, can't drink, not while Rosie is missing. He shows her through to a formal interview room. Camera on the ceiling, two plastic cups of water on the table. One for her. One for – who?

Her question is answered when DCI Jack Ellis comes into the room. He's less friendly, forehead furrowed. He tries a smile; it doesn't reach his eyes. He holds a folder in his hand. Thick, filled with a good centimetre of paper. He asks her to sit down.

'Thank you for coming in this morning, Maria,' Ellis says. 'Just so you know, we're recording this interview, and you're under caution.' He repeats the warning again. *May be given in evidence.* For what? For what crime? 'Do you want a lawyer present?' he asks.

'Do I...? No. Why would I need a lawyer?'

'We're sorry we had to bring you to the station,' he continues, but he doesn't sound sincere. Not sorry at all. 'I know this is the last place you want to be right now.'

'Better than being at home,' Maria says, aiming for humour, but Ellis doesn't respond. She's never noticed his eyes before. Grey-blue. *Cold, like a serial killer.* The thought pops into her head before she can stop it, but it's true.

'How long have you had problems in your marriage?' he asks.

'We haven't…' she begins. But what's the point? The whole world knows. 'Since Rosie was born,' she says. 'Tony's not… He's not great with children.'

'Is Rosie your child?' he asks.

Maria reels. She stares in surprise.

Ellis scratches at his chin, calm, waiting. She notices a patch he's missed shaving, just under his jaw.

'Maria?'

'I am Rosie's mother. A hundred per cent.'

'Not her biological mother.'

'No.' Maria juts her chin forward defiantly. How dare he question who Maria is. She's Rosie's mother. Who cares who gave birth to her?

'Who is?' Ellis sighs and sits back in his seat. 'Because this is important, Maria. As you know, we believe Rosie has been abducted, so we need to consider the possibility that either her biological mother or biological father has her.'

Maria shakes her head quickly. 'No. Neither of them does. I can tell you that now.'

'Let us find out for ourselves. Who are they?'

'It doesn't matter—'

'Do you want to find your daughter, Mrs Logan?'

'Yes.'

'Then let us do our jobs. Who is Rosie's mother?'

Maria clamps her mouth shut. She shakes her head again.

'Who's Rosie's father?' Same response. 'Why won't you tell us? What could be so important that you're prepared to risk your daughter's life?'

Maria remembers. Nearly four years ago – the tears, the story that made Maria sob with frustration and guilt. History repeating. And the solution that fixed all their problems.

'I promised,' she says.

'Who?' But Ellis doesn't wait for an answer this time. 'Did you adopt her? There's no official record.'

'It was a private arrangement.'

'We couldn't find a birth certificate for Rosie Logan either.'

'She has a birth certificate.'

'Under a different name? What name, Maria?'

'No. She doesn't have Rosie. Why can't you let it go?'

Ellis stares at her again, his eyes locked on hers. He must sense her resolution because his gaze drops to the file on the table. He opens it to the first page. He doesn't show it to Maria, but she can see what he's looking at. A photograph – white powder in a small plastic bag. Maria can't breathe; a trickle of sweat runs down her back.

Ellis looks at it for what feels like a lifetime, then he flips it over and takes the next photo from the folder. It's a rectangular blue tin. He turns it around and pushes it towards her.

'Do you know what this is?'

'It's...' Her mouth floods with saliva; she's going to be sick. 'It's the tin you found the drugs in.'

'Correct.' He gives her a small smile. Smug bastard. 'We found MDMA in that tin. And do you know whose fingerprints we found on the front? We ran them through the system. They came back to a woman, cautioned in 2008 for shoplifting – Maria Madden. That was you, wasn't it, Maria?'

'That was a long time ago,' Maria mutters.

'But this was yesterday. They're your drugs, aren't they, Maria?'

She's fed up with his games. Fed up with being in a room with this man, who thinks he knows everything about her. His arrogance, his complacency. She's not having it.

'Have you ever been so hungry your stomach hurts? So starving you think you can smell baked beans through the tin?' Ellis doesn't flinch. 'I needed to feed my child, so yes, I got done for shoplifting. They let me off with a caution. I haven't done anything wrong since.'

'Who are Rosie's biological parents?'

'And yes, it's mine. A bit of Molly, who gives a shit. It's not coke, not heroin. I wasn't selling it. Nobody knew I had it. So I need a little something every now and again. I don't take much, just enough to wake me up, a little pep to keep me happy. More effective than antidepressants, cheaper than coke. To help me forget who my husband is fucking. To get through yet another mind-numbing day.'

'It's a class A drug. Possession for a class A could get you seven years.'

'Is that how this works?' Maria looks him right in the eye. 'You threaten me with a drugs conviction, and you hope I'm going to break my word. Well, no. Do whatever you like. Charge me. And we'll see how much that helps your little investigation.'

Ellis narrows his eyes. She's got him there. However much the press and the public don't like her at the moment, it's still not going to go down well if the police arrest a mother for a ridiculous possession charge in her hour of need. Wasting time when they should be finding her daughter.

And the drugs aren't a big deal. Not compared to what she used to indulge in. Pills, powder, you name it, she'd take it. But that all ended the moment she met Sean. Just being around him was a drug. The rush, the joy of being that much in love. She's never felt it since, not with any of the men that followed and certainly not with Tony.

She needs something to get through the day. The Molly isn't any different from other drugs – from the caffeine, the socially acceptable alcohol. Gin o'clock, the influencers laugh, necking goldfish bowl-sized cocktails, their children playing in the background. All she needs is a fingerful, rubbed into her gums, and she's ready to go.

Ellis takes a long breath in, looking up at the ceiling for a moment, then back at her.

'Is that who you were meeting at the park?'

His words stun her. She blinks, dumbfounded, until she realises. Her mobile phone bill. How could she have been so *stupid*?

'Give us the name of your dealer.'

'He hasn't got Rosie.'

'How do you know? How can you be sure, Maria?' He leans forward across the table. 'You're asking us to do our job with our hands tied,' he says, frustration creeping into his voice. 'Do you know how much time we've wasted running around after you? After your husband and his affairs? When we could have been out there, looking for Rosie? Please,' he adds, his voice softer, almost begging. 'It's been forty-eight hours. *Please* help us find your daughter.'

She swallows. 'His name's Bleecker. Like the street in New York. I don't know any more than that.'

'That's enough. We can find him. And the name of Rosie's biological parents?'

She made a promise – to a vulnerable young woman. She knows what it's like to be scared – terrified of what you've done, and what your future might hold. It's not her secret to tell.

'No,' Maria repeats, and Ellis's face turns dark again.

'We'll find out,' he says. 'You're just wasting our time.'

'She hasn't got Rosie.'

'How can you be so sure?'

But before Maria can reply, there's a bang on the door. Ellis gives Maria another long look, pauses the recording then gets up, opening it. DC Lawrence is there; he talks to Ellis in frantic, whispered tones, then Ellis claps Lawrence on the back and the DC leaves.

When Ellis comes back into the room, his whole manner has changed. He's buoyant, bouncy. He smiles at Maria across the table.

'You can go,' he says. 'We'll get a car to take you home.'

'What's happened?' Maria asks, pleading.

'We don't need you to tell us,' Ellis replies, holding the door open. 'We know who Rosie's biological mother is.'

CHAPTER THIRTY-EIGHT

'It was the bank payments that gave it away,' Lawrence explains to Jack as they walk towards the car park. 'One every month, and it's been going on for nearly a year and a half now. Gus tracked down the recipient.'

'Absolute genius,' Jack mutters, resolving to buy their new intelligence analyst a huge bottle of something when this case is over. First locating fingerprints for Maria Madden, and now this.

The DNA still isn't back on Rosie Logan – but Jack's bluff paid off. Maria has admitted that Rosie isn't hers, and now the second piece of the puzzle is falling into place.

Jack leaves Lawrence at the nick, and takes his old Mercedes up Hill Lane and The Avenue, heading at full speed towards Bassett. Uniformed officers have gone ahead of him with the search warrant – it's amazing how quickly those things can be authorised when a missing child is involved.

By the time he arrives at the address a crowd has gathered. Teenagers, students, Jack assumes, jostling in annoyance as they watch the PCs file in and out of the house. Spoiling for a fight, ready for an opportunity to earn their stripes. A nice little rebellious caution to disgust Mummy and Daddy over afternoon tea.

The group moves aside as Jack gets out of the car, his smart suit marking him out as the man in charge. The front door is open; it's a grand house, five or six bedrooms but identifiable as student digs from the weeds and long grass in the driveway, the flimsy curtains, pulled shut over most of the windows.

But the lie-ins are over. All the residents are up, woken from their hangovers by burly coppers banging on the door. A uniform greets Jack at the doorway.

'The place is empty. Nothing but a few joints and stolen road signs.'

'Bugger,' Jack mutters. He points into the house. 'She's here?'

'Waiting for you in the living room.'

He thanks the officer and goes through.

The decor inside is better than Jack imagined. Simple, basic, but clean. A door to a bedroom is open as Jack passes – the resident sits on her bed, glaring as Jack walks down the corridor into a tidy, bright living room. There is a flatscreen television on the wall, not huge, but decent. Stacks of DVDs line up next to a half-empty vodka bottle. On the wall, posters range from Ghostbusters to Godzilla and Harry Potter – an eclectic mix of taste displayed alongside photographs of the housemates. Friends, family; broad grins, big hugs.

And sitting on the sofa is Chloe. She's wearing jogging bottoms and a hoodie, clutching a mug of tea. She scowls as Jack walks in.

'I don't have her,' she says. 'I would have told you. You didn't need to send the cavalry.'

'New information has come to light.' Jack takes a seat on a worn sofa opposite her. He rests his hands on his knees and leans forward. 'Where's Rosie, Chloe?'

'I don't know.'

'Are you her mother?'

Chloe's face pales. She glances towards the kitchen where Jack assumes her housemates are waiting.

'That's none of your business,' she hisses.

'I'm getting tired of people saying that to me,' Jack replies. 'While I'm looking into her disappearance, everything to do with Rosie is my business. Most of all: who her parents are.'

'Maria and Tony are her parents.'

'Not biologically. And you knew that, when you came in to speak to me yesterday.'

'It's complicated.'

'Try me.'

Chloe glances to the door again, then back to Jack. 'Fine. But not here.'

'Back at the station?'

'Am I under arrest?'

'Not yet.'

'Then no. We'll go into the garden. I need to smoke.'

Chloe stands and Jack follows. She slips trainers on her feet, grabs a coat from the rack, then leads the way out to the overgrown garden.

It's small – no more than a patch of long grass, trampled by multiple pairs of large boots in the last half an hour. Traffic cones line the concrete path down the side, and Chloe stops next to one of them, taking a pack of Lambert & Butler out of her pocket and lighting one.

'Aren't you studying medicine?' Jack asks.

Chloe regards him with a wary side-eye. 'Better than vaping,' she says. 'We're only just starting to discover what those chemicals do to your body.' She holds up the cigarette. 'At least with these guys we know how they'll kill you.'

She takes another long drag; Jack pulls his coat tighter around him, lifting the collar against the bitter February wind.

'Talk,' he says.

Chloe blows up a long plume of smoke, staring into the near distance until finally, she speaks.

'Yes, Rosie's mine.' So quiet, he can hardly hear.

'And the father? Is it Tony Logan?'

She turns to look at him. 'Fuck's sake. What makes you think that?'

'The bank payments.'

'You think I slept with Tony Logan and he's paying me to keep quiet? Is that it? You cops – it's all blackmail and rape and murder with you guys. How do you sleep at night?' She sighs, wearily. 'I was sixteen when I got pregnant. A mistake, my first time. You can't get pregnant on your first time, can you? Who could be that unlucky?' She utters a bark of laughter. 'That's what he said. He was older, I trusted him. Stupid,' she spits. 'I was three months along before I realised. Do you know the baby's the size of a lime at that age?'

Jack shakes his head, staying quiet.

'I knew I couldn't keep it. I wanted to go to university, to be a doctor. I was getting the grades – I knew it was possible. But not with a baby. I was ready to go to the clinic, do what had to be done, when Eddie guessed. We were good friends by that point, and I thought I'd hidden it well, but somehow, he knew. And he told me not to go through with the abortion.'

'Eddie did?'

'Yeah. I would have ignored him, putting it down to some right-wing, misplaced toxic masculinity bullshit, but he said, "For you. Don't do it for you. You'll regret it."'

'He told you you'd regret it?'

'Yeah. And his face when he said it, I thought he was going to cry. I'll never forget – he said that it would eat me up, that I'd always wonder about that baby. Who she might have been.'

'You knew it was a girl at that point?'

'No, not at all. But he definitely said "her", like he could see into my future. It made me stop and think, but I still didn't want to have a baby. And then Maria came to see me. She said she couldn't have any more children of her own, and that her and Tony desperately wanted them. I could have as much involvement with the child as I wanted – be a part of her life, or just let her go – it was all up to me, as long as I kept the baby. Plus, they'd pay me. Any expenses before the baby was born – and then for university after. That's what that money is for. All my tuition, plus a grand a month until I graduate. You think I'm an awful person, don't you? Selling my child? But it wasn't that. I knew how well Maria and Eddie got on – I knew she'd be loved. So I agreed.'

Jack frowns. 'But why didn't you go through the proper process for Rosie's adoption? There's no legal record of it.'

Chloe smiles ruefully. 'I couldn't. Because then he might have found out.'

'He?'

'The father. I couldn't take the risk that he would realise and apply for parental responsibility. I was crystal about that. I didn't want him to have any hold over my life. I didn't want to see him again, full stop, and I sure as hell didn't want him anywhere near Rosie.'

Jack leans forward. 'Who?' he asks.

Chloe takes a last draw from the cigarette, then stubs it defiantly against the red plastic of the traffic cone. Silent tears run down her cheeks as she exhales in jerky plumes into the freezing air.

'Derek Pope,' she says. 'Maria's stepdad is Rosie's father.'

CHAPTER THIRTY-NINE

Jack's lack of sleep is starting to get the better of him, because right now he can't make the pieces add up.

'But how do you know Derek Pope?' he asks. 'Maria is estranged from her mother and her stepfather. Hasn't seen either of them in years.'

'She may not have seen them, but I did. He came by, out of nowhere one day when I was at the house, seeing Eddie. Claiming to be Maria's stepfather, Eddie's step-grandad. Eddie wasn't convinced but I...' She gives a long sigh. 'I was young. Stupid. And he was attractive, in a silver fox kind of way. Eddie told him to leave but later, when I was walking home, he caught up with me. Insisted on walking me back. Said it was dangerous, a young, pretty girl like me, walking alone. Bullshit, of course, but I liked it. Boys my age were, well, kids. And he was older, confident. He asked for my number, I gave it to him. He called.' She shrugs, feebly. 'He told me I was the only one for him. That I was beautiful. That he had to have me, and no other man could ever make me happy. Ridiculous, isn't it?'

Her face is flushed; she looks at Jack, hoping for absolution.

'You were young,' he says. 'It wasn't your fault. What happened? Did he hurt you?'

'No.' She wrinkles her nose. 'Not really. He wanted to take me away for the weekend. A romantic getaway,' she says, her tone mocking. 'We went to Bournemouth. Some stinking B and B, miles away from the beach. But he said we weren't there to sightsee.'

'He raped you.'

'No.' She shakes her head, defiantly. 'No, he didn't.'

'You were sixteen. He must have been...'

'Fifty-eight. Yeah, it's disgusting. But it was consensual. I let him, and after, he went out for a smoke and didn't come back for two hours. When he did return, he was drunk, stinking of booze, and I realised I'd made a huge mistake. He wanted to do it again, but I ran out of there. Called my mum. She came to pick me up.

'I wanted to put it all behind me but of course, three months later, I realised I was pregnant. And by then Maria had told me all about her stepfather. What he used to do to her, how he'd hit her, bring women home and sleep with them, her mother in the room next door. A real shit. I didn't want a man like that anywhere near my child, so I said it was some kid at school and Maria believed me.'

'Do you think she knows?' Jack asks quietly.

'No. And she mustn't. She'd look at Rosie differently if she knew her daughter had his blood in her veins. And she certainly wouldn't want that man near her baby girl.' Chloe pauses, her eyes widen. 'Do you think he has Rosie?'

'It's a possibility. But is there anyone else you can think of? Anywhere she might be?'

Chloe shakes her head, tears starting to fall. 'I'm sorry. I have no idea. I've told you everything. I swear.' She looks back to her student house, now empty of police. 'Fuck knows what I'm going to tell my housemates,' she mutters. 'They always tell me off for being boring. For babysitting when I should be out drinking.'

'Maybe you should tell them the truth,' Jack says. 'It feels better when you do.'

They head inside, Jack holding the back door open for Chloe. Together they walk through the house, silent with their own thoughts.

They'll get on to Derek Pope as a matter of priority, but instinct tells him it's going to be a dead end. The style of the woman's boot doesn't suit what he knows about Maria's mother, and he can't get a grip on motive. How would Derek Pope have even known? Surely he'd want to distance himself from the sixteen-year-old he groomed into having sex with him?

They stop at the front door, and Jack turns back to face Chloe.

'You'll tell me when you find her?' she says.

'I will,' Jack confirms.

He walks to his car. Even after everything they've done today – interviewing Sean Madden, working out the owner of the drugs, finding Rosie's biological parents – Rosie is still missing.

And there is so much to do.

They need to find Derek Pope, search the house. Speak to the drug squad about Maria's dealer – they're sure to know the mysterious Bleecker – and rule him in or out. He updates Amrit as he drives back to the nick, but the moment he puts the phone down it rings again. He answers it straight away.

'Soph?'

'You promised me,' she snaps. 'You said you'd tell me everything that was going on with Theo.'

'I did. I will—'

'You said nobody was investigating it and that things would take time.'

'Nobody is—'

'So why did your little mate turn up at my mum's house today?'

'My little—?'

'Halliday. The dog handler. She was there. She knows all about the case – she's looking into it, trying to find Theo. Why didn't you tell me?'

Jack's jaw grits together. 'She's doing what?' he manages.

'You haven't changed. You're exactly the same – keeping secrets from me. I shouldn't have trusted you,' Sophie says, then hangs up.

Jack's stomach burns. He pulls the Mercedes in a sharp U-turn, heading back the way he came. Lucy Halliday has some explaining to do.

CHAPTER FORTY

'What did I tell you? What did I say?'

Jack stands on Lucy's doorstep.

She takes a step back. 'Jack, I—'

'I don't want your excuses. You promised! You said you'd stay away.'

'I said I'd do my best. But Jack—'

'Hasn't that family been through enough? Sophie called me. What did you tell them?'

'Please can you just come in?'

'What did you say?'

Lucy stubbornly stands on the threshold, the door open wide. Jack – sensing he's going to get no further by bellowing on her doorstep – sweeps inside.

He spots the paperwork on the kitchen table, the piles of case notes, the comments scrawled on her pad, mostly punctuated with question marks. There is still so much uncertainty. Disparate information that needs one common thread to pull it together.

Jack points to it sarcastically. 'And? Have you solved the case yet? Have you caught Theo's killer?'

Lucy gives him a look. 'Don't be facetious. If it was easy, it would have been solved thirty years ago.'

'So you agree it's a waste of time reopening the investigation?'

She's seen Jack like this before: the middle of a case, skin grey, cheeks hollowing.

'Sit down,' she says. 'Have you eaten today?'

'I don't want to eat. I want you to leave Wendy and Sophie alone.' His voice is cracking, on that dangerous line between angry and upset. 'I told you yesterday, and you ignored me. Why can't you just do as I ask?'

'Because it's important. It's important to Wendy.'

'Stop and think, for once in your life, about how what you're doing affects others. Your ridiculous crusades. It was fine when you were searching for Nico – that was your misery, your problem. But this is Wendy's. This is… This is mine.'

He stops, his fist resting on his breastbone, as if he's protecting his own heart.

'Wendy, she's family to me. Even after all this time. When Theo and I were friends, they looked after me. When my own mother barely spoke to me, Wendy was there with food and hugs and… and love. She treated me like I was one of her own and when Theo disappeared, so did they. I lost more than my best friend that day. I lost everything. It's taken this long to come to terms with the fact that we will never see Theo again. Now you're digging…'

'We've got his T-shirt, Jack. We know where he went. That's a solid lead.'

'It's been thirty years! What's left to find?'

'I've already noticed discrepancies. I have a feeling. This witness, Angela Joseph—'

'You can't run a case on a bloody feeling, Lucy. Just you, on your dining room table. Murder investigations need a team, they need…' He stops. Glares. 'Who have you dragged into this?' Lucy doesn't need to reply. 'Amrit. For crying out loud, Lucy, she's my DS, the only one I have. Hasn't she got enough to do with Rosie Logan? Leave it alone.'

'I will not. I won't contact Amrit anymore, and I don't want to upset you or Wendy, but—'

'But nothing. Leave it alone. I thought you and I were friends. I thought—'

'I'm doing this for you!'

'You're not! You're doing it because you can't help yourself. Get a life, Lucy. Stop interfering in other people's.'

'I have a life. I have a job. Why are you so scared? What are you worried I'm going to find?'

'It's not what you will find. It's the fact you won't. Me, Wendy, Sophie – we've lived for thirty years under this crippling blanket of hope. That someone will find Theo. That he'll turn up alive. Why do you think Wendy hasn't moved house? Because some part of her thinks her forty-year-old son might knock on that door again. It's the hope that kills you. That kills *me*, every single day. And you – what you're doing… I've protected you, time and time again. Why can't you just do this for me?'

Lucy frowns. 'I never needed protecting. When I was looking for Nico, I knew I was risking my job, but it didn't matter. I would have done anything to find out what happened to him.'

'And it nearly destroyed you.'

'But it didn't. Look at me now. Finding Nico meant I could move on, start living again.'

'Theo isn't your narcissistic, violent husband. He was an eleven-year-old boy with his whole life ahead of him.'

'But you could have closure.'

Jack scoffs. 'You don't have closure. Nico created just as much shit after his death as he did when he was alive.'

Abruptly, Jack's manner changes. He steps backwards, straightens. His gaze shifts and he silences, his hand covering his mouth.

Lucy stares at him. 'What?' she asks slowly. 'What are you talking about?'

'Nothing. I…'

'Jack… Was there something about Nico's case you didn't tell me?'

'No. And I'm not here to talk about Nico. Keep your nose out of Theo's investigation. That's all I want to say.'

They stand for a moment, glaring at each other. But the look on Jack's face isn't anger. It's fear.

'What are you so afraid of, Jack? What do you think I'm going to find?'

But Jack doesn't hang around to answer. He strides to the door, pulling it open and walking out into the cold. It slams behind him; she listens until his car fades to nothing.

She turns back to her darkened kitchen. To the scattered notes and the endless questions, lying unanswered on her dining room table.

Because Jack's warning hasn't put her off investigating. She's more determined than ever.

CHAPTER FORTY-ONE

When faced with something difficult – a decision she doesn't want to make, a calamity in her life she can't solve – Lucy has two options. The first – drinking until she passes out comatose – has a certain appeal, but she has responsibilities nowadays. Which brings her to the second.

She makes a mug of coffee and heads out to the garden. Both dogs look up from their bed boxes at the squeak of the back door; she opens their kennels, and the dogs happily gambol out onto the lawn. They circle and sniff; Lucy watches them for a moment, then sits on the cold hard concrete of her step, back resting against the closed door. It's cold out, so she clutches her mug of coffee to her, considering Jack's words. The fury behind them.

His reaction, it seems disproportionate. Yes, she shouldn't have gone against his wishes, and yes, involving Amrit was wrong. But he seemed almost scared. As if he couldn't face the reality of what happened to Theo that night. Denial, or something more?

It's been three days since Rosie Logan went missing, and as the SIO, that responsibility lies with Jack. A heavy load to rest on shoulders already bowed by Theo's disappearance. It's a lot for one person to bear.

The dogs finish their business and join her. Iggy, the younger but bigger dog, wants to play, nudging her with his nose, then bringing her presents – small sticks and twigs which he lays at her feet. She gets up and fetches his favourite plaything, a red plastic bobbly creation, and Lucy thinks, not for the first time, how much it resembles a sex toy for the anatomically ambitious. She holds it above her head.

'Do you want this, huh?' she says, and his ears lift, eyes bright. His head tilts quizzically as she squeaks it, and he backs up, poised as she hurls it down the garden. He races after it, ears back, picking it up in a flurry of legs and waving tail, then joyfully throwing it around, like a cat torturing an animal.

Moss doesn't try to compete with the bigger dog, taking advantage of Iggy's playtime to get some love from his owner. Lucy settles back on the concrete and rubs the spaniel's fur, scratching up and down his body and receiving happy grunts in return.

'What would you do, Moss?' He lifts his head, his ears high, listening. 'Nobody else is going to find Theo, and we're actually on to something now.' She pulls her phone out of her pocket, sets her empty mug on the ground, and calls Cal.

'You must be a mind-reader. I was just about to phone you.'

'About that number?' Lucy shifts as Moss settles his fuzzy rump into her lap.

'Yes. We didn't get far with the old number format, but when we translated it to the new Southampton code, we got a hit. For a flat in Southwood.'

A chill runs down Lucy's back. 'In Fletchers?'

'Yeah. Number thirty-one. How did you know?'

'Woman's intuition,' she says vaguely, not wanting to give too much away. 'Is the number still in use?'

'No, we tried that. Cut off. But don't go out there by yourself, Lucy. Promise me. Get a team in.'

'I will.' It's a promise she knows she'll keep. If she wades in there alone, without a warrant, possible evidence could be compromised. She wants to make sure any conviction related to Theo sticks.

'And Lucy? Clock's ticking.'

'Fuck's sake,' Lucy mutters, and hangs up before Cal can ask any more. Iggy has returned and looks at her, the red toy hanging out of his mouth like a disturbing cigarette. She reaches forward and scratches behind his ears; he slumps at her feet, giving Moss a nudge for good measure.

It's starting to drizzle, raindrops settling like tiny glass beads on Iggy's fur. She runs her hand across his back and sighs.

It's getting late. Dusk has settled across the garden, and she pulls herself to her feet, dusting off the dirt and going back into the house. The dogs follow her, nails clicking on the floorboards, knowing they've been fed but ever hopeful for a second dinner.

Instead, she opens her laptop and settles at the kitchen table. She pulls up a Google Street View of Fletchers, the tower block distorted and silent, a moment of rare calmness from a place where drug dealers come and go all night, where outbreaks of violence are constant, both in the street and behind closed doors. She needs a warrant. And it's going to take more than a thirty-year-old phone number to get one.

While she's studying the screen, her email pings – a message from Sturridge, the DI in charge of the paedo house search where they first found Theo's T-shirt. It's a simple note, with several files attached.

House search complete. Samples taken, pending lab. No further children's clothing (belonging to Theo Nkosi or otherwise) found. Multiple photographs recovered – should be a successful prosecution once we narrow down our offenders. Have attached some images that might be of relevance to your case. But be aware, they make for difficult viewing.

Lucy narrows her eyes, then clicks on the first one. It loads, and initially she's confused. It's a scan of a Polaroid photograph, the colours faded. Barely more than monotone, little gradient in the darkness. But when she realises what it is, her breath stills in her chest.

It's the back of a small child. Dark brown skin, head bowed, spine jutting. Naked, the top of his buttocks just in shot. There are abrasions across his skin, raw scuffs, blood oozing from the cuts. She clicks away. Selects another. And this is worse than the first. She can see his face this time. It's clearly Theo, and he's filthy. Streaks of dirt run in rivers down his cheeks. His eyes are half-closed. Semiconscious, dying, who knows. The next, and the next. Lucy can see why Sturridge warned her of their content.

Polaroid after Polaroid, a man – a white man, from what Lucy can see – sometimes in shot but never clothed, never his face. But the rest. Lucy can see the rest. An erect penis, large hands, a bulbous, hairy stomach. And the boy. He's always with the boy.

The room darkens around Lucy. The dogs, sensing the mood of their owner, stop their nagging for food and lie motionless at her feet, ready for when they might be needed. Her vision narrows, locked on one thing and one thing only – reviewing these hideous photographs.

For this is a catalogue of abuse. One ugly, evil man documenting what he did to Theo Nkosi. How he raped him, abused him. Killed him.

Lucy closes the last file. She touches her face; her cheeks are wet, and she realises she's been crying. She feels sick, spent. She closes the laptop, but the images persist, rotating inside her head.

That poor boy. What he went through. How he died. If she was ever in doubt about pursuing this case, there is no hesitation now. Not for Jack, not for his family. It's time to get retribution for Theo.

She will catch this man. And they will make him pay.

DAY FOUR – SATURDAY

CHAPTER FORTY-TWO

When Lucy finally manages to sleep, her dreams are broken – full of scattered limbs, bodies screaming with fear. She wakes, her duvet tangled around her legs. She gets up, groggy, the sun still low, and stands in the garden in the freezing cold while the dogs sniff and scratch.

She thinks about Jack. She wonders how the investigation into Rosie is going and frowns, looking around for her phone. She goes inside, eventually finding it on the kitchen worktop, drained of battery. She plugs it in, feeds the dogs, makes breakfast.

She missed dinner last night, and eats her first slice of toast standing up while she waits for her fried egg to cook. Her phone bursts into life with an array of beeps and alerts, and curious, she picks it up. Her heart sinks.

There are three messages from Pete. The first is gentle; the second, rising in tone; the last a curt *I give up*. Too late, she remembers their plans to meet and her stomach drops. It's getting familiar, this feeling. Disappointing the significant people in her life – people who should mean more to her than broken promises and forgotten dates.

She's steeling herself to phone Pete back when she hears a light tap on the door. The dogs go mental – Moss twirls in circles in the hallway, Iggy barks from the garden like Lucifer himself is trying to break in. Lucy ignores them and opens the front door.

Pete's standing there. The moment he sees her, he turns to leave.

'Pete, wait. Please. I'm sorry.'

'The skipper gave me your address – I only came to check you're okay. And you are. So.' He turns again, and this time Lucy catches his arm. He glares at her hand on his bicep, then shakes her off.

'I'm sorry,' she says again. 'I was sent something about the case. I got caught up in it and I didn't realise my phone was dead and—'

'And what? I thought we were getting along well—'

'We are.'

'—but I won't put up with you treating me like this. Running out halfway through an evening. Leaving me waiting at home for your call.'

'I know, it's just…' She looks back into the kitchen where her laptop sits on the table. 'This case. It's got under my skin.'

'It's not even *your* case.' He shakes his head. 'You say there's nothing between you and Ellis, and I believe you, for what it's worth. But you have an obsessive streak that's self-destructive. There's no space for anyone else in your life, and you and I…' He shakes his head. 'You don't let me in. We've been… I don't know… dating? If you could even call it that. For nine months, on and off. And I still don't know anything about you.'

'You do! You know plenty.'

'Not what matters.'

He stares at her for a moment, the hurt in his eyes. He's right. They talk about work, the dogs, the offenders they catch. He shared that he split up with his last girlfriend about a year ago, but she rarely talks about Nico.

'I just need time,' she says quietly.

'I get that,' he replies. 'And that's fine. But I won't put up with being forgotten. If we make plans, you stick to them, unless there's a bloody good reason. If you can't give me that basic courtesy then I'm sorry, but that's my limit.'

He takes a step away from the door. And that's when it all goes wrong. Lucy reaches out for him, but in one swift move he bats her away and his arm comes into contact with hers. There's no pain, not enough to even bruise, but just the lift of his hand induces something in her – a primitive reflex, a jolt in the pit of her stomach. She flinches, her legs weak. She backs away, her heart racing, but she's not looking and the step catches her heels. She falls backwards into her hallway, landing heavily on the carpet, her hands instinctively up and over her face in seconds.

Pete sees what's happened, raises his hands in defence and confusion. He takes a step towards her but something about the look in her eyes makes him stop.

His mouth opens in shock. 'I didn't… I wouldn't…' he says. 'Lucy—'

'Just go,' she says, the words catching, choking in her mouth. 'Please.'

He blinks, hesitates, then in three quick strides, he's gone.

She hears his engine fade into the distance, and sits up, resting her head between her knees, trying to catch her breath. She needs to calm. To reset. Moss stops circling and sits at her side, sticking his nose over her shoulder. She puts her arms around him, buries her face in his warm fur.

She has no one. Not Jack, not Pete.

What a fucking mess she's made of everything.

CHAPTER FORTY-THREE

Jack stayed in his office until well after midnight, desperate for a distraction after his argument with Lucy. The team sent their progress reports and left; Amrit, ever the dedicated second-in-command, stayed until Jack sent her home.

Despite the team's hard work – their diligence in following up every lead, scouring every inch of CCTV and running every number plate – they're no closer to finding Rosie. Uniforms have searched Derek Pope's home and car, even brought him in for a voluntary interview, but there's no reason to arrest him. To Jack's annoyance. Jack had instructed the team to keep tight-lipped about Rosie's parentage, but he would desperately like to charge Pope with something. Grooming? Child endangerment? But Chloe was sixteen, and, by her own admission, everything undertaken that day was consensual. Disgusting, but not illegal.

Jack had left the nick feeling twitchy and frustrated. He drove home, went to bed, but his mind wouldn't switch off, and in the early hours he found himself circling back to his fight with Lucy.

He nearly told her – blurting out in the heat of the moment, about how she might have a sister. Maybe. Potentially. Jack has no way of confirming whether what Nico said was the truth. She's happy and settled. She has moved on, she's living again, as she told him last night. Why upset the apple cart now?

That matter resolved, at least in his mind, his thoughts shift to Theo. Jack knows Lucy well enough by now: there's no way she's paid any heed to his warning last night. Especially, as she says, if she is making progress. For the first time he discovers he's curious, desperate to know what she has found on the case.

He gets up before the sun rises, rubbing his scratchy eyes and staring at himself in the bathroom mirror. Lit only in the harsh overhead light, his skin looks jaundiced and puffy, his eyes bruised by lack of sleep. He shaves quickly, showers, then gets dressed in his one remaining clean shirt and suit. Life can only go on hold for so long.

The radio blares as he drives in to work, happy pop songs, punctuated by the news bulletin, reminding him of his failure to find Rosie. The newsreader can't offer much, only that the search is ongoing and putting out a fresh appeal for information. That's something, at least. The news gives way to One Direction and Jack switches it off, finishing the drive in silence.

Jack's convinced the answer to where Rosie is lies down another line of enquiry. Someone they haven't considered: an acquaintance, a friend of the family, or worse, a random taking Rosie for purposes Jack doesn't want to consider. He debates contacting the MET team – a group dedicated to working with missing children at risk from exploitation or trafficking. He hasn't spoken to them yet because Rosie doesn't fit into the usual categories – those families with mental health problems, drug and alcohol dependency, or unstable relationships, just to name a few – but maybe his own bias is impeding the investigation. Drugs are certainly a factor now; he goes to put in a call, then realises it's the weekend. Some people have a life.

Not his team, it seems. Lawrence, Bates and Amrit all trickle in before nine, putting a fresh pot of coffee on and trailing aromas of bacon sandwiches and fresh croissants in their wake. Jack's stomach rumbles, breakfast missed, once again, and his gratitude towards Amrit grows as she appears in the doorway to his office, greasy paper bag and takeaway cup in her hand.

She places them both on his desk.

'Tea, milk, two bags, just the way you like it. Almond croissant.'

'Amrit, I love you.'

'Hold that thought until I've finished talking.' She sits down slowly in front of his desk. 'I've been helping Lucy Halliday.'

'Right,' Jack says calmly. He takes a bite from his croissant and chews slowly.

'Not much. Just helping her trace a witness and follow up on some enquiries.' A blush creeps up her neck from her shirt. 'I thought it would be okay, and you wouldn't mind. And it didn't get in the way of the work I was doing on Rosie Logan. But then you disappeared and came back in a terrible mood, so...' She winces, trying to read his expression.

'You thought you should tell me before I went postal at you too.'

'Yes,' she says quietly.

Jack continues to eat his breakfast. He's not sure whether it's the sugar hit or the mortified expression on Amrit's face, but he doesn't feel as angry as he did last night. As much as he hates to admit it, Lucy is right. They do need to follow up on this lead now, before the discovery gets out into the general public.

'It's fine, Amrit. I know.'

'You do?'

'Lucy told me. And it's fine.'

'It is?'

Her surprise makes him smile. 'I don't like that you went behind my back, but I know your motives were pure. You're a good detective – you want to find Theo. And I can only be grateful for that.' He sighs, balling the empty paper bag and chucking it in the bin. 'Nobody's done anything to help Theo in nearly thirty years, and now he has two of the best detectives in Hampshire on the case, all I do is get angry about it.' He shrugs. 'It's a confusing time.'

'Maybe you should tell that to Lucy, too?'

'Don't push your luck.' But Amrit gives him a warm smile, which he returns. 'From now on our priority lies with Rosie, right?'

'Right, boss.'

'Could you get the team together for a morning briefing?'

'Yes. Yes, of course.' She stands up. 'I know that you're my DCI, but if you ever want to talk...?'

He nods. 'Thank you.'

Jack finishes the last gulps of tea. Amrit was right, just the way he likes it. He looks out into the incident room where the team are settling, mugs of coffee in their hands. Gus has arrived, the analyst pulling a chair next to Amrit, laptop in hand.

Jack comes out to join them. 'Morning.' Murmurs all round. He turns to Bates. 'How were the family when you left them last night?'

Bates frowns, waggles her head with indecision. 'Tense. As you'd expect. Maria made dinner for her and Eddie – Eddie's still not speaking to her because she didn't tell him his dad was out of prison, but he did take a bowl of pasta back to his room. Both of them are ignoring Tony. He spends most of his time in his study. Do we have an update I can take out there today?'

'We've ruled out several lines of enquiry, Sean Madden included. What mood was Madden in yesterday?' he directs to Lawrence.

'Pensive,' Lawrence says. 'We let him go just after half-five without charge. Kept him there for the full twenty-four hours. He said he was going to head back to Cornwall, but I don't believe him. I told him stay away from the Logans.'

'Good. Bates, keep an eye out. Make sure he doesn't go near, unless he wants a black eye from Tony. Gus, where have we got to with the cars that morning?'

The analyst sits up straight. 'It was my main priority yesterday – running every plate through the databases and calling anyone I could get hold of. But so far, nothing. The majority are local residents, presumably heading to work. No criminal records on the RMS or the PNC.'

'And the rest?'

'A mixture of dog walkers on their way to the New Forest or retired pensioners stopping for tea and cake in town. Still about a third to work through.'

'Good. Have we managed to track down our friendly neighbourhood drug dealer yet? Bleecker?'

Amrit puts her hand up. 'I called the drug squad, and DCI Perry—'

'Excellent, can't wait to work with him again.'

Amrit smiles at Jack's sarcasm. 'He's putting feelers out. Rural Fordingbridge isn't his neck of the woods, but he's confident he'll find him.'

'That's good news. Any more reports from the helpline?'

'That's me,' Lawrence speaks up. 'Some, but nothing worth pursuing.'

'Shit.' Jack gives an exasperated grunt. 'What is our working hypothesis at this point? Where the bloody hell is she?'

The whole room is silent. Nobody wants to say it.

'She's not dead,' Bates says quietly.

Out of all the detectives, Bates has been closest to the family. She's seen the photographs and the toys – it's impossible for her not to get emotionally invested.

'So where is she?' Jack asks gently.

'We're looking at roads and cars, but we know Rosie was walked out of the woodland, we have the video to prove it. What if she's in a house somewhere locally?'

'Wouldn't someone have seen them?' Lawrence says.

'Not if they didn't go far. The uniforms did an initial door to door around the estate closest to the park, but they were looking for witnesses, not a child. What if they do it again, but looking for Rosie this time? Evidence that a child's staying there.'

Jack raises his eyebrows. 'It's a good shout. I'll get on to the duty skipper of R and P. See if we can get some lads from Wiltshire, too. Any more good suggestions?'

'What about canvassing local shops?' Gus chips in. 'Anyone seen buying toddler clothes or food? Assuming they didn't plan to take Rosie, they would need provisions.'

'And what if they did plan it?' Amrit counters.

The team falls silent.

'No, it's good,' Jack says. 'I'll get R and P on this, too. They're going to love us this morning,' he mutters. 'Anything else?'

‘More background into the family?’ Amrit suggests.

‘Haven’t we done that already?’

‘The last few years, yes. But they moved house in 2018 as well as the move here in 2021. Where were they living before Swindon? And why did they move?’

‘More problems with Tony?’ Lawrence says.

‘Maybe,’ Jack confirms. ‘Let’s find out. You all have your tasks, crack on. Report back to me when you find something.’ Everyone stands up, about to head off. ‘Amrit,’ Jack says. He inclines his head back towards his office; Amrit’s head bows once they’re inside and he closes the door behind them.

‘Tell me about this witness,’ he asks.

‘The one who saw you and Theo?’ Amrit says. ‘Angela Joseph?’

Jack nods, resting his bum on the edge of his desk.

‘Must be late forties by now. Lives in a nice house in Ampfield. Married, no children. Lucy went to see her, didn’t believe a word she said, then followed her to an address in Southwood.’

‘What was she doing there?’

‘Looking for someone, apparently. She gave me the address Angela Joseph went to, asked me to look into who lived there in 1997. It came back this morning – I haven’t had a chance to tell Lucy.’

‘I’ll tell her,’ Jack says. ‘What’s the name?’

CHAPTER FORTY-FOUR

The last person Lucy expects to see on her doorstep as she returns from her dog walk is Jack Ellis. And it doesn't look like he's in a good mood: hunched shoulders, head bowed. He looks up with a deep frown as Lucy stands in front of him.

'I'm not here to apologise,' he begins, once Moss has finished his enthusiastic greeting – muddy paws all over Jack's clean trousers. Iggy is more restrained, nudging him with his nose until his ears get a stroke.

'I can see that,' Lucy says. 'Do you want to go in? I'll take the dogs around the back.'

She opens the front door, and leaves Jack while she fills water bowls and towels the dogs dry. She leaves them in their kennels, abandoning her wellies and coat by the back door and padding towards the kitchen in her socks.

Jack has made himself at home. Kettle boiled, he's adding milk to tea, coffee for her. She can't tell what's prompted this new visit. He hasn't started shouting, but neither is he contrite.

He sits down at the table. She takes her cue and does the same.

'Tell me about the flat. The one your witness went to.'

Lucy studies him for a second; his face is stern but interested. She pushes her notes towards him.

'Tower B, thirty-one Fletcher Towers. And before you say anything, it's definitely significant. Wendy was getting crank calls in 1994 from a Southampton number. I asked Cal to trace it—'

'You've involved Cal in this?'

'He doesn't know anything significant, Jack. He won't publish until we give him permission.' Lucy refrains from mentioning the possible future article about Jack's past – she doesn't want to make his mood worse. She continues: 'And guess where the number came back to.'

'Same place?'

Lucy nods. 'Are you… Is MCIT working on this now?'

Jack sighs, chewing on his lower lip. 'Part of me is desperate to know what happened to Theo. And the other…' He glances upwards, blinking.

Lucy reaches out and gently touches his arm. She wants to offer reassurance, that nothing they'll discover could be worse than what's in his head, but she doesn't need to imagine. She's seen it with her own eyes.

'Theo deserves to be buried by his family, peacefully. Once and for all.'

'He does.' He swipes under his eyes with his fingers, then looks at her. 'What else do I need to know?'

Lucy tells him about the witness, and her doubts about her walking her dog, if she was even there at all. She talks about the conversations between the detectives at the time and the newspapers, but stops at mentioning his parents, and the real reason the press went after his family.

'And Jack,' she says, 'they've found photographs.'

'Photographs?'

'Polaroids, at the house on Randall Road. Of Theo.'

His jaw tenses. Jack's been a copper for long enough, he knows what they'll show.

'I don't want to see them now. Anything else?'

'No.'

He reaches into his jacket pocket and takes out a piece of paper. He lays it on the table in front of Lucy.

It says one name at the top: *Robert Chaplin.*

'Who's this guy?'

'The house in Randall Road is currently owned by Robert Chaplin. Same guy who owned the flat in 1994. All paths lead here.'

Lucy pulls the printout closer. 'Robert Chaplin,' she reads. 'Born 1953. Convictions for theft, armed robbery, drunk and disorderly. Multiple stints inside, including one from 1993 to 1996 for GBH. Currently serving a life sentence for murder.' She looks up. 'Nice bloke. But he couldn't have been involved with Theo's disappearance.'

'Doesn't look like it.'

'So why did Angela Joseph go to his old address yesterday?'

'Why don't we ask her?'

–

Lucy's unsure what's brought on this change of circumstances. Yesterday, Jack wanted nothing to do with the investigation and was furious with her for getting involved. Now, here he is, tagging along.

But however much confusion she has about Jack's change of heart, it can wait. She's just as keen to speak to Angela Joseph again as he is, find out what the woman is hiding.

Twenty minutes later, Jack pulls into the smoothly tarmacked driveway and cuts the engine. Lucy points to the two cars outside. 'I'm guessing her husband is home,' she says. 'But Jack, you can't be near this.'

'It'll be fine. The first sign of anything definitive and I'll back off. I promise.'

She hesitates. As someone with close personal involvement in the case, Jack should stay away, but she knows that pull only too well. Of wanting justice, seeing it with your own two eyes.

He senses her indecision. 'What? You're going to make me wait in the car?' He points to the front door. 'This woman's statement put me in the firing line. It ruined my life. I just want to see her reaction when you question her.'

'Fine,' she agrees reluctantly. 'But get behind me.'

He does as she says, letting her take the lead as she knocks on the door. It's opened to tantalising smells of cooking, warming central heating, laughter and the sound of a television. A man stands on the threshold, thinning grey hair swept back from his forehead, wearing a diamond-patterned jumper and smart trousers. He's confused when they pull their IDs.

'I'm sorry, I was expecting a friend of mine. I've got a tee time booked in an hour. Can this wait?'

'We're actually here to speak to Angela, Mr Joseph,' Lucy says. 'Is she in?'

He doesn't need to call his wife. Angela appears behind him, apron on, a tea towel in her hand. The paragon of middle-class respectability.

'Angela, we met before, I'm…'

But Lucy doesn't get any further. Angela's gaze locks onto Jack, standing behind her. Smart suit, full height; she starts to cry.

'It's you, isn't it? That kid. You're Jason Kent. I saw you on the news, last summer. It's you.'

'Mrs Joseph…'

'I'm sorry,' she says. First to Jack, then to her husband. 'I'm sorry, Michael. I never meant this to happen. I didn't think…'

'Angie, what…?'

She turns back to Jack.

'I'm sorry,' she repeats, over and over, mumbling through her tears. 'I didn't want… I didn't know… You shouldn't have got in trouble for what I did.'

Lucy's skin prickles. Thirty years is a long time to hold onto guilt, and in the face of the child she wronged, now a grown man, there's no stopping Angela Joseph.

'I killed him,' she says. 'That little boy. I killed him.'

CHAPTER FORTY-FIVE

The arrest is swift, the caution clear. Neither Lucy nor Jack have cuffs on them, but this isn't a woman causing trouble. Before Angela can say any more she's got her shoes and her coat on and is in the back of Jack's car.

She cries all the way to the police station. Jack drives, Lucy sits next to her in the back. Every now and again, Lucy catches Angela staring at Jack, then quickly looking away.

Her tears eventually subside to silence and an occasional sniff, staring at the balled-up tissue in her shaking hands as they pull up behind the police station.

Jack gets out first to announce their arrival.

'He seems so normal,' she says to Lucy. 'Jason Kent. DCI Ellis. After all this time, what I did… What I must have put him through.' She starts crying again. 'That poor boy,' she says, and Lucy's not sure whether she's talking about Theo or Jack.

'We'll talk more inside,' Lucy replies, keen to get any important information on record in an interview room, knowing how Jack's quiet façade hides years of damage.

The passenger door opens; a uniformed cop beckons Angela out and through to custody. Lucy and Jack follow, answer questions about the nature of the arrest, the offence. Angela cries harder at the mention of murder. Job done, they leave the custody sergeant to complete the rest of the paperwork, take her fingerprints, photographs and DNA.

Lucy pulls Jack to the side. 'What I don't get,' she says, 'is how this woman fits with the squat. Women aren't typically paedophiles, so why would she kidnap a small boy?'

'Rose West?' Jack answers succinctly.

A serial killer, an enabler to her husband's crimes.

'So who was she working with?' Lucy says.

'I guess we'll find out soon.'

'Not you, Jack. You know what I'm going to say.' She sees him about to protest. 'You've done too much already – we want this confession to be watertight. We don't want some lawyer claiming you coerced her or doctored the evidence. Stay well away.'

Jack hesitates, but he knows Lucy's right. 'I'll be watching,' he says. 'I'll go and speak to DCS Weaver. Get him up to speed and ensure he's happy with you interviewing. I'll send Amrit down to be your second.'

Lucy watches him go. On the surface he seems measured and calm, but Jack must have a thousand emotions running through his head. She needs to get this right – for him, but also for Wendy and Sophie and Leo and Harry. And most of all – for Theo.

She finds a quiet corner and gathers her thoughts, scribbling questions on her pad. She hopes that the half an hour in custody wouldn't have dulled Angela's resolve to come clean. Or worse, that she will have asked for a lawyer.

But all her prayers are answered when Amrit comes to find her.

'She's in interview room one, ready to go,' Amrit says. 'I've got the file.' She smiles. 'And she's declined legal representation.'

Lucy takes a long slow breath in, then lets it out. She pulls her shoulders back and stands up, meeting Amrit's resolute gaze.

'Ready?' Amrit says.

'Ready.'

–

The video is running, introductions have been made, the caution given. Angela fidgets constantly, glancing around the room with wide eyes then at the file in front of Amrit.

But Lucy's not about to begin there.

'Angela,' she begins softly. 'When you came to the door, you said to me and DCI Ellis that you – and I quote – "had killed him". Could you explain what you meant?'

Angela starts crying again; Amrit passes her a tissue. She blows her nose, before looking up at Lucy, her face full of resolve.

'When you turned up on Thursday, I knew it was only a matter of time before you'd come back. I knew you'd find me.'

'Who are you saying you killed?'

'That little boy.' Her voice cracks. 'The one that disappeared.'

'Theo Nkosi?'

'That's his name, yes. I killed him.'

'And how did you kill him?'

'I was there, that afternoon. You know that – you caught my car on camera. So I lied. I had to say I was walking my dog and saw those boys playing. I'd heard Jason Kent's name on the news – I knew he was a suspect. I needed to give the police somewhere else to look.' Tears run down Angela's face as she talks; her words are frail and wet.

'Why were you there, Angela?'

'We shouldn't have been. I knew it was a bad idea, going out that day. But Jimmy, he persuaded me. He said it was going to be a good night – that people would be out at the pub, in friends' gardens. That we could maybe break into some places.'

'Jimmy who?' Lucy asks. She has to fight to keep her words measured; her heart is beating double speed in her chest, almost desperate with anticipation.

Angela looks at her, her gaze level. 'No. I won't give you his surname. You'll arrest him and he'll know it was me. He'll find me, and my husband.'

'We can protect you—'

'Not from him.' She shakes her head, tears dropping to the table. 'I got away once. I won't manage it again.'

Lucy glances to Amrit. Lucy can see her colleague's frustration, but it won't pay to push Angela now.

'Tell us about that night.'

Angela's gaze drops again.

'Jimmy was my… my dealer, I suppose you'd call him. Things weren't good for me back then. I left home when I was seventeen, found myself on the streets. He took me in, but he was into drugs – and soon, so was I.

'For the first few years, I was whacked out of my head on H most of the time. Jimmy slept with me, said he was my boyfriend, but he went with everyone. If it had a pulse, he'd fuck it, he always said. And then he got me sleeping with other men. Just his mates at first. Bit of cash. I could pay off my debts, but all it meant was I stuck more needles in my arm. Then came the strange men. The ones I didn't like. But what could I do? I owed him. He was my whole world.'

Lucy stays quiet. Her life was never that bad, but she certainly knows what it's like to love a man that's no good for you.

'What were you doing that night?' Lucy prompts.

'He wanted to break into a few houses. It was early, but he figured we could case some places, see who was in, who wasn't. It was Jimmy's car – he bought it – but it was in my name because he was banned from driving and wanted me to take his speeding tickets when he got caught. Figured I was useful for something, at least. We were both off our heads. Can't remember what on. I was driving because he was practically paralytic. And then… And then…'

She takes a heaving breath, snot, tears, dripping from her face onto the table.

'I thought it was a dog at first. Something big. I must have been going fast, because I heard this thump. I stopped. I did, I swear. Got out of the car. And there was this boy. On the road. Not moving.'

'You hit Theo with the car?'

'He was just lying there. On the concrete. I panicked. I wanted to call 999 but Jimmy said no. I said we could leave him in the road, phone an ambulance, nobody would ever find us, but Jimmy told me to get in the car.'

'What happened next?'

'He opened the boot. Picked up the kid's body and put him inside. Then told me to drive home. I drove to where I'd been staying with some other girls, other girls Jimmy liked to pimp out, like me, and Jimmy got in the driver's seat and left. Next thing I knew, that kid was on the news.'

'What did he do with Theo?'

'I don't know. Honestly, I don't. I asked him the next day and he said to forget about it. I reckon he buried the body somewhere. Every day, for the past thirty years, I've thought about that boy.'

'You phoned his mother, didn't you? You apologised.' Angela looks stunned. 'Theo's mother kept records of the calls she received. And we traced one back to that flat at Fletchers.'

'I just wanted to say sorry.'

'Why didn't you come forward, Angela?'

'I couldn't. Jimmy would have killed me. And… and I was scared. It was murder. I killed him.'

'Except you didn't, Angela.' Angela looks up sharply. Lucy reaches across and takes the file from Amrit. She places her hands on the top of it, knowing what horrors lie inside and doubting whether she has the strength to look at them again, to share them with Angela. But she must.

Lucy continues. 'You didn't kill him.'

Angela blinks in surprise as Lucy opens the file. On the top is the photo of the T-shirt found at the squat.

'This T-shirt belonged to Theo Nkosi. Do you recognise it?'

Angela gawps. 'He was wearing it. That evening.'

Lucy nods slowly. 'We found it at a squat. Twenty-two Randall Road. Do you recognise the address?'

'In Southwood. Yes, I know it. Jimmy used to take us there sometimes. To meet men.'

Angela's speaking more slowly now. Desperate to make sense of what Lucy's telling her.

'We found other evidence at that house. Blood, belonging to Theo. And photographs.'

She selects one from the pile and pushes it across to Angela. It's by far the lesser of the images, but Angela recoils.

'But… he… what?' She quickly turns it over, won't look at it again.

'From what you've told us today, it's my belief that you injured Theo with your car, but you didn't kill him. This man, Jimmy, your boyfriend, took Theo to twenty-two Randall Road, where he imprisoned him, abused him, and eventually killed him.'

'He… what… oh my God.' Her hand flies to her mouth and she stares at Lucy with wide eyes. 'So I didn't… but he…'

'We believe so. And Angela, we need your help. At this point, you're facing charges of failing to report an accident, conspiring to hide a body, and causing serious injury by dangerous driving under the influence, but if we don't believe you, we could push for joint enterprise murder. That you and Jimmy conspired to kill Theo.'

'I… I didn't… I didn't know…'

'So help us find this man. And help us find Theo. He deserves to be laid to rest properly. For his mother and his family to be able to grieve. Please. Help us.'

Angela looks at her, tears running unabated down her cheeks. And she nods.

'Jimmy Smith,' she says. 'That's the guy you're looking for.'

Lucy raises her eyebrows. She glances to Amrit – she has the same look of disbelief.

'Jimmy Smith?' Lucy repeats. 'James Smith? One of the most common names in the UK? Can you give us anything else? Where he lived? Age? Date of birth? Middle name?'

Angela shakes her head. 'I'll give you everything I can remember. Maybe something will help.'

-

Over the next few hours, Angela tells them everything she knows about the elusive Jimmy Smith. They pore over a map, Angela identifying houses she stayed in, the hangouts of Jimmy's friends.

Aliases, people he knew, drug dealers he used. But nothing pulls them closer to identifying the man.

Lucy leaves Angela with Amrit, trying to tease out some fragment of knowledge that might help, and joins Jack in the corridor. He looks how she feels – knackered, disappointed. Another dead end.

'She identified the squat and the flat,' Lucy says. 'Both places she used to live with this guy.'

'Both owned by Robert Chaplin in 1994, the one person we know couldn't have done it.'

'But he might know who did.'

'A career criminal, inside for murder? What incentive does he have to talk to cops?'

'Look, Jack. You're right to be pessimistic. Thirty years of nothing is telling you we're going to get nowhere. But we're closer than we've ever been, you have to believe that.'

'I just… I can't even dare to imagine we'll find him.'

'Then let me be the optimistic one for a change. Let me hope. You just need to be there. Will you come with me to see Robert Chaplin?'

He pauses for a moment, then nods.

CHAPTER FORTY-SIX

For once, events are working in their favour – Robert Chaplin is being held at HMP Winchester. The governor approves the visitation request in record time and they are on the road, heading up the M3.

It's started to rain, huge droplets on the windscreen, and Jack feels disorientated as he drives, like he's being swept along by floodwaters, tossed and turned towards an unknown destination. He had watched Lucy and Amrit interview Angela Joseph, looking for some trace of recognition in her older, lined face. Had he seen her driving that day? Had they passed him as he walked home, a blue Ford Fiesta, anonymous, with Theo's unconscious body in the boot? So many regrets, now one more to add to the list.

They pull up at the prison gates and show their ID. They're waved through; Jack parks in the nearest space. But once he puts on the handbrake, he turns to her.

'Lucy, I need to apologise.'

'Okay?'

'For shouting at you. I was scared. Still am. Of facing everything that happened that day. It's been… a lot.'

There's silence, Lucy seemingly waiting for him to say more. But he stays quiet, bottling the rest inside.

She half looks at him, then sighs. 'And I'm sorry. For pushing the issue about Theo.'

'No, you were right. We have an opportunity now – we should take it.' He points out of the windscreen to the prison. It looms, large and imposing, through the rain. 'At last, we might get some answers. However awful.'

Lucy nods. 'Come on. Let's go talk to this guy.'

They hurry through the rain to the entrance, shaking out their coats as they take them off for the security scanner. They sign in, offer police ID, and surrender their mobile phones and valuables into the lockers.

Jack's stomach is in knots as they're escorted through locked door after locked door to the interview suites on the West Wing. Visiting a prisoner is no big deal, he's done it a hundred times before, but not when so much is at stake. They're shown into an interview room. They sit down. Lucy takes her notes out of her bag and places them on the desk. It feels like any normal police set-up – video cameras overhead, a digital recorder next to them.

Just a normal day at work, he tells himself.

He notices Lucy looking at him. 'Jack, should you be here?' she asks. 'You're too close, this is too personal—'

But he interrupts her. 'It's fine,' he says. He squares his shoulders, rolls his head from one side to the other, feeling his neck crack. 'I need to do this,' he finishes, and before she can object the door opens and a man is escorted inside. He's wearing a woolly black jumper, grey tracksuit bottoms and white trainers. No handcuffs. He looks older than his police photo would indicate, but he's been inside for sixteen years. It's no surprise.

Chaplin sits down. Lucy pushes the file across to Jack, a small gesture that says, *It's yours*.

'Mr Chaplin…' Jack begins.

'Bob's fine,' he says.

'Bob. I'm DCI Jack Ellis and this is PC Lucy Halliday. Thank you for agreeing to meet with us.'

'Nothing else to do. I was curious. What's this about? The guv'nor said it was to do with a cold case. Must be – the time I've been in here.'

'You've been inside since 2009 for murder, is that correct?'

'You've got the file.'

'This is to do with a crime that was committed in 1994. That summer.'

'Then you know I was inside, an' all. GBH. Didn't get out until ninety-six.'

'Can you tell us about a property you own? Twenty-two Randall Road?'

His eyes narrow. 'That's still mine? Shit. Would have thought someone would have taken it off me by now. Horrible place. I only bought it because it was going cheap, and my mate said it was an investment. You wouldn't know now, but I was quite the businessman once. Owned a few places. Dreams of a property empire, you know.' He laughs. 'What bullshit.'

Jack smiles weakly. 'Did you go back there when you go out?'

'Yes,' he says slowly.

'Who else was living there at that time?'

'Nobody, just me.'

'And who was living there while you were inside?'

Jack asks the question as mildly as he can, not wanting to flag it with the significance it deserves.

Chaplin regards him with wet, rheumy eyes, debating. 'Think it's about time you come clean with what this is about, or we're not going to move much further forward. I've not got my lawyer. I don't want to, you know, incriminate myself. I could be up for parole in a few years, don't want anything getting in the way of that.'

Jack studies the man, debating. Bob's an old hand at dealing with cops. He doesn't have to be here if he doesn't want to be, and as yet he's been civil. It's time to trust the man who might hold the key to this entire case.

'In July 1994, an eleven-year-old boy went missing. Theo Nkosi. Last week, we found his bloodied T-shirt at twenty-two Randall Road.'

Chaplin tilts his chin up. A fraction of an inch, but Jack can tell that something he just said has hit home.

'Where in the house?'

'There was a hidden room at the back of one of the cupboards. In the bedroom at the front.'

'That wasn't a *room*. It was a hidey-hole.'

'You know it?'

'Yeah.' He frowns, leaning closer to study Jack's face. 'You're that detective, aren't you? We were talking about you in here, over the summer. The murder suspect who became a cop.'

'I was Theo's best friend. And a suspect in the investigation, yes.'

'Tell me. What made you go this way.' He gestures with his finger, up and down, at Jack. 'Rather than here.' Points to himself.

'I wanted to make sure nobody else went through the same experience as I did. And I wanted to find my best friend.'

Jack feels Lucy's eyes on him. Up to now he's let Lucy believe he never went near the case, when the truth is all he did when he first became a detective was look into it. He found the same files as she did, read those transcripts, watched that VHS tape of his interview on that fateful day.

'And how did that go?' Chaplin asks.

'I failed.'

'Until today.'

Jack looks up sharply. Chaplin's wearing a different expression now. Disgust, hatred, but not towards Jack or Lucy.

'We built that hidey-hole to stash stolen goods. If we were ever raided by the police. TVs, cash, clothes. Stuff like that.' His lip curls. 'Not *kids*. That fucking *cunt*.'

Chaplin says the last word with feeling, to himself rather than to Jack.

'Who are you talking about, Bob?'

'I wasn't there for long. After I got out in ninety-six, I went back, got a few hours' shut-eye, then headed up north to where a mate said he had a job for me. The place was empty when I arrived. It was empty when I left. It didn't even occur to me to look in the hidey-hole. I assumed nobody else knew it was there.'

'Who was staying at your house in July 1994?'

'I owned a few places, as I said. That house, a flat in Fletchers. A few other properties. I made a good little income from the rent. I could have had a decent life, you know, if I hadn't been greedy.'

'Please, Mr Chaplin,' Jack says. He can feel Lucy tense next to him, rigid with anticipation. 'This is important. This child has been missing for thirty years. His mother needs to know what happened to him.'

'Eleven years old, you say?' He pauses. 'Did you find a body? At the house?'

'No. Bob, please.'

'Do you know how I've kept sane in here? I get privileges. I don't get caught up in the rucks. I don't take sides. The boys leave me alone. You know the fastest way to get fucked up? Talk to the coppers. I'm no snitch.' He senses Jack about to say something and silences him by holding his finger in the air. 'But I also know what's right and what's wrong. Sure, I stole some stuff. Only people that punishes is the insurance companies. Yeah, I hit a guy. But he deserved it, nasty piece of work. And now I'm in here for murder. But I only meant to punch the geezer. Hit my woman, he did. So I stuck up for her. Just happened he went down too hard, and the police said I did it on purpose. Lost everything I had – because of that one punch. Had to sell most of the houses to pay for the lawyers – fat use that did. Except for that shithole in Randall Road, but only because no one would have it. One thing I won't tolerate is those bastards that do things to the kids. Kids and animals – the only innocents in this world.'

He pauses, looks from Lucy to Jack, then back again. He leans forward.

'Jimmy Smith. That's the cunt you're looking for. There was always something off about him. I could get into trouble but Jimmy – it was like he looked for it. Drugs, women, hookers. I didn't like the way he slapped them around, but I stayed out of his business. Made sure he had a roof over his head, thought that if I let him stay, he might keep on the straight and narrow.' He scoffs. 'Fat chance. He used to rent it out, pretend it was his. Little bastard.' He narrows his eyes, takes in Jack's reaction. 'But you knew his name, didn't you? Knew that before you came here.'

Jack nods. 'We did. But it's too common, we don't know anything else about him.'

Jack opens the file and plays his trump card. The photos Lucy didn't want to show him, images that will haunt Jack for the rest of his life. He places one on the table – a man in the middle of the shot, a black tattoo in full focus as Theo lies on the floor underneath him. Thick bile rises in Jack's throat, but he swallows it down.

'Does he have a tattoo like this?' Jack asks.

Chaplin considers it, gives a long sniff, then nods slowly. He looks at Jack. 'I didn't do anything then, but what sort of a man would I be if I stand by and let this go. If he did something to a kid, he deserves everything he gets.

'Jimmy Smith is my half-brother. And I'll tell you exactly where you can find him.'

CHAPTER FORTY-SEVEN

There is no delay: the warrant is authorised in moments, patrol cars stream to the address.

The enforcer breaks down the door and they're in. Jack doesn't wait, he follows closely behind the house entry team, joining in the shouts as each room is declared clear. Except for the last. In a living room at the back, the air thick with cigarette smoke, a thin crumpled man sits in front of a decrepit television set.

Jack approaches him; the man looks up through saggy yellowed eyes. Jack expects some sort of recognition, that even after all this time, the man would know who he is. The police officer whose life has been dedicated to finding his best friend, who's spent the majority of the last thirty years alone, blaming himself for his disappearance. But all the man sees is another copper. A detective about to ruin his day.

'Can't you wait,' the man croaks. 'I want to know whodunnit.'

The television is playing an episode of *Midsomer Murders*; Jack reaches for the heavy remote control and mutes the sound.

'Jimmy Smith?' Jack asks.

The man sneers. 'What d'you think I've done this time?'

'I am arresting you on suspicion of the abduction, rape and murder of Theo Nkosi in July 1994. You do not have to say anything, but it may harm your defence if you do not mention when questioned something you later rely on in court. Anything you do say may be given in evidence. Do you understand?'

Jimmy's face crinkles into a frown, every line adjusting and settling into a new expression, like a tree growing over time. 'Who d'you say?'

'Theo Nkosi. He was eleven.' Jack should stop, stop right now and take him into custody, but he needs to see the realisation as it dawns on this man's face. He wants to see some sort of guilt, or regret, or even anger, that he's finally been caught. 'Your girlfriend Angela hit him with her car in July 1994. You took him. You held him captive. You abused him. And then you killed him.'

Jimmy blinks. Jack can see his eyes flicker, searching for a glimmer of recognition in his addled skull. He frowns, latching onto a memory, then looks back up at Jack.

'Yeah. Yeah, that kid. I remember. He were no good. Angie did a number on him when she hit him with the car – he were too injured to be much fun.' A leer forms. 'I know you. I saw you on television. You were his mate. Now you… You were more my type. Rich little white boy. I would have had more fun with you.'

Each word hits Jack like bullets to the chest. The hatred, the rage burns. For the first time, Jack understands why people kill. How, in a moment of fury, you could place two hands around another human's neck and squeeze until you feel their last fetid breath express on your cheek, until they're helpless and limp in your hands. Jack's barely breathing, barely able to think.

He takes a step towards Jimmy. There's only the two of them in the room. Nobody to stop him. The man stares up, limp and defenceless in the armchair.

'Go on,' the man wheezes. 'Give in. Get your revenge. Give me the ending I deserve.'

Jack forces his arms back to his sides. He opens his fists, stretches stiff fingers wide. This man deserves to be locked up in a prison cell with a thousand hardened criminals – vicious men who dislike paedophiles more than any other. Who will rip this man to shreds, day after day. He doesn't deserve to die peacefully, here in his own home. Theo demands justice.

Jack steps back; Jimmy sags in his seat as two uniforms enter the room.

'Take him out of here,' Jack manages, his voice little more than a croak. 'Get him out of my sight.'

Jack turns, retraces his steps. Outside, it's still pouring, but the cold provides relief as Jack tips his head up to the sky, letting the rain soak his hair, his face. Wash him clean of the hatred, the anger that still burns in his muscles.

He hears shouts, calls from the back garden. His name bellowed over the pounding of rain on concrete.

He follows the noise through an open gate, out into the overgrown back garden. Brambles grasp at his trousers, nettles spike his skin, but he doesn't stop, striding across to the small figure on the opposite side, a dog lead gripped in her hand.

He can just make out the small black spaniel in the darkness. He's leaping joyously, a ball on the end of a rope in his mouth. And Jack knows what that means. The dog has done his job.

He has found a body.

Lucy looks over at him. Her face is pale, lit only by torchlight, her mouth downturned. She's standing next to a blue tarpaulin. What might have once been a vegetable patch, bordered by rotted planks of wood.

He should wait for the SOCOs, but nothing is stopping him now. He pulls on blue latex gloves, and bends down, moving one of the rocks from the corner of the tarp. The plastic is immediately caught in the wind, fluttering and cracking as it tugs away, revealing a patch of wet, dark mud. Jack grabs the corner and reveals the rest of the dirt, a small square patch of ground. The click of a torch and, for the first time in thirty years, Jack is back where he belongs. Where he always felt happiest. Next to his best friend.

For in the mud, worn away by years of decay, is an unmistakable sight. What Jack's been waiting for most of his life.

Small white bones, emerging from a shallow grave.

CHAPTER FORTY-EIGHT

In that moment, everything collapses. Jack's mind splinters – the sight of that white bone, the freezing cold rain, everything he's thought and worried about and been accused of – it all comes down to this.

He steps away from the grave, his legs weak as he rests his hands on his knees, back bent. Tears mix with the rain on his cheeks; he wipes them away his hand, then presses his palm against his chest, trying to assuage the pain, the thumping of his heart. He gasps; small, stuttered breaths, and then he's on his knees in the mud, still staring at that white, *white* bone as people bustle around him. Theo's face flashes in his head. His grin, his impression of a T-rex that would reduce Jack to peals of hysterical laughter. This – this white, *white* bone – is all that's left.

He feels hands on his shoulders, someone next to him. A wet nose shoves into his face, soaking black fur settles in his lap. He ignores the pouring rain, the dirt, the noise, and lowers his head, meeting Moss's black muzzle. The dog licks his face; he doesn't react. Doesn't mind.

'Jack. Jack, please.' Lucy's voice. She tugs at his arm, trying to pull him to his feet. But he's tired, so fucking tired. He doesn't want to move. Can't.

He tries to protest but his voice breaks and the only noise that comes out is somewhere between a grunt and a cry.

'Jack, we need to go,' she says. 'You can't be here anymore.'

Another hand on his arm. A face peers down at him, a ghostly figure in a crime scene suit. Fran. The forensic pathologist called out to view the body.

The body.

Theo.

He gulps back a sob, and is suddenly aware of the people around him. Watching – a DCI, the senior officer at a crime scene. He staggers to his feet; with Fran's help, Lucy pulls him away to her car, forcefully pushing him into her passenger seat. She closes the door, and he hears her coax Moss into the boot. She gets in next to him.

'I'm taking you home,' she says. He nods, gaze fixed on the dirt drying on his hands, crusted under his fingernails. The same mud—

The same mud that's been surrounding Theo for the last thirty years.

Lucy drives, turning heaters to full blast. It makes no difference. Jack's soaked to the skin, infused with a chill that's eaten its way to his bones, frozen him from the inside. He starts to shiver.

He doesn't remember the drive. Only Lucy heaving him out of her car, propelling him up the driveway to his front door. She has his keys, somehow, he doesn't remember giving them to her, but he must have, she has them, how does she have them? Thoughts rotate in his head, mangled and confused as she helps him inside. She places two hands on his face, forcing him to look at her.

'Are you okay? Jack? Do I need to call someone?'

Who? Who would she call? He feels numb, utterly exhausted. He can't talk, can't think. He could collapse here, in his hallway, nobody would care. Least of all him.

'You're shaking.' She takes his hands in hers. 'You're freezing. Fuck. We need to get you warm.' She starts tugging at him again, up the stairs towards his bedroom. He walks on autopilot, little more than a shuffle, dripping on the carpet, muddy footprints.

He hears running water, and then he's back in the rain, but this time it's warm, soothing. He looks up. He's in his shower. Fully clothed. Doesn't care. He doesn't care about anything anymore. He slides down the glass to the floor, slumps at the bottom, watching the mud run from his clothes, his hair, his shoes.

'Stay there,' Lucy says from outside. As if he's going anywhere.

He hears her footsteps thump away.

He is alone. His best friend is dead. Killed, tortured, abused. The images from the photographs flash in his head and he squeezes his eyes shut but there they remain, indelibly carved on his brain. The confusion, the fear, the pain Theo must have experienced before he died. Crying out for his mother.

Nobody came.

He died alone.

Jack can't hold it back now. Small cries break as he places his hands over his face and lowers his head to his knees. His shoulders shake, great racking sobs as the tears come, as everything he's held in, everything he's tried to forget comes to the fore. That's it. Here. Now. This is what he's reduced to. A grown man, howling, while the mud from an unmarked grave, from the boy he failed to find for thirty years, washes in circles down the drain.

CHAPTER FORTY-NINE

Lucy stays with Jack. She's checked on Moss – dried him off and fed him, leaving him contented in the back of her car – and now she sits cross-legged on the tiles next to the shower as the bathroom fills up with warm steam. She waits. His shoulders convulse, but his head stays bowed. He doesn't look at her. Time ticks by until she senses his tears abating and looks over. He's staring at her. Hair plastered to his forehead, clothes stuck to his skin.

'You shouldn't be here,' he croaks.

'Why not?'

'You should be... with him.'

'Fran's looking after Theo. He's in good hands.'

He's no longer shaking; his skin is restored to a healthier shade of pink. She gets to her feet, turns the shower off, then reaches out her hand. He takes it; she pulls him to his feet, hands him a towel.

'Get changed,' she says. 'I'll cook you something.'

'Hell, no,' he says, with a flicker of a smile. The normal Jack returning. Reassured, she heads downstairs.

Cooking, for her, is no more than shoving a ready meal in the microwave, something even she can't mess up. Luckily, Jack has a pizza in his freezer; she unwraps it and throws it in the oven while she checks on Moss.

The spaniel is fast asleep in his crate in the back of her car, filling the estate with the musty smell of warm dog. As she opens the boot, he gets to his feet.

'Do you want to come in?'

His eager panting answers the question and she opens the grate, grabbing a dog towel and directing him in through Jack's open door. As the pizza cooks, she towels Moss off for a final time, the dog accompanying the rub-down with satisfied grunts.

She can hear movement upstairs, and wonders at Jack's state of mind. Rosie Logan is still missing, and his reaction to finding Theo's body was so all-encompassing she can't see how he can possibly go back to work. But the Jack that emerges ten minutes later seems more his usual self. In grey joggers and a sweatshirt; he smooths his towel-dried hair down with his fingers and sits at the table.

'How are you doing?' she asks.

'I'm sorry,' Jack replies, staring at his feet as he puts socks on. 'I'm sorry you had to see that.'

'Jack.' She waits until he looks at her. 'I get it. I've been there. Grief – it's changeable. Sometimes it's nothing, like a touch of nostalgia, and sometimes it hits you like a freight train. It's been over two years since Nico first disappeared and some nights I miss him so much I feel physically ill. You need to take some time. To process all of this.'

Jack shakes his head. 'Not this week. Not while Rosie's still missing.'

'There are other detectives who can take over. Other—'

'No. My priority right now is to get Rosie home safely.'

Lucy studies him closely. He's still pale but the look on his face is sheer determination. 'Jack,' she begins. 'It's been four days. You and I both know that the chances of bringing Rosie home alive diminished within forty-eight hours. We're looking at murder here.'

'Do we have a body?'

'Jack—'

'Do we?'

'No.'

'Until we have a body, I have to assume that Rosie's still out there.' He catches Lucy's expression. 'I'm not an idiot. I know the most likely explanation is that either someone has abducted her, or she's dead. But I'm going to choose to assume the former, until I know otherwise. There's nothing I can do for Theo right now, but I can help Rosie.' He glances around. 'Is something burning?'

'Oh, shit!' Lucy jumps to her feet and opens the oven. A plume of black smoke emerges, along with a charcoaled pizza. She plonks it on the oven top and stares at it disapprovingly, hands on hips, as if it's the pizza's fault. 'It's not *completely* ruined.'

'Beans on toast it is,' Jack replies.

Beans on toast works just fine. Lucy smothers hers in salt and pepper and cheese; Jack opts for a more restrained sprinkling. They eat in silence, and by the time they've finished a little more colour has returned to Jack's cheeks.

He places his knife and fork together on his plate and looks at Lucy. 'Will you do something for me?'

'Anything.'

'Will you phone Fran?'

Lucy glances at the clock. 'She won't know anything yet. She'll have hardly got the bones out of the ground.'

'She'll have a preliminary assessment. I need to know. Please.'

Lucy sighs. She has her misgivings about Jack being privy to the ongoing investigation, but she knows how much that desperation burns. As a police officer your mind turns over the worst scenarios, until the line between reality and the horrors you've seen through your career blurs.

She places her phone on the table between them and calls Fran on speaker. When she answers it's clear that Fran's still at the crime scene.

'Lucy, it's early days, you know that.' Fran almost shouts to be heard over the noise of the rain drumming on canvas.

'I know, but… Jack is with me on speaker. Can you tell us anything?'

A long pause. Then, 'Hold on a moment.'

There's rustling, squelching footsteps and a car door opening and closing. A long sigh as Fran comes back on the phone.

'That's better. At least I'm in the dry now. Hi, Jack. You shouldn't be involved, you know that.'

'I know. Lucy's told me already.'

'I can tell you what I know so far, and it's not much. The body has been in the ground for a long time. We're talking complete skeletonisation, but I'll need to get a forensic anthropologist to date the bones more accurately.'

'But?' Jack says.

'But I believe this is Theo Nkosi, yes. I'm sorry, Jack. There are fragments of clothing on the body. Natural fibres like cotton or linen decompose fairly quickly but this was polyester, rubber, plastic. A pair of shorts. And trainers.'

Jack puts his hand over his mouth and screws his eyes shut.

'What colour were the shorts?' he says after a moment.

'Navy blue. Same as—'

'Same as Theo was wearing. It's him, Fran. Have you found any damage to the bones?'

'We're still getting him out of the ground. But yes, I've noticed two previously healed breaks – his right humerus, and right clavicle.'

'He fell off his bike when he was nine. Broke his arm and collar bone. Any new fractures?'

Another pause. 'Two broken ribs, fractured skull. For now.'

'Injuries consistent with being hit by a car?' Lucy asks.

'Maybe. I'll know more when I'm able to properly examine the bones in the mortuary. Probably tomorrow, before you ask. I've got to go.'

Fran hangs up. Jack runs his hands down his face.

'Stop staring at me,' he says. 'I'm fine.'

'You're not fine. An hour ago, you were almost catatonic in my car.'

'I'm better now. It was a shock. It's still a shock. I don't need a babysitter.'

'I just want to know you're okay.'

Jack turns to her, two deep ridges between his eyebrows. 'I am not okay. I will never be okay. Would you say you are?' Lucy frowns, then shakes her head. Jack continues, 'I will always regret not walking back with Theo that day. That we were running late, that I was more worried about my mother being angry with me than making sure Theo got home. I am furious with the detective in charge of the investigation for not being able to find out what happened in thirty years – thirty bloody years! – when it took you three days.'

'I had a lead to pursue,' Lucy says softly.

'But you were suspicious of that witness. And you followed up on her, something he should have done in ninety-four. My heart is breaking for what happened to Theo, but if I feel bad, I can't imagine how his family is feeling right now. And I hate myself for being too scared to call Sophie, for not knowing what to say, how to help her.'

Lucy picks up his phone and holds it out to him. 'Say that. What you just told me. Be honest about how you're feeling. And be there for her. That's all that matters.'

He takes the phone from her with a faint smile. 'Thank you,' he says. 'For persisting. And for finding Theo.'

Lucy returns his smile and gets to her feet. 'Call me. Anything you need.'

'I will. You'll follow up on the post-mortem?'

'Tomorrow,' Lucy says, and, with a final squeeze of Jack's shoulder, she calls Moss to heel and leaves, closing the front door with a quiet click behind her. She waits for a moment, listening, then hears the murmur of Jack's voice, talking on the phone.

She's glad he's reaching out – that he'll talk to Sophie and Wendy and maybe they'll end up reconciled. She's glad he has someone.

She thinks about her own family – her father with his new wife, up in Newcastle. And her mother, dead. None of them have been there for her. After everything she's been through it takes a lot for her to trust someone and she can count them on one hand. Fran. Jack.

And more recently, one other.

She takes her own mobile out of her pocket. Pulls up a number on the screen, and dials.

'Pete?' she says, when he answers. 'Can I come over?'

CHAPTER FIFTY

Lucy's never been to Pete's before. The address he's given her takes her to the last house in a quiet cul-de-sac. It stands out from the others: detached, distinctive with a high fence running the whole way around the boundary. There's a sign next to the buzzer:

> RING THE BELL. DO NOT ENTER. WARNING: DOGS.

She presses the button, smiles as a cacophony of barking rings out.

'Come in,' the voice says at the other end. 'Pepper! Shut the fuck up.' Then it cuts and an electronic buzzer releases the gate. Moss at her heels, she shuts it firmly behind her and walks down the gravel drive, past Pete's police Ford Mondeo and his own huge Volvo XC90. The front door opens as she gets closer and Pepper barrels out, greeting Moss with a bounce and a sniff.

'This is nice,' Lucy says with a meek smile. 'Friendly.'

'I live in a fenced compound, I know,' he replies. He leans down and says hello with a chaste kiss on the cheek. 'But early days I had more than one GSD – and the last thing I wanted was the postman being savaged. Now he just lobs the parcels over the gate and lets Dax do his worst.'

He shows her inside to a warm, cosy living room. The spaniels immediately get comfortable on a sofa covered with dirty blankets, curling themselves into a single warm, furry ball.

'Is Dax in his kennel?' Lucy asks.

'Yes, I don't let that reprobate in the house. Iggy at home?'

'Best place for him.'

Pete nods. 'Tea? Coffee? Something else?'

'A beer would be amazing, if you have one.'

'Peroni okay?'

'Thank you.'

The conversation is stilted, reduced to awkwardness by their previous argument. Pete's manner is subdued; she senses he doesn't want to start anything new – the ball is in her court to make things better. She sits down on the nicer, cleaner sofa and waits.

He returns with two beers, hands one to her and takes a seat at her side. He's dressed in off-duty casual: worn jeans, a woolly jumper with a hole in the sleeve. His hair is unstyled in soft peaks, slightly fluffy. It's a good look. She likes it.

'I want to explain,' Lucy begins, unsure of where to start. She remembers her advice to Jack. *Tell her how you feel.* 'You've heard about my husband?' she says.

'I've picked up some. Rumours around the nick.' He shrugs, apologetically. 'I'd prefer to hear it from you, though.'

Lucy takes a long breath in. She has to trust him, otherwise where will this lead? She desperately wants to find out. 'He was… He was a shit. He was abusive, both physically and emotionally, especially when he drank, which was most of the time. He had his good side, but as our relationship progressed, I saw less and less of the man I married, and more of a man I hated. But I stayed. Because I loved him. Even though he stole confidential information from me that nearly lost me my job. Even though one day he beat me so severely I thought he might kill me. Then he went missing, and I lost my mind, until I – or rather Moss – found him. And we discovered he was tortured, and then murdered, and you can't hate a murdered man, can you?'

This all comes out in a garbled rush, Lucy staring at her hands. After she stops, she barely dares to look up at Pete. When she does, he's staring at her, his brow furrowed.

She can't make out his expression, and in his silence, she tries again. 'He was often jealous. And that made him angry. And when he was angry—'

'So when I was jealous about Ellis?' Pete says, his voice soft. 'And I was angry? That was the worst thing I could do.'

'I didn't think you were going to hit me,' Lucy adds quickly. 'But yes, I reacted instinctively. I just wanted to get away from you. Fight or flight. I fell over. That wasn't your fault, I'm sorry.'

Pete shakes his head. 'No, I'm sorry. I have no claim on you, Lucy. You're free to do whatever you want with whoever.'

'But I don't want. I mean – with Jack.' Lucy tries for a smile; it comes out slightly twisted. 'Jack and I, we're just friends. There's nothing going on between us.'

'Are you sure? Because you seem close.'

'We are, I guess. But not in that way. He was there for me when I was searching for Nico. He was the only one who believed me. So this week – when everything went wrong for him, I wanted to help. In any way I could.'

'You found the boy, didn't you? Tonight. I saw search teams had deployed and SOCO had been called.'

'Yeah. We found him. It's awful, Pete. For all this time.'

He reaches out, encloses her hands in his. He's warm and reassuring. 'You did a good job. You and Moss.'

Moss opens an eye at his name. 'Stay there, mutt,' she directs to him. She's close to tears; she's tired, but she feels so restless she might never sleep again. 'And it's only the start. There's the post-mortem, the interview. I know I could hand it over now, but I want to see it through. That part at least.'

'I get that.' He hesitates. 'How can I help?'

'Just being here, that helps. I know I haven't been the easiest person to be around. Work taking over, standing you up last night. Tomorrow's my last rest day. I'm back at work on Monday.'

He looks up at her, his head slightly tilted down, his dark, irresistible eyes meeting hers.

'Are you busy now?'

She smiles. 'Not for the next few hours.'

'We can do a lot in a few hours.'

'We can? Like what?'

He leans forward and gently kisses her, winding his hands into her hair. She responds, kissing him deeper, and as they fall back on the sofa a flurry of brown and white and black fur leaps on them both.

'Fuck! Dogs!' Pete exclaims, as two overzealous spaniels force their way between them. Pete jumps up. 'No, you jealous monkeys,' he says to Moss, as the dog settles next to Lucy, a smug expression on his face. 'This is not about you. Come on.'

He whistles; both spaniels look up eagerly as he coaxes them out into the kitchen. After a moment, Lucy hears the familiar slam of a wooden kennel door, then Pete returns.

'Gave them a Kong each from the freezer. That'll keep them busy.' He grins. 'Now, where were we?'

'I believe you had your tongue in my mouth,' Lucy says as Pete collapses next to her.

'That can't be right. How ungentlemanly.' He slides a hand up her top. 'I would never do such a thing.'

'You wouldn't? That's a pity. Because I was hoping you would do it again.' She reaches down, toying with the button on his jeans. 'And maybe a little more.'

'Really? You mean like this? And this?'

And Lucy groans, appreciating Pete's efforts, and she wonders why she's put this off for so bloody long.

CHAPTER FIFTY-ONE

With Lucy gone, the house suddenly feels empty. Jack regrets letting her go, but he's a grown man. He's survived by himself for this long, he'll be fine.

Sophie hadn't answered the phone when he tried to call her. Unsurprising; she needs to be with her family. He left a message. Jumbled, hesitant: formal words of condolence mixed with stuttered apologies. He hates himself for who he's become. This mess of a man.

To distract, he busies himself tidying the kitchen, then heads upstairs with a bin liner to find his suit, abandoned in a muddy, wet pile on his bathroom tiles. He'll never wear it again and pushes it inside the bag, then mops the soaked floor as best he can with the nearest towel.

That'll have to do. He can barely think; he's exhausted. He flops into bed, pulls the covers over his head, wishing for oblivion. His brain doesn't comply, spitting out memories of Theo, his face, smiling, laughing, interspersed with rain and mud and white, white bone.

When the doorbell first rings, he imagines it as part of his dream world. But then it comes again, and again, and he pulls himself to a sitting position, squinting at the clock. It's late, just past midnight, and the thought of who it might be pulls him into a panic, his heart racing. Something else has happened, something worse. Scenarios scroll through his mind as he takes the stairs two at a time, throwing open the door. He expects Lucy, or a copper in uniform; he's thrown when he sees Sophie.

She's in a big coat, scarf up to her nose. The rain has stopped but the cold air is biting. He ushers her inside.

'Sophie… are you…? What's happened? Are you okay?'

'Yes, I'm fine. I—' She shrugs, shaky as she unbuttons her coat. 'As fine as I can be, given…' And her face collapses and she starts to cry. Jack reaches forward, enveloping her in a tight hug. His tears mirror hers, but he doesn't hesitate, just holds Sophie to his chest, pressing his face into her hair. After a moment she lets go, looking up at him with a halting laugh.

'I was coming here to see you,' she says, swiping first at her face and then gently reaching up to his. 'I didn't want to make things worse.'

'Never. Here, come through. Sit down.'

He ushers her into the kitchen, aware of what a state he must look. Tracksuit bottoms, sweatshirt, hair askew, haggard from days without sleep.

'Would you like tea, coffee?'

He doesn't wait for an answer, but goes to the kettle, putting it on and trying to smooth his hair down in the reflection in the window. She joins him, watching him for a moment. Then she wordlessly reaches up, takes two mugs down from the shelf. He opens the cupboard, holds out the teabags; she nods.

They make the tea without conversation, Sophie fetching milk from the fridge, Jack dropping the teabags into the bin. He passes her a mug, and together they go into the living room, sitting on the sofa.

He waits for her to speak. She's cupping the scalding mug in both hands, looking into the depths like it might hold her future. He can't imagine why she's here.

'How's your mum?' he asks after a long pause.

'Not good. Harry and Leo are with her.' She looks up at last. 'I got your message.'

The voicemail seems inadequate now. 'I'm sorry,' Jack says. 'I wanted to come and see you, but I didn't want to intrude.'

'You are always welcome.' She swallows. A single tear rolls down her cheek; she wipes it away. 'He was there, all this time? In that man's garden?'

'We think so, yes.'

'And he was alive? In that house? For how long?'

'We don't know yet. I'm sorry, Sophie. We'll find out more over the next few days.'

'But they can do that? Work out what happened?'

'I hope so.'

She looks up to the ceiling, her mouth stiff, obviously trying to stem the flow of tears. Feeling helpless, all he can do is watch, knowing how she feels.

'I keep on imagining him there,' she says, her voice choked. 'What he must have gone through. And how we… they… did nothing.'

'They tried—'

'They didn't! They went after you! And us. Focused on his family, and his eleven-year-old best friend. What sort of detective does that?'

Jack shakes his head. There are no excuses. Would he have done any different if he'd been in charge? He can't help but make parallels to Rosie – his first thought that day was Maria and Tony Logan. And there are still so many questions left unanswered. Who is the woman in the video? Is the drug dealer involved? Where is Rosie now?

Is she safe?

Is she dead?

Can he find her?

'And how are you?' Sophie asks.

'I'm… you know.' He smiles, weakly. 'I had a minor breakdown at the grave site. Lucy had to drag me home.' That burn of embarrassment again. What his colleagues must have thought, seeing him like that.

'Lucy…' Sophie says quietly. 'She's the one who found him.'

'She is.'

'She's a friend?'

'A good one. Nothing more,' he adds after a pause.

Sophie looks at him, stifling a grin. 'I didn't ask.'

'You didn't need to.' He hesitates, desperate to know. 'And you?'

'No. There was. A teacher, at my school. He was nice, handsome. Kind.'

'I hate him,' Jack says, meeting her eyes with a smile.

'We broke up. He didn't understand. It's hard, you know. Explaining. Why our family always feels incomplete. The place missing at the table. He said I was always holding back.' She shrugs. 'Maybe I was. Difficult to believe in a happy ever after when you know first-hand how things can go wrong.'

He looks across at her. A few curls fall gently across her face; she's beautiful, here, in the dim light of his living room. Nothing has changed. He still loves her. Always has.

'Why are you here, Sophie?' he says. Then realising his bluntness, quickly backtracks, 'I'm glad to see you, more than you know, but I thought… you and I… we were over.'

'Even though we're not together, you're still an important part of my life. When I heard about Theo, that they'd found him, when I stopped worrying about Mum, the first person I thought of was you.' She pauses; Jack waits, not knowing what to say. 'Can I stay tonight?' she continues. 'Not like that. Just… I want to be near you.'

'Of course. The spare room—'

'With you.'

'Okay.'

He doesn't know what this means, but he's too tired to care. He places his empty mug down on the side table, and gets up, holding out his hand and pulling her to her feet. They walk upstairs, turning lights off as they go, still hand in hand until they get to the bedroom. His duvet is rumpled, his room is a mess, but he points to the bathroom. 'You use the en suite. Do you want something to sleep in?'

She nods; he hands her a clean T-shirt from the drawer, and she goes into the bathroom. He uses the one down the hall, and when he comes back, she's in bed, just her head poking out of the covers. He turns the light off and climbs in next to her, still in his joggers and T-shirt. He's not sure what she wants, but the last thing he wants to do is overstep, so he turns his back, keeping firmly to his side of the bed.

He can hear her breathing. He tenses as she shifts next to him, hyper aware of every movement she makes until he feels her warmth, her breath on the back of his neck as she nestles against him. Her arm wraps over his body and finds his hand. He grips it, gently rubbing his fingers against her thumb.

He hears her crying softly, wet tears soaking into the back of his T-shirt. He doesn't let go and slowly she calms. Her breathing slows; her hand releases his. She sleeps.

He's glad he's provided some comfort to Sophie. But her sorrow only reminds him of the people left behind. Of Tony and Maria Logan, trapped, waiting to hear news of where Rosie has gone.

When he joined the police force, his resolution was to solve the case. Whatever it was. Find the killer. Give peace to those left behind. And with Rosie Logan, he's failing.

He can't let the Logans go thirty years without knowing.

He left his team alone for most of the day, and while he's safe in the knowledge they're tireless in their work, he's also aware he's deserted his post. That can't happen again.

Next to him, Sophie has rolled away, and now he turns onto his front, resting the side of his body near hers. Just her being here, it's enough. Enough to soothe, to let him slip away. A few hours' sleep. And then, he resolves, tomorrow. All this will end tomorrow.

CHAPTER FIFTY-TWO

A few hours turn into more, and by the end of the night, Lucy has a new-found appreciation for Pete Nash's athleticism. After, Lucy lies sleepy in the crook of Pete's arm. His hand idly caresses her hair, until it pauses, drops, and she realises he's asleep.

She shifts carefully away from him then lies on her side, watching him in the dim light from the half-closed curtains. She wonders how she got this lucky. From what she's seen of his house, the private Pete Nash is no different from his outward persona. He doesn't seem bothered by material goods; his furniture is comfortable but worn, clothes simple but nice – T-shirts and jumpers bought in the multiple when he finds something he likes. In the kitchen, mugs are mismatched, all adorned with mutts of various shapes and sizes, no doubt presents over the years for an uncomplicated man with no interest other than dogs.

And boy, does he love his dogs. Lucy's known that from seeing him working with Dax and Pepper, but from the fences around the perimeter to the blankets on the sofas, his whole house is built to suit them. She likes that about him. She likes that Moss and Iggy fit into this arrangement without fuss, that Pete understands a life that revolves around two messy animals.

And as she drifts off to sleep, for the first time in a while, she can see a future.

–

The deep sleep doesn't last for long. She wakes while it's still dark, Pete's arm thrown over her body, and takes reassurance in the solid pressure, the comforting warmth of him. In the night, Theo has returned. His bones may have been found but the case is far from settled.

She wants to finish what she started. For Jack, and for Theo. To sit down, face to face with the man who put Theo in the ground. Who stood guard over his body for thirty years and said nothing. She needs to speak to Fran about how Theo died, be there for the post-mortem.

She gently moves Pete's arm from on top of her; he groans quietly and rolls to his side. She climbs out of bed, groping for her clothes and putting them on. The air is cold; she longs to get back into bed, push her naked body against Pete's, but the desire for a resolution is stronger. She can't resist one last kiss on Pete's stubbly cheek; he half opens an eye.

'You're going?' he croaks, his voice husky.

'Just for now,' she says. 'I'll be back.'

He smiles, sleepily, and closes his eyes, almost immediately back in slumber, while she tiptoes out, picking up her boots on the way. She opens the back door, conscious of the noise she is making in the still of what can only be early dawn. Around the back to the kennels, praying she doesn't wake Dax. She opens the door to the spaniels, peering into the bed box. The two dogs are curled peacefully together, and Moss looks up, a black head emerging from the ball of fur. Pepper seems to sense that this is Moss's wake-up call, not hers, so stays inside while Moss gets to his feet, trotting out into the night.

She opens the car, Moss jumps inside, and she gets into the front. She looks at the time. Six thirteen a.m.

She starts the engine. And to her surprise her phone rings.

'Jack,' she says. 'I thought you'd be sleeping.'

'I knew you wouldn't.'

Knowing what she was up to until the small hours, she elicits a small chuckle.

'The *dogs*,' he clarifies, wearily, and she's cheered to hear humour back in his voice. 'You're always complaining about the early starts.'

'I am. How can I help?'

'I had a voicemail late last night from DCI Perry from the drug squad. They've tracked down Maria Logan's dealer – apparently, he had a lot to say. I need you to formally interview with me.'

'Don't you have a team for that?'

'I'm giving them a lie-in. And I knew you wouldn't be able to resist.'

He's right; Lucy's curiosity is on full. 'Why? What did he say about Maria?'

She hears him take a long breath in. 'Not Maria,' he says, and there's decisiveness, steel in his tone. 'Eddie. Everything Eddie Madden has told us is a lie.'

PART THREE

DAY FIVE – SUNDAY

CHAPTER FIFTY-THREE

The drug dealer, Bleecker, is actually called 'Beaker', and it's a nickname. Perfectly suited to this man in front of Jack with his bulbous red nose and shock of bright ginger hair. DCI Perry had easily tracked him down, found him outside a club in Portswood, distributing pills like a Viagra salesman on a Saga cruise. An arrest followed, with an overnight stay at Southampton's finest.

Beaker hasn't appreciated being hauled out of his cell before breakfast, and sits glaring on the opposite side of the table to Jack and Lucy.

'Tell us what you told Perry, and we'll let you go with a caution,' Jack says.

'An' that's all?'

'That's all. But only if you help us find Rosie.'

'You'll give me my pills back?'

Jack gives him a withering look.

Beaker sighs. 'Like I told the guy last night – I don't know where that kid is.'

'But you know Maria Logan and Eddie?'

He regards Jack suspiciously. 'Yeah. For a few years now. I used to see Eddie around. At clubs and the like. His music tastes are more metal than mine, but I like the rockers, they're good for the green. I'd pass on a bit of weed, he'd sometimes come back to mine for a smoke.'

'Just a bit of weed?'

'Recently, yeah. But when I first met him, he was more into ket.'

'Ketamine?' Jack glances to Lucy, her expression echoes his concern.

'He said it chilled him out, worked better than the weed. And he was no trouble, not like some of the guys we get hanging round. He'd shove a bit up his nose and then bliss out for a few hours. Wake up at dawn and get his mum to pick him up. Can you imagine? I don't see many parents that chill.'

'And that's how you met Maria?'

'One day she just said, could I get her something? Out of the blue, looking all posh in her big Land Rover. Baby in the back an' all. Said could I get her some Molly. And she was specific. Didn't want pills, only powder. Some people like it that way – can control how much they take. Charged over the odds, she didn't seem to mind. But then she got to be a pain.'

'Pain, how?'

'She wanted me to drive out to meet her, and do you know how many clients I got out in the New Forest?'

'Not many?'

'Fuck all. She offered to pay for my petrol, but it was the time, y'know? I'm a businessman.'

'You've got overheads,' Lucy murmurs with a hint of a smirk. 'Time is money.'

'Right? She gets it,' Beaker says, jabbing a finger at Lucy. 'I said that was it – on Wednesday. I knew she were trouble. Now look where I am.'

'But you didn't see Maria that morning?'

'No. By the time I got to the park it was full of cops, so I left, quick smart.'

'You didn't speak to Maria? Didn't see Rosie? Or Eddie?'

'No. And I haven't seen Eddie for ages. Like I told that drug cop, not for a few months. Reckon he's embarrassed, like.'

'Embarrassed, how?' Jack asks.

Jack had only managed a quick exchange with Perry that morning, in the car park, standing next to a huge tactical support van. Perry had been his usual egotistical self, standing with his arms folded, legs unnaturally wide apart, jaw jutting like a bulldog.

'Got a situation down at the docks,' Perry said. 'Sunday morning, who's got the energy for that?'

'I owe you one.'

'Yeah, well. Anything to help find that missing child. Reminds me of my kiddies, I'll do anything for those girls. Just ask Beaker about the last time he saw Eddie. Reckon it's not what you expect. Kid's been lying to you.'

Jack had wanted to ease Beaker gently into the revelation, but now they're here, Jack can't hold back.

'What happened the last time you saw Eddie?'

Beaker regards Jack closely, realising this is his ticket out. 'He was off his face, completely out of it. Reckon he'd taken something in the club too, because he wouldn't shut up, just kept on going on about some baby.' Beaker sits back, relishing his moment. 'How he could have been a dad, but she wouldn't let him.'

'She?' Jack says. 'She who?'

'Dunno. Didn't say. He was crying an' all. It was all a bit much, brought the mood right down.'

'But he definitely said he could have been a dad?'

'Yeah. "I would've made a great father." Word for word. Now can I go?'

Jack exchanges a look with Lucy. Beaker's testimony solves nothing, just raises a thousand new questions, none of which Jack can answer.

'Yeah,' Jack says wearily. 'You can go.'

CHAPTER FIFTY-FOUR

'Is Eddie Rosie's father?' Lucy says the moment they're free of the interview room.

'We're still waiting on the DNA results, but he could be,' Jack replies. 'He and Chloe are good friends.'

Jack had filled Lucy in on the salient points of the case pre-interview over a strong mug of tea, and now they walk up to the incident room, trying to make sense of it all.

'But why would Chloe lie,' Lucy asks, 'and say the father is Maria's stepdad? It seems odd. Are you going to get Eddie in?'

'Soon. We need those results back. We need to know for sure before we speak to him. And even if he is, it doesn't answer where Rosie is now.'

'Some connection to the drugs? Maybe Eddie had another dealer?'

'Kidnap a three-year-old for some low-level ket and weed use? Doubt it. Besides, Eddie hasn't left the house since Rosie was taken. He's done nothing to make us think he's involved.'

'Unlike Maria, who screams dodgy at every turn.'

Jack huffs with frustration as he holds the door to the incident room open for Lucy. He hates to admit it, but Lucy's right. Going to the park to buy drugs, lying about everything – from Rosie's biological parents to seeing her ex-husband. Is there anyone in that family telling the truth?

The two of them pause in front of the whiteboard. Five days into the investigation and it's covered in photographs, crime scene images, scribbled notes from multiple hands. Ticks and cross-throughs adorn to-do lists, lines of enquiry ruled out by hours of painstaking work.

Jack glances across to Lucy as she takes it all in. It's still early, just after eight, and harsh overhead bulbs cast Lucy's face into yellow. He knows he must look the same: tired, jaundiced approximations of human beings.

He got four, maybe five hours' sleep before Perry called. But for that time, he slept deeply, not shifting a muscle, better than he had all week. Had it been because Theo had been found? Or because Sophie was there with him? There's no doubt that Sophie's presence has always been a balm to his frazzled mind; even at the worst times in their relationship being with her was always better than being without. But what did it mean, her turning up last night? He hasn't got the brain space to dwell on it now.

'What would you do?' he asks Lucy.

'Start again,' she replies. He tilts his head, curious. She meets his gaze. 'Even I couldn't work like this,' she continues. 'This mess, this disorganisation. And knowing you as I do, I'm surprised it doesn't bring you out in hives. Take it all off. Start again. What do you know for sure about Rosie? Where did she go that day, who saw her, when? And what are the unanswered questions?'

Jack doesn't reply, just starts methodically removing the documents, the printouts, the photos. He lays them on the table next to them, then waits as Lucy finds a damp cloth and wipes it clean.

Already, Jack feels a sense of relief. At the beginning of a case the huge empty white space can feel insurmountable but today, Jack is cleansed.

He scrabbles through the piles and pulls out their first lead – the still from the video that confirmed that on Wednesday morning at ten forty, Rosie Logan was alive.

He points to the foot.

'Five hundred and sixty pounds' worth of designer ankle boot. You don't wear that if you're taking the dog for a walk.'

'Or if you're a poor student like Chloe Winters.'

'Old person boot,' Jack says with a smile. 'Apparently.'

'So we're looking for someone with a decent income, let's say forty or older—'

'Hey,' Jack replies. 'I'm forty. Forty isn't old.'

'You are to kids like Eddie and Chloe.'

'Point taken.'

'Female. With reason to take a three-year-old away from a park, and then not come forward.'

'Which is?'

Lucy sighs. 'Why do people abduct children? Because of a loss of their own. Because they're related to the child. Someone connected to the family, for revenge?' She pauses. 'Paedophiles.'

'Who fits into those categories?' Jack goes back to the mess on the table; he takes photos out and sticks them on the board in turn. 'Chloe Winters and Derek Pope – biological parents, apparently, not that he's aware of that fact. Adelaide Pope – grandmother, as far as she knew, although weirdly, also stepmother, as she's married to Derek. Sean Madden – wants to be with Maria again, so, potential stepdad. Bridget Daley – Tony's mistress. And Gary Ballard. Paedophile, whose car was seen in the area at the time.'

'Who you've since cleared,' Lucy adds.

'We've cleared all these people, one way or another. Searched their houses, checked their alibis. Accounted for every known sex offender in the area.' Jack takes a step back from the board. 'So what are we missing? *Who* are we missing?'

'Could it be a random stranger? Saw an opportunity, took it?'

'Then how did they get Rosie out of there? There's one road in and out, we're going through every number plate.'

'They walked.'

'Not far. Rosie's three. My experience with kids is limited, but I'm guessing your average three-year-old isn't a big fan of walking. Plus, nobody saw them, you've got zero witnesses. They must have hidden her quickly.'

'A car parked a few streets away, near that estate?'

'Then we really are screwed.' Jack runs a finger along the row of photos. Their suspects, one by one. 'What was your first thought when you heard? When you were called out to the park Wednesday morning?'

'That either we'd find her quickly...'

'Or?'

'Or the family had done something to her.'

'That's what I thought, too. But we've been through the Logan family – Maria, Tony, Eddie. Even if Eddie is the father, how does that help us? We know where the three of them were when Rosie disappeared.'

'So you're back to Chloe,' Lucy says. 'The biological mother who wanted nothing to do with her adopted daughter, yet babysat for the family even after they moved away.' Lucy stands closer to the photo of Chloe. 'She lives in Bassett. The Logans live in Fordingbridge. That's a forty-five-minute drive. And she says she did it to earn a little extra cash? Bollocks. She could have worked in a bar. She cares about her daughter. She wants to be part of her life.'

'We searched her house. We found nothing. And, for what it's worth, I believe her.'

Lucy gives him a look but before she can reply, her phone rings. She answers it, listens. 'I'll be there,' she says. She hangs up and turns to Jack. 'I've got to go.'

He saw the name on the screen; he knows where she's going.

'Okay,' he replies. 'And Lucy? Thank you.'

She nods, and he's alone.

He doesn't say anything, barely moves except to organise the last of the evidence. Puts a few photos of the park on the board, next to the map. Summarises the exhibits in his small, neat capitals:

> BLOOD DROPLETS IN WOOD. LOGAN HOUSE CLEAR. DRUGS – MDMA – FINGER-PRINTS, MARIA LOGAN.
>
> EDDIE – FATHER? NEED DNA BACK.

The team arrive, one by one. They take their coats off, join him wordlessly at the board. Amrit, Lawrence, Bates, Gus.

Amrit takes a step forward and presses her finger against the new statement about Eddie. She raises her eyebrows; Jack shrugs.

There's little to say.

Five days since Rosie's disappearance. And they have nothing.

The parallels between this misper and Theo's case, thirty years ago, are clear. If things carry on like this, Rosie will become a statistic. Yet another missing child, whose body won't be found for decades. If at all.

They have to find her. And soon.

CHAPTER FIFTY-FIVE

It doesn't feel right to see bones this small. A lump forms in Lucy's throat as she enters the mortuary and notices the white skeleton laid out on the stainless steel table. Fran stands at the head in full PPE. She spots Lucy and indicates towards where the white coveralls and masks are kept on the far side. Lucy suits up and joins her.

'It took all night to get the bones out of the ground,' Fran says. 'Would have taken longer except he was so close to the surface. The team are still there now.'

Lucy frowns. 'Another body?'

'We don't think so. But best to be sure.'

'Have you slept?'

'Forty winks in my office while the technician was prepping. Otherwise, no.'

Lucy gives her a grateful smile and secures the mask over her face.

'Let's do this, shall we?' Fran pulls her shoulders back, clears her throat. She is no longer a mother of two, she's a pathologist, with an important job to do.

'We're still waiting on DNA, so in the meantime I referred the bones to a forensic anthropologist, Dr Allinson from Southampton University. He knows the circumstances of this case and was keen to come in this morning. He has confirmed what we thought: bones belong to a prepubescent child, aged between ten and twelve, approximately a hundred and forty centimetres tall.'

'Male or female?'

'Hard to tell. Assuming the bones are complete, we can work out sex from the size and shape of the pelvis. However, in this case, the child hadn't yet hit puberty, so the pelvis remains equally paedomorphic, which doesn't help us here. The same applies to other anthropological markers, like the external occipital protuberance and the mastoid process, and the supraorbital ridging above the eyes.'

'But he knows height and age?'

'With a reasonable degree of certainty. Given the close correlation between height and age in children and the predictable rate of growth in the long bones – that is the main bones in the arms and legs, humerus, radius, ulna, and so on – we can say what height we would expect a child to be at a certain age. This child was approximately a hundred and forty centimetres tall, putting them between ten and twelve years of age. And this fits with other findings – there is no second molar, which erupts about age twelve, the pisiform bone in the hand has formed, which happens about age eight in girls, ten in boys, and the ilium has only just started fusing, a bone that combines with other parts of the hip joint between eleven and fifteen. We'll wait for the DNA before we confirm for certain, but Dr Allinson was confident in his findings. We believe this is the body of Theo Nkosi.'

Lucy nods solemnly, looking at the skull, the eye sockets, the teeth. All that remains of the living, breathing child, the son, the brother, the best friend. She takes a centring breath.

'And cause of death?'

'Intracranial haemorrhage as indicated by a fracture of the parietal bone.' She gently picks up the small skull and turns it over in her hand, showing Lucy the fracture lines running along the back of the head. 'A common injury from victims of pedestrian versus car – the force of the car braking sends the victim flying off the bonnet, hitting the back of the head on the concrete. You can see the stain inside the skull, caused by the blood pooling over time.'

'Would he have been conscious?'

'For a while. It's tough to say how long the brain bleed went on for before he lost consciousness, but he would have been confused, vomiting, slurring his speech. Maybe even having seizures.'

Lucy swallows down the sorrow, the hatred towards the person who did this to him. 'This boy would have been obviously ill?'

'Very much so. And in a lot of pain. We found fractures to his right ulna and radius, as well as two broken ribs. Fractured pelvis on the right side, same to right tibia, consistent with being hit by a car. We can't say for sure as we don't have any soft tissue, but he would have been bruised and bleeding. This was one sick child.'

'How long might he have survived like this?'

Fran shakes her head. 'Twenty-four hours, at most. And unconscious for a lot of that.'

Lucy stares down at the skeleton. She can't help but imagine Theo's last hours in the hands of this monster. Her only hope is that he lost consciousness soon after arriving at that terrible place.

'If they'd called 999 when he was hit by the car, might he have survived?'

'It's impossible to say. He had a significant brain bleed, who knows what damage that might have caused. But it would have saved his parents years of worry. And Theo's last moments would have been with his loved ones.'

Lucy thinks about those photographs. The abuse on a small body already injured beyond belief. That someone could look at a child lying in the road, bleeding, and see an opportunity for their sick perverted mind, rather than calling an ambulance.

'When are you doing the interview?' Fran asks, reading her mind.

'In an hour. I wanted to know more from you first.'

Fran steps away from the body and pulls the hood down.

'Do you want a cup of tea?'

'Coffee. And make it strong.'

Fran indicates towards her office and they both pull their suits off. Fran heads to the kitchen and while Lucy waits, she picks up a small toy car from where it sits on Fran's desk and runs it over her hand.

Fran's kids are younger than Theo was. But Lucy knows what this signifies: Fran bringing a keepsake to work, something to keep her close to her own children, to remind her how precious they are. She replaces it on the desk and smiles as Fran comes in, carrying two steaming mugs.

'Raff gave that to me when I left last night,' she says, nodding at the car. 'It's like he knew where I was going.'

'I'm sorry, Fran.'

'You don't need to apologise,' Fran replies with a sympathetic smile. 'You did your job, I'm doing mine. It's important we completed the PM as soon as possible. That family shouldn't have to wait any longer.' She looks at Lucy. 'How's Jack?'

'He was better when I left last night. A bit more colour in his cheeks. But I worry. Rosie Logan still missing. Now this. It's a lot.'

'Did you say that to him?' Lucy nods. 'And what did he say?'

'That he wasn't dropping the case. As I expected. I'll keep an eye out. He'll be okay.'

'It's good he has you.' Lucy tilts her head to one side, studying Fran's face for any hint of an ulterior motive. Fran notices. 'I mean that,' Fran says. 'I like that you're friends. You're good for each other.'

Lucy sips her coffee slowly. 'Pete thought there was something going on between me and Jack. I think I managed to convince him otherwise.' She can't help a small smile; she meets Fran's astonished gaze. 'Last night.'

Fran's eyebrows shoot upwards. 'You… You and Pete Nash?'

'Uh-huh.'

'And?'

'It was good. Really good.'

'I bloody knew it.' Fran chuckles. 'How do you feel about it all today?'

'Fine. Honestly, I do. He's a good man. He's not like Nico.'

'He's not. Now just don't fuck it up.'

Lucy laughs. 'I'll try.'

The moment of levity is appreciated. What happened to Theo weighs heavy on Lucy's mind but now she's filled with resolve, rather than anger and sadness. Her phone rings, Amrit on the other end of the line.

'His lawyer's here,' she says. 'They're waiting.'

'I'm on my way,' Lucy confirms.

CHAPTER FIFTY-SIX

Jimmy Smith has been assessed medically fit to be held in police custody and interviewed, despite what his appearance might suggest. In the harsh light of the interview room, his skin looks yellow and saggy, as if it's cleaving away from the bones of his face under sheer force of gravity. His remaining few strands of hair are wispy and greasy, stuck to his scalp. Nicotine-stained fingers shake.

Lucy starts the recording, recites the cautions.

'It's about time. I've been in there all night,' he says. 'I need a cigarette.'

'You've had food and drink?'

'I need a fag. It's my right.'

'Nicotine is not a human right, Mr Smith. But if you tell us all we need to know then we'll make sure someone takes you out for a cigarette after.'

He glares. 'I've no idea why I'm here.'

'So let me be clear. You were arrested last night for the murder, abduction and rape of Theo Nkosi. Officers searched your house, and while you were in custody last night, you were further arrested for the possession of extreme pornographic images and possession of prohibited images of children. Do you understand now?'

'No comment.'

Lucy glances to the lawyer next to him. The man looks uncomfortable; no lawyer, not even one in criminal defence, wants to be representing a man arrested for crimes as hideous as this.

'I want you to prove it,' Smith says. He looks at his lawyer. 'Don't they have to prove it?'

'You admitted as such to my colleague last night,' Lucy interjects. 'You confessed.'

'I did no such thing. You're making it up.'

'Any witnesses to this so-called confession?' the lawyer says. 'Can you prove my client was under caution?'

Lucy grinds her teeth with frustration.

'I'll take that as a no, PC Halliday,' the lawyer continues. 'So, if you could run through the evidence, that would be a great help.'

'Fine.' Lucy opens the file to the first page. She pushes across a photo – a police mug shot taken less than twenty-four hours ago in this very police station. 'Do you recognise this woman?'

Smith barely glances. 'Should I?'

'Her name is Angela Joseph. She used to be known as Angie Burns.'

His eyes flash. 'That slut. What's she been saying?'

'That on the twenty-eighth of July 1994, she hit Theo Nkosi with her car. And that you placed what she believed to be his dead body in the boot, and drove him away. But we now know that Theo was alive, and you took him to an address in Southampton. Twenty-two, Randall Road. Do you remember that house?'

'I don't remember what my name was in 1994, let alone where I was living.' He chuckles. 'All the drugs. Fucked me up.'

'Okay, fine.' Another photo. An older police mug shot this time. 'This man is Robert Chaplin, known as Bob. Your half-brother. He gave us a statement yesterday stating that in July 1994 he gave you permission to stay at his house on Randall Road. An address you've been living at, on and off, ever since. Giving permission for other people to stay there, a fact corroborated by another witness we arrested this week. Gary Ballard.'

Smith's lip curls. 'That fat fuck. The one time I try to be nice.'

Lucy ignores him, placing another photograph on the table. 'This is a T-shirt found in a locked cupboard in that house. It has since been matched to the DNA of a missing boy, Theo Nkosi.'

Lucy pushes a photo across to Smith. He looks at it with a leer; she pulls it quickly back. 'You don't need to remember him because we can prove you were there. Semen was found on that T-shirt, and this has now been matched to you.'

'So I spunked on a T-shirt. So what?'

'So what?' Lucy can barely believe what she's hearing. She clenches her jaw, feels the pressure ricochet to her forehead. 'You kept Theo in that house. And you abused him.' More photos, copies of the Polaroids, and this time Lucy can't contain her anger. She slaps them down in front of him, one after the other. The lawyer looks briefly, then blanches and turns away. Lucy searches for the one she needs, then pushes it forward, her finger pointing out a part of a back. 'That's you, isn't it, Jimmy? That's your tattoo. We have others, too. Other tattoos, other shots, that we can now match to you. You were there. You abused Theo Nkosi. You raped him. And then, when he died from the horrific brain injuries that Angie inflicted with her car, you took him home and buried him in your garden. We have his body. We know how he died.'

Lucy leans forward, pushing down her repulsion. 'You could have saved him. You could have called an ambulance. But you didn't. You raped a critically injured eleven-year-old boy, you let him die, and then you buried him in a shallow grave in your garden.'

Jimmy glares. 'I didn't know that body was there.'

'No? So why haven't you moved in thirty years? We spoke to the council. They told us that they've offered you countless other properties. Nicer flats. Houses without the damp and the mould that are actually fit for human habitation. But you fought them every time. Why was that, Jimmy? Was that because you knew that the moment you moved out, someone would look under that blue plastic tarp in the garden and they'd find your guilty secret? And you'd go to jail and be beaten into a pulp by the other prisoners for being the dirty, murdering paedophile that you are?'

'No comment,' Jimmy says with a snarl.

Lucy sits back. She gathers the photographs together and pushes them into the file. 'Do you know what, Jimmy? We don't need your statement. We don't care. We have all the evidence we need. You are going to prison for the rest of your pathetic life.'

She picks up the file and stands up; next to her Amrit does the same.

'You've got it all wrong.'

'Save it for your cellmate, Jimmy.'

'I don't give a shit about going to prison. You think I care about a few beatings, the life I've led? Three square meals, health care on site. Nice and warm and dry? No. That wasn't why I stayed in that house all this time.' Lucy turns and the split-second hesitation spurs Jimmy on. He has her attention now. And he likes it. This pathetic man. He has lost everything, but he still wants to gloat. One last time.

'The boy,' Jimmy says. 'I saw him lying there, in the road, and I wanted him. He was mine. For those few hours, we had fun. Me and the boy. And when he died, I wanted him close to me. Forever. That's why I buried him there. So I could go back. See his body. Remember him.'

Bile rises in Lucy's stomach as Jimmy makes a lewd one-handed sign over his groin.

'He'll always be mine,' he says. 'Down here.'

Lucy can't take it any longer. She rushes out of the room, leaving Amrit to conclude the interview, and doesn't stop until she reaches the toilets. The door hits the wall on the other side as she runs into a cubicle, doubles in two and throws up. Again and again, until there's nothing left in her stomach.

CHAPTER FIFTY-SEVEN

Sunday is normally Maria's favourite day of the week. The chores and shopping all done, house clean, it is the day when she will let Rosie do what she likes. No restrictions on sugar or screen time, the two of them will often sit on the sofa and watch Disney and Pixar movies, singing along to *Moana* and *Frozen*. Rosie will put her Anna princess dress on, and Maria will be Elsa, with a long blonde plait. Sometimes even Eddie will emerge and can be persuaded to play Sven if the plot requires a reindeer, Rosie climbing onto his back and shrieking with glee as he gallops around the living room.

But with Rosie gone, there is nothing. The quiet consumes the memories like a black hole, a gaping void where Rosie once was. Maria lies in bed, staring at the ceiling as tears drip down the sides of her face. She makes no attempt to wipe them away, letting them wet her hair, her pillow. Why bother trying? Why move, or eat, or talk? It's been five days.

She closes her eyes. She sleeps. Not properly – she hasn't slept deeply for days – but in a light doze, her senses on alert, waiting for the phone to ring or the bell to go. So when there's a light knock on her bedroom door she wakes with a sharp inhale of breath.

'Mum?' She opens her eyes as Eddie pokes his head around the door. 'Mum, can I come in?'

'Yes, sure.' She sits up, keen to see Eddie and make amends. He's barely spoken to her since he saw Sean and discovered he'd been out of prison for nearly six years without his knowledge. Coming to Maria today must be significant, an easing of his resentment. She hopes so. He edges into the room; Maria pats the bed next to her and Eddie perches on the side.

This boy – this man – who used to be red-faced and angry. Oh, such a furious baby, his hands in tiny fists as he screamed. It seems insane this is who he is now – this six-foot lump, with stubble and a faint smell of sweat. He turns to face her, and Maria is shocked to see he's crying.

Maria reaches out, touches his sweatshirt. He doesn't resist, so she wraps her arms around him and he leans into her, his shoulders starting to shake. She pulls him into her chest, resting her face on the top of his head; his hair smells faintly of weed and tobacco, edged with that bubblegum vape he likes so much. They stay that way for a few moments, until she senses him move away.

Eddie sniffs and wipes his nose with the sleeve of his sweatshirt.

'You should have told me,' he says, 'about Dad.'

'I should have. I'm sorry. I just thought… I worried.'

He looks at her. 'What about?'

'Sean got out in 2018, and you… You weren't doing so well. I worried that seeing your dad would make it worse. When Sean went inside, he was bad news. I didn't want him near you.'

'But Dad's doing okay now?'

'I think so. That's what he says.'

'I'd like to see him. If I can.'

'He'd like that.'

They sink back into silence. A truce, and Maria's glad.

'Mum?'

'Yes, sweetheart?'

'Is Rosie coming home? Are the police going to find her?'

Maria sighs, a lump in her throat. Astonishing she can still cry, after the tears she's shed this week. 'I hope so. I really do.'

Eddie nods. 'I looked up some stats. It said that eighty-one per cent of children are found within twenty-four hours, and ninety-one per cent are found within two days. What does that mean for Rosie?'

'I don't know.'

'Is she dead?'

'*Eddie*. Don't.'

The breach of a wall; the unthinkable, said aloud. She shifts away from him, pulls the duvet back over herself, as if protecting herself from the monsters. He gets to his feet but instead of walking out, as she expects, he makes his way to the other side of the bed, climbing in next to her.

They lie that way for a moment, Maria listening to her son's breathing. Then he turns, his head on the pillow looking at her.

'This is my fault,' he says. She blinks at him, confused. 'It's karma. For… what happened.'

Maria sags. 'Oh, Eddie. This has nothing to do with Maisie.'

He flinches at the mention of her name. 'I feel like the universe is punishing us. Punishing me. An eye for an eye.'

'You don't believe in God. Nor do I.'

He turns away then, his head shoved into the pillow, and she only just hears his words.

'Maybe we should,' he replies.

CHAPTER FIFTY-EIGHT

The DNA results are back. Eddie Madden is not Rosie Logan's father.

'So Beaker was lying?' Lawrence says, clicking on the email repeatedly, as if refreshing will change the data within. 'Shall we get him back in?'

'What's the point?' Jack sags into the chair next to Lawrence, putting his head in his hands. He shouldn't have been so stupid – so eager for leads that he was taking drug dealers at their word. 'Do the results give any indication of her parentage?'

'No familial match to any of the Logan family. Match to Chloe Winters. She's definitely the mother.'

'That's something, at least. Gus, where are we on the full background into the Logans?'

The analyst looks up from his computer. 'We know before Fordingbridge they were living in Swindon – moved there in 2018. And before that they were just outside Manchester, in Didsbury. I'm still digging.'

'Keep me updated.'

Whatever determination Jack had gained from speaking to Beaker early this morning has evaporated. He pulls himself to his feet and goes back into his office, slumping behind the desk. He glances up at the clock. Nearly midday – time marches on, tea gets drunk, biscuits are eaten, but all the sugar and the caffeine in the world won't help them if they can't find one single lead. Just one, he mutters, tilting his head back and running his hands through his hair. Just one.

'You okay?' He looks up. Lucy is standing in the doorway. 'I heard. About Beaker.'

'Yeah.'

'We got him, Jack.'

It takes a moment for Jack to realise what Lucy's talking about, but when he does his consciousness slows into half-time. There is a buzz in his ears; the room shifts to the left.

'Whoa. Put your head between your legs.' Lucy's next to him in seconds, her hand resting on his back. 'Breathe.'

He takes two gulping breaths, staring at the floor. His head swims.

'And again. In, out. When was the last time you ate?'

'Yesterday, with you,' he manages between gasps.

'You told me you'd had breakfast. Fucking hell, Jack. Keep breathing.'

He does as he's told and slowly his vision clears. He sits back up, wobbly but better.

'Theo's killer?' he croaks.

'Going to prison for a long time.' She crouches in front of him. 'Confessed to it all. No way he's coming back from that. I'll get you something to eat.'

'I can't eat. Just feel sick all the time.'

'I don't care. A minute ago you looked like you were going to pass out.'

She straightens up, heads to leave.

'Lucy?' She pauses in the doorway. 'Thank you.'

She nods, with a smile. 'You'd do the same for me.'

He watches her go. This strange friendship, one he's come to treasure – last summer he could barely tolerate Lucy and now she's someone he relies on every day. He hasn't been fair. He told himself he kept the news about her sister quiet to protect her – because she'd been through a lot and he didn't want to pile more on when she was still grieving her husband – but looking at her now, he realises he doesn't give her enough credit. She's come out stronger, with more resolve and determination than he's ever had.

His own instinct for privacy – to bottle up concerns and worries and manage them all himself – it's destructive. Where has it left him? Until last summer, he was alone. Shifting from placement to placement within the force, resolutely single, coming home to an empty house, night after night.

Since meeting Lucy, and being a part of the team at MCIT, he's realised that life can be something more. Yes, it hurts, but it can also be beautiful, and warm, and loving. Where colleagues know exactly how you like your tea and bring you hot food when you're stuck on a shift; where they pull you away from crime scenes when you're having a breakdown.

He realises with a sting that Lucy's parting words were misplaced – he wouldn't do the same for her, he hasn't. He's kept her in the dark, for nine months. Made no effort to find out if Nico's dying words hold any truth. He certainly hasn't used all his rest days and worked every hour to help her. He resolves that once this is over he will be honest. He will tell Lucy and, most of all, he will do everything in his power to get to the bottom of Lucy's missing sister.

He looks up as Amrit and Gus appear in his office doorway.

'You okay, boss?' she asks. 'You look a bit… peaky.'

'I'm fine. Thank you – for getting that bastard locked up.'

'My pleasure.' She beckons Gus inside and the two of them sit at his desk. Gus looks almost comically large in Jack's flimsy office chair; when he leans forward the wood creaks ominously. Amrit nudges him.

'So, as well as looking into the family, I've been doing some work on Chloe Winters, her housemates, anything we can find online.'

'And?' Jack says hopefully.

'And there's nothing. She lives with four med students, second year, like her. None of them have a criminal record, their social media accounts are boring travel photos and drunken nights out. Chloe herself is much the same, minus the social media. She's not on any of the usual sites.'

'Twitter, Instagram?'

'Nope. She's on Facebook, but rarely posts. The only photo is one her mother took – afternoon tea at a nice hotel somewhere.'

Jack pauses, narrows his eyes. A memory surfaces, one of a photograph on the wall at Chloe's house. Her and another woman. Shorter hair, blonde, slim. Older, but definite similarities.

'Tell me about the mother.'

Gus consults his notes. 'Again, not much. Thirty-nine years old—'

'Sorry? Her mother is thirty-nine?'

Gus looks skyward, doing the maths. 'If she had Chloe when she was nineteen, more than possible.'

'I guess...'

'She lives in North Baddesley, just outside Southampton. Moved a year ago.'

'When Chloe moved here to go to university?'

'Presumably.'

Amrit leans forward, taking over. 'And what's more – her name is Rosemary. Rosemary Winters. Chloe named her daughter after her.'

'You're kidding me.'

'Would I?' Amrit smiles. 'She's Rosie's grandmother, she moves house to stay in the same city as her daughter. I'd say they were close, wouldn't you? She would have known Chloe was pregnant – and what happened to the baby. And Jack.' She diverts his attention back to the Facebook photo. 'Here's the best part: look what she has on her feet.'

Jack stares, mouth half-open. He takes in the full body shot. The dress. The coat. *The boots.*

There's no time to waste.

'Let's get down there,' he says, grabbing his coat. 'Let's knock on some doors.'

CHAPTER FIFTY-NINE

Lucy arrives at Jack's office just in time to catch him. She holds out the sandwich.

'Best I could find,' she says. 'Cheese and pickle.'

'No time now,' he replies, slinging his jacket on. 'Got to go. We've found the boots.'

'Then I'm coming, too.'

'What about your dogs?'

'They're fine.'

'Then come on.'

She grabs her coat and follows him and Amrit. They take a pool car; Amrit drives, Jack sits in the front. Lucy's aware she's superfluous to this expedition, but she saw the way the blood drained from Jack's face earlier, and she feels like she needs to stick around. He shouldn't be working, not after last night.

She shoves the sandwich through the gap in the seats.

'Eat it,' she says.

He huffs a sigh, but grabs it, opening it and taking a bite.

'You haven't got a warrant, have you?'

'Nope,' Jack says, his mouth full. 'No time, and I suspect a couple of photos of similar-looking footwear isn't going to cut it. But we have motive – a grandmother desperate for time with her granddaughter. It makes sense.'

'No witnesses, no ANPR?'

'Nope.' He pauses, swallows. 'We're hoping she'll just let us in.'

'Which there's no way she'll do if she has Rosie.'

'Then that answers our question?' Lucy looks at him, dubious. 'I know, I know. But it's worth a try, isn't it?'

Lucy sits back in her seat, marginally reassured as Jack finishes his food.

The house isn't far away from the nick, fifteen minutes, and they park up outside, looking at the pleasant semi-detached with a police officer's eye. A light on in the top window, car in the driveway: somebody home. Minimal entry and exit points – just the front and a side gate, leading to a garden and a back door, no doubt.

'Amrit, go round the back,' Jack says. 'Lucy and I will take the front.'

Amrit nods and the three of them climb out, heading towards the house. Jack goes to knock while Lucy peers in the front window. A living room – television, sofas, coffee table. No sign of toys or anything that would indicate a child being there.

Lucy joins Jack as the front door is opened by a slim, blonde-haired woman. She seems younger than Lucy, hardly a grandmother. They show their ID.

'Mrs Winters? DCI Jack Ellis, Hampshire Police,' Jack begins. 'This is PC Lucy Halliday. Can we come in?'

Lucy smiles broadly, aware she's out of uniform, in jeans and a sweatshirt. But the woman only has eyes for Jack, in his smart suit, looking every inch the respected police detective. And an attractive one at that.

'Rosemary, please,' the woman says. 'And I'm not married.' She moves out of the way to let Jack and Lucy inside and Lucy can't help but smile at her eagerness. 'Is this about Rosie?'

'You're aware she's missing?' Jack says as they're shown through to the same neat living room that Lucy saw through the window. Amrit joins them, sharing a quick introduction and a warrant card.

'Chloe told me. We're both worried sick. I was wondering if you would come and see me. Would you like something to drink? Tea, coffee?'

'No, we're good, thank you. Would you mind if my colleague takes a quick look around?'

'She's not here, if that's what you're thinking. But yes, whatever you like. No shoes upstairs, please.'

Amrit does as she's told and heads up, as Lucy and Jack take a seat on the sofa. Rosemary joins them opposite.

'So you know you're—'

'Rosie's grandmother, yes.' She runs a self-conscious hand through her hair. 'Not that I look it. You don't meet many grandparents that look as good as me, do you?'

Lucy suppresses a grin as Jack flushes, unaccustomed to such direct attention.

'I think, er… no,' he stutters.

Amrit saves him, appearing at the door to the living room, holding a pair of boots, now encased in an evidence bag. Jack beckons her inside; Amrit places them in the middle of the coffee table.

Rosemary looks from the boots, to Amrit, then to Jack again. 'But those… They're not the same.'

'Same as what, Ms Winters?'

'Same as the ones in the photo. Chloe told me. You have a video, or a photo or something. Of a woman taking Rosie away. She thought it might be me, at first. But then… look.' She glances to Jack. 'Can I?'

Jack nods.

Rosemary leans forward and turns the boots around in the bag so that the material presses against the see-through plastic. 'These are last season, see? I got them in the sale, super cheap.'

Jack peers at the boots, then takes a copy of the photo out of his pocket and compares the two. He can't make head or tail of what Rosemary's getting at but both female coppers realise, sitting back on the sofa with a quiet, 'ohhh'.

'What?' Jack says, confused.

'These are suede,' Lucy points out. 'And the ones in the photo – they're leather. See? The way the light reflects off the boot. No way you'd get that shine with suede.'

'Besides, Rosie went missing on Wednesday. I was at work at the hospital. All day – double shift. No way I could have taken her.'

Lucy can see Jack's disappointment, but he recovers fast.

'Does Chloe have any brothers or sisters?'

'Anyone else who might have Rosie, you mean? No. Chloe's an only child. I think that's why she hangs around with that boy. He was always bad news.'

'What boy?' Jack asks.

'Eddie Logan. Or Madden. Whatever his name is. I warned her about him. But she never listens.'

'I thought they were friends?'

She scoffs. 'Yes, I suppose so. But who encourages their friend to make a decision like that?'

Lucy's puzzled. She looks to Jack; his forehead is furrowed.

'Having Rosie,' Rosemary continues. 'Not having an abortion. I told her at the time – that would be the best thing. It was early, no more than a few months along when she realised. It wouldn't have been a problem.' Her gaze shifts to the photographs on the wall – Chloe, varying ages, the focus of all. Her tone turns wistful. 'I didn't want her to make the same mistake I did.'

And then, to Lucy's surprise, she starts to cry. Almost daintily, a small sniff, followed by gentle tears. Jack hands her a tissue from the box on the side.

'Thank you. Look at me, getting all emotional,' she says, dabbing at her eyes. 'Twenty years old and my daughter is brilliant and beautiful and my best friend, but I still think about what I might have had.' She looks at Lucy. 'You must think I'm awful.'

'Ms Winters...'

'Rosemary, please.'

'Rosemary,' Lucy says. 'You're obviously upset. Maybe Rosie going missing has affected you more than you think.'

'No, well, yes. I suppose so. She is my flesh and blood. I remember those early days. They're so vulnerable, aren't they?' She looks at Jack. 'Have you any idea where she is?'

'We're following up on some leads,' Jack mutters, non-committal. 'How well do you know the family?'

'Not very. I met Eddie a few times before Chloe got pregnant. I didn't meet Maria and Tony until Chloe asked me to go with her. For a proper introduction, to see if she wanted to give Rosie to them. And I liked them. Maria particularly. She seemed determined, but also keen to have a baby. Desperate, you might say. I thought that whatever happened, she would look after Rosie. But Eddie.' Her face darkens. 'I didn't like that boy. Especially at the beginning, when I assumed he was the father. He's not, is he?'

'No, he's not,' Jack confirms. 'Do you know who is?'

Her face clouds. 'That man. The one she was with. I wanted to call the police, but Chloe wouldn't let me. I didn't want to make things worse.' She chokes out a laugh. 'And then she was pregnant. At sixteen. Stupid how these things repeat themselves.'

'Chloe's dad isn't on the scene?' Lucy asks.

'Hell no. I was eighteen when I fell pregnant with Chloe. He wanted nothing to do with us. And I was happy with that. But I had plans. I was going to travel, see the world. Then get a degree, become something. Chloe always wanted to be a doctor – that's why I thought she should get an abortion. I didn't want her dreams to become nothing, like mine.'

'Do you know why Eddie was so determined she should keep it?' Jack asks.

'No, not a clue, although Chloe knew something. She said that Eddie didn't want her to make the same mistake he had, whatever that means. I pushed her but she wouldn't tell me any more. But I do know they've moved around a lot. Something rotten in that family. I wish Chloe hadn't given them Rosie. You want to know more about that family, ask him. That boy's not as innocent as he seems.'

–

Lucy, Jack and Amrit leave Rosemary Winters, walking back to the car. They take the boots, just to be sure, but all of them know: she's not got Rosie.

'She asked me to give you this,' Amrit says, passing Jack a scrap of paper. 'In case you needed to "get in touch",' Amrit adds, complete with air quotes.

Jack flushes an even brighter shade of red while Lucy and Amrit smirk.

'Piss off, both of you,' Jack mutters, screwing the piece of paper into a ball as they all get in the car.

'I wish it was that easy for me to get a cute guy's phone number,' Amrit says.

'I thought things were going well with Raj?' Lucy asks, poking her head between the front seats as Amrit drives.

'Too into his gaming. But still on and off.'

'That analyst likes you – Gus?'

'Do you think? He's hot, right?'

'Definitely.'

'I am here,' Jack interrupts. 'And I am your boss. Amrit – leave the poor man alone, he has a job to do. Lucy, stop encouraging her.'

'Roger that, *boss*,' Lucy says with a smirk. She sits back in her seat, mulling over the case and the relationship between Chloe and Eddie. Something's not making sense.

'Explain one thing to me,' she says, sitting forward again. 'Chloe met Eddie when they lived in Swindon, right?'

'Yes,' Amrit replies. 'Gus says they moved there at the end of 2018. Before that they were near Manchester.'

Lucy frowns. 'And then they moved again to Fordingbridge in 2021?'

'Because Tony Logan kept on having affairs.'

'So why move from Manchester?' Lucy says. Jack stares at Lucy. 'That's what I'd be asking. If I was investigating.'

Jack's mouth drops open.

'It's annoying, Halliday,' he says. 'Just how often you're right.'

CHAPTER SIXTY

Jack always forgets that Eddie Logan is twenty years old, a full-grown adult, because here he is in their interview room, six foot tall, and looking every inch like their average offender, pulled off the streets.

Jack reads the standard wording, and Eddie bristles.

'I thought I'm not under arrest. I said no to a lawyer, do I need one now?'

'That's completely up to you. You're not under arrest, but we have to give the caution, even for a voluntary interview like this one. Thank you for agreeing to come in.'

'Mum said I had to,' he mutters. 'Anything to help find Rosie. She said I have to tell you anything you want to know.'

'That's helpful, thank you.'

Jack has Bates by his side; she's smiling warmly, and Jack hopes that her familiar presence will help.

After visiting Chloe's mum, they went straight back to the station. Lucy's assistance has been invaluable, so he's asked her to watch on the video feed, reading through the file, in case something else pops. It annoys him that he missed this, but he's not been top of his game. Theo's case distracted him, and good grief, he really needs some sleep.

'As part of an investigation like this one,' Jack begins, 'we always look into the family and their background in the hope that it turns up something helpful. And we'd like to talk about what we found on you.'

'Me?' Eddie says. 'What about me?'

He shifts awkwardly in his seat, looking at Jack from the corner of his eye.

'Can you tell us about life in Manchester?'

'That was ages ago. What does that have to do with Rosie?'

'We don't know yet. But it's worth asking, in case it helps, right?' Jack tries to keep his tone light, but Eddie is already looking reluctant. His face has turned solemn; he sniffs, and wipes his nose with the back of his sleeve. Jack readies himself for his knockout punch. 'Can you tell us about Maisie Clark, Eddie?'

The mention of the name has the desired effect: Eddie shies away, face pale, pushing back in his chair, distancing himself from Jack as much as he can.

Jack steadily opens the file and pushes a printout across the table. It's a photo of two kids in shorts and T-shirts, standing next to a net, holding tennis racquets.

'We didn't find this before because you used the name Edward Logan instead of Madden back in 2017. Why the name change?'

'I realised that Tony was a dick,' Eddie says.

'This is you and Maisie Clark, isn't it, Eddie? You two were a force to be reckoned with in 2017. Mixed doubles county champions, right?'

'And singles,' Eddie adds, sulkily. 'Three years in a row.'

'You must have been good friends?'

'She was my best friend,' he mumbles to the tabletop.

'What happened, Eddie?'

Eddie stares at his fingers, laced together so tightly they're mottled red and white. Jack lets the silence hang, watching his hunched shoulders. A single teardrop runs down his nose and falls to the table.

'She died, didn't she?' Jack asks softly.

Eddie nods. He sniffs; Bates hands him a tissue. He takes it, wiping aggressively at his eyes.

'She killed herself,' Jack adds.

'It wasn't my fault,' Eddie says. He looks up at Jack, eyes desperate. 'It wasn't.'

They'd got this far. Gus had scoured newspaper archives, finding the reports by accident, assuming Eddie had the same name as his mother. Jack read them in disbelief, the articles showing a different picture of a teenage Eddie than the lad he has met. Muscular, tanned, with short hair and a big smile, they told the story of a tennis prodigy, a boy only reaching his potential when he teamed up with Maisie Clark, a girl from his school who was just as talented. Sports scholarships were discussed, the potential of both of them going pro. And then, in 2018 – nothing.

It all stopped.

Nothing about Edward Logan. Nothing about Eddie Madden.

But plenty about Maisie Clark.

'What happened?' Jack asks.

'She's gone!' Eddie explodes, slamming both hands on the table and looking Jack right in the eye. Bates jumps but Jack doesn't move. 'Okay? Is that what you want to know?'

'What happened?' Jack asks again, evenly.

'She was my best friend. We played tennis, every day, all day if we could. And we were good. I mean, really good. I knew where she'd be when the ball was hit, knew how she'd return it. We first played together when we were thirteen, just kids, and then...'

'You fell in love,' Bates says.

Eddie looks at her, stunned. 'Yes,' he replies. 'We were in love. It wasn't what they said. I didn't talk her into it. I didn't have to persuade her. I didn't want us to sleep together until we were sixteen, but she was one month older than me, and she said it was okay and...'

'And you wanted to,' Jack finishes for him. 'You were a young lad. Of course you wanted to.'

'I guess so,' Eddie says, quieter now. 'But she got pregnant. It was a shock, for both of us. But then...' He shrugs. 'We thought it might be okay. We loved each other.' He cackles at that, a strange noise. 'How naïve we were.

'Her mum went nuts. Said we were ruining our lives – how could we possibly bring up a child? All we knew about was tennis. And... well... we let them convince us. Or rather, Maisie's mum convinced her. Mum said that she would be happy to take the baby on. Bring it up as if it were hers and Tony's, but Maisie's mum had already booked the appointment. They went and… and it was gone.'

Eddie pauses, tears, snot dripping from his nose, looking much younger than his twenty years. Jack watches the boy, and wonders at these parents. These people who thought they were doing the right thing for their children, who unwittingly destroyed them with their actions. He takes a long breath in, knowing what happened next. He has his interviewee on the ropes, ready to talk. And for the first time in his career, he can't bear to ask. So much misery, so much pain. Jack's not sure he can take any more.

But Bates steps in. 'What happened to Maisie?' she says.

Eddie doesn't move, his focus locked on the table. 'Maisie's mum thought that everything would go back to normal. Tennis, GCSEs, the lot. But Maisie wasn't the same. She took her to the doctor – physically she was fine, but mentally. Mentally it destroyed her. She wouldn't stop crying. She didn't want to see me. She wouldn't leave the house, let alone go to school, go to the tennis club. In the end, her mum had to put her in a hospital. You know, one of those mental institutions. And that's where… where she died.' His hands ball into fists; he thumps them both on the table, making the drinks slop and spill. 'She said it was my fault. Maisie's mum,' he says, his voice hard. 'She blamed me. But it was her. If she hadn't… If we had kept the baby, things would have been different.'

'That's why you moved away?'

'Yeah.' Eddie looks up at Jack, his lip curling. 'Tony got involved. He paid Maisie's mum to keep quiet, and we moved to Swindon. Started again. But Tony blamed me. His job wasn't paid as well, he didn't like it much. He said he was bored, and that's why he started sleeping around.'

'It wasn't your fault, Eddie,' Bates says. 'None of it was your fault.'

'I know,' Eddie says, but he's shaking his head, still locked in his guilt.

'And that's why you didn't want Chloe to have an abortion?'

'You know about that?' Eddie replies. 'Did Chloe tell you?'

Bates nods. 'Not about Maisie. Just about Rosie and that you wanted her to keep her.'

'I knew she'd regret it. I didn't want Chloe to feel the same way as Maisie. And Mum agreed. So Rosie became my little sister.' Eddie wipes his eyes even though the tissue is no more than a small white ball. 'But what's this got to do with Rosie? Maisie's dead. That was five years ago. Maisie didn't even know Chloe. Rosie hadn't been born.'

Jack sits back in his seat, Bates's expression mirrored on his face. He's as baffled as she is.

Eddie's friendship with Maisie Clark is sad – desperately so – but it brings them no closer to finding Rosie. Before going in they hoped that Eddie's confession about Maisie would lead to something else. A new revelation: a snippet of something to take them closer to the truth. But all they have is a broken young man, stuck in the trauma of his youth.

Jack's about to admit defeat when there's a bang on the door. Bates gets up as Jack pauses the interview; when she opens the door, Lucy's standing there. Flushed and eager, she holds out a piece of paper.

'I need to talk to you,' she says. 'Now.'

CHAPTER SIXTY-ONE

Lucy could be at home. She could be chilling out, on the sofa with her dogs. Or better yet – in bed with Pete. Yet here she is, in a semi-darkened room, reading through case files while the interview from next door plays on the monitor.

Poor kid. From the sounds of it, everything went to shit for Eddie after Maisie's death. He gave up tennis, flunked his GCSEs and never made it to college. Snorted ketamine with some drug dealer in Portswood and now hangs out in his room, smoking weed, unemployed.

Lucy flicks through the newspaper clippings, the melancholy growing as Eddie tells his and Maisie's story. They were just kids – absurd to think the two of them were prepared to bring up a baby. In love, delusional, or incredibly mature, they'll never know. She turns the page, and here is a photograph of Eddie and Maria next to Maisie and her mother. All smiling proudly, a large silver trophy resting between them. Lucy looks closer at Maria. She seems happy here, almost carefree.

She turns to the next article, when something catches. A glimmer of recognition, a nebulous thought. She looks again at the photo of the kids and their mothers. Does she know Maisie? She's never lived in Manchester, it's ridiculous. But still, something lingers. Like a bad taste on her tongue. She sits back, the page in her hand. Leans over and turns the light on full, so she can look closer.

And that's when she realises. It can't be. *It can't.*

She opens her laptop, logs on to the RMS and types in the name. It comes up blank. She goes back to the case files, rifling through the pages until she finds the one she needs.

The name on the top. The surname's different, a bit less weight, but it's her. It has to be.

She gets to her feet, papers flying, and rushes out of the room, banging on the door without hesitation. Amrit answers. Lucy looks past her to where Jack is watching, confused.

'I need to talk to you,' Lucy says. 'Now.'

'What?' Jack asks when he's out in the corridor, door closed.

Lucy thrusts the witness statement in his face. 'Look,' she says. 'Look at the name.'

'Gemma Brogan?'

'She was the witness. The woman who first helped Maria in the park. She called 999. I saw her. From a distance, but I recognised her.' She holds up the photo of Maisie and her mother. 'This,' she says, pointing to Maisie's mother, 'is Gemma Clark. Gemma Brogan. They're the same woman.

'Maisie Clark's mother was there in the park that morning. At exactly the time Rosie went missing. That can't be coincidence. Can it, Jack?'

CHAPTER SIXTY-TWO

Jack feels light-headed; how could he have been so *stupid*? The woman they've been looking for has been right in front of them the whole time. When they went for Chloe's mother they had the right motive, but the wrong person. A different woman, grieving a child she has lost.

No, it can't be a coincidence. But nor does it make sense. If Maisie Clark's mother, Gemma Brogan, had been there at the exact moment Rosie went missing, where had Rosie been? And how did Lewis finding Rosie in the woods fit into it all?

Whatever the answer, they have to find this woman. And fast.

Amrit goes back into the interview to interrogate Eddie on everything he can remember about Gemma Brogan. Jack heads towards the incident room but Lucy pauses in the corridor.

'Jack, I need to go.' He can see how much she's torn. 'I have to get back to the dogs.'

'It's fine. I get it.'

'I'm sorry. I want to help, but—'

'You've babysat me enough. I'm not going to pass out in the corridor.' He reaches across and gives her a quick hug. 'Go. I'll call you later.'

And he hurries away to be with his team.

Gus is fast, but they quickly realise – there's not much. Gemma Brogan is fifty-three, has been divorced from Maisie's father, John Clark, since 2020. Maisie was their only child. Last known address is in Didsbury, Manchester. Calls are made to Greater Manchester Police and patrol cars stream to the address on file for both Gemma and John.

Gemma drives a red Seat Leon; the number plate doesn't match any of the cars recorded in the area that day, and hasn't been seen since. Units are dispatched to Fordingbridge to scour the area for her car, but in a town with a population of six thousand over nearly fourteen square kilometres, that could take hours. She has no social media accounts except for Facebook which she hasn't touched since her daughter died. Amrit returns, Eddie knows nothing about Maisie's mum. He hasn't seen her since Maisie's funeral. Hasn't heard from her. And why would he?

It makes no damn sense.

They listen to the 999 call. The voice is distorted, wind blowing loudly across the receiver but there's no doubt what she says. She gives her name, her phone number. And then: 'A little girl's gone missing. Rosie Clare Logan. She's three and a half.'

Jack looks at Amrit. 'That level of detail – that's odd. She knows her full name and exact age, when she's only just met Maria by chance in the park that morning?'

'Maria could have told her before she made the call?' Amrit counters.

'Or she was targeting them? Get a trace put on that phone number.' He turns to Gus. 'Go back to the transactions from the shops in Fordingbridge. Cross-reference with Gemma Brogan.'

'I've done that already. Nothing.' He pauses. 'But she might have paid in cash. Let me look at the withdrawals.'

'You have those?'

Gus gives him a look. 'Not a chance. But we do have the CCTV from the cashpoints in the town. See if we can spot her.'

A recent photo of Gemma is distributed, and the team get to work. There are three main cashpoints: one at NatWest, one near the Co-op, and the last one near Tesco. They have footage from all three, given to them in the hope that Rosie passed that way on Wednesday.

By the end of the next hour, they find Gemma Brogan on camera, taking money out of a cashpoint on Salisbury Street, just outside the Tesco Express at fourteen fifty-six that Wednesday afternoon. They speak to the manager who finds the CCTV – she bought whole milk, Petits Filous, baby wipes, bread, carrot sticks, houmous, pasta, tomato sauce, cheese strings, Pom Bears, and chocolate buttons, bundling them into a carrier bag and heading left out of the store.

Rosie wasn't with her, but her shopping and her hurried manner suggests she has the child, and she was attempting to look after her.

Jack consults the map: the left-hand turn out of the store doesn't narrow it down. Back towards the park, or further into town? There are no more sightings on CCTV, no way of knowing where she had gone.

Jack hovers around the team like an expectant father, waiting for the warrant, waiting for something, anything, until Manchester Police phone.

Jack takes the call in his office.

'No answer from Gemma Brogan's residence,' the sergeant says. 'And the neighbours haven't seen her for a week or so. Car's not outside.'

'Can you check the M6 toll?'

'Already done, nothing, but that assumes she went east of Birmingham. Most likely she would have taken the M5, south past Worcester. Plus there's nothing from the Central Ticket Office so chances are she stuck to the limit.' The sergeant senses Jack's frustration. 'I have a number for John Clark if that's any help? The ex-husband. We've checked him out – he was travelling for work all week, only got back on Saturday. Not your guy. But you could phone?'

Jack takes it eagerly and thanks him. He makes the call; John Clark picks up on the first ring.

'DCI Jack Ellis from Hampshire Police. I was hoping you could provide some insight into your ex-wife.'

'Gemma?' he repeats. 'I can share what I know, but I haven't heard from her in… oh… eighteen months? What's this about? Manchester Police said it was to do with a missing girl. I can't imagine Gemma being involved with something like that.'

'A three-year-old called Rosie Logan went missing on Wednesday morning. We know Gemma was there at the time, she made the initial 999 call. We're trying to find her.'

'Logan... Oh, Christ. Not related to Eddie and Maria? Surely not.'

'It's Eddie's sister. Maria and Tony's daughter. You haven't seen it on the news?'

'I've been away. Taiwan, South Korea. I work in manufacturing – I was visiting customers. Oh, Christ,' he says again. 'Why would Gemma want anything to do with that family? After Maisie died, we were glad to see the back of them. It was difficult enough, Maisie being gone, without seeing them around. Knowing they were responsible for her death.'

'I'm sorry for your loss, sir. But responsible, how?'

'If it hadn't been for him – Eddie – pressuring her to have sex, she wouldn't have got pregnant. Maisie was a sensible girl. She knew not to do anything that would risk jeopardising her future.'

Jack remembers Eddie's version of events. They were young, in love, and teenagers are prone to doing stupid things. It's unfair to blame Eddie, but he keeps quiet. A grieving parent is allowed their opinion.

'Did Gemma feel the same way?' Jack asks.

'Yes. Probably more so.' He sighs. 'It was why we split up in the end. We were both grieving, missing Maisie, but Gemma... she wouldn't let it go. She wouldn't eat, sleep, lost a ton of weight. I loved Maisie, but I needed to move on with my life. She pestered the police, wanted Eddie charged with something, God knows what. Then she started on the hospital. Said they had failed at their duty of care. That they shouldn't have left her alone that day, should have known she was suicidal.' His voice cracks. There's a pause. 'Didn't matter in the end. The inquiry found nobody was negligent. That Maisie had been determined, and there was nothing anyone could have done to stop her taking her own life. Oh... It was Valentine's Day. It was on Wednesday.'

'Maisie died on Valentine's Day?' The day Rosie went missing. Another coincidence. It's too much. 'Do you know where Gemma is now?'

'No, as I said, I haven't heard from her for a while. I've no idea where she even lives.'

'Would she call you back if you left her a message?'

'I doubt it. She hates my guts. Says I was desperate to forget about Maisie, but it wasn't that at all. I just couldn't live my life in the past.'

Jack thanks him and hangs up. He looks at the paperwork in front of him: the photo of Gemma Brogan, her address, her phone number.

'Is the trace back on the mobile?' he shouts out of his open door.

Amrit gets up and stands in the doorway. 'The warrant came through ten minutes ago,' she says. 'Raj is working on it. But we've found her on ANPR. That number plate was captured late Tuesday night, arriving in Fordingbridge via the A338 from Ringwood. Hasn't been spotted since.'

'So she's still there?'

'Looks like it.'

'That's something. She hasn't left – at least not by car.'

'Unless someone came to pick her up.'

'Then we have nothing.'

Amrit pulls a face and goes back to her desk.

Alone again, Jack thinks about Gemma Brogan. Why was she there, that morning? Grieving for her lost daughter, she drives down on the evening before the anniversary of her death to confront Eddie, or even Maria. Did she follow them to the park? Whether deliberate or planned, what must her state of mind be like now? She's trapped in Fordingbridge, surrounded by police and concerned members of the public. What might she do next?

He looks at the phone number. He debates for a moment, then picks up the receiver. Dials the eleven numbers. And waits.

It rings. Three, four, five times. And just when Jack thinks it's going to cut to voicemail, the line clicks open. Nobody speaks. Jack listens. He can't hear much, a television in the distance.

'Hello, Gemma?' Jack says.

Another beat. And then, 'Who's this?'

The voice is quiet, tremulous. Jack decides to opt for the truth.

'Gemma, my name is Jack. I'm the detective in charge of finding Rosie.'

'Leave us alone,' she whispers, and is gone.

Jack lowers the phone slowly. 'Shit,' he says.

She has Rosie. And now she's aware that the police are on the way, there's no knowing what she'll do.

CHAPTER SIXTY-THREE

Lucy doesn't have a chance to do much before the phone rings. She stands in her garden, dog leads in hand as she answers it.

'Have you got her?' Moss does excited twirls while he waits; Iggy picks up one of her shoes, lying next to it on the grass and looking at her reproachfully.

'No, but we have a last known location,' Jack replies. 'They managed to get a ping before she turned it off – to a house in Fordingbridge. Amrit and I are heading there now.'

Lucy hears a voice in the background, then Jack reply, '…break in if you have to.'

'What's going on?'

'Uniforms have found a red Seat Leon at the property,' Amrit says, 'but there's no noise or movement within.'

Jack takes over. 'The place is deserted—'

'Then get away,' Lucy interrupts.

'Lucy?'

'She can't have gone far, right? Not if her car is still there, and not with a three-year-old in tow. Iggy and I can track her. But only if they don't fuck up the scene.'

'They could have left days ago,' Jack replies. 'Someone could have picked them up.'

'Then if that's the case, the trail will have gone cold and we won't be able to find it. But if it is there, keeping the area clear will give us the best chance.'

'You can't get here in time.'

She's already ushering the dogs towards the car. 'I'm half an hour away. And I have sirens.'

'You heard the dog lady,' Jack says to Amrit. 'Clear the area.'

CHAPTER SIXTY-FOUR

Iggy stands next to Lucy – forty-two kilograms of muscle and fur, ready to go. He looks up eagerly, waiting for her command.

The whole team are watching – from the uniforms on patrol, to Amrit and Jack. Particularly Jack. He's silent, but she can feel the burden of expectation. Gemma Brogan is aware the police are on to her. Nobody knows for sure why she took Rosie, but Lucy can make a fair guess that this is an emotional, distraught, desperate woman.

She crouches down to Iggy's side, hand outstretched to the ground.

'Seek,' she says.

Multiple police officers have walked around this house, there must be numerous scent trails to lead Iggy off track. There's no way of knowing which one he'll pick up. She waits while the dog sniffs, letting the long line spool through her hands. She watches his body language; nose to the ground, Iggy's doing what he loves – going hunting. Instantly he finds a scent, his muscles tense as he picks up speed – only to lead Lucy back to one of the waiting police cars. She rewards him briefly with a chew on his favourite toy, and on they go – with the same result. Lucy curses – her job would be easier if well-meaning PCs didn't do quite so much exploring – and refocuses Iggy with a determined, 'Seek on.'

A new trail, and this time it takes him away from the house. She lets out more line, letting him sniff, first in the air and then back to the concrete. The day is good for tracking – it's rained overnight, and the ground is still wet. Iggy has no problems following this particular trail. They make their way into the woodland – the same place they found the badger cam – then across the road, past the outbuildings, and through the car park to the trees on the other side.

Iggy's picking up speed, losing the scent occasionally, sniffing the air, the grass, finding it again, tail high, wagging with enthusiasm as his keen nose does its job.

It's darker as they enter the next copse of trees. Lucy can hear the rush of the river, swelled from the recent influx of rain, but also a voice. A cry. The wail of a small child, a tantrum about to begin. Lucy jogs to catch up with Iggy, following him as they break out of the trees.

And there they are.

Gemma Brogan is a tall woman, hunched over with the cold, wearing only a jumper and jeans, holding Rosie in her bright red coat on her right hip. She's thin, almost gaunt. She regards Lucy and Iggy warily, her grey hair curly and wild around her face. Behind them the river swirls, a mass of basalt grey, fast-flowing and threatening.

'Don't come any closer,' Gemma shouts.

Lucy commands Iggy to a stop. 'My name is Lucy. PC Lucy Halliday. Are you okay? How is Rosie?'

'We're fine. Just leave us alone.'

There are no more than ten metres between them, a distance that Iggy could cover in a few bounds, but Lucy can't risk Iggy catching Rosie, or any harm coming to the child if she were dropped.

Lucy bends her face to her radio. 'Suspect in sight. Near the rugby club. Request assistance.'

She looks back to Gemma. 'I can't do that, I'm afraid. Rosie needs to go home to her mummy.'

At the mention of the word, Rosie starts to cry. 'Mummy,' she repeats, her face red and blotchy.

'Your mummy lost you,' Gemma says. 'Your mummy didn't look after you.'

'You can't keep her. Everything will go much better from here if you pass Rosie to me and we can all go somewhere warm to talk.'

Gemma backs away. Two paces, three, moving ever closer to the river.

'Gemma,' Lucy repeats. 'Please. Don't make me send my dog.'

'You think I care about your dog?' Gemma's shouting now, desperate to be heard over the crying child as Rosie's screams escalate. 'You think I give a shit about anything?' She shifts Rosie to her other hip, the one closest to the water. 'You or your dog come closer, and I'll go in. Both me and Rosie.'

'You don't want to do that. You love Rosie.'

'I can't lose her. I can't lose another one.' She's crying, her desperation plain, and Lucy doesn't like what she's seeing. A grieving mother, brought to the brink by the loss of her daughter. 'I came down here to confront them. The Logans. I wanted them to see what they'd done to me, to Maisie. How dare they carry on like nothing had happened. I found them, online. Tony, plastered all over his company website. Talking about his family. Where they lived. Their new baby.' She swallows a sob. 'I wasn't planning… I didn't want to take Rosie. But then I saw them at the park, Wednesday morning, and Maria had lost her. Stupid bitch,' she spits. 'Lost her daughter in an empty playpark, who does that? And she was useless, hysterical. I wanted to help.'

'You called the police.'

She looks up, fixing on Lucy for the first time. 'I remember you. That morning. You were here, with this dog.'

'I was.'

'Couldn't find her though, could you? Police didn't know what they were doing so I left Maria and looked for her myself. She was over there.' She points to the trees where they found the badger cam. 'And she was bleeding. I just wanted to help. And I did, didn't I, baby girl?' She talks to Rosie, trying to soothe her, bouncing her on her hip, only making her scream louder. 'I took her to the place I was renting. Cleaned her up. I meant to call the police, I did, but…'

'But you fell in love.'

Gemma's face changes – fury behind the tears. 'I couldn't take her back. To *her*. She'd lost her once, she'd do it again. She's much better off with me.'

'You know that isn't possible, Gemma. Please, pass her to me.'

'No. No, I won't.'

'Look at her. Rosie's upset. Let's go somewhere warm.'

'No. No.' Even from this distance, Lucy can see Gemma's shaking, her whole body convulsing as she takes two steps further back. She presses her face against the screaming child, kisses her on the forehead. 'I can't. I can't lose another one. I'd rather… I'd rather…'

Gemma glances to her right, to the fraction of riverbank left between her and the swirling current.

'No, Gemma, don't—'

'I can't let you take her,' she sobs. 'I can't…'

'Gemma—'

Shock snatches the next words from Lucy's mouth; with one last look, Gemma takes the final step from the bank into the river.

Lucy barely has time to process what has happened. Jack appears from behind her, letting out a howl of dismay as he sprints to the edge of the riverbank, watching as the two figures are carried downstream.

Lucy's mind goes into free fall. All they've gone through over the last few days. Jack's desperate search for a child who was here all along; Theo's white bones in a shallow grave; the sorrow on Wendy Nkosi's face as she talked about her missing son. And Maria. Another mother who's going to be broken into a thousand pieces when she finds out what's happened to her daughter.

'Hell, no,' Lucy mutters. She drops Iggy's lead, shrugs her tac vest and coat to the ground, and jumps into the river.

CHAPTER SIXTY-FIVE

The freezing water hits Lucy like a slap to the face; a punch that winds her, renders her breathless, unable to see or think. Her body goes into survival mode, flapping, scrabbling, kicking to the surface where she takes a deep lungful of beautiful, clean oxygen. It takes every effort to swim; her clothes, boots weigh her down, but she remembers her training, leans back and floats, letting the current carry her swiftly downstream, only too aware of time ticking by and the child in the water with her.

She can hear shouting from the riverbank, dogs barking, frantic voices. She pulls her head up and scours the surface. Rosie. Rosie, where are you? She's freezing, water in her ears, up her nose. She coughs, gets little more than a mouthful of river for her efforts. Tries again, and that's when she sees it. A glimmer of red, off to her right.

The stream is carrying them away fast, but arms pumping, legs kicking, Lucy thrashes towards her. She has the current on her side and makes up the few metres in seconds. There, so close. One final grab and she has a fistful of coat; she tugs it towards her, rolls onto her back and pulls the bundle into her chest.

Lucy finds herself barrelled and bashed, but somehow manages to turn Rosie in her arms until she's face up. Eyes closed, skin grey. And she's silent – so bloody silent. There's nothing Lucy can do; it's taking all her energy to stay above water. For the first time she catches a glimpse of the riverbank. People running, black uniforms, the blue of the sky, but so far, far away. She needs to get out, get help, but the more she kicks, the further she seems from the bank. The current pulls them fast downstream; Lucy's tired, growing more helpless by the second as the cold saps her energy. She can't. But she must. She must…

People drown every day. Parents, going after their children. Men, trying to save their dogs. Today, it's going to be her. Rosie is going to die, and Lucy will be the collateral damage if she doesn't get out soon. She kicks again, goes under, tastes mud, river water. Spits, curses. And senses something next to her, something large, splashing, stupid. Big paws, striking her chest. She reaches out and grabs. Fur. Iggy. Summons every ounce of strength she has to lock her fingers around the handle on the dog's harness, and suddenly they're moving. Towards the riverbank, towards helping hands, pulling at her jumper, tugging, wrestling her towards safety.

And then she's out. She lies on her back, mud, grass underneath her, cold air on her skin. Rosie is wrenched away and Lucy's gasping, choking. She can see blue sky, bright flashing lights. Iggy licks her face, his soft muzzle pressed into her cheek as she starts to shiver.

A face comes into view. Pete.

Pete – what's he doing here? Kind, concerned Pete, repeating her name.

'Lucy, Lucy? Are you okay? Talk to me.'

'I'm fine. Fine. Just… just cold. Rosie…' She tries to sit up; Pete helps her, putting a silver, crinkly blanket around her shoulders.

'Jack's with Rosie. Going in after her, that was crazy.' Pete shakes his head in disbelief. 'Just glad Iggy decided to get you out, otherwise I would have had to go in too.' He smiles. 'Can you stand? We need to get you to the ambulance, get you warm.'

'Just sort out my dog. He'll be freezing.'

'Iggy's fine, see?' Pete points: Iggy's shaking furiously, a spray of droplets soaking everyone around him to annoyed yells. He cups her face in his hands, warm against her chilled skin, and kisses her gently. 'But I'll get the dogs home. No more heroics while I'm gone?'

'I promise,' Lucy says.

She allows Pete to pull her to her feet. He guides her on wobbly legs to the ambulance where two paramedics are waiting.

'Get inside,' the woman says. She opens the doors, and a gust of super-heated air greets them. 'Once you're in, take all your clothes off.'

'Everything?'

'Everything,' the paramedic confirms, closing the doors.

'And you didn't even take me for a drink first,' Lucy mutters through chattering teeth as she complies, stripping off her sopping garments and dumping them in a pile. The paramedic gets to work, patting her dry and then wrapping her in blankets.

'Better?' she asks, a sheen of sweat on her forehead in the insane heat. 'Put this on,' she adds, handing Lucy a white Tyvek suit.

'Yes, thank you.' Lucy can feel her fingers again, her skin itching as blood rushes to the surface. 'Is that the best you've got?'

'Unless you want to go out there naked?'

'Covid coverall it is then. How's Rosie?'

The paramedic's face falls. 'I don't know, I'm afraid. Non-responsive when she came out of the river. They've taken her straight to Salisbury District Hospital.'

She turns away and Lucy gets dressed, every muscle weary. She thinks of Rosie. How long was she in the water? A few minutes, five, maybe ten before Lucy got to her. What damage might that do to a small brain?

Lucy slumps back on the bed and sends a silent prayer out into the world. Please, after all of this, please may that little girl be okay.

CHAPTER SIXTY-SIX

The lights of the police car flash blue on the bedroom wall. Maria stares, paralysed with fear. Bates always arrives in her own car; this is something new – the moment she's been dreading.

She gets up and peers out of her bedroom window – Emma Bates is walking up her driveway, her gaze fixed to the floor. Maria stares at her trying to gauge: what news is she bringing? Is this the end of her world? The doorbell goes. She swallows the tears and heads downstairs.

Tony is already standing with her in the hallway. Bates looks up as she nears.

'Tony. Maria—'

'Just tell us.'

'Rosie's been found. She's at the hospital.'

'Hospital? Why?'

'I'll explain on the way. Call Eddie. We have to go now.'

Coats and shoes are collected, and they bundle into the police car – all three of them in the back, Bates in the front. As they drive, Bates explains how Rosie was found in the estate nearby, and in the resulting altercation, Rosie ended up in the river.

'River. Oh, God.' Maria feels faint. 'Is she… Did she…'

'She was pulled out by one of our officers and went by ambulance to Salisbury hospital. I don't know any more than that.'

'Who took her?' Tony snaps. Bates looks hesitant. 'Tell us.'

'We know her, don't we?' Maria says.

'Rosie was abducted by a woman called Gemma Brogan. You met her Wednesday morning. She was the woman who called 999.'

Maria frowns, trying to think back. In her panic, she hadn't paid much attention to that woman, but she remembers thinking she recognised her. From the town, a neighbour? Gemma Brogan – the name doesn't ring a bell.

'You know her as Gemma Clark.'

'Maisie's mum?' Eddie gasps. 'So she did take Rosie. But why?'

'It's my understanding that she didn't plan to abduct Rosie. She was there to see you, confront you, and came across Rosie once she'd gone missing. And then, she just kept her.'

'To punish us? Some sort of warped revenge?'

Bates presses her lips together. 'No. I think she just missed her daughter.'

The whole car falls quiet. Gemma Clark, Maisie's mother. A woman Maria despised at one point, who pushed Maisie to get rid of a baby that Maria wanted to keep as her own.

Eddie was never the same after Maisie's death. Her energetic, athletic son turned inwards, angry at the world. She looks at him now. Unkempt hair, picking at his nails, sullen. She reaches out, holding his hand, and he responds, lacing his fingers into hers. It's not too late, she thinks. Eddie's only twenty, he has so much life ahead of him. She will do her best to mend his relationship with his father, pay for therapy, if he's open to it. There's still time.

Maria tries to summon hatred towards the woman, but all she can feel is sorrow. So many lives ruined, when Maisie died. No mother should lose a child. She grips Eddie's hands tightly, willing Rosie to be okay. She feels sick. She can't – *can't* – lose Rosie now.

They arrive at the hospital; Bates rushes them into the Emergency Department. There is no waiting, no hesitation: a nurse meets them at the door and shows them quickly through.

And that's when Maria hears it. An ear-splitting cry – her daughter screaming blue murder. And this isn't a child in pain – this is anger. This is Rosie, in full tantrum.

Maria runs towards the noise – and there's her daughter. Red-faced, plump, a perfect halo of blonde curls framing her furious face. She spots Maria and the noise intensifies, evolving from anger to upset as she holds her arms out to her mother. Maria grabs her, pulling her tight to her chest and showering her with kisses. Her tears mingle with Rosie's as she collapses to the hard floor, mother and daughter as one, rocking, crooning to her, saying she'll never let her go, never let her out of her sight again. She feels Eddie's arms around them, and then Tony's, and for the first time in days she doesn't push her husband away. She wants them all here, together. Her family.

–

Time passes and Rosie's crying abates. Maria releases her, just a little, enough so she can look her over. She takes in her warm, chubby cheeks, her bright eyes. She's dressed in pants and a vest, but she feels warm and clean, especially in the stifling heat of the hospital. Tony and Eddie leave to go to the canteen and while they're gone, a woman arrives, smart trousers, smart shirt, an NHS lanyard around her neck. She watches them, smiling, then introduces herself.

'I'm Dr Gandhi, I've been treating Rosie today.'

'She's okay, isn't she?' Maria asks.

The doctor nods. 'Yes, in a nutshell. Your little one is lucky to have got away as lightly as she did. We've done a standard primary survey and a few other routine investigations, all of which were unremarkable, and for completeness our intensive care colleagues even did a quick ultrasound of her chest, which didn't have any signs of aspiration. We've carefully rewarmed her, and our paediatricians are keen to keep her in overnight, but otherwise I think she's been really lucky. She's had a little something to eat and drink. Her main complaint was that she wanted her mummy.'

Maria feels tears threaten. 'And...' She barely dares to ask. 'The last few days?'

'She looks fine, in good health. Good weight, well hydrated.' The doctor smiles. 'She's been well looked after. There was a small but deep laceration on Rosie's right hand. It looks like it's been cleaned over the last few days and is well on the way to healing nicely, so we've just re-dressed it and left it alone.'

Rosie realises what they're talking about and holds up her hand, fingers splayed – the white dressing looks huge on her tiny palm. Maria pulls a sad face and lifts it up to her mouth, kissing it gently. Rosie grins.

'And there's someone who would like to see her?' the doctor continues. 'If that's okay? Chloe Winters? She says she's a friend of the family.'

'Chloe, yes. She can come in.'

The doctor leaves and after a moment, Chloe arrives. She hesitates in the doorway, tears in her eyes, but Rosie spots her, her whole face lighting up.

'Woo-wee!' Rosie squeaks and Chloe smiles.

'Come in,' Maria says. 'Say hello.'

Chloe does, resting a gentle hand on Rosie's head. 'I'm glad she's okay,' she says softly. 'I was terrified.'

'I know.' The two women share a smile. 'Listen, Chloe, after this is all over and we're home, I'd like you to be more of a part of Rosie's life. If you want to, of course.'

Chloe frowns. 'As her babysitter?'

'No. I'd like her to know who you are. We'll need to find a way to explain it to Rosie, but she should know. After everything that's happened, I think it's time we're more honest, don't you? I'm sick of all these lies.'

'I'd like that. Whenever you're free.'

'We have plenty of time,' Maria says, placing her lips against the top of Rosie's head, breathing her in. 'All the time in the world.'

DAY SIX – MONDAY

CHAPTER SIXTY-SEVEN

Lucy refuses to go to the hospital – all she wants is to be home. Safe, with her dogs; have a long bath and go to bed. Jack calls when she is warm and dry, tells her that Rosie is fine but they are still searching for Gemma. He promises to come around in the morning.

Her sergeant has already been in touch, granting an extra day's leave. 'Weaver said you've been busy,' Andrews grunts. 'Have a lie-in. I'll see you on Tuesday.'

She breaks all the major rules of dog handling, and spends the evening curled up on the sofa with both her dogs. Iggy was reluctant to come into the house at first, but soon got the hang of it, acclimatising to life on a soft warm sofa far too quickly. It is teaching him bad habits, and this lack of consistency is going to be hell to untrain later, but she wants the comfort of her massive dog by her side. The dog that saved her life, that will put his own safety ahead of hers, time and time again. He deserves some reward for that, she thinks, scratching his ears. He pushes his head against her hand, looking for more.

But the home comforts have to end, and when it's time for bed, both dogs saunter cheerfully back to their kennels.

She sleeps deeply, wakes long after she should, squinting at the sunshine creeping through the curtains. She goes downstairs, lets the dogs out into the garden and returns to the kitchen to make a large mug of coffee. While the kettle boils, she starts to tidy away the mess on her table: the photographs, the notes, the case files from the investigation into Theo. She gathers them all up into one large pile, the map on the top.

She remembers the woods when she looked around, the distance from Jason's house, Theo's in the opposite direction. She runs her finger along the network of roads, imagining that time of day. Residential streets, people returning home from work, the summer sky still light. Yet nobody saw Theo.

She opens her laptop and turns it on, logging in to the RMS and pulling up Angela Joseph's statement. She finds what she's looking for, then turns to the map. Here. She draws a small red cross on the road. Angela Joseph says she hit Theo with her car here, yet it's in the opposite direction to Theo's house. It's no wonder nobody saw Theo that night – he wasn't going home.

'What were you doing, Theo?' she whispers.

She sits down, pulling Jason's – Jack's – witness statement out from the pile. Were the discrepancies the result of an addled mind, or had Jason been dishonest? The detectives were convinced he was lying. Had something else happened that day? She spreads the photographs and documents out again, gently runs her fingers over the mass of paperwork, thinking.

The kettle clicks off and she gets up, making her coffee, still frowning. Theo has been found; his killer has been caught. Whatever it is, does it matter? She heads out to the garden, sitting on the steps, watching the dogs, cheerful in the winter sunshine, until a noise distracts them. Iggy's ears go up, he barks furiously, rushing to the gate and standing up on his hind legs. On the other side, Jack recoils.

'I preferred visiting when it was just Moss,' he shouts over the clamour.

'Iggy, quiet,' Lucy yells and the dog silences immediately, taking his place at her left side. Moss continues to wag his tail by the gate, happy in the knowledge that this is not his job. 'You can come in now,' Lucy says to Jack.

'Sure?'

'Sure,' Lucy laughs. Jack tentatively slides the bolt on the gate and edges inside. Iggy watches him, tongue lolling, all teeth on display. She gets up, her half-drunk coffee in her hand. 'Come in. I'll make you breakfast.'

'I've already eaten,' Jack says, following her to the kitchen, his stance never fully relaxing until Iggy is locked in the boot room.

'That bird food is not breakfast,' Lucy says. 'I'll cook you some eggs.' Seeing Jack about to resist, adds, 'I can do poached. And I haven't eaten yet, so it's no trouble.'

'Fine,' Jack replies, putting on the kettle and heading to the fridge. He hands her bread, eggs, then busies himself with mugs and teabags.

'You didn't have to come around, I'm fine,' Lucy says.

'I can see that,' Jack replies, but stays quiet. Lucy cooks, regarding him out of the corner of her eye. Tea made, he sits at her kitchen table, turning the mug around in his hand. He should be relaxed now that Rosie has been found, but he still looks like he has the weight of the world on his shoulders.

'Rosie okay?' Lucy asks.

'Yes. She'll be heading home today. Fit and well, thanks to you.'

'Thanks to Iggy.'

'I'll leave you to thank the dog,' Jack says, with a small smile before his face turns grave again. 'They found Gemma Brogan this morning. The divers.'

Lucy winces. She expected this news. 'Dead?'

'Very,' Jack replies. 'I'll wait for Fran's official report from the PM, but her initial verdict was drowning.'

'Poor woman,' Lucy mutters. She catches Jack's look. 'I know she shouldn't have taken Rosie, or tried to kill her for that matter, but nobody should end up in that state. So deranged after the death of her daughter that stealing someone else's seems like an option. She should have got help. Someone should have been there for her.'

Jack nods, thoughtfully. His gaze drifts to the mess on the kitchen table, the case notes.

'And how are you, Jack? Did you manage to get some sleep?'

'Not much.'

He rifles through then picks up the map, running his finger along the red line that Lucy had drawn between the woodland and Theo's house, then the small red cross.

'Was this where Theo was hit by the car?' he asks. His voice sounds thick, laced with sorrow. Lucy pauses making the breakfast, leaves the eggs uncooked on the side. She joins Jack at the kitchen table.

'Jack,' she begins. 'What happened that day?'

He looks up, his eyes full of tears. 'Everything they said about me, they were right. Theo… It was all my fault.'

CHAPTER SIXTY-EIGHT

Nothing was going right for Jack that day. The constant heat made everybody grumpy – his mother especially, and she had taken her displeasure out on her son. She didn't like him going out every day with Theo; she wanted him at home, reading or studying.

'To get ready for secondary,' she said. 'There will be smart children there, smarter than you. You need to make the most of the advantages you've been given in life. And here you are, wasting your time. Playing with *that boy*.'

Theo was always *that boy* to his mother, said with a disdainful wrinkle of the nose. Like he was a bad smell, or a stain on his clothes she just couldn't shift.

'He's my friend,' Jack replied, abstaining from the full truth, that Theo was his only friend, and always had been.

'You'll make new friends,' she said. 'When you get to secondary. More suitable friends.'

Jack was eleven but he wasn't stupid. He knew she meant *rich* friends. Or worse, *white* friends, but she'd never articulate that second one, never be so blatant with her racism. She'd never tried to get to know Theo, never invited him around for dinner, while Theo's family was the opposite – welcoming Jack with open arms, serving him huge steaming bowls of whatever delicious lunch Wendy had prepared that day. Jack had caught his mum peering at his T-shirt once, sniffing at a deep yellow stain. He knew she was turning her nose up at the spices, the exotic flavours when her idea of seasoning was adding a pinch of salt to the leathery gammon chops she would serve for his dinner.

But she let him go. The last thing Jack's mother wanted was to actually spend time with her son, so he ran free, sweat soaking his T-shirt as he sprinted to the woods to meet Theo.

When he got there, Theo was already covered in grime, digging a hole in the scorched earth with a stick. Jack emptied his pockets onto the dust, dropping fruit salads, black jacks, love hearts and other brightly coloured sweets in front of them. And then his crown jewels – four packs of World Cup football stickers. The two of them had been collecting all summer and they only had a few more to get – maybe it would be their lucky day.

Jack dropped to the ground, cross-legged, and opened a fruit salad, sticking it in his mouth and chewing contentedly.

'Pocket money day?' Theo said, looking down at the bounty.

'Something like that,' Jack replied, his mouth full.

'I don't believe you.'

Jack squinted up at him, his round tummy silhouetted against the bright sunshine. 'What d'you say?'

'I said I don't believe you,' Theo repeated. He wouldn't look at Jack, running his toe in circles in the dirt. 'You get your pocket money on a Friday, like me. You've nicked it.'

Jack paused, swallowing, the sweet a lump in his throat. 'I haven't.'

'You have. Cash from your mum's purse. Or these from the shop.' He gestured behind to the detritus and litter from the past week. 'Like that lot. You didn't buy them, like you said. You nicked them.'

'Why does it matter? You weren't complaining before.'

'I should've.' Theo bent down and picked up one of the unopened packs of stickers. 'Did you, Jay? Just tell me, I won't be cross.'

His mother said that. And his mother was always cross, no matter how truthful Jack was, receiving a slap around the backs of his legs for his trouble. Or worse, if his dad was home.

'I didn't.'

'You did. And unless you tell me, I'll ask them.'

Jack's skin prickled. He'd done everything in his power to keep Theo away from his mother. He didn't want his best friend to see her disgust, that disdain. Especially if Theo was asking something like this.

'I didn't nick money from my mum. I took them from the shop.'

'From the Patels?' Theo cried. 'I like the Patels. They always let my mum off when she's a bit short.'

Jack shrugged. 'They can afford it then.'

'You gotta take them back.'

Jack stared at him, unaccustomed to his friend's disapproval. 'I won't.'

'If you won't, I will. I won't say it was you.'

'You'll get in trouble!'

'Doesn't matter. It's wrong. You shouldn't steal.'

Jack's shoulders sagged. There was no way he was going to let his friend take the blame for it. 'Fine. I'll take them back. But later. I'm not walking in this sun. Let's just play, yeah?' He smiled up at his best mate; Theo still refused to look at him. 'Look, I'm sorry, alright. Don't stay angry at me all day.'

He got to his feet, then shoulder barged him, Jack's skinny frame barely shifting Theo an inch, but it elicited a reluctant smile. Theo pushed Jack back and in the ensuing scuffle, Jack was reassured. Everything was back to normal, and Theo would have forgotten about it by the end of the day. Jack wouldn't have to apologise.

But Theo didn't forget. If anything, his resolution hardened with the setting sun.

'I'll come with you to the shop,' Theo said, once their water was long drunk and their limbs were black with dust. 'It won't take long.'

'It's in the opposite direction – we'll both be late for dinner. My mum will go nuts.'

'Should have thought of that sooner then.' Theo paused, looking at Jack with an expression he had seen one too many times at school. The look Theo gave someone before he defended the kid that was being bullied, or stood up to a teacher about an unfair mark. The look that always got Theo, and Jack by association, into trouble. 'You've got to go. You said.'

'Sod that. They'll call the police on me.'

'Not if you apologise.'

'I won't do it again, Theo. I promise. Let's just go home.'

'No. You stole from the Patels. You have to own up.'

Jack glared at Theo, folding his skinny arms across his chest. 'No.'

'Don't be such a scaredy cat.'

'I'm not, I'm just...'

'Scared.' And Theo let out a meow, mocking Jack.

'Fuck off.' Theo's eyes widened. That was the worst possible word, one only bad people used.

'Jay...'

'Fuck you.'

And Jack walked away. Turned his back on his best friend and marched from the woods.

'If he wants to own up, he can sodding do it himself,' he muttered and the dread, the fear that Theo had so correctly identified, coursed in his veins.

Yes, he was scared. If he went to the corner shop and owned up to what he'd done the Patels would call his parents. And then what would happen? Even though it was Jack who stole, Jack who broke the law, they would blame Theo.

And Jack's parents would never allow him to see Theo again.

–

That was the last time Jack saw his best friend. Theo never made it to the shop – he was hit by a car just around the corner, his broken body thrown into Angela Joseph's boot, and taken to 22 Randall Road where he was beaten and abused until he died.

'All of this,' Jack says now, pointing to the notes, the photos, the scribbles as Lucy investigated Theo's case. 'Was my fault. If

I hadn't stolen from the shop, if Theo hadn't been such a *bloody good kid*,' he spits, furious with himself, with Theo, with the whole sodding world, 'then he wouldn't have been anywhere near that road. He wouldn't have been hit by that car. He would have gone home, eaten dinner and still be alive today.'

His mouth is dry, his throat raw. He feels like he's been talking for hours, blurting it all out to Lucy. The shame, the guilt he's felt for thirty years cowers him, reduces him to a shell, his shoulders caved in, his head bowed.

The kitchen is silent. He doesn't move, stays staring at his fingers, laced together on the table. He hears Lucy shift in her seat, clear her throat.

'Theo's death wasn't your fault.' She reaches out, gently touches two fingers to his shaking hand. 'Jack? Listen to me. It wasn't your fault.'

He looks up, hesitantly meeting her eyes with his own. 'If I hadn't—'

'No. Jack. Theo's death wasn't your fault.'

'I stole from that shop.'

'But you didn't know that would happen. You didn't make Theo—'

'But if I'd gone—'

'Then you might have been hit by the car instead. Jack, you don't know. It was a perfect storm of terrible events. Five minutes earlier, and Theo wouldn't have been hit by the car. Or maybe he'd have been hit by someone else and they would have called an ambulance. He might have died anyway. It was a hideous set of circumstances that led Jimmy Smith and Angela Joseph to take Theo that day. But Jimmy Smith killed Theo. It was his fault, nobody else's. Certainly not yours.'

Jack reaches out, moving the mess around on the table. 'You knew, didn't you?'

Lucy shakes her head. 'I didn't. Not for sure. But there were a few things I couldn't make sense of. Nobody saw Theo walk home. The place Theo was hit – it wasn't on the way from the woods to Theo's house. The mess in the woodland – the litter and the wrappers. More than two eleven-year-boys should have been able to afford. And what Wendy said about Theo – that he had such a strong sense of right and wrong. I couldn't make it add up. And the timings were conflicting. In your initial interview you said you left the woods at six, but your mother said you weren't home until quarter to seven.'

'I couldn't go home. I was terrified of what Theo was going to do so I just walked around.' His voice catches. 'While Theo was dying, I was cursing him for doing the right thing. Praying he wouldn't tell the Patels it was me. How shitty is that?'

'You were *eleven*, Jack. You were a child.'

But Jack ignores her. 'And everything that happened after,' he says. 'The press coming after me, having to move, change my name – I deserved that. I'm just sorry I put my family through it all. It's no wonder they barely speak to me now.'

Lucy frowns. She opens her mouth but closes it again instantly.

He sees her hesitation. 'What?'

'There's something you should know. Cal sent me some of the notes and recordings from around that time. And the reason the press went after you – it was because of your parents.'

'Sorry, what?'

'Your dad. He made a racist comment. And that was all they needed. In their eyes, you were the same as them.'

'I never—'

'I know. But the press…'

Her voice trails off; Jack sits back in his seat, stunned.

'Listen, Jack,' Lucy says. 'What you told me today – it changes nothing. You made one mistake when you were eleven. You've had thirty years making up for it. You're a DCI. You've put away more crooks than either of us can count. Retribution is swayed in your favour.' She stops, waiting for him to look at her. 'Trust me, Jack, please. Don't ruin the rest of your life because of this. Get some therapy, or do what I've done and get a dog. Get two.' Jack laughs, despite himself. 'Maybe not. But speaking to someone – a professional – wouldn't be such a bad idea? Right?'

'I'm fine,' Jack says. 'I'm okay.'

'Sure, you are. But maybe you deserve to be better than okay. Don't you deserve to be happy?'

Lucy looks at him a moment longer, then taps him on the hand. 'Now. Those eggs. Scrambled okay? I'm terrible at making poached.'

Jack smiles. 'Scrambled would be perfect.'

And for the first time in six days, he's absolutely starving.

CHAPTER SIXTY-NINE

Jack leaves Lucy's house with his stomach full, and yet feeling lighter, as if the millstone has been removed from his neck. For nearly thirty years he's carried this burden like a tumour, a cancer slowly eating away at his insides. But now he's laid it on the table, the relief is immeasurable. He has a long way to go yet – and maybe Lucy's suggestion of therapy isn't a bad one – but he can finally start to see it for what it was. A mistake. Childhood rebellion that misfired in the worst possible way.

Jack's been told to take the day off, but he drives home, resolving to have a shower and a shave, then head back to work. As he pulls into the driveway, he spots a figure hunched on his doorstep; she looks up and smiles softly as he parks up and gets out of the car.

'Sophie, how long have you been here? You must be freezing.'

Her hands are thrust into her armpits, her lips blue. She stands up. 'Not long. I wanted to see you.'

'You should have called. I could have been hours.'

'I was just debating breaking a window.'

Jack opens the front door. 'Come in, come in.'

Inside the heating has been on, and the rush of warm air is instantly welcoming. Jack shows her through to the kitchen, aware of the mess from the last few days – the washing-up in the sink, the dishwasher he hasn't emptied.

'Do you want tea? Coffee? And shouldn't you be at work?' He's aware he's gabbling and turns his back to compose himself, putting the kettle on.

'I've got a few days off. Compassionate leave. Hard to face a room full of rowdy thirteen-year-olds when your missing brother has just been found after thirty years. And coffee, please. Black.'

Her tone is glib, but Jack recognises the hurt bubbling under the surface. 'Three sugars?'

'One nowadays,' she says with a smile. 'Trying to cut down.'

Sophie sits at his dining table, and silence descends. He doesn't dare to ask why she's here: they haven't spoken since she stayed over on Saturday night, since he ran out Sunday morning desperate to find Rosie.

He brings her the coffee and sits down next to her, cradling his own mug of tea. Her eyes remain averted, holding the mug in both hands and looking down into the liquid, reluctant to meet his gaze.

'I keep on coming here, to see you. Almost like…' She frowns. 'Mum and Leo and Harry – they're devastated, I know they are, but all they can talk about is arranging a funeral. And it… it just…' She looks up, meeting his eyes. 'It just feels too soon. Like we've only just got him back and now they want to put him in the ground again.'

'But he'll be at peace, Soph,' Jack says softly. 'And you'll be able to visit him anytime.'

'That's what Mum says. And she's right, I know. I guess I just thought… I thought that once we found Theo, that I'd feel better. That something would lift. But instead, it's just…' She sighs. 'Different.'

He nods slowly, waiting for her to continue.

'I still don't have a brother. Knowing what happened to him doesn't change that. If anything, it's worse, knowing how he died. How his last moments were in pain and fear.'

Jack reaches out, covers her hands in his. She doesn't move.

'And some part of me, some ridiculous part,' she acknowledges with a wan smile, 'hoped he was still alive. That he was out there somewhere, living his life, and one day he'd come back. Knock on Mum's door.' She sniffs, wipes her nose on a tissue from her pocket. 'I feel like I'm grieving for that, too. The dream. The forty-year-old man I'll never get to meet.'

'I always wondered about that,' Jack says. 'What he'd be like as a teenager, an adult.'

'And what about me? What would I be like if he hadn't disappeared?'

'I'd still be Jason Kent.'

'Little Jay. Did you know we used to call you that? Even though at eleven you were taller than most of us?' Jack shakes his head with a smile. 'Affectionately, though. Mum was always fond of you. Still is. You should come to see her.'

'I will. Soon. Would we have got married, Soph? Had kids?'

Jack says it without thinking, and as she looks up quickly, he worries he's said the wrong thing.

But it's what he's always wondered. When he and Sophie split up, it was always the 'what if' he considered. If Theo hadn't disappeared, would he and Sophie have still got together? And could they have made it work?

The question stills the room. Jack wishes he could take it back, but part of him wonders why she's here.

As if reading his mind, Sophie says, 'Since they found Theo – since *you* found Theo – I can't stop thinking about you.'

Jack opens his mouth to speak, but she stops him.

'Let me finish. I keep on telling myself, we didn't work. We were together five years. You never proposed, I never wanted you to. There was a reason for that.'

'Which was?' Jack asks, almost a whisper.

'Theo,' she says, her eyes full of pain. 'I looked at you, and all I could see was my brother. You two, running around together. At the beginning, it was good. Because you understood what I was going through, and you remembered him too. But by the end all I could see was the life he never got the chance to live. And you were so scared – of your bosses, of the world finding out who you really were. The murder suspect turned cop.'

'I was stupid. I should have been more honest—'

'You were doing your best, Jay. Same as we all were. But it wasn't enough.'

'And now?'

She pauses. 'Now I wonder whether we missed our chance.'

Jack's shoulders sag. She turned up here, again, and he hoped, wished, that she was there to rekindle what they once had.

'Wouldn't you rather know?' he says.

She looks up, her forehead furrowed.

'All this time, for the last thirty years, I've worried about what might happen. What the press would do to me if they discovered I was Jason Kent. Whether I'd lose my job. How finding Theo might destroy me, all over again. But now it's all happened I've realised: it's better to know. The reality is never as bad as you imagine. It's not true – what you don't know *can* hurt you. It will ruin your life.'

'But Jack, last summer, we did try again—'

'Not really. One night, and for some stupid reason I believed you when you said it was too hard. It's not – it's harder being without you. It's harder not knowing what could happen between the two of us, if we just *tried*. It's different now. Theo – we found him. We can actually move on with our lives.'

She looks at him, her eyes pleading. 'I'm not sure I could take losing you again.'

'So why are you here?' He's being deliberately confrontational; bullish even, confidence, relief, whatever it is, finally coming to the fore. 'You turned up on my doorstep today because you wanted to see me.' He leans forward, clasping her hands tightly. 'We don't even need to do much. We could take it slowly. Go on a few dates, get to know each other again. At least then, we'd know. That we gave it – us – a chance.' He pauses; she still looks unsure.

'Please. Sophie?'

Slowly, she extricates her hands from his. She stands up and he thinks, *Shit, this is it, it's over*, until she takes a step closer, standing over him. He turns himself around in his chair to face her and she moves, until she's straddling his legs. He puts his hands up to her waist; she sits down so they're eye to eye and, tenderly touching his face, she kisses him. He responds, softly and slowly, like nothing has ever come between them.

'I need you,' she whispers, her mouth still against his. 'I need this. I need this to work.'

'It will.'

Her fingers entwine in his hair; his hands explore her back, down to her bum, pulling her closer. His previous declaration to take things slowly is almost forgotten as she starts to undo the buttons of his shirt.

He reluctantly pulls away.

'I thought we were...' he says.

'Stop thinking,' she replies.

Jack doesn't need to be told twice.

CHAPTER SEVENTY

Rosie is home. Rosie is *home*.

Maria pauses in the hallway, looking through the open door into the playroom where Eddie and Chloe are sitting around a ridiculously small table, drinking pretend tea with Rupert the rabbit. Rosie peals with laughter as Eddie pretends to butter some plastic toast and eat it, her cheeks pink, her lips rosy red.

The doctors were happy to discharge her yesterday, telling Maria to return if she had any concerns, but Rosie has been the picture of health. Eating, drinking, sleeping – Maria in the bed next to her, still unable to let her out of her sight.

Rosie seems nonplussed by her 'holiday', as Maria's been calling it. She asked, 'Where's Gemma?' at breakfast – 'Gemma made me pancakes' – but seemed satisfied with Maria's reply that Gemma has left, and we won't be seeing her again. Maybe something will rise to the surface of her consciousness later, maybe it won't, but Maria resolves to tell her about this terrible week one day. When she's old enough to google her name and discover that once Rosie Logan's photograph was plastered all over the country.

But that isn't today.

The doorbell rings, and Maria goes to answer it.

'Eddie, your father's here,' Maria calls, when she sees Sean on the doorstep. It still feels strange – Eddie's father – when for so long it was just the two of them. But Maria has resolved that things will be different now. Honesty. Forgiveness. Another chance, for all of them.

'Coming,' Eddie calls from behind her as Sean takes a step into the hallway. He's smarter today, in a navy-blue jumper and jeans. Maria remarks on it.

'Making an effort, aren't I?' Sean replies with a grin. The jumper brings out the blue in his eyes and as he looks at Maria, she remembers what it was like to be scrutinised by that gaze. Sean may have made his mistakes – huge ones – but she never doubted his love for her.

'Can we talk?' Sean says, turning serious, keeping his voice low. 'When I get back?'

'Sean—'

'I'm not expecting anything. Just a chat.'

'Sure.'

Eddie returns, coat in hand. His cheeks are flushed, he's excited to be heading out with his dad and it warms Maria's heart. She knows what Sean's going to say. He's already hinted at it a few times – he wants to move close by, to be a family again. Maria likes the idea, but slowly, slowly. She won't be rushed, not on something as important as this.

She waves Sean and Eddie away, but her good mood is immediately quashed by the sight of DC Emma Bates coming up the driveway. She waits while the police officer approaches, trying to read the meaning behind her smile.

'I'm sorry to disturb you,' Bates begins. 'But we need to talk.' She holds up the notebook in her hand. 'Some paperwork we need to conclude.'

Maria nods and shows her inside. Bates takes off her coat and shoes, looks through to the playroom where Chloe is still playing with Rosie.

'How's she doing?'

'She's fine. Look, I'm sorry to be rude, but why are you here?'

'Is Tony about?'

'Gone,' Maria confesses. 'Packed up and moved in with his new girlfriend. Mutual decision. Best for all of us. Do you need him here?'

'No. No, this only concerns you.' Maria knows what this is about then. She shows Bates through to the kitchen, feeling like she wants to sink through the floor.

'The drugs,' Maria says.

'The MDMA, yes. Some of the things we uncovered while we were investigating Rosie's disappearance were concerning, both for the ongoing welfare of the child and from a legal perspective.'

Maria feels sick. 'They've all gone. I promise. And I won't be doing it again. Please don't take Rosie away.'

'No, no. That's not going to happen. But we have made children's services aware, and I would strongly suggest you make use of these.' Bates passes her a handful of leaflets: drug abuse charities. 'Your family had a scare this week, and we are all thankful that it turned out well. Mostly,' she adds, a dark cloud crossing her face, and Maria knows she's thinking about Gemma Brogan. 'So please, take this as an opportunity and stay well away from the illegal drugs.'

'I will. I have. And Eddie will, too.'

'Plus, you lied to us. You lied to the police. That's a serious offence.'

'I know.' Maria glances back to Chloe. 'But I didn't know what else to do. I couldn't betray Chloe's trust and I knew she'd never take Rosie.'

'But *we* needed to know. You wasted our time.' Bates sighs. 'Look, we're not going to take it any further, but let this be a warning. No more lying. And formalise that adoption.'

Bates gets up and Maria shows her to the door, still clutching the leaflets. A final polite handshake and the police officer has gone. Out of their lives, for good.

Maria walks through the house towards the open door of the playroom, already smiling at Rosie's giggles, Chloe's laughter. She sticks her head around; Chloe has made a makeshift den out of blankets and pillows and the two of them are inside, *The Gruffalo* clutched in Rosie's hand.

'Room for one more?' Maria asks. Chloe pats the rug next to her and Maria clambers in between them, putting her arm around her daughter and breathing in the smell of her shampoo.

Things will be different now.

Everything is okay.

Rosie is home.

EPILOGUE

It rains for six days straight. Roads flood, rivers break their banks, but by the day of Theo's funeral the sun has returned. A blue sky shines down on mourners in their bright colours – reds and pinks and purples and, in Iggy and Moss's case, bright yellow bandanas. Iggy has already managed to chew a corner off his.

Lucy holds Iggy on a short lead; Pete has taken charge of Moss for the day. Both dogs are behaving impeccably. So far.

Wendy had called herself. 'It was down to them we found Theo. And you, of course,' she added, humour in her voice. 'All of you should come.'

Lucy looks across at her now. She's wearing a bright blue dress, flowers in her hair, flanked by two tall almost identical men – Leo and Harry, who Lucy met earlier. Wendy looks tired, her features distorted with grief, but her shoulders are straight and strong, a determined mother about to give her boy the send-off he deserves.

They're standing in the middle of a woodland, surrounded by birdsong and flowers. Daffodils push through the grass; new shoots threaten at the ends of branches, buds of new life, about to burst into leaf for another season. It's a peaceful place; Lucy likes it here.

The service was short but full of love. The village hall was bursting, people who knew Theo back then, Wendy's friends now. The celebrant offered words of joy; memories were shared by Sophie and Wendy, some sad, all full of pride. And now, as Wendy lowers Theo's ashes into the earth, Jack steps forward. He's wearing his usual dark grey suit, his favourite *Jurassic Park* T-shirt underneath, out of place but wholly appropriate. He stares at the piece of paper in his hand.

'Wendy asked me to say a few words, and I've prepared a speech, but I don't... I don't know. It doesn't seem...' He hesitates, looking down into the wet, brown earth, then back up again. He folds the speech in half and tucks it in his jacket pocket, before looking up, taking in the gathered mourners for the first time.

'Theo and I used to play somewhere like this,' he begins. 'A woodland, near where we lived. Just the two of us, hour after hour. We didn't need anyone else. He was a superhero, a football player, a movie star. A cowboy, Luke Skywalker, Indiana Jones. Sometimes even a *Tyrannosaurus rex* – nobody could do a T-rex impression like Theo.' A ripple of amusement, and he smiles, lost in the memory. 'But most of all, Theo was my best friend. The only trouble Theo got in was because I caused it. He got into fights, defending me. He would be late for dinner because I didn't want to go home. He was loyal, caring, funny as hell. And I loved him.' His voice breaks and he swallows heavily, his lips pressed together. His head is bent, eyes screwed shut. Nobody speaks; Lucy blinks back tears as she watches her friend take a few hitching breaths. He sniffs, wipes at his nose, then bends and picks up a handful of dirt, throwing it into the hole. He steps back. 'I've missed him every day since I was eleven. I'm glad he's finally here. Back with his family. Where he belongs.'

He looks up then, meeting Lucy's gaze across the circle of mourners. A glance passing between them, acknowledging her part in bringing Theo home. He's finally crying, wiping away the tears with shaking fingers as he rejoins the group next to Sophie, her hand slipping easily into his. Lucy noticed that when they arrived: Jack and Sophie, back together. She likes that they've found each other again. Hopefully for good this time.

Lucy glances up at Pete, standing next to her, looking ridiculously handsome in a smart black suit, peacock-blue shirt. She catches his eye and smiles. Life has been simple these past few days – just them and their dogs, working, walking, running, cooking together. Sometimes at hers, often at his, where there is more space for the dogs. And the sex isn't bad either, she thinks, her cheeks flushing at the thought of last night, when she screamed his name so loudly she woke the dogs and the resulting ruckus of barking German shepherds set off the neighbour's alarm.

'What?' he whispers, catching her expression.

She stands on her tiptoes and plants a soft kiss on his cheek. 'Later,' she replies.

Slowly, Wendy, Sophie and the rest of the group take turns to drop fine earth onto the box and the mourners slowly head off. Some murmur with conversation, others are silent. Back to tea and cake, at the hall. Lucy waits her turn, then says a silent wish.

'Sleep well, Theo,' she whispers, then moves away.

Jack's waiting for them as they meander up the gravel path. He shakes hands with Pete, an awkward greeting between the two men in her life.

'You both scrub up well,' he remarks.

'He's pulling it off better than I am. Can't wait to get back into trainers.'

Jack smiles. 'Lucy, can we talk? Pete, do you mind?'

'No, mate. I'll take these two reprobates back. Meet you there.'

Lucy hands him Iggy's lead, and he leaves them to it.

'Good speech,' she says as she walks by Jack's side. He gives a quick reticent smile.

'Did you hear?' She looks up at him, puzzled. 'Derek Pope, Rosie's father, Maria's stepdad – he was arrested this morning.'

'What for?'

'Meeting a child following sexual grooming. Fifteen, this time. The mother managed to intervene before anything happened. Called the police.'

'Shit.'

'Yeah. From what they told me there's evidence he's been doing it to other girls too. Chloe wasn't the first.'

'I hope they lock him up and throw away the key.'

'Quite.' Jack's face turns grave again.

'What is it? What aren't you saying? You didn't need to send Pete away to tell me that.'

'I need to talk to you,' he says. He looks at her from under lowered brows, his strange blue-grey eyes locked on her. 'I need to tell you something.'

Lucy pauses on the path, a strange sense of foreboding taking over. Jack stops next to her. 'About Theo?' she asks.

'No. Nico. I haven't been completely honest with you.'

Lucy nods slowly. 'Do I want to know?'

'That's not up to me.'

She looks up the path to the car park, where Pete is loading Iggy into the boot. He's laughing at something the dog is doing, and in that moment she feels nothing but calm contentment.

Life with Nico was anything but. At best, he was a whirlwind, full of ideas and plans. And at his worst, he destroyed her life.

If Jack has something to tell her that involves Nico, it's not going to be good.

'Can it wait?' she asks him. 'It's just…' She shrugs, weakly. 'Things are finally settled, or heading that way, at least. Can't I have that? For now?'

Jack smiles. 'Yes. You can. You can have anything you want, Lucy.'

She looks up at him, the sincerity etched on his face. She can tell that whatever it is, it's a heavy weight on his shoulders. And after everything that's happened – with Theo, his guilt around his murder – she doesn't want to add to that.

'Tomorrow,' she says.

'Tomorrow?'

'Come over. Tell me then.'

'Are you sure?'

'Yes.' She starts walking again, linking her arm through his. 'If I've learnt anything from this past year, meeting you, losing Nico, it's that uncertainty is never the way forward. You can try to ignore it, try to get on with your life, but it always pushes to the surface.'

'Fresh shoots of spring?'

'Or maggots in a rotting body,' she says, with a grin.

He smiles and shakes his head, laughing quietly. 'Tomorrow, then. And you'll be fine. I have no doubt you can take anything life throws at you, single-handedly. And if not, you have an attack dog and a six-foot-tall bloke to defend you.'

'And Pete.'

'I meant Pete. I'm shit in a fight. Don't think for a moment you can count on me. Do you know how much dry-cleaning costs?'

Lucy knocks into him with her shoulder, and together they walk up the path towards the hall with tempting smells of freshly cooked bread and coffee. Pete's waiting for her at the door; in the car park she can hear Iggy furiously barking at someone who's deigned to come near the Ford estate.

'Everything okay?' Pete asks as Jack goes on ahead.

She leans up and gives him a soft kiss on his cheek. 'Everything's fine,' she replies with a smile.

AUTHOR'S NOTE ON THE LOCATIONS

First off, while the beginning of this book takes place in the town of Fordingbridge, eagle-eyed residents will spot I have taken some liberties with the layout and nature of Memorial Park and its surroundings. I wanted a large, public area, but one that wasn't too busy, with plenty of places for a search dog to sniff. So, apologies, but there is no patch of woodland and no badgers.

Secondly, the suburb of Gathurst in Portsmouth, where Jason and Theo live as children and where Theo disappeared, simply doesn't exist. Gathurst means 'the way through the wooded hill' and I thought it worked. I considered using existing places but as I'm not particularly nice about the area, I decided on using a pure figment of my imagination.

Sometimes, it's easier to make things up. It is fiction, after all.

ACKNOWLEDGEMENTS

Writing a book of this nature would be impossible without the incredible technical experts who regularly take time out of their busy lives to help me.

Firstly, thank you to Paul Sainsbury from the Hampshire Police Dog Section for providing astonishing insights into Lucy, Pete, Moss, Iggy, et al. It is no exaggeration to say that I wouldn't have been able to write this book without you. Thank you to Paul Shutler from the PolSA team for painstakingly taking me through how a misper search like Rosie's would be carried out, both in the present day and in 1994.

As always, I am in the debt of Dr Matt Evans, my long-suffering medical expert, who answers my ridiculous questions at all hours of the day and never complains (to me, at least!). Thank you to PC Dan Roberts and Charlie Roberts for taking me through a missing child investigation, all the way from the 999 call to the boots on the ground; and to Laura Stevenson for paramedic advice on fishing hypothermic victims out of rivers.

All mistakes, whether deliberate or otherwise, are down to me, and me alone.

This book is dedicated to my writing life support – to Fliss, Heather, Jo, Clare, Kate, Niki and Rachael who collectively put up with more of my wittering and angst than any sane person should. And thank you to the rest of the Criminal Minds gang – to Dom, Barry, Tim, Victoria, Simon, Adam, Elle, Polly, Liz, Rob, Harriet and Susie. Of these, particular thanks must go to Dominic Nolan for a much-needed first read (and second opinion), to Tim Kinsey, the number one expert on badger cams, and to Harriet Tyce, for legal help on charging decisions.

Thank you to Sorrel and Paul Morganti for introducing me to their gorgeous German shepherd, Otto. According to my husband, getting a GSD is taking research a step too far, so I had to make do with a fun morning with Otto instead. (And thank you to Fliss Chester for the introduction!)

Thank you to my family: to Chris and Ben; Dad; Susan, Jon, Megan and Anwen (your names are here! But no, you cannot read it yet); and Tom, Mel, Leo and Henry. I love you all.

Last but very much not least, to the publishing side!

A massive thank you to Louise Cullen, Alicia Pountney, Nicola Piggott, Iain Millar, Thanhmai Bui-Van, Kate Shepherd and the rest of the incredible team at Canelo.

Thank you to my wonderful agent, Ed Wilson, for the motivational talks, and to Anna Dawson, Hélène Butler and the rest of the team at Johnson and Alcock.

Thank you to Russel McLean for the structural edit, Miranda Ward for the copy edit and Jenny Page for the proofread.

Thank you to Dan Mogford for the beautiful covers. (And sorry for making Moss black. I know that doesn't make your life easy.)

A massive thank you to all the readers and booksellers. It is a dream to be able to do this job – and you make it all possible.

And Max – you are a ridiculous dog, but wake up and pay attention, I've written another book about you. And stop eating sticks, you'll make yourself ill.